She had his desire—
would she ever have his love?

Kinyan rose in the tub, the water streaming from her body like rivulets of tears.

Colter caressed the wispy tendrils that framed her face, the fine arch of her throat, her gentle curves. He ached with the need to cover her, to warm her body, sear her soul. He closed his eyes. . . . He needed her.

For a moment, Kinyan considered yielding him his freedom, but she lifted her hand to his sharp cheekbone. Colter exhaled fully, a deep, sighing sound of surrender, and turned his head slightly to kiss her palm.

"Oh, my love," she whispered.

Colter swept her slick, wet body into his arms, bringing her mouth to his, splaying his large hand across the base of her spine, urging her against him. . . .

Colter's Wife

Joan Johnston

PUBLISHED BY POCKET BOOKS NEW YORK

This novel is a work of historical fiction. Names, characters, places and incidents relating to non-historical figures are either the product of the author's imagination or are used fictitiously. Any resemblance of such non-historical incidents, places or figures to actual events or locales or persons, living or dead, is entirely coincidental.

Another *Original* publication of POCKET BOOKS

POCKET BOOKS, a division of Simon & Schuster, Inc.
1230 Avenue of the Americas, New York, N.Y. 10020

ISBN: 0-671-60472-4

First Pocket Books printing November, 1986

10 9 8 7 6 5 4 3 2 1

POCKET and colophon are registered trademarks
of Simon & Schuster, Inc.

Printed in the U.S.A.

For my sister, Jackie Green,
whose loving support,
unflagging encouragement,
and well-aimed criticism
have meant so much to me.

COLTER'S WIFE

CHAPTER 1

1875
Wyoming Territory

KINYAN HOLLOWAY HAD to make a choice in the next few moments that could change the rest of her life. Her mind raced, remembering the past, imagining the future. Time was running out. Rides-the-Wind had demanded her decision. The Oglala Sioux warrior and the white woman who stood facing him, her waist-length hair whorled in eddies about her by the gentle morning breeze, etched a stark silhouette on the golden predawn horizon. A dog barked and was promptly shushed by an abrupt guttural command from inside one of the many tepees that surrounded them. The four horses tethered nearby stomped and snorted and swished their tails on general principles, warming up for whatever the day required. An older Sioux, wearing only a breechclout as a concession to the already miserable August heat, supervised two impatient youths as they checked the packs on the four mounts in preparation for the coming journey.

The old man's voice, hoarse with age, interrupted the soft murmuring of the couple as they said their farewells. The choice had been made.

"Rides-the-Wind, the day comes."

The warrior clutched the woman to him one last time, then let her go. He took two steps away, then pivoted, speaking to her in a low, urgent voice.

"Don't leave me."

Never had Kinyan thought to hear a Sioux as proud as Rides-the-Wind make such a plea. She clenched her teeth to stop the quivering of her chin. When she thought she had regained control, she opened her mouth to speak, but no sound came out. She swallowed hard, but the lump in her throat didn't get any smaller. It hurt.

Suddenly, Kinyan hurled herself into the arms of the Sioux brave. Her nose and chin dipped into his smooth black hair as she let tears of sorrow fall upon his broad shoulder. She inhaled the man-scent of him, so different from John's. His arms held her tight. Her soft calico dress provided little more barrier between their flesh than his simple buckskin breechclout.

"I'll miss you!" she cried.

Rides-the-Wind grabbed a handful of Kinyan's silky black hair and pulled her head back, baring her anguish to his piercing gaze. Sharp onyx eyes stared down at her. His arrow-straight nose flared with desire, and his thin, tightly pressed lips showed the effort exerted to check that desire.

"You can choose to stay, Kinyan. Your white husband is dead now. You would have been my wife eleven winters ago if Soaring Eagle had not given you as wife to the rancher John Holloway. Only you can quench the fire that burns within me. I have waited for you, I have not taken a wife. . . ." Rides-the-Wind paused when Kinyan shuddered in his arms.

No warrior should be without a wife to care for him, Kinyan thought, and it was her fault that Rides-the-Wind was alone after all these years. Why hadn't she told him long ago she no longer felt the same love for him that they'd shared when they were fourteen- and fifteen-year-old youths? Those first few days, those first few weeks after her father had forced her to marry John Holloway, she had ached with loneliness. Yes, she must have loved him then. After all, hadn't she run back to Rides-the-Wind not once, but twice?

Each time, her father had returned her to the white rancher, threatening on the second occasion to beat her mother, Wheat Woman, if she ran away again. And while Soaring Eagle had never beaten her mother, not even when

2

he had first captured her from a wagon train on the Oregon Trail, neither had he ever broken his word. So she had stayed with her white husband.

At first she had feared Rides-the-Wind would marry someone else. It was only much later that she began to fear he would not. Summer after summer, when John allowed her to visit her parents, she had expected to find that Rides-the-Wind had taken a wife. Yet it had been his sister, Willow, who had cared for all his needs. If the gossip of the tribe could be believed, he had shared a blanket with other women. Yet he did not ask any one of them to become his wife.

Kinyan had suggested once that he should marry, but he had sworn he could never love another woman. That was all the balm her conscience had needed, and she had never brought up the subject again. Over the years, his unchanging devotion was her lifeline to the world she had left behind. So she had never told him that her husband had usurped the love that had once been his. And the reason she didn't say something now was sheer cowardice.

She had waited too long.

Now, after eleven years of marriage, John was dead, killed in a freak range accident. Twenty-five years old, a widow with three children, heiress to the Triple Fork, the largest ranch in the Wyoming Territory, Kinyan was free to marry whom she chose. She should have guessed that when she came to her Sioux family for solace, Rides-the-Wind would ask her to become his wife. Kinyan now felt the full weight of these eleven years of deception. The twins had been born within a year of her marriage to John, and even with John's constant consideration and kindness, it had taken her that first year to come to understand that she loved her sometimes solemn, sometimes temperamental husband.

Kinyan's fingers went to the engraved gold heart that hung together with a feathered amulet on a short thong around her neck. John had added the heart to the Indian keepsake on her fifteenth birthday, shortly after the birth of the twins. How proud he'd been of his two sons! How he'd cherished her! Kinyan swallowed again, but the lump stayed in her throat.

She glanced over at the two fidgeting boys standing by the horses. They were dressed in buckskin breechclouts, elk

3

bones adorning their necks, their hair in short braids. It was little comfort to know that even if she had loved Rides-the-Wind, she couldn't have accepted his proposal. Her sons deserved the heritage their white father had left them.

An inner voice argued, *An Indian would not need to own the land. An Indian would only need so many things as she could carry with her on her own back or pack on the back of her horse.* Well, maybe once it had been that way, Kinyan thought bitterly. But the world of the Oglala Sioux she had fought against leaving eleven years ago was no more. Things had changed. She had changed. She had become a misfit—born into one world, belonging now to another. But that wasn't the reason she chose not to marry the Sioux brave.

Quite simply, Kinyan wouldn't agree to marry Rides-the-Wind because she didn't love him. But she had let the lie fester for too long. She couldn't bear to hurt him by telling him the truth, nor was she willing to cut the final cord that bound her to the Sioux. So she told the warrior another truth—one that was equally valid—to explain why she would not become his wife and live once again among the Oglala.

"I can't consider only what I want for myself. I have to think what's best for Josh and Jeremy and Lizbeth."

"I will love your children—"

Kinyan put her forefinger to the warrior's lips to stop him. His lips were soft and warm, and Kinyan waited for a spark of something—anything—to light at the touch. But she felt only regret for the pain she was about to inflict.

"I've never questioned your love for my children, and they return it. But look around you. How can I, when I see the disease, the starvation, the degradation endured by all in this camp, look with hope at a future for my children among the Sioux? If I live among the white man, I know my children will grow healthy and sturdy and strong. I cannot stay with you. I cannot be your wife."

She had spoken bluntly, brutally even, about a situation that was unspoken yet that could not be denied. The band of Oglala were confined to the Red Cloud Agency camp, situated on the south bank of the White River near the mouth of White Clay Creek. The surrounding land was flat and grassy as far as the eye could see in any direction, with only the cottonwoods that grew along the banks of the river to break the brown and green monotony. The buffalo no longer came

4

here, and the tribe's forays for food were discouraged by the soldiers from Fort Laramie, not far to the southwest. So a once proud and self-sufficient people had become wards of the white man, at the mercy of pitiless Indian agents.

Kinyan could see the effect of her words in the Sioux's tightening facial muscles, the defiant tilt of his head, the snarling curve of his once-soft lips. She knew he could imagine as well as she the dull-eyed Sioux children whose sharp ribs pressed out beyond their thin skins and whose cheeks were hollow with hunger.

"And if the white man were gone from the land and we could once more freely hunt the buffalo, would your answer be the same?"

"The white man is here to stay. Things will never be as they were."

"There are others besides myself who do not agree with you. When we have forced the white man from the face of the land, I shall ask you again to become my wife."

"It's hopeless to fight the white man. There are too many of them. They have rifles and an endless supply of bullets. Think! Think!"

Frantic with fear, Kinyan grasped the Sioux's shoulders, and would have shaken him like a disobedient child, except his solid strength prevented it. She let her hands fall to her sides, feeling helpless. How could she make him understand? There were too many white men who thought the only good Indian was a dead Indian. It was almost a joke in Cheyenne. So long as the Sioux stayed in the various agency camps and didn't complain too loudly when the agents fleeced them of their rightful rations from the United States government, all was well. But let soldiers or cowboys catch a buck hunting buffalo too far from camp, and it was liable to be the Indian's hair that left his scalp.

"You can't just—"

"It is day. You must go now. I will miss you, Kinyan, but I can wait a little longer to have what has always been mine. Have a good journey to the white man's ranch." The warrior had dismissed his woman.

"Rides-the-Wind—"

This time it was Rides-the-Wind who put his fingertips to Kinyan's lips. He had stopped her from admitting she did not love him. If she had thought her confession would keep

5

him from fighting the white man, she would have forced him to hear it. But she was well aware of his rebelliousness; it was what had caused her to fall in love with him at fourteen. She would only hurt him again, and for nothing.

Kinyan tore herself away and raced for her stallion, Gringalet. A figure stepped out of the shadows, startling an exclamation from her. "Mother!"

Kinyan's impetus carried her into her mother's arms, which were open in welcome. Wheat Woman calmly stroked her daughter's hair until Kinyan's breathing steadied.

"I'm all right now."

Wheat Woman gave Kinyan one last hug before she released her. The flaxen hair that had given Wheat Woman her name gleamed as the golden morning light streaked between the tepees. Not even years spent in the sun had darkened the warm, honey-toned skin that attested to her whiteness, and which she had passed along to her daughter.

"I wanted to look upon you one last time before you left. I hadn't planned to let you see me," she admitted.

"Oh, Mother, I'm so glad you did! Why didn't you tell me about this talk of war?"

"So you could worry over what cannot be changed? No, it was better left unsaid. Rides-the-Wind was foolish to speak of it to you."

"I told him I wouldn't marry him because of how the tribe must live. He said when the white man is gone, he'll ask me to marry him again. But, Mother, things will never change, and even if they did . . ."

"You don't love him."

Kinyan's eyes widened for a moment, then closed as she fought not to confirm the point to her mother.

"So you will go back to the ranch. I can see the choice has been difficult for you, but it is where your sons belong." Wheat Woman paused before adding, "And I think now you belong there also."

"I'll be so alone."

It was a confession Kinyan hadn't intended to make. Rides-the-Wind had forced her to think about marriage when she was a mere three-months' widow. Would she ever be able to accept another husband after John? He had been all things to her: father, because he'd been old enough and wise enough to be one; friend, because she had needed one when

6

she'd been forced from the Indian world to that of the whites; and lover, awakening the maiden she had been to the woman she had become. Without John's anchor, Kinyan had felt adrift between two worlds, and she'd leaned first toward the Indians and then toward the whites, unsure where she belonged. Until Rides-the-Wind had forced her to make a choice.

Wheat Woman's voice interrupted Kinyan's musing.

"You'll have John's mother, Dorothea, and the children, and we're always here if you're lonely, Kinyan. But I expect you'll be too busy taking care of your children and running the Triple Fork to have time to think about being alone. And now you'd better get started if you expect to get home today."

Kinyan returned her mother's fierce embrace until it seemed they must crush one another. Then, without giving herself time to think, she mounted her stallion and clapped her heels to the horse's flanks. Gringalet bolted into a gallop that raised clouds of dust in the overgrazed area surrounding the agency camp. Kinyan never looked back, but she could hear the sound of her sons' ponies and Soaring Eagle's pinto, following close behind.

Kinyan spent the morning and most of the afternoon in thoughtful silence. The fourteen-year-old Indian maiden who had been forced to leave the Oglala Sioux and become the wife of the rancher John Holloway had been lost somewhere over the passage of time. And Kinyan Holloway hadn't been able to find her. She was a white woman now. Rides-the-Wind was, would always be, a Sioux brave. Once, their lives would have intertwined. Now they would never meet. Her father had sent her footsteps among the white man, and it was there Kinyan was convinced she would find her destiny.

Yet she had no idea how she was going to manage to hold on to the Triple Fork now that John was gone. That he'd kept her in virtual ignorance of the workings of the ranch was not so unusual. But the result was that squatters, aware there was no man to challenge them, had already settled on the northeast corner of the ranch. The Triple Fork's foreman, Dardus Penrod, had informed Dorothea about the invasion, and that had prompted John's mother to send for Kinyan.

7

Because she'd already had condolence visits from the owners of the adjoining spreads, Kinyan knew the white ranchers expected her to resolve her dilemma by either selling the Triple Fork or remarrying. Kinyan had rejected the idea of selling. John had loved the Triple Fork, and his last wish had been for his sons to have it. Neither, on the other hand, would she ever again marry someone she hadn't chosen herself.

That left a third option, which Kinyan had been mulling in the month she'd spent among the Sioux: why couldn't she learn how to do what needed to be done on the ranch herself? She rode as well as any man, and while she was small, she was sturdy. She was quick to learn and not afraid of hard work. Kinyan had been in the white world long enough to perceive the one fatal flaw in her plan—the white man's aberrant attitude toward the ability of a woman to do much more than make babies, knit, sew, and cook. Never mind that before she'd married John, Kinyan's life among the Sioux had meant heavy labor from dawn to dusk. A white man's wife had responsibilities limited to caring for the children and the chickens. Well, the good citizens of Cheyenne were about to get their first taste of something a little different, Kinyan thought. At least she was going to give it a try!

By the time she reached this momentous decision, the small party had been riding over Triple Fork land for several hours and only had a short distance to travel before they reached the ranch house. The coolness of the pine forest mantling the Laramie Mountains, which formed the western border of the Triple Fork, beckoned to her and Kinyan wanted—needed—one last flirtation with freedom before she again submitted herself to the strictures of the white world.

"I'll race you to the trees!"

With Gringalet prancing in excitement beneath her and a grin of pure pleasure on her face, Kinyan turned first to the right and then to the left to check for agreement from the two ten-year-old boys who flanked her on their ponies. She already knew the response she was going to get, and it pleased her to think how well she knew her sons.

"Sure, Ma, on the count of three!" Josh agreed without a second thought as he gathered the reins and crouched forward until his hawklike nose stuck well into the dark mane of his buckskin gelding.

"Hold on!" Jeremy countered with a squeaky shout. "First we gotta get the rules straight!"

Kinyan's grin broadened. Everything was as it should be—Josh, the elder twin, ever impulsive; Jeremy, the younger, ever practical.

"We'll let Grandfather give us the go. Whoever reaches that big pine at the base of the mountains first, wins."

Kinyan glanced over her shoulder at her father, who sat straight and tall as a war lance on his spotted pony, to get his concurrence to Jeremy's announcement and suddenly saw him not as he had been, but as he was now. The years had not been kind to him—certainly no kinder than the white man to the Sioux—for he had survived long enough to become a war chief with no war to fight.

Kinyan didn't allow herself to feel sorry for him. She would never forgive her father for manipulating her marriage to John Holloway in order to pay a debt of honor—notwithstanding the happy result. She ignored the inner voice that urged her to pardon him for that one transgression before it was too late. She simply couldn't.

"I had not realized you were in such a hurry to be home," Soaring Eagle said.

Kinyan felt the squeeze begin around her heart at the word *home*. She was headed for the place that had become her refuge. Yet no husband waited there to hold her in his arms, to send her pulse racing when he kissed her in that special place behind her ear. She must put the past behind her, where it belonged. She must see only the future.

"You know you are welcome to return and stay among us," Soaring Eagle offered in response to the tautness of Kinyan's features.

"I need to get back to the Triple Fork."

"What can you hope to do about those thieves upon the land that your foreman is not already doing?" Soaring Eagle asked.

"I don't know," Kinyan admitted. "But I have to go back. Dardus wants to talk to me about the squatters, and some of John's friends have stopped by to see if I need help. Dorothea has kept my absence a secret for long enough. I am bearing my grief well in the solitude of my room," Kinyan

9

said, her lips quirking in amusement as she gave the excuse she and Dorothea had made up for those well-wishers who had had to be turned away.

"You have borne your grief well."

No expression showed on the face of the Sioux chief. Through long practice, he had learned to keep his feelings hidden. Yet in his heart, Soaring Eagle smiled. There was no comparison between the hopeful young woman with sparkling eyes who faced him now and the devastated widow who had arrived at the Oglala Sioux camp a month ago with her two sons.

Soaring Eagle had watched Kinyan try desperately to belong once again to the world she'd left behind at fourteen, when he'd commanded her to marry John Holloway. He had known the moment when Kinyan realized she could never come back to live among the Sioux. With his onyx eyes, broad, flattened nose, and almost nonexistent upper lip, he looked little like his half-white daughter. Yet he understood her better than she did herself. He had always known she would return to the white man's ranch.

He had come to regret his decision to give her to the white man, but he had made a promise and he never broke his word. Had he known at the outset that the price he would pay for keeping his vow was his daughter's love, he would never have agreed to the improbable scheme when it had been suggested to him so many years ago.

Yet Kinyan had not changed completely from the mischievous girl he remembered. Unheeding of the proprieties demanded by the white world, she had efficiently gathered up the flowing skirt of her calico dress and tucked it under her thighs so it wouldn't whip about in the upcoming contest, leaving a goodly amount of thigh showing. Soaring Eagle chuckled, a low sound that never passed beyond the depths of his broad chest. Kinyan's name, which meant "One-Who-Flies" in Sioux and which she had acquired because of her habit of racing to get from one place to another, suited her well even now.

"If you are ready," Soaring Eagle announced, "I will start this race and then follow to judge who first reaches the tall pine at the edge of that far gully."

The three racers lined up their horses, but Kinyan forced them to hold the start while she tucked the skirt of the calico dress even higher up under her thighs so it wouldn't get in her way. Of course in the past she'd pulled her buckskin dress up just so, but white women didn't do such things. Kinyan defiantly gave the calico an extra tuck. She wasn't ashamed of the trim brown thighs and slender calves that lay exposed to view. It was the Indian side of Kinyan that had chosen the red dress. She would not wear black and mourn as the white man. Besides, the white voice within her reasoned, there was no one here to see her.

"Come on, Ma!" Josh urged. "Hurry up!"

"I'm ready now." Kinyan leaned forward, her eyes focused on the mountains ahead, waiting for the command to start.

At her father's guttural "Go!" Kinyan spurred her mighty stallion, bounding forward into the lead. With a hoot of laughter, she taunted her sons, "I'll be waiting for you at the finish line! Don't be too long!" She leaned forward to burrow her face in the chestnut mane and laid her hand on Gringalet's neck. It was a signal between them, and the stallion began to run full out for the sheer love of it.

The pounding hooves faded back on either side of her, until Kinyan heard only the roar of the wind that sent her long black hair whipping and snapping like streamers on a gonfalon behind her, felt only the warm afternoon sun beating down upon her shoulders and the bunching muscles of the straining animal between her thighs. The acrid sweat of her horse and the fresh, pungent pines blended in a wild perfume that caused her nostrils to flare in an attempt to absorb as much of the tantalizing odor as possible.

Kinyan increased her distance from her sons with each stride of her magnificent chestnut stallion. Behind her, she heard Jeremy's gleeful war whoop. She glanced over her shoulder and grinned as she watched both of the half-naked, berry-brown boys swinging their stone and rawhide war clubs in fearsome arcs about their heads. She laughed aloud when her sedate father joined the boys, his shrieking war cry hauntingly fierce, enough to shatter the nerve of any enemy.

Her eyes blurred by the blinding wind, Kinyan put her worries behind her and concentrated instead on the powerful muscles that moved between her thighs, taking her ever forward to the beauty of the cool mountains and away from the sadness of the recent past. Kinyan pressed her cheek to

11

Gringalet's mane as she neared the tall pine that signaled the end of the race. In a moment she would have to rein in the stallion to keep him from charging headlong into the pine forest.

One second Kinyan was lying close to the neck of her great stallion, the next a steel-thewed arm had wrapped itself around her waist and she was torn from the saddle, lifted bodily into the air, and crushed against a hard, muscular chest. For a moment Kinyan didn't comprehend what had happened to her. Her horror, when she perceived the gun aimed at the three who followed her, forced the air from her chest in what would have been a cry of warning. But before she could utter the scream rising in her throat, a callused palm snaked around from the other side and clamped across her mouth. Her waist-length tresses tangled around her, impeding her struggle as she writhed and scratched like a wildcat in her captor's embrace.

Kinyan froze when a harsh male voice snapped, "Hellfire! Shut up and be still, or you're liable to get yourself killed!"

CHAPTER 2

KINYAN'S TERROR GAVE HER strength far beyond her diminutive size. She managed to pull the cowboy's fingers far enough away from her mouth to screech a muffled, "Help!" before his strong hand once again silenced her.

The cowboy tightened his painful hold on her waist and mouth. Kinyan kicked at the villain's legs with her spurs, but the heavy rawhide chaps designed to protect him from hardy brush deflected the brunt of her efforts. Her wriggling caused him to yank her further up onto the saddle, where she was in a better position to elbow his ribs, which she did. It was little satisfaction to hear his grunted "Ooomph!" because the cowboy didn't release his fierce grasp the least bit.

Kinyan had no doubt what fate the dust-laden drifter probably had in mind for her. But her fear for herself was eclipsed when she saw the cowboy aim his .44 Colt revolver at the three tightly bunched riders who were riding pell-mell directly toward them. Kinyan thought her heart might stop beating, so tightly was it constricted by fear. Yet it was that same fear that gave her the strength to claw at the binding hand across her mouth until she caught a forefinger in her teeth. She crunched hard on the firm flesh until she tasted blood.

The man jerked his wounded hand away and at the same time bound her with his gun arm as he alternately sucked at the blood streaming from the two precise half-circles of tooth marks and swore furiously under his breath.

"This is some rescue," the drifter muttered, shaking his head in disbelief. "Damn fool woman! If you don't shut up, you're going to get us both killed!"

Kinyan's incredulity at the cowboy's announcement that he planned to *rescue* her left her mouth agape. But only momentarily.

"You idiot! You dumb, loco cowboy! Just who are you supposed to be rescuing me from anyway—my own father and my sons? And don't call me a fool! You're the fool for being on my land, where you don't belong!" Kinyan ranted in the Sioux tongue to which she reverted whenever she was truly angry.

Benjamin Colter narrowed his eyes in consternation at the strange exhortation. The little lady had just cussed him out in a language that sounded distinctly Indian! But before he had a chance to grasp the significance of that revelation, the three braves galloping into the ravine drew his full attention. Colter unconsciously relaxed his hold on the woman to ready himself to confront the Sioux, and she quickly escaped from his grasp.

As the Indians drew closer, Colter could see that two of them were no more than boys. He shot the woman an irate glance, not a little vexed that her cries had made it necessary for him to shoot at the young Sioux. Yet all too aware their youth didn't make them any less deadly, Colter aimed his .44 at the Indian in the lead.

"NO!" Kinyan screamed. *"Don't shoot!"*

Acting instinctively to prevent the catastrophe that appeared to be only moments away, Kinyan flung herself at the cowboy's gun arm and hung on for dear life. She could feel the cold blue barrel of the army revolver pressed against her flesh, and her breath came in heaving pants as she fought to keep him from turning the gun on her father and her sons. Kinyan's desperation increased as she realized she was slowly but surely losing the battle. Despite her efforts, the throbbing muscles in her shoulders and arms were giving way. Knowing she couldn't hold off the cowboy much longer, she chanced a look in the direction of the three riders.

At that moment, the cowboy wrenched the gun from her grasp. Kinyan's fury overcame paralyzing despair and sent her flying once more into the face of the Colt as, with a cry of enraged pain, she attacked the man on horseback. Her efforts were as doomed as a newborn calf abandoned by its mother. The cowboy simply swept her up in his arms, pulling her securely into his lap.

"Whoa, hellcat!" he snarled as his sinewy arm pulled tight against a full, rounded breast.

Kinyan continued fighting until, from the corner of her eye, she saw that Soaring Eagle had recognized the danger. Her father slid down to the side of his horse away from the cowboy, so that only his leg was visible across his pony's back. With a high yip, he warned Josh and Jeremy, and they mimed his action instantly. The three riders sprinted past the struggling couple to safety in the thick pines. After they had pulled their horses to a stop amid the dense forest, the only sound to be heard was Kinyan's heavy breathing.

Her intense relief at seeing her loved ones safe left Kinyan's muscles useless. Her entire body trembled, and she slumped forward over the cowboy's arm.

"There's obviously been some mistake here," she dimly heard the cowboy say. "And I'm willing to admit it may have been mine. If you'll just sit tight a minute, maybe we can sort this all out."

"We've got you covered, mister," Josh yelled from somewhere above and behind Colter. "You just let my ma go, and I won't have to kill you."

Colter released a stream of expletives. The buck must be her husband and the two boys her half-breed kids! Even as that thought came into his head, Colter realized he couldn't be right. The boy spoke perfect English, and the woman wasn't dressed like a squaw. Well then, what was she doing with the Sioux, and why were the boys all decked out in breechclouts, bones, and braids! He wanted some answers, and he wanted them fast, before the kid decided to scratch his itchy trigger finger.

"Hold on, boy. Just give me a minute to parley with your ma." Colter tightened his grasp on the woman in a no-nonsense manner and demanded, "Start talking, lady. What's going on here? What are you doing with those Sioux?"

In English, Kinyan answered, "Soaring Eagle is my father. The boys, Josh and Jeremy, are my twin sons."

Colter stared at her in disbelief. The woman didn't look

15

old enough to be mother to the two strapping boys. He found himself waiting for the delicately accented, almost musical sound of her voice as she continued.

"We were just racing, *racing,* when you snatched me from Gringalet's back. Now you tell me—what are you doing here on my land?"

Colter perceived the woman's rising irritation as she made her explanation, but he found his attention distracted by something even more pleasant than the timbre of her voice. Several buttons on her calico dress had been ripped away during their struggle and a pair of luscious, peachlike breasts heaved with exertion practically under his nose. Colter thought, *How careless the man who left this delicious fruit to be plucked by any passerby!*

Colter ignored her question and asked instead, "Where's your husband that he lets you ride alone?"

"I wasn't alone. I—"

Colter had tried to deny to himself the importance of the question, but when the woman avoided answering it, he lost patience with her.

"Answer my question!" he snapped.

"None of your—"

The rock-hard arm that held Kinyan cut off her breath so completely she couldn't finish her sentence. The low growl rumbling in the cowboy's throat warned that further defiance was not likely to be tolerated. Forced to remember events she'd been trying for the past month to forget, Kinyan spat, "My husband is dead! Is that what you wanted to hear, Mister . . ."

Kinyan left the sentence hanging, hoping the gruff cowboy would identify himself.

But he didn't.

"I'm sorry, ma'am," Colter said quietly as he loosened his grasp. Colter was sorry the woman had lost her husband but at the same time inexplicably relieved she didn't belong to some other man, which was crazy because he really had no intention of getting involved with her himself. He couldn't explain his attraction to the tiny spitfire. He'd barely had a good look at her perfect, heart-shaped face. Naturally he'd noticed the large, luminous eyes that flashed fire at him, the lashes so long they swept the honey-gold skin of her cheeks when she blinked, her windswept silky black hair that

16

smelled of fresh air and sunshine, and the tiny, slender figure that curved in all the right places. He was suddenly conscious of the warmth of her breasts and the rapid beating of her heart under his arm.

Colter felt the familiar quickening in his loins that preceded full arousal. There was no sense tormenting himself. He would never touch a respectable woman without the benefit of matrimony, and nowhere in his careful plans to start over in the Wyoming Territory had he accounted for a wife. The pain of losing one wife was enough. Besides, there were plenty of women who could satisfy the need he felt right now. Of course the ones he knew were all back in Texas, he thought wryly. Better to get this hapless encounter over with and be on his way.

"I thought you were in trouble, ma'am, and needed rescue from those three bucks chasing you. Seems I was wrong," Colter admitted with a grin. "If you'll just tell your father and your boys to put their weapons down and come out here where I can see them, I'll be leaving."

Kinyan shivered as the cowboy's soft, slow drawl caressed her, compelling her to turn around in his embrace. Her first glimpse of the man revealed a flashing smile of perfect white teeth and thick black hair falling over his collar in gentle curls. It wasn't at all what she had expected to find! She tilted her head back, anxious to see if the rest of the man fit the mental image of the villain she had pictured. Kinyan caught her breath when she at last focused on his captivating visage.

The man looking back at her possessed a surprisingly fine-boned face stubbled with dark beard, except where a jagged scar ran the length of his bronzed left jaw. Her eyes traced the slashing scar from just below his ear to where it ended, an inch or so to the left of his slightly cleft chin. She followed the line of the shallow cleft up to a sensual mouth, the lower lip fuller than the upper. The small natural indentation above the lip led her to the sharp blade of nose and upward to large, wide-spaced blue eyes that stared back at her in tolerant amusement. Kinyan realized he was patiently allowing her to examine him while he performed an examination of his own.

Kinyan unconsciously licked her lips, like a cat tasting cream, unaware of the provocative picture she provided.

17

Her gaze dropped to avoid the man's incisive perusal, coming to rest on the dusty black scarf knotted loosely around his neck, and then on the white, salty rim inside the open neck of his black shirt. She imagined his skin must taste equally salty. Appalled at the absolutely ridiculous train of her thoughts, Kinyan let her eyes drop even lower until she perceived the Texas five-point star stitched in red on the pocket of his black leather vest.

Kinyan squirmed in the cowboy's arms, uncomfortably aware of his rising passion, for under her hip a ridge grew along the skintight denim jeans that were encased in the well-worn rawhide chaps. Knowledge of the cowboy's desire excited Kinyan, evoking feelings she found particularly disturbing because she'd felt nothing like them since John's death—and because she felt them now, toward a perfect stranger. When it became apparent her movements had only aggravated the problem, Kinyan stole a peek at the cowboy's face. His full lips quirked in a knowing, sardonic smile.

Kinyan ducked her head once again in embarrassment and peered sightlessly at the wall of green that surrounded them. It didn't help. Her body began to respond to the lusty male in whose arms she found herself, and Kinyan realized she had no inclination to remove herself from the cowboy's lap. How had that happened? What was it about him she found so attractive? Kinyan's curiosity sent her flashing eyes back to meet the cowboy's compelling stare, but the look in his eyes had changed again. She found herself challenged by intense blue orbs that burned with a longing so fierce it sent a jolt of desire spreading from her center outward in fiery tongues of radiating pleasure.

Desperate to escape the entangling sexual sparks flying between them, Kinyan looked down again. This time, she detected the beginning of another ragged scar at the base of his throat, which she supposed must run down his chest. How had he come to have such marks of violence? He was dressed as an ordinary cowboy, from his Texas crowned hat to his two-inch roweled Mexican spurs, and the double cinch rigging on his saddle attested to the fact he'd done some hard roping from the back of the roan. Yet the smooth, walnut-butted revolver that seemed to belong in his left hand and the holster tied down on his thigh belied that simple occupation.

18

The hungry blue eyes she could feel devouring her were not kind like John's, Kinyan decided, but neither were they cruel, and though she had no reason to trust the man, she did. That was fortunate, because she really had no choice in the matter. Kinyan jerked her head away as though her chin had been physically held by the rugged cowboy and wet her lips nervously before speaking.

"Everything's okay, boys. You can put away your guns and come on out now. This man thought you were chasing me, and he was only trying to help."

"Can this man be trusted?" Soaring Eagle questioned in Sioux.

"I believe he can," Kinyan answered in kind.

"Ma, I ain't puttin' myself at the mercy of no gunslinger," Josh argued in English for the benefit of the cowboy.

A frown of disapproval worked its way onto Colter's face at the boy's evaluation of him. But it eased as he conceded to himself that the kid had reason to be wary. Still, the boy owed his mother the right to be wrong.

"I guess this calls for a little trust on both sides, son. I'm going to holster my gun. I expect you boys'll be gentlemen enough to oblige me by doing the same," Colter said to appease the chary child.

"I ain't your son," Josh replied belligerently. "But you get shuck of that iron and we'll do the same."

Colter put away his .44, then eased Kinyan carefully down along his leg to the ground. When Colter held up both hands to show they were empty, Soaring Eagle, Josh, and Jeremy slid hurriedly down the hill behind him and circled until they faced him head-on. Colter noted that although the boys were unarmed, the older Sioux cradled a Winchester rifle comfortably in his muscular arms. Clearly, the Indian's trust didn't extend to carelessness.

"You all right, Ma?" the dark-haired boy asked, moving to his mother's right side as the towheaded boy moved to her left.

"Yes, Josh. I'm fine," Kinyan replied.

Colter thought the boys must be fraternal twins, from the disparate look of them. Attired only in beaded breechclout and moccasins and wearing a polished bone necklace as a collar, Jeremy stood a good two inches taller than his brother, who was dressed similarly. Where Josh was lean

19

and wiry, Jeremy was heavier, broad-shouldered, and narrow-hipped. Although Jeremy's spread-legged stance was wary, his green-eyed gaze was open and almost friendly. Colter even thought he detected the flicker of a smile on the lightly freckled face!

But there was certainly nothing funny about the situation as far as Josh was concerned. Colter empathized with the boy, knew his kind. He stood alone, at war with the world. Josh's sin-black hair and coppery skin hinted at his Indian heritage, and the boy's challenging demeanor would have made any warrior proud to call him son.

Colter looked quickly from Josh to his mother and was startled to find the same azure blue eyes staring at him from both faces. Unless he missed his guess, the young woman was probably at least half white.

Colter's speculation was interrupted by Jeremy, who suggested, "Ma, we'd best get started home again if we want to make it before dark."

Kinyan glanced up at Colter.

"I'm sorry if I hurt your hand." The words were sincere, even though the hint of mischief dancing in Kinyan's eyes seemed to add, *but after all, you brought it on yourself.*

Colter grinned ruefully as he examined his tooth-marked finger.

"Don't worry about it. It's nothing."

That wasn't exactly true. The bite was deep enough that he was going to have a permanent reminder of this fiasco.

Kinyan continued, "It all seems so silly now. I can see how you might have misunderstood the situation." Then, on impulse, she added, "We're heading south. Would you care to ride along with us?"

Colter answered more harshly than necessary because he found himself on the verge of saying yes, and getting involved with a woman—any woman—was just not part of his plans.

"No. I've got business that needs tending."

Kinyan didn't understand the stab of disappointment she experienced at the cowboy's curt refusal. "So long, then, and good luck," she said. She stepped forward and offered her hand to the cowboy as he looked down on her from his roan.

Her hand was softer than Colter had expected—only lightly callused, not as rough as it would be if she did heavy labor around a ranch house. He wondered who did the work for her. Colter examined the lovely face carefully: the mischievous blue eyes, the impish nose, the regal cheekbones, the stubborn set of the generous mouth, and the proud tilt of the chin, setting the inconsistent features in his memory to be taken out and enjoyed at his leisure. Then he let his gaze drift down over the sensuously disheveled red calico dress that hugged her slim waist and flared in loose gathers over her rounded hips.

"You gonna sit there holdin' her hand all day, mister?" Josh demanded.

"Joshua!"

Kinyan turned to find Josh glaring malevolently at Colter. Kinyan despaired of how the high-spirited boy would end up now that John was dead. Josh's behavior had changed drastically in just a few short months. He'd begun using the rough slang of the cowhands, as though by simply talking like them, he could be a man. Every time a neighboring rancher offering condolences had so much as given her a second glance, Josh had bristled like this and warned the man off. Kinyan had hoped some time among the Sioux would ease the pain of John's death for all of them, but apparently it hadn't helped Josh.

"You will apologize immediately," Kinyan commanded.

"I'm sorry," Josh said. But it was clear from his sullen expression he was anything but.

"I think you owe your mother the apology, son. She's the one embarrassed, not me."

"I ain't your son and I ain't never gonna be," Josh erupted in a shout, "so don't be tellin' me what to do!"

Colter could see the boy was hurting, but he kept the sympathy from his face, knowing it would only press the youth to further rebellion. The kid's pa must have been some kind of man, Colter mused, to engender this fierce loyalty to his memory. Well, he couldn't bring back the boy's pa. Time would have to heal that wound. Besides, this was a family matter and best handled by the woman, although he could see from the exasperation on her face she had no idea how to stop the kid from acting this way. He opened his mouth to

21

offer a word of advice and snapped it shut again. Hellfire! He was getting out of here before he interfered where he didn't belong!

"Have a good trip home, ma'am," Colter said, tipping the curved brim of his black felt hat. He tipped the battered hat once more in respect to Soaring Eagle as he met the Indian's dark eyes, and the Sioux acknowledged Colter's farewell with an equally respectful nod. Colter turned the angular roan and kicked him into a mile-eating trot in the direction of Cheyenne.

"I'm sorry, Ma," Josh said when the cowboy was gone. Josh's contrition was genuine. He couldn't seem to control these emotional outbursts lately. "I promise I won't do that again. I promise," he repeated. "Just don't be mad, Ma."

Kinyan's voice trembled with fury and frustration as she spoke. "I know you miss your pa, Josh, but there's no excuse for the way you behaved toward that cowboy!"

Josh kicked a pine cone with the toe of his moccasin, and seemed to find the arrangement of the crunchy bed of dead pine needles of great interest.

It was at times like this Kinyan's ache for John grew unbearable. Kinyan had never realized how much she'd depended on John until he was gone. She had moved from the safe bosom of her Sioux family to John's protective arms and now, for virtually the first time in her life, she had no one to rely on but herself. John's death had ripped away Kinyan's safe cocoon, and ready or not, the caterpillar must become a butterfly. Kinyan sighed. Lately she'd spent a lot of time on the ground just batting her wings and getting nowhere.

"Father, we can make it home from here by ourselves."

Seeing the distress on Kinyan's face, Soaring Eagle longed to enfold his daughter in his arms and comfort her. However, because of a decision made eleven years ago, that closeness was lost to him. He nevertheless made it clear he would welcome her return to his fatherly embrace.

"I am ever there if you truly need me," Soaring Eagle said. "For now, do not be too harsh with the boy. He fights the death of his father. Soon he will realize that Wakan-Tanka will not return what he has taken, and your son will accept his loss. Be well, my daughter."

Kinyan struggled to keep from showing her feelings. Once

22

upon a time, Soaring Eagle had been a wonderful father. But magical fathers who never did wrong belonged in the white man's fairy tales. She would never forgive Soaring Eagle's betrayal. She managed to make her voice hard, though her words were not.

"Be well, my father. Thank you for your thoughtful words. I will take them to my heart."

The Sioux threw his foot easily over his spotted pony's back. With a piercing yell, he sent his mount out of the pines and back east across the endless plains that only a few scant years past had belonged to the buffalo and now had been claimed by the whites.

Kinyan whistled for her stallion, which was grazing not far away. After the three travelers had remounted and started on the last leg of the journey home, Kinyan pondered the life before her. She was a widow with the vast Triple Fork ranch to manage, and no idea at all how to do it. If she hoped to survive without remarrying, however, she would just have to learn somehow what needed to be done on the ranch and do it.

Seeing his mother lost deep in thought, Jeremy signaled for Josh to fall back, and they reined in their mounts until they trailed behind the pensive woman.

Once they were out of earshot, Jeremy said quietly, "You know, Josh, sometimes you can be a real horse's tail."

Before Josh could retort, Jeremy continued, "Have you thought about who's gonna run the ranch now that Pa's dead?"

"Dardus can manage the hands and—"

"And who's gonna tell Dardus what to do?" Jeremy interrupted.

"We can, I guess."

Jeremy snickered. "Face it, Josh. Who's gonna take orders from two ten-year-old boys?"

"Then Ma can do it," Josh said stubbornly.

"Ma don't know nothin' 'bout ranchin'. We gotta have a cowman to take over the Triple Fork, and that means Ma's gotta marry."

Seeing Josh stiffen, Jeremy hurried on.

"I'm not sayin' we gotta take the first gent who asks, but we gotta be lookin' for some man to help run the ranch, not scarin' them off willy-nilly like you've been doin'."

23

"You thinkin' of somebody like this no-'count drifter we met today, maybe?" Josh asked, a grown-up sneer distorting his features.

"Maybe."

"Ain't nobody *ever* gonna take Pa's place!" Josh spat.

"No, prob'ly not," Jeremy agreed. "But somebody's sure gotta marry Ma."

Josh glared at Jeremy, then turned his head away to study the far-flung fields of grass that would one day belong to them both. He shook his head in an infinitely small arc from side to side, denying the future Jeremy envisioned.

"Not if I can help it," Josh vowed solemnly. "No sirree, bob. Not if I can help it."

CHAPTER 3

"MAMA! I MISSED YOU!" Lizbeth shouted, leaping into Kinyan's arms and wrapping her legs around her mother's waist. "Hi, Josh! Hi, Jeremy!" she called over Kinyan's shoulder to her two brothers, who were hard at work in the adjacent stalls of the huge barn, rubbing down their horses before letting them out in the corral. "Grandma Thea sent me to get you. Someone's here to see you. You have to come! Hurry!" In her excitement, Lizbeth's childish lisp was more pronounced, but it was welcome to her homesick mother's ears.

Kinyan hugged her six-year-old daughter tightly, then swung the giggling girl up onto Gringalet's bare back. Kinyan grabbed a handful of Gringalet's mane, backing him out of the stall and then urging him down the center aisle toward the barn door.

"Josh, Jeremy, we've got company. Don't come to the house until you change out of those breechclouts," Kinyan warned as she passed from the fly-buzz quiet of the shadowed barn into the June-bug riot of the dusky evening.

"Grandma Thea let me give the two men lemonade, but it's all gone now," Lizbeth spouted.

"Two men?"

It was only then that Kinyan noticed the darker outline of two horses in the umbrella of shade created by the immense two-story house John had finished building only last year. When her eyes adjusted to the failing light, Kinyan recognized the distinctive black and white Appaloosa that be-

25

longed to Ritter Gordon. That meant the dun probably belonged to Ritter's constant shadow, Willis Smithson, one of the ranchers whose land bordered the Triple Fork to the east.

Ritter Gordon was a force to be reckoned with in Laramie County and had been elected to take John's place as head of the Laramie County Stock Association. In the last months before John's accident, he and Ritter had disagreed violently on the attitude the Association should take toward small ranchers and sheepmen settling in the Territory. John had been much more willing to encourage newcomers than Ritter.

Although she'd seen him frequently at social functions over the past seven years, Kinyan had spoken with Ritter rarely. Their most recent meeting had been three months ago, the day after John died, when Ritter had made his condolence call. She wondered what possible purpose Ritter could have to visit her.

"Let's go and see our visitors, shall we?" Kinyan said, her curiosity aroused.

Lizbeth laughed gaily when her mother tugged her down from Gringalet's broad back and set her on her black-booted feet in the dust of the barnyard, sending three speckled hens clucking away in a dither. Then Kinyan opened the corral and let Gringalet run free within. As Kinyan and Lizbeth headed hand in hand toward the ranch house, Kinyan reached down to straighten the grimy white pinafore over Lizbeth's marigold-yellow calico dress.

"Guess what Prissy did!" Lizbeth lisped in sudden recollection of the momentous event that had occurred in her mother's absence. "She had five kitties on my bed!"

Wishing to greet her company without the inquisitive child in tow, Kinyan seized the opportunity the kittens provided to keep Lizbeth occupied.

"I can't wait to see Prissy's babies. Why don't you go find them now and make sure they're all right."

Lizbeth readily scampered off the covered front porch and around past the trellis of blue morning glories to the back of the house, where her grandmother had firmly relegated the new litter.

Kinyan tucked her Indian amulet beneath her dress. Then she opened the front door, paneled in intricate designs of leaded glass, only to discover Josh and Jeremy practically tumbling on her heels. Hearing their mother's announcement of company, they had rushed to finish with their mounts, released their braids, and changed into the plaid shirts, jeans, and boots they'd carried in their bedrolls, afraid they might miss something. Now they bounded past Kinyan into the wide hallway that divided the lower floor of the house in two, and then scampered on through the doorway on the right into the combination parlor and study. They immediately vaulted onto either arm of the burgundy brocade-upholstered settee situated perpendicular to the gray stone fireplace. Willis Smithson roosted uncomfortably in the center of the settee, and the twins flanked the wide-eyed rancher like two bronzed bookends.

"Welcome home, Mrs. Holloway," Ritter Gordon said as he rose sinuously from the comfortable dark brown leather wingback chair that had been John's. "John's mother said you were indisposed today and you wouldn't be able to join us. She got called to the cookhouse to tend an injured cowhand and we were just about to leave. Now I'm glad we waited."

"Yeah, welcome home," Willis Smithson echoed, bobbing up from his perch on the settee.

Kinyan ignored the tone of accusation in Ritter's voice, bluffing, "Yes, I felt better and decided to take a ride. I guess I should have told Dorothea I was leaving."

She paused for a moment to let her eyes adjust to the glow of the cut-glass kerosene lantern on the mantel. There were more lanterns scattered on the several simple pine end tables located near the settee and on the two leather chairs across from it, which she and John had habitually occupied. Her hand slipped down to her throat to touch her amulet beneath the calico, and she became aware of the missing buttons on her dress and how dusty and disheveled she must look. Well, there was no help for that now. But she could imagine what a man like Ritter, so conscious of appearances, must think.

Ritter owned the second largest ranch in Laramie County, bordering the Triple Fork to the west, and most of the land in Cheyenne. Luckily, his wealth made it possible for him to hire a surrogate to run his ranch, the Lazy 6, because he was fastidious to a degree that would not have been possible had he been required to actually play the role his clothing proclaimed. He was dressed, as always, in an immaculately clean pale blue shirt and brown leather vest. Nary a speck of dust marred the rawhide batwing chaps that encased his Levi's. A pearl-handled .44 Colt rested comfortably in a hand-tooled brown leather holster that sat just below his beltline. His polished silver spurs gleamed in the lantern light, but they were given a fair contest by expensive boots, polished to a spit shine. No band of sweat rimmed his hat. Kinyan ventured a guess that the pure white scarf around his throat had never cleared the sweat from Ritter's brow, let alone the dust from his horse's nostrils after a hot summer afternoon on the prairie. She spoke to curb her rising amusement over Ritter's appearance of exaggerated cleanliness.

"Can I get more lemonade for you two gentlemen?"

"That'd be just great! I'm shore 'nuff dried up!" Willis blurted.

"No thank you, it's late," Ritter contradicted Willis. He took two quick steps and reached out to take Kinyan's hand. "May I say again how sorry we all are that you've lost John."

The hand that grasped Kinyan's was huge, powerful, and decidedly possessive. John hadn't been a jealous man, but Ritter had been forward enough with Kinyan on one of their prior meetings for John to step between them. John had later raged to Kinyan when she tried to excuse Ritter's advances that Ritter's handsome face was no better than a scab over an infected sore. It merely covered up the slimy foulness growing underneath.

There was no one to protect her now from Ritter's subtle assault on her. Before Kinyan had a chance to regret the gesture that put her on more intimate terms with this man, Ritter employed his Southern-born charm and graciousness to completely dispose of her reservations about being friendly to him.

Ritter raised Kinyan's hand to his lips and pressed a kiss to her palm, bringing a quirking smile to Kinyan's face because the unexpected kiss tickled. Kinyan found herself entrapped by eyes the color of brandy. In a sweeping glance, she noted hair the color of tobacco, a mobile mouth, a fine, straight nose, and an outthrust chin that might have seemed arrogant, except Ritter's overall pose was so decidedly humble. Looking at Ritter now, Kinyan found it difficult to believe John could have been right.

"Yeah, it's shore a shame John got all mangled up like he did," Willis said. He jumped up again and thrust a bony hand toward Kinyan, nearly knocking her over in his exuberance.

Kinyan blanched at Willis's disturbing reminder of how John had died and withdrew quickly from Ritter's grasp, at the same time moving away from Willis's outstretched hand.

Willis finally perceived Kinyan's shocked look and stuttered an apology for whatever it was he'd said wrong. He was a simple, harmless man, with large innocent brown eyes and a tall, almost emaciated form that ended in two extraordinarily large feet. He worshiped Ritter as the epitome of everything he would never be—strong, virile, and dominating. Willis would have done anything to please his idol, and he'd been happy to come along on this occasion to confirm Ritter's claim that some of the Association members had their eyes on the Triple Fork's grass, even if it wasn't precisely true.

"Well, what is it you two fellas want here, anyway?" Josh piped up impatiently.

Josh had never been one to mince words, but Kinyan shot him a look that promised retribution if he didn't mind his manners.

"I'm glad you asked that, son," Ritter began.

Josh opened his mouth to deny the parental relationship but caught Kinyan's sharp glance and clamped down on his jaw with an almost audible snap, his eyes narrowing dangerously.

Ritter hadn't missed the look between mother and son. In fact, his plans depended to some extent on Kinyan having trouble managing her unbridled boys without a man around the house. He proposed to become a model father figure for Kinyan's children—at least until he had the Triple Fork ranch in hand.

"I have some serious business to discuss with your mother that concerns you two boys as well. Why don't we all sit down, Mrs. Holloway," Ritter suggested. "You must be tired after your ride."

Ritter hid his repugnance for the woman before him. He

didn't care much for the windblown look of Kinyan's hair, and the dusty red calico dress gaped open at the top, where two buttons were missing. She was too thin for his taste, and her skin was not pale enough to suit him. Worst of all, her eyes were too direct for a woman. Once she was his wife, he would rectify that.

Ritter took advantage of the opportunity to put his arm solicitously around Kinyan's shoulders, tucking her small form neatly against him as he escorted her to a small leather armchair.

"Boys, make yourselves comfortable."

"We are comfortable," Josh responded, cocking his leg up to rest his left boot on his right knee. He didn't like the turn events were taking at all. His mother seemed entirely too willing to be touched by this smooth-talking man, and the man was acting like he already owned the place.

Ritter sat down in John's chair and leaned forward, his elbows resting on his knees and one large hand cupped in the other, to speak confidently to Kinyan.

"You may recall, Mrs. Holloway, that John and I didn't always see eye to eye with regard to small ranchers and sheepmen moving into the Territory. As it turns out, since John's death, the Laramie County Stock Association has decided unanimously to oppose new settlement by anybody who's not a member of the association."

Kinyan stared blankly at Ritter, unable to imagine what his speech had to do with her. She raised her gaze to Ritter's face and his yellow eyes, rimmed in black, bored into her own as he spoke.

"It's the government land we're really trying to protect from squatters."

When Kinyan continued to stare in confusion, Ritter explained, "Like most of the other ranches around here, the greatest part of the Triple Fork is actually government land. John's only claim to the range was the one he enforced with his Winchester."

Kinyan knew that what Ritter said was true. John had explained it to her once when she'd asked him how the Triple Fork had become the largest ranch in the Territory. Over the years, the government had occasionally made it possible to take land free. John had gotten 160 acres free under the Homestead Act of 1862. He'd acquired another 160 acres free under the Timber Culture Act of 1873. Taking advantage of the common practice of having cowhands file for land under the homestead laws and then purchasing the land within forty-eight hours, John had extended his holdings by another sixteen hundred acres. But considering each steer required from 20 acres of the best rangeland to 130 acres of the poorest, John still owned barely enough land for forty or fifty steers.

So over the years, John Holloway had proceeded to claim, by right of possession, over 300,000 acres of government land. With the good water provided by Lodgepole Creek, Horse Creek, and Little Bear Creek, he'd been able to increase his herd to almost eight thousand head of cattle. John had placed his ranch headquarters on his homestead, where he could control a stretch of Lodgepole Creek, but Kinyan knew the Triple Fork wouldn't have been much of a spread without the government lands John had confiscated and that he had, when necessary over the years, fought to control.

"Did you know, Mrs. Holloway," Ritter continued earnestly, "that since John's death, squatters have settled on the northeast corner of the Triple Fork?"

Of course she did. That was the reason she'd cut short her visit to her parents and returned to the Triple Fork. But Ritter never gave her a chance to answer the question before he continued, "With John laid to rest, it occurred to me you might need some help removing those squatters. I'd be more than happy to lend you a hand. Of course, you'll have my help indefinitely if you need it," Ritter reassured Kinyan. "But have you given any thought, Mrs. Holloway, to how you'll keep the Triple Fork from being overrun by squatters, from being plagued by riffraff drifters, or from being squeezed by rustling cowboys and renegade Indians?"

Kinyan fought hard to listen to what Ritter said and not succumb to the melodic baritone voice. Kinyan had the most extraordinary feeling that if she could have seen herself, she'd resemble nothing so much as a rabbit being hypnotized by a snake before being swallowed whole.

"After all, with John dead, the Triple Fork no longer has the benefit of the protection provided by the Association to its members. You'll have to deal with intruders by yourself."

Kinyan's eyes widened as she finally understood the ex-

31

tent of the danger to which she was now exposed. There were at least twenty outfits belonging to the Laramie County Stock Association, including those of both Ritter and Willis. Another fifty or so smaller ranches ground out a living in the Territory. Kinyan could fully expect that some or all of them would attempt to appropriate the government lands that comprised the Triple Fork. Ritter was right about one thing: she would have to make a decision, and soon, about what she was going to do.

"I know this must be a very difficult time for you," Ritter continued smoothly. "There are, of course, alternatives for a woman in your position."

"Such as?" Kinyan kept her face blank, afraid that if she showed any expression at all, it would reveal her fear of losing everything because she couldn't handle a .44 Winchester.

"You could always sell out."

"No way!" Josh exclaimed.

"We're not leavin'!" Jeremy confirmed.

Kinyan was too busy thinking to contradict the suggestion.

However, Ritter concluded from her silence she was in accord with her sons. *The woman and her two brats aren't going to be so difficult to manipulate after all,* he thought. Ritter offered the next alternative in as normal a tone as he could muster in his jubilance.

"And naturally, you can always marry a member of the Association."

"My ma ain't gettin' married," Josh said flatly.

"Until she finds the right man," Jeremy added quickly.

"Did you have someone particular in mind?" Kinyan asked with wide-eyed innocence, suddenly very aware why Ritter had made this visit.

Taken aback by Kinyan's perceptive question, Ritter recovered quickly enough to say, "I've taken the liberty of making it clear to the members of the Association that I personally will not tolerate an intrusion on Triple Fork land until you've made your choice. However, just so there wouldn't be any bad feelings, I'm afraid I told a little white lie."

Kinyan focused on the beautiful—and it was beautiful—male face not three feet from her.

"What lie was that, Mr. Gordon?"

"I told the Association I've been courting you and that our wedding is imminent."

"That's not true!"

Kinyan rose angrily to her feet, and the twins jumped off the settee to stand protectively on either side of their mother.

"Of course not," Ritter explained with an unctuous smile. "But would you rather I'd threatened to shoot them if they started running cattle on the Triple Fork? I wanted to avoid bloodshed if at all possible. Don't you?"

"Yeah, there were some ranchers wanted to just split up the Triple Fork in little pieces, but Mr. Gordon here wouldn't let 'em," Willis offered.

Ritter beamed a smile of approval at Willis, whose tail would have wagged if he'd had one.

Kinyan closed her eyes momentarily, but snapped them back open when her hand was entwined with another that was dry and smooth and cold, like a snake. Ritter smiled at her again, and Kinyan felt her stomach turn. How could he make such a presumption! Things were different in the white world. He couldn't just announce he was going to marry her without getting her consent first. Could he? Kinyan's stomach turned again. He already had.

Ritter helped Kinyan back into her chair and turned to the two boys, who glared defiantly at him.

"Why don't you boys sit down and give your mother an opportunity to think," Ritter ordered.

"Josh, Jeremy, I'm all right," Kinyan said softly, aware of the response Ritter's tone was likely to provoke. "Please sit down."

Josh opened his mouth to retort, but one look at his mother's flashing eyes told him this wasn't the time to vent his spleen, so he turned back to the settee in obedience to her wishes.

Ritter had thought this scene out very carefully beforehand. His next words were calculated to relieve the fear he'd instilled in the young woman.

Ritter knelt down and took Kinyan's hands in his own again, looking deeply into her blue eyes. "With your consent, the lie I told the Association could become the truth," he said fervently. "I've admired you for a long time, Mrs.

33

Holloway. I know this seems sudden, but circumstances warrant my speaking now. Will you do me the honor of becoming my wife?"

Josh felt the hairs on the back of his neck stand on end. Jeremy's face scrunched up in disgust. They watched their mother anxiously to see how she would respond.

Kinyan's brain whirled with the enormity of the offer Ritter had just made, but he was not *demanding*, he was *asking*. And that made all the difference. Kinyan was free, suddenly, to consider rationally Ritter's offer of marriage. If she married Ritter, she would have someone to protect the Triple Fork. There would be no need to fear the future. Accepting Ritter's proposal made perfect sense.

Except, she didn't love Ritter.

But then she hadn't loved John at first either.

The boys obviously didn't like him.

But Ritter was gracious and well mannered and could teach her sons to be gentlemen.

Ritter had lied to the association.

But he had done so to avoid bloodshed.

It was too soon after John's death to accept another man in his place.

But the danger to the Triple Fork was imminent, and there was no time to waste.

Kinyan had one final objection to which there was no answer: she didn't trust Ritter. It was just a feeling, but it was a strong one, and she would have given next year's calf crop to know whether John had been right. Did Ritter's beautiful face mask a hideous inner nature? Kinyan shuddered. She racked her brain to think of some other man who was a better choice.

When the face of the cowboy she had just met came to mind, Kinyan almost laughed aloud. She knew even less about him than she did about Ritter! Except, she trusted him. Remembering bold, blue eyes, Kinyan felt the constriction of inner muscles and a tingling fullness in the tips of her breasts that revealed something else very important about the cowboy. He made her feel . . . alive again. Kinyan shook her head as though to clear a fog. He was long gone by now, and she'd probably never see him again. It was just dreaming to think about marrying the cowboy. Ritter was reality.

"I wish there were more time to let you get to know me, but I'm afraid your decision will have to be made soon."

Ritter didn't doubt Kinyan would be receptive to his offer, because there was no one else to whom she could turn in this situation. He had checked thoroughly. She was totally alone.

By marrying Kinyan, Ritter would have the Triple Fork without the cost of buying it or the aggravation of fighting the other members of the Association to prove his claim. Although he didn't find her particularly attractive, Ritter hadn't overlooked the advantage of having a handy female to fulfill his baser needs instead of having to ride all the way to Cheyenne to see Rosie McLaughlin at the Variety Palace. Of course, he saw no reason to give Rosie up entirely just because he was getting married.

If Kinyan refused his offer of marriage, Ritter was prepared to do whatever was necessary to force her to sell, although another suspicious accident might make the Association question his eventual ownership of the Triple Fork.

Considering everything, Ritter preferred to marry Kinyan. She had seemed meekly obedient to John on the occasions when Ritter had seen her, so he expected her to capitulate readily to his proposal. Ritter had been very careful and thorough and correct in everything except his evaluation of Kinyan Holloway. That became apparent with the next words out of her mouth.

"I'm not really ready to marry again," Kinyan said in a deadly calm voice. "I'll need some time to think about your offer. I hope you'll be patient with me."

Patience was not one of Ritter's virtues.

"Two weeks from today, then," he said, taking Kinyan's hands possessively, turning them palms up, and kissing each one. "I'll be here for your answer. And, Mrs. Holloway, we know what that answer will be, don't we?"

Two weeks! How dare he! Kinyan seethed. *How dare he treat her as though she were some helpless, defenseless widow without any choice except to marry him!*

Suddenly, the truth of the situation hit her. She had no idea how to run the Triple Fork herself, no idea how she could get rid of the squatters, no idea how to deal with rustlers or drifters, and there was no man she could turn to in her time of need. Her Indian family, which had been a well-kept secret all these years, knew no more about ranching than she did and no Indian would be allowed to represent her interests to the Association anyway. Ritter knew exactly what he was doing. She *was* a helpless, defenseless widow! She could hardly blame Ritter for being the first in what she supposed would be a long line of such suiters. But Kinyan wasn't in the habit of giving up that easily.

"The Triple Fork needs a man to run things, Mrs. Holloway," Ritter pressed.

Still fighting the inevitable, Kinyan retorted, "My foreman, Dardus Penrod, is a very capable man and my sons and I will certainly do our part. In fact, I've been thinking seriously about running the Triple Fork on my own."

Ritter dropped Kinyan's hands and rose, no longer a supplicant. He was quite frankly shocked by her suggestion. She was obviously overwrought by John's death, but such ideas needed to be nipped in the bud.

"Mrs. Holloway, a woman belongs in the home taking care of her children and her husband. You'd be a fool to try to do otherwise!"

Ritter perceived the stubborn set of Kinyan's mouth and chin, and his mask of civility slipped momentarily in light of her contrariness. "Whether your foreman can run this ranch or not is beside the point," he continued irritably. "What about those squatters? You let them settle in, and soon you won't have any ranch to manage! My offer of help still stands. I'll send some boys over to burn them out. You just say the word."

Kinyan hesitated. She was sure that if she just had someone to teach her what to do, she could manage on her own. Dardus Penrod had worked with John since he'd started the ranch, and while her relationship with him hadn't been particularly friendly in the past, surely they could manage together without the need for her to marry. However, shouldn't she at least let Ritter handle the squatters? No, Kinyan reasoned. Then she would be indebted to Ritter, and she didn't want to be indebted to anyone just yet.

"I can handle the squatters," she said, displaying all the confidence of the truly naive.

"If you reconsider, you know where to find me," Ritter replied with a pleasant smile that didn't reach his eyes. Too late Ritter realized it had been a mistake trying to push Kinyan to an immediate commitment, especially when it wasn't necessary. He was certain she would eventually make the right decision. There were too many people out there ready to take the Triple Fork away from her, and too many ways he could hasten her change of mind. For instance, what if the foreman she mentioned were no longer around to help out?

"Come on, Willis. Let's go."

As Ritter rose to leave, he reached for his hat, which he'd left on the end table by the chair; but it wasn't there. He turned in a small circle but had no better luck locating it.

"You lookin' for this?"

Josh pulled the crushed Stetson out from under his hip.

Just loud enough for Josh to hear, Ritter snarled, "A leather strap will take some of the vinegar out of you, boy. I'll look forward to it."

"I ain't afraid of you!" Josh shot back.

Ritter ignored Josh, turning to Kinyan with a charming smile, which was the third one that hadn't reached his eyes.

"I hope you'll consider my proposal carefully." Ritter glanced down at the crushed hat in his hand. "I feel I could be of some assistance in helping these two young gentlemen improve their manners. Good day, Mrs. Holloway."

"Yeah, good day, ma'am," Willis repeated as he obediently followed Ritter out the door.

When the door slammed behind the two men, both Josh and Jeremy flew off the settee to confront their mother.

"You *can't* marry *him!*" they blurted in unison.

"Jeremy and I will help, Ma. Pa taught us how to use a Winchester just fine."

All through the discussion with Ritter, Kinyan had been harboring hopes of learning to manage the Triple Fork on her own and of someday finding a man she could love enough to marry. Josh's comment brought that selfish desire into perspective. She would not forego a decision about marriage to Ritter until her sons ended up planted under the Wyoming grass.

"You know it's not what I want, but I don't know the first thing about how to run the ranch," Kinyan acknowledged bitterly. "If I don't marry Ritter, we could lose the Triple Fork."

"You can learn how, Ma! I know you can!" Josh cried.

"Dardus could teach you, Ma," Jeremy suggested. "He knows all there is to know about ranchin'."

That suggestion was so in accord with her own thoughts that, coupled with the imploring looks on the two distraught faces turned up to her, it caused Kinyan to hedge her stand.

"All right," she agreed, sighing raggedly. "Ritter will be back in two weeks wanting an answer. We'll give it a try on our own until then. But if it doesn't look like it's going to work," she warned the two now-ebullient faces turned trustingly up to her, "I'm going to . . ."

Kinyan never finished the sentence because she realized she didn't know what she'd do. She had been backed into a corner. She had vowed never again to allow herself to be forced to marry. Yet it was a fine line she walked, for she would willingly choose Ritter rather than put her children in mortal danger.

"If it doesn't work," she repeated, "I'm going to have to marry him."

Unvoiced was the cry of her indomitable spirit: *Or come up with another plan.*

CHAPTER 4

CHEYENNE WAS A YOUNG city, barely eight years old. Born of the Union Pacific Railroad, then abandoned to its fate, it was brash and loud as any unsupervised youngster, going in all directions, unable to make up its mind to do any one thing for very long. The city boasted a collection of hotels and stores stuffed, like a greedy child's mouth, with wares of every kind. The small dot of rambunctious humanity, appearing almost like a mirage on the barren plains, was a mecca for every traveler, every lonesome cowboy looking for some hell-raising fun. Thus, Cheyenne also enjoyed a proliferation of theaters and saloons and gambling houses, many of them, like Rosie McLaughlin's Variety Palace, a rowdy combination of all three.

Colter had found Cheyenne a highly hospitable place. From the moment he'd entered the Variety Palace, Rosie McLaughlin had made him feel right at home. He'd asked about a bath and a shave, and she'd escorted him out back to a room full of wooden tubs with a fancy barber's chair set off to one side, the spiffed-up barber sitting in it. Nor had Rosie's cordiality ended there. It hadn't ended, in fact, before Colter found himself upstairs in Rosie's elaborate, pink-ruffled canopied bed, which had come, she'd proudly announced, all the way from St. Louis.

Colter lay in the big bed with the naked woman draped half across his fully clothed body and tried to figure out why he didn't feel more satisfied. The woman was attractive, skilled at her work, and she'd even seemed a little caring—

no mean accomplishment, he thought, for a whore. All he'd been able to think about the whole time, however, was that young woman he'd met on the trail. Rosie hadn't come off too well in the inevitable comparison.

About all Rosie had in common with the unidentified woman was her petite stature and a hint of the same spitfire spirit. It was the latter that had attracted Colter to Rosie in the first place. But when he'd looked into Rosie's large, spiky-lashed, caramel-colored eyes, he'd thought of eyes the clear blue of a prairie sky. When he'd squeezed Rosie's melon-sized breasts, he'd thought of another delicious fruit—softer, sweeter, and more to his liking. When he'd run his fingertips through Rosie's coarse, heavily perfumed hair, he'd thought of raven tresses soft as silk and fresh as sunshine. So even though his body had found the physical release it had needed, he was left with an overall sense of having missed something.

Rosie didn't share Colter's sense of dissatisfaction. Because the mysterious scarred drifter had intrigued her, she'd readily agreed to his proposal, made as he lounged in one of the bathtubs she provided out back, that they spend the rest of the afternoon together. She had quite honestly wanted a closer look at the scar that began in the curly black hair at his throat and trailed down enticingly beneath the soapy water. In that she had been disappointed because, even in bed, the drifter had kept most of his clothes on. But she hadn't regretted her decision.

Though it had been a frantic coupling, Colter had been concerned for her needs. She had to admit it hadn't taken much to satisfy her, she'd been so ready for him, but he'd made her feel like a desirable woman. Yet there had been a quiet desperation in his actions Rosie recognized all too well. She wondered for a moment who the other woman was. Still, Rosie wasn't one to allow wasted jealousy to deprive her of the pleasure time spent with the drifter promised.

The afternoon shadows had deepened, leaving the room in darkness. Rosie reluctantly rose from Colter's embrace and lit a lantern beside the bed. She felt no modesty about her nudity. Her body was perfectly formed, her breasts large and high, her hips in good proportion to her small waist. Her legs tended to be a little heavy at the top, but she excused that small flaw because at least they were firm. With her youthful body, she could have been any age from eighteen to thirty. Actually, she was a very well-preserved thirty-five. Rosie slipped on her unmentionables, then sat down at her dressing table and began the repair of her makeup that would keep her looking as young as she pretended to be.

"I've got to get down to work now. I'll be dealin' at one of the poker tables. You comin' down to play some later?" Rosie asked.

"Yeah, I'll be down."

Rosie wondered what it would be like to have a man like Colter love you. Her first impression, of a strong man who probably didn't realize his own strength, hadn't changed. He fought some private demons. He'd muttered a woman's name in anguish when he'd come—but what man didn't? He was a considerate lover, and that usually said a lot about a man. She didn't get into an argument with herself about whether she deserved to have such a man love her. Hell, she'd done a few rotten things in her life, but a woman alone had to do what she had to do. Which reminded Rosie about Ritter.

She had come to Cheyenne two years ago with half the money she'd needed to buy the Variety Palace, and when she'd asked where she could borrow the difference, the owner had sent her to Ritter Gordon. If Rosie had known then what a sonofabitch Ritter was, she'd have hightailed it back to Denver. Ritter had loaned her the balance of the money she'd needed to buy the Variety Palace on the condition that she would do all the work and he would get half the take; but she could never buy him out. They were partners to the death, so to speak—like a married couple. Only Ritter would never marry her.

Oh, he had all the liberties of a husband, all right, but without any of the responsibilities. He came and went as he pleased, used her body abominably, and had exhibited outrage the first time she'd taken another man upstairs besides him. She'd decided then that what Ritter didn't know couldn't hurt him. For the past two years, when she'd wanted a man, she'd invited him upstairs when Ritter wasn't around. So the next words out of Colter's mouth caused her a bit of consternation.

"Will I see you later tonight?"

"Depends."

"On what?"

On whether Ritter comes in tonight, she thought. But Ritter was supposed to be busy at his ranch making plans for the association's fall roundup, and Rosie couldn't bear the thought that she might never get a chance to see the rest of that scar on Colter's chest.

"Hell, sure I'll see you later. After I'm through dealin' poker, we have a date."

Rosie got up from the dressing table and stepped behind the nearby lacquered screen that covered her to a spot just above her nipples. She pulled a shiny pink dress from where it lay across the screen and stepped into it.

Colter felt a vague irritation. He certainly had no claim to the woman's time, but it had appeared she wanted to put him off in the hope that someone better might come along to entertain her. He reached into his vest pocket to get some money.

"You can pay me later," Rosie said.

Colter paused with his hand in his pocket, then smiled. She expected to see him again. No whore who planned to pick up someone else was going to send a customer away without making him pay.

Rosie stuck an enormous black-sequined pink feather headdress into her piled-up hair and stepped from behind the screen. She crossed to Colter and turned around so he could button her into the dress. Rosie smiled ruefully at the deftness with which his fingers accomplished the task. He was no stranger to a lady's boudoir. When he was done, she leaned over to press a soft kiss of thanks on his mouth.

"I'll see you downstairs," she murmured against his lips.

She looked even better with the flashy gown on, Colter thought. But it was the way she acted, proud and fine, not at all like the kind of woman who sold her body for money, that made him wonder, briefly, how she'd ended up here.

Rosie saw the admiration in Colter's eyes and endured a moment of painful regret. She was stronger than the pain, stronger than the regret. Rosie stood and raised her chin and then pulled her shoulders back, which brought her upthrust breasts even higher out of the square-cut gown. Damn Ritter Gordon! And damn all the other cruel, greedy bastards just like him!

42

Rosie returned Colter's look of admiration. He was a fine man, all right. And for tonight, at least, he was hers.

Ritter's need to vent his frustration on a woman's flesh had spurred him through the dark to the Variety Palace, with Willis close on his heels. He'd had one stop to make, to set some wheels in motion. So when he stepped down at last from the saddle into the noisy, dusty street in front of the Palace, it was almost midnight. Beyond the slatted doors, Ritter could hear the whistles and claps of approval for Samuel Finfrock's Fabulous Fiddle as the last musical show of the evening drew to a close. Ritter left Willis to handle the horses as he shoved through the swinging portals in search of the one woman who knew best how to satisfy him.

It was Saturday and the bar was crowded, but Ritter could see Rosie seated at one of the felt-covered gambling tables that littered the right side of the smoke-hazed bar room. Ritter's entire being was concentrated on the voluptuous redheaded woman dressed in an alluring ruffled pink satin gown as he elbowed his way single-mindedly through the stinking horde to his goal.

"Come with me," Ritter commanded Rosie huskily as he laid a hand on her soft, bare shoulder. His mouth had gone dry from the thought of kneading and pinching the pink cleavage exposed to his view.

"That won't be possible," a baritone voice drawled from across the large table.

"What!"

Ritter's incredulity arose as much from the fact that someone had dared naysay him as from his sudden awareness of a stranger at the table. Ritter was well known in Cheyenne, and he wasn't used to being contradicted.

"We haven't played out the hand, and as you may or may not have noticed, there's a considerable pot in the center of the table," the same calm voice responded.

Ritter addressed himself to getting rid of the poker players so he could have Rosie to himself.

"Hank, Jeff, Steve, Whitey," Ritter quickly greeted the cowhands he recognized around the table as his eyes adjusted to the darkness. "I'm sure it would be agreeable to all of you to have back double your ante," Ritter offered confidently. Of the cowhands, only Hank, the youngest, worked for Ritter. The other three rode for Hoot Beaumont's Double B brand. Ritter didn't recognize the fifth player, but the newcomer would soon learn that he could be generous if accommodated. Ritter reached into his vest pocket and pulled out a wad of bills to assuage the greed visible in the eyes of the cowboy closest to him.

" 'Fraid not," the fifth man answered.

So far Rosie hadn't said anything, but she could see Ritter's rising irritation. Anxious to head off any violence, she said, with a smile meant to charm, "What say we finish this hand, Ritter? Then I'll join you."

"That won't be possible," the quiet voice contradicted. "Or have you forgotten you have a prior commitment, Rosie?"

Rosie blushed, an unusual reaction for an experienced whore, and struggled to maintain her composure at the drifter's teasing grin.

Rosie realized now that she should have explained the situation to Colter. Ritter had always come first. Although she regretted having to make a choice, as a businesswoman Rosie knew her best bet was to hold Colter off, if possible. Ritter was going to be here forever; the drifter might be gone tomorrow.

"Surely, mister, we can make it another night," Rosie purred, batting her long eyelashes coyly.

Colter bridled at Rosie's tone, which suggested a hell of a lot less intimacy than they'd shared.

"No."

Rosie's painted ruby-red mouth rounded to a perfect circle in surprise. As she met Colter's dazzling blue eyes, a shiver of anticipation swept through her. To hell with business! Rosie thought. Although he'd paid for the privilege, sex with Ritter meant pain. The drifter's seductive eyes and strong, slender hands promised to repeat what had been an infinitely more pleasurable experience.

"Go see Nell, Ritter. She'll take care of you," Rosie said. Unconsciously, she wet her full lips with her small pink tongue.

The bulge in Ritter's britches grew, and at the same time, he realized that because of this drifter, Rosie had just denied him what he'd ridden fifteen miles to have.

"What the hell!" Ritter exploded. "Rosie, who is this cowboy anyway?"

"My name's Colter. Benjamin Colter. And you're interrupting my game."

Ritter had endured about all he could take in one evening—first the Holloway woman telling him she didn't want his help or his hand in marriage, and now Rosie turning him down because she'd promised the evening to some drifter!

"Just who the hell do you think you are?"

"I just told you. Weren't you listening?" Colter said in a deceptively calm voice.

The muffled guffaws and titters of the cowboys at the surrounding tables infuriated Ritter. He could see a handsome, toothy grin under the battered black hat, but that was all. He couldn't see the steely glint in the dark blue eyes that would have warned him he wasn't dealing with an ordinary cowboy.

"Just what exactly are you doing here in Cheyenne, Colter?"

"That's my business."

A hum of agreement could be heard around the room. It was plain bad manners for Ritter to ask. A cowboy was coming from nowhere and going to nowhere, leastwise until he said differently, of his own accord.

"There'll be no job for you around here now, so you can be on your way."

"Who said I wanted a job?"

"Riffraff drifters in Cheyenne tend to find themselves at the business end of a rope."

"Thanks for the information." Then, dismissing Ritter, he said to Rosie, "I'll take a card."

A collective gasp could be heard, and then a hiss as the great intakes of air were all let slowly out. This drifter apparently had no idea he was playing with fire. The cowpokes who knew Ritter's short fuse were amazed the evening hadn't already erupted in violence, but now they were certain it was only a matter of time.

The other players looked on uneasily as Rosie glared warningly at Ritter and dealt Colter a card. Ritter could hardly believe his eyes. He was not only being dismissed, he was being censured and ignored.

"Saw some good grassland just north of here. Thought I might see about getting me some of it," Colter said amiably to the cowboys at the table. He folded his cards in a small, neat pile in his callused hands, waiting for the next player to take his turn.

"Last good grass to be had was 'tween here and Fort Laramie, and it got bought up in seventy-three. Anyway, cain't buy no land, cain't have no roundup, cain't do nothin' 'round here now less'n yer a member of the 'Sociation," Whitey mumbled through the wad of tobacco pouched in his cheek.

Whitey sent a leery glance at Ritter, who had backed off to lean against the gold-papered wall and now watched the men at the table through slitted eyes. Then Whitey spewed an arc of spittle toward the shiny brass vessel in the corner—and missed. The sawdust covering the hardwood floor quickly absorbed the dark brown puddle.

"I'll take two."

Colter raised a questioning eyebrow, and Whitey continued.

" 'Sociation's a group of ranchers that banded together two years back to put a stop to thievin'. They got some laws passed that make it damn hard on any cowpoke bent on rustlin'. 'Sociation holds a big roundup fer ever'body in the spring 'n fall. Ain't nothin' 'portant happens 'round here now less'n the 'Sociation's involved."

"Then why not just join the Association?" Colter asked.

A grin split Whitey's leathery face, and Steve and Jeff also looked amused. Hank, too scared of displeasing his boss to smile, looked down and noisily ruffled his cards.

"Sure," Whitey agreed with a chuckle. "Ya jus' go out an' join the 'Sociation."

Seeing his chance to humiliate Colter, Ritter moved in close to the table, held out his huge palm, and gibed, "Sure. Just hand over your five-dollar membership fee and I'll sign you up tonight, Colter. Of course there'll be monthly dues of fifty cents and assessments to pay the Association's detective his hundred and fifty a month. . . ."

A general snicker made its way around the poker table. A working cowboy might be able to come up with the membership fee and dues, but no way was he going to be able to pay the assessments when they came due.

Colter glanced at Whitey, who said, "Ritter's head of the 'Sociation."

Colter narrowed his eyes, then slowly stood up so his face came momentarily into the light. He reached into his vest pocket and pulled out a handful of cash. He peeled off five dollar bills and counted them out as he laid each one firmly in Ritter's outstretched hand. Then he added a fifty.

"Sign me up, and put the difference on my account. For assessments," he explained when he saw Ritter's pursed lips. Then he sat back down.

Ritter silently fumed at the way he'd been outmaneuvered. Where the hell had this drifter gotten that kind of money? Ritter shot a glance at the scarred face, then shook his head at a memory that kept slipping from his grasp. There was something familiar about the drifter, but he just couldn't seem to place him. His unease gave way to chagrin when he looked at the bills in his hand. Ritter swore under his breath.

"I'll be damned!"

"Probably," Colter agreed. "It's your play," he reminded Steve.

"I'm afraid I can't accept this money after all," Ritter interrupted, looking for a way out of the trap in which he found himself. "You can't belong to the Association unless you're voted in by the members."

"When do you meet?" Colter inquired.

"Monday nights, usually, but—"

"This month we're meetin' on Wednesday afternoon 'cause we gotta plan the roundup," Willis interrupted over Ritter's shoulder. He'd finished with the horses and searched the bar room until he'd located Ritter. Then he'd come to stand reverently in the shadow of his idol.

"I'll be there," Colter assured Ritter. "Keep it till then."

"Wouldn't be much point in that. You won't find any land around here anywhere that hasn't already been spoken for by some other member of the Association," Ritter said.

"There's that Holloway ranch," Willis intoned, trying to be helpful. The Holloway woman hadn't actually said she didn't want to sell, nor had she accepted Ritter's proposal.

If looks could kill, Willis would have shriveled on the spot from Ritter's glare. Instead, Willis cleared his throat and, for once in his life, remained silent.

"Willis is mistaken," Ritter snarled, daring anyone to deny it.

"What about the Holloway ranch?" Colter asked Whitey, since it was obvious Ritter wasn't going to volunteer any more information.

Seeing the fury building again on Ritter's face, Whitey hesitated. He scratched the short gray and black whiskers growing on a deeply receded chin that left his front teeth bucked. Then he pulled his sweat-stained hat down lower over his small, beady eyes. There was a limit to how far Ritter could be pushed, and Whitey began to think maybe that limit had been reached. He'd seen the results of Ritter's vengefulness before, and they weren't pretty.

"Don't know nothin' 'bout that ranch," Whitey answered blithely.

Colter searched the inscrutable faces of the other cowboys at the table one at a time, challenging them to give him the answers he needed, but each hazarded a glance at Ritter and then stayed silent, unwilling to put himself in range of the dynamite about to explode between the two men.

Ritter crossed his arms across his chest and leaned back against the wall, a smug look on his perfect face. The visage became distorted moments later when Ritter realized Colter had simply dropped the subject and returned to his game.

"Your play," Colter said to Jeff.

"Two cards," Jeff replied nervously.

"I'm out," Hank blurted. "Think I'll get me a beer." The fuzz-cheeked seventeen-year-old abruptly scraped his chair back from the table and headed for the slick mahogany bar on the opposite side of the room. In the forty-foot marbled mirror that ran the length of the bar, he could more safely watch the melodrama being played out behind him.

The suspense mounted minute by minute as the game dragged on, until finally Colter had won yet another hand.

"You got the luck o' the devil, Colter," Steve grumbled.

"It's been a long evening. How 'bout you boys gettin' yourselves one last drink 'fore the bar shuts down," Rosie suggested.

"Sure, Rosie, sure," Steve agreed. He dragged himself up and, spurs jangling as they raked the sawdusted floor, dispiritedly followed Whitey and Jeff over to join Hank at the bar.

Rosie eyed Ritter surreptitiously, noting he'd made no

move to seek out Nell as she'd suggested. The last thing she wanted tonight was two cowboys shooting up her place for the privilege of bedding her! As long as she'd been in the business, she'd managed to avoid that kind of insanity. What had come over her to make her, for the very first time, turn Ritter down?

There was no denying Ritter was a handsome man. He stood just under six feet tall and had strong, muscular shoulders that narrowed to a trim waist. If his body was a little long and his legs a little short, the deformity wasn't remarkable, except that the shortened stride of his legs denied him grace. However, Ritter being the eloquently courteous kind of man he was (and deadly with a .44), that small defect was never commented upon.

Rosie made a leisurely examination of the clean-shaven Colter. Although he was an inch or so taller than Ritter, he was leaner, all sinew and bone. Nor did he have Ritter's perfect facial features. Oh, the mouth was gentle and the eyes burned with a fire that scorched, but the refined cheekbones were high and sharp and the nose too strong. Yet Rosie knew, perhaps better than most women, that there was more to a man than his looks.

"Jake can shut this place down. You ready to come upstairs, Colter?" Rosie asked with an anticipatory smile.

"Yes, ma'am," Colter replied. He came around the table to hold Rosie's chair for her courteously as she stood.

"Why, thank you." Rosie flushed under Colter's solicitous regard. This was another in a series of firsts for Rosie and only served to convince her she'd made the right decision. The last time a gentleman had held a chair for her had been . . . well, she couldn't rightly remember the last time it had happened.

If there had been any way to get around Ritter, Rosie would have taken it, but the embittered man had placed himself so he lounged negligently against the carved oak newel post at the base of the winding staircase.

By now, word of what had happened between Ritter and Colter at the poker table had spread, and it had been whispered more than once that Colter better have said his prayers, because he wasn't going to get another chance to do so. A hushed nervousness came over the crowd in the saloon as Rosie approached the stairs, her arm linked in Colter's.

Colter assessed the situation, then released Rosie's arm and sent her up the stairway past Ritter without him.

"I think I'll have just one more drink before I join you," Colter explained when Rosie turned around to see if he was coming.

Rosie's eyes narrowed to slits. Well, she hadn't figured the drifter for a coward, but he sure didn't seem to relish the prospect of crossing Ritter. It was a shame the man didn't measure up to her first impression of him, but then it was probably better this way. She would have had hell to pay with Ritter.

"Sure, Colter," Rosie said, doubt seeping into her tone. "I'll be waiting for you." There was a world of promise in her words that every cowpoke in the room envied. Every bleary eye watched Rosie's sensuous, hip-swaying ascent until the last black-lace-trimmed pink ruffle flounced from sight. It would almost be worth facing Ritter to find Rosie in your bed at the top of the stairs. Almost.

Ritter stepped into the small space at the bottom of the steps, blocking Colter's access to the stairway, his face a smirk of mocking triumph. He had jumped to the same conclusion as Rosie. When it had come time to put up or shut up, the drifter had shown a yellow streak.

"Would you care to join me?" Colter invited Ritter, gesturing toward the bar.

Having seen it all before, the cowboys in the saloon had a pretty good idea what was coming now. The drifter would try to soft-talk Ritter to avoid having to draw his gun, and Ritter would provoke the drifter until he slapped leather. Then Ritter would kill him.

"I don't drink with low-life yellow-bellied curs," Ritter sneered.

"I usually don't either," Colter replied pleasantly, "but I was making an exception." Then he turned his back on Ritter and sauntered over to the bar. "Whiskey," he said to the bartender.

Ritter gasped at the drifter's audacity.

More than a few of the cowboys sat up and took notice. For a yellow-bellied cur, the drifter showed a considerable amount of nerve.

"Don't bother to pour that whiskey, Jake," Ritter commanded the bartender. "This drifter has decided it would be better for his health to have his drink somewhere other than Cheyenne."

"Now I don't recall having decided anything of the kind." Colter turned to face Ritter, leaning back with his elbows on the bar. "That's a somewhat inhospitable way to treat a new member of the Association, wouldn't you say?"

"You're not a member yet."

The cowboys drinking at the bar began to edge away toward the center of the room, clearing a space around Colter.

"I'll take that whiskey," Colter repeated quietly.

Jake looked to Ritter, who finally nodded. Why not let the man have a drink? It would be his last. Ritter could be very magnanimous when he was certain he was going to win.

Colter picked up the small glass and sipped the bitter, burning liquid.

Ritter changed his stance slightly so he faced Colter at the bar and dropped his hands casually to his sides, the fingertips of his right hand resting against the base of his holster.

"Are you going to walk out that door right now, or are you going to need some help leaving?"

If the saloon had been hushed before, now it was so quiet that the lazy stomp of a horse's hoof could be heard as the animal shifted position outside the slatted doors.

"Can't leave now. Wouldn't be polite. Rosie's waiting for me," Colter quipped with a smile and a wink at Ritter.

Colter had measured his man well, and the words and gesture that were intended to incense Ritter did their job. The red flush that rose from Ritter's neck spread across his face, and the hands at his sides clenched into furious fists.

"I'll make sure she doesn't miss you," Ritter said through gritted teeth.

Colter thought Ritter a fool to start a gunfight over a woman. If he hadn't minded moving on, this disagreement wouldn't matter. He could just leave. But Colter had meant what he said about the grassland. He was staying. If he wanted to hold his head up around Cheyenne, he couldn't back down from Ritter's challenge either. On the other hand, it could hardly endear Colter to his new neighbors if he killed the head of the Association.

51

"It certainly seems a shame to kill a man over a woman who sells her favors," Colter said finally, shaking his head sadly.

Again, Ritter heard only what he wanted to hear, and the placating words of the drifter sounded defensive to him. Colter hadn't shifted his position at all and still leaned back with his elbows on the smoothly polished surface of the bar and one bootheel caught in the brass rail at its base. Ritter couldn't understand why the drifter just lounged there. He should be standing up, flexing his hands, getting ready to draw.

"This is your last chance. You can leave on your own two feet or get carried out. It doesn't matter to me," Ritter warned.

"Pour me another drink, Jake," Colter replied, setting his glass down on the bar.

Ritter drew first.

In the blink of an eye, Colter spun around, pulled his .44, shot the gun from Ritter's hand, and reholstered his smoking weapon.

An astonished Ritter looked from his blood-spattered blue shirt to the blood streaming from his right hand. He'd barely gotten the gun out of his holster! Ritter glanced back at the perfectly relaxed Colter, before he howled in outrage and pain.

"It really just doesn't make sense to kill a man over a woman who sells her favors," Colter repeated. "I'll see you Wednesday afternoon. Better have someone look after that hand."

Then, ignoring shouts of "Get the sheriff!" and without a backward glance at the bedlam breaking loose behind him, Colter strode past a bleeding Ritter up the stairs to Rosie.

When Rosie heard the single gunshot downstairs, she fluffed her henna-dyed hair over her shoulder. Shortly, she would be entertaining a gentleman caller. She watched the reflection in the mirror as the door opened and then closed behind her.

"Good evening."

A pleased smile suffused Rosie's face. She turned down the lamp on the dressing table, then slowly swiveled to face Colter.

"Did you kill him?"

"No, although I have a feeling I'll regret it someday."

She'd have hell to pay herself later, Rosie thought. But she figured it was worth it.

"There's no doubt you've made a powerful bad enemy. He's as smooth-talkin' as the snake in Eden. That's how he got to be head of the 'Sociation. They're all a little awed by his manners and 'fraid of his gun. Course, now that'll change some," she said, grinning broadly.

Colter stood to the right of the door, staying well clear of the canopied bed. The pink sheets had been turned down again temptingly, but this time Colter balked at accepting the invitation. Rosie held her seductive pose on the small upholstered stool before her dressing table a moment longer, then stood up. Her filmy lavender nightdress left little to his imagination.

Rosie fit her curved form in the niches of Colter's body as she wrapped her arms around his expansive shoulders and slid her hands up into the black curls at the nape of his neck. Her lips touched the scar at his throat seductively.

Colter spread his fingertips along the sides of Rosie's breasts and worked his hands knowingly down the lush curves to her hips, but surprisingly, he felt nothing at all. As Colter put his lips to the racing pulse beneath Rosie's ear, he murmured, "I want to know about the Holloway ranch."

"Hell, Colter," Rosie said breathlessly, her senses heightened by the fiery grasp in which she found herself enfolded. "Can't we talk business later?"

"The ranch," he repeated insistently. Colter nuzzled the hennaed hair away from a soft ear and ran his hands from Rosie's full hips up her arched back, waiting for his body to respond. It didn't.

Between tantalizing kisses on Colter's face and throat, Rosie explained, "John Holloway was killed in a range accident three months ago. Horse threw him and dragged him. He left a wife and some kids. The Triple Fork is the largest ranch in the Territory. Word around Cheyenne is the widow's been losin' stock to rustlers and that squatters are movin' in. Ritter considers it's just a matter of time 'fore that land is his. He ain't gonna like it if you go buttin'—"

Colter ended Rosie's speech by covering her mouth with

his own. He had almost all the information he needed except— Colter nibbled Rosie's full lips as he asked, "Where's the ranch, Rosie?"

"Northwest of here, some fifteen miles or so. Big white house and lots of outbuildin's. You can't miss it."

Rosie began unbuttoning Colter's black shirt. She wanted to see that scar on his chest he'd kept hidden from her earlier. She had to. Just then, Colter leaned over and blew out the lamp on the table beside the bed. The only light in the room came from the slivered quarter moon. Rosie's groan in the darkness was a cross between dismay and desire, for Colter had taken up his delightful conquest of her breasts and belly with the nimble touch of a gunslinger. Rosie dug her fingers through the pelt of wiry hair on Colter's chest, and she could tell from the smooth ridges along the taut skin which way the scars ran. How strange his desire for darkness, Rosie thought. But soon she wasn't thinking at all.

Colter worried over the fact he'd been north of Cheyenne today and hadn't seen any ranch buildings. Maybe he just hadn't gone far enough west. Then again, that tiny woman had said he was on her land, and her husband was dead. Could she possibly be Holloway's widow? He pressed himself against the grinding hips that met his own in fevered excitement, determined not to let the memory of the respectable female he'd met earlier in the afternoon rob him of the comfort of Rosie's flesh—flesh he'd shot a man to enjoy in peace. But the picture of the tiny woman he'd so carefully branded in his memory insinuated itself in his thoughts and refused to go away.

Colter deftly released the ties at the shoulders of Rosie's silken gown, and as it slipped to the floor, he pushed her back up against the door, pressing his full length against her naked body. Then he sought the pulse point behind her ear with his lips. He'd please her, oh yes, he'd please her, the tiny, haunting woman!

Rosie knew something was wrong even before Colter dropped his forehead to her shoulder. A muffled groan issued from his lips. Rosie's head dropped back against the door and her eyelids sank closed.

"I know I'm not the woman you want, but I'm here and I want you. Will you just spend the night with me?"

At her plea, a wave of loneliness such as he hadn't felt in years swept over Colter. It was surprising, because he'd believed he'd conquered the need to be close to another human being. He wondered what had caused that feeling to reassert itself so strongly now. A softly smiling, heart-shaped face appeared before him, bringing with it a surge of longing he fought against—to no avail. There was no sense staying with the whore. What she offered could not assuage his need. He bit down the cruel retort to Rosie's query that had sprung to his lips. It wasn't Rosie's fault she was who she was.

"No thanks. I can't stay," Colter finally responded with what he hoped was an appropriate amount of wistfulness as he buttoned himself back into his clothes. "I have some miles to travel tonight." Colter managed a flip grin. "It's been nice knowing you, Rosie."

"Likewise, I'm sure," the naked Rosie replied, gamely returning his grin as she relit the lamp by the bed.

"Is there a back way out?"

"Does a dog have fleas?"

When Colter's grin had relaxed into a smile, Rosie continued, "Last door down the hall on the left leads to an outside stairway."

As Colter reached for the money in his vest pocket, Rosie put a tentative hand out to stop him.

"My door is always open," she whispered.

The soft lamplight had stripped the years from Rosie's face, and as her grin faded she looked young, and surprisingly innocent. For a brief moment, Colter reconsidered his decision. His thumb caressed the top of Rosie's hand gently, then fell away.

"Good-bye, Rosie."

A draft of air cooled Rosie's sweat-dampened body as the door clicked closed behind Colter. She leaned against the smooth wood and closed her eyes. He would be going to Kinyan Holloway now. Rosie felt a rising emotion and was chagrined to discover it was envy. She shook it off, but when she felt regret taking its place, she fought again to feel envy, jealousy, anger. Her anger came to rest on Ritter.

As though she had summoned him, he appeared, pounding furiously on her door. She barely had time to turn and move away before Ritter's booted foot kicked the door open. It hit the wall with a bang, and Ritter, gun in hand, was through the door and had slammed it shut again before Rosie had a chance to cover herself.

"Well, well. What have we here? A bitch in heat?"

"Get out, Ritter." Rosie made no move to cover herself, her soul impervious to Ritter's lusting eyes, her anger hidden by her calm response.

Ritter laughed. It wasn't a pleasant sound. Before Rosie could react, he reached out and grabbed her hair, pulling hard, bending her over backward.

"Where's that drifter? I expected to find him here."

Rosie's hands went to Ritter's wrist in an attempt to control the pain.

"Colter's gone. Is the sheriff looking for him?"

Ritter yanked Rosie's hair in anger as he admitted, "Damned Wiley Potts! Said from all accounts it was a fair fight. Wouldn't even agree to question the cowboy. Doesn't matter. I'll take care of Colter in my own way. But first," he said, holstering his gun, "you and I have some unfinished business."

Ritter cupped Rosie's breast in his blood-splattered hand, which had merely been scratched by Colter's bullet, his fingertips pinching cruelly.

"Don't *ever* say no to me again," he warned in a low, vicious voice. "You're my private property, and I keep what's mine."

Then Ritter's mouth dropped to a nipple and he bit down until Rosie bled.

Rosie knew better than to cry out. It only made Ritter more cruel. She made her mind blank and thought back to a time when she had been loved, revered by a husband. They'd had a small ranch of their own, with good water and grass, and had a baby on the way. Then the husband had been killed by land-grabbing neighbors, and she'd been raped and beaten and had lost the baby. She'd survived, but had been thrown by circumstance into a far different kind of life. She'd learned to draw more subtle lines of right and wrong. She'd made a moral niche for herself in which she felt comfortable, and she stayed faithfully within it. She might have to deal in business with scum like Ritter, but she wouldn't be threatened. And she wouldn't be owned.

At that moment, Rosie began to make her plans to be free of Ritter. She'd always wanted to see San Francisco. Of course it would be best if she waited to leave Cheyenne until the Association's fall roundup was over. The thirsty cowboys who hit town with their pockets full at the end of the roundup would spend plenty at the Palace. But once she had their roundup wages, she'd leave. She had escaped from the clutches of unscrupulous men before, and she could do it again.

Rosie wondered whether she should try to find the drifter and warn him, then decided against it for the time being. Colter seemed the kind of man who could take care of himself. If he was heading for that Holloway woman, it wouldn't be long before he found himself in conflict with Ritter. At the thought of Colter with the widow, a pailful of envy sloshed over Rosie. She took the dousing, and came up sputtering. Rosie McLaughlin wasn't going to drown in self-pity. She was stronger than the pain, stronger than the regret.

I wish you luck, Mrs. Holloway, Rosie thought. I could have used some when I was in your shoes. But then, you may not need it as much as I did. No Benjamin Colter ever showed up at my door.

CHAPTER 5

"I TOLD YOU these steers should've been treated for blowflies before you left, Miz Holloway!"

"Then why weren't they treated, Dardus?" Kinyan snapped back at her foreman. She used her anger to hold at bay the nausea that threatened to rise in her throat as she turned away from the sickening infestation of larvae on a downed steer. Kinyan remounted Gringalet, then walked her chestnut the few steps over to face Dardus Penrod, who sat rigidly on his dun, trying to decide whether to give this woman the gamy piece of his mind he'd let ripen for the three long months since John Holloway had died. When Kinyan raised an accusing eyebrow and cocked her head expectantly, Dardus exploded.

"Why, of all the rank, shiftless, no-good green, half-cocked . . . ! Miz Holloway, I ain't got no more turpentine! I asked you twice now to order more and you just ain't done it. I only brought you out here 'cause I thought maybe if you seen how bad the problem is, you'd know I wasn't just complainin' to hear myself talk!"

Kinyan wiped the sweat from her brow with the sleeve of her white blouse and kept her arm up just a little longer than necessary to hide the blush of shame that had flushed her face. She'd asked the aging foreman to be honest, and he had been. But this certainly wasn't the way she'd pictured things turning out when she'd started the day.

After Ritter's visit, Kinyan had advised Dorothea of both

Ritter's proposal and her options of selling or trying to run the ranch herself. Dorothea hadn't admonished her to let Ritter handle things or argued against selling, as Kinyan had feared she might, but rather had offered her support for whatever decision Kinyan made. Kinyan had spent the night doing some serious thinking. Perhaps, just perhaps, with Dorothea's help, she and the boys could make it on their own. Kinyan had approached Dardus Penrod at cock's crow this morning and asked that he fill her in on everything that needed "the boss's" attention, insisting she wanted to learn what she needed to know to manage the Triple Fork. She'd had no idea he would so promptly take her at her word.

Kinyan took one more quick look at the infested steer before she stiffened her spine, lifted her chin, and said determinedly, "I'll have some turpentine available for you first thing tomorrow morning. And, Dardus . . ."

Kinyan waited for the older man to make eye contact, but the closest he came was focusing on her hands. When she realized he wasn't going to look her in the eye, she added, "Next time I forget to do something important, I won't expect you to be so understanding."

A sound something like "Hummph" came from Dardus, and Kinyan assumed, since it was a response she'd often heard him give to John, that he'd concurred with her. She smiled, thinking some things stayed the same after all. Dardus hadn't changed in the eleven years she'd known him. With Dardus, you always knew exactly where you stood. He'd disapproved of her marriage to John, and he hadn't hesitated to make his feelings known at the time.

"Why the girl's young enough to be your daughter!" he'd bellowed to John.

"And old enough to be my wife and the mother of my children," John had replied calmly.

And that had been the end of that. Kinyan had never heard another disparaging word from Dardus, even though she knew the two men were never quite as close after. John would have been glad to have Dardus join them for supper in the house, but Dardus said he felt too much like a fifth leg on a cow, so he spent his evenings with the hands in the bunkhouse.

But the two men had remained inseparable on the range. It

was the one place where Dardus had been able to have his old friend to himself. Kinyan had never intruded on that domain until now. She knew Dardus had been hard hit by John's death, like a hen who'd lost its one chick, and the fact he hadn't gotten the turpentine himself testified to how busy he'd been the past three months without John. Kinyan felt more confident about her position when she admitted that however much he might resent it, Dardus could use some help.

"How many head have we lost?" Kinyan asked as they slowly rode the perimeter of a small buffalo wallow toward the meager shade of an isolated juniper.

" 'Bout twenty, I'd guess. But them flies ain't the worst problem."

Kinyan's head came up with a jerk. "They aren't? Then what is?"

"Rustlin', Miz Holloway. Near as I can figure, we've lost three hundred head from along the west boundary since John passed on. There was some rustlin' even before John's accident, so I just kept up what John ordered then. I've had the boys out ridin' every night, tryin' to catch the thieves in the act, but they're just too smart. They seem to know where we are, and they hit us someplace else.

"Then there's them squatters that settled 'bout a week ago. I been waitin' for you to get back so's you could tell me what you wanta do."

"What would John have done?" Kinyan asked, thinking that was probably the easiest way to unknot this particular coil.

"I dunno."

"You don't know? You worked for John twenty-six years. Surely this problem came up before!"

"Sure it did," Dardus defended himself. "But John never handled the situation the same way twice. He always sized up the individuals involved first, then planned what he was gonna do."

"Which was?" Kinyan prodded in exasperation.

"Well, sometimes he just talked 'em into leavin' or bought 'em out."

Kinyan felt relieved she wouldn't have to use violence, until Dardus added, "Then there was the times he had to shoot their stock and burn 'em out."

Kinyan looked down at her hands. Could she do those things herself or order them done?

"Then there's those got invited to stay here permanent like, only not where they'd take up any space," Dardus finished.

Kinyan turned Gringalet away from Dardus because she didn't want him to see the uncertainty on her face. Even though she hadn't appreciated being scolded like a child for failing to order turpentine, at least that was a problem she could remedy simply by sending a cowboy to Cheyenne. But dealing with blowflies didn't compare with the prospect of capturing rustlers and facing down squatters.

Well, now she had the reins of control in her hands all right, only to find out the horse had the bit in his teeth and was running wild. Kinyan rubbed a sweaty palm along the leg of the Levi's she had borrowed from Jeremy as a symbolic token of her changed status. It was quite a revelation to discover that her experienced, capable, wise, and all-knowing foreman expected *her* to tell *him* what to do!

Kinyan pivoted in the saddle to demand that the wizened cowboy just take care of the rustlers and squatters however he thought best. The sight of the old, grizzled man unconcernedly rolling a cigarette brought her up short.

Dardus poured a precise line of tobacco on a thin paper, then pulled the string on his tobacco pouch closed with his nicotine-stained teeth and one-handedly stuffed it back into his calfskin vest pocket. At the same time, he rolled the makings expertly in the other hand, licking the paper before making the final twist and setting it between his sun-browned lips. He flicked a match against a chipped fingernail and sucked deeply on the burning tobacco.

Kinyan realized the foreman was no less now than what he'd been when John was alive—a cowboy who took orders and made sure they were executed, not one who gave them. If only she had known that before she'd told Ritter she would handle the squatters on her own! Kinyan fiddled with the amulet around her neck. Her thumb caressed the gold heart; her forefinger smoothed the feather. She had never had to make important decisions. The very newness of it made her next orders sound tentative.

"I'll go visit the squatters tomorrow," she said, deciding to do so simultaneously with her announcement to Dardus.

"I have to admit I don't have any idea right now how we can stop the rustlers," she added, her lips pursed in thought. "But I'm sure if I put my mind to it, I can come up with something. Meanwhile, I'll send somebody into Cheyenne for turpentine. If there's anything else I should order, let me know now."

An astonished look crossed Dardus's lined face, and the cigarette dangled from his lips as his mouth opened in surprise.

"Well, you don't have to act quite so surprised. I told you I planned to learn everything I need to know to run this ranch, and I meant it."

Dardus's mouth worked futilely, the cigarette bobbing up and down awkwardly, but he couldn't seem to get any words out. It was not until the arrow sank into the fleshy part of her own arm that Kinyan realized they'd been attacked. Kinyan gasped in pain, then gasped again in horror when Dardus fell forward on the neck of his horse and she recognized the feathered shaft extending from his back. A Sioux arrow! Attacked by her own people?

Kinyan shouted a greeting in Sioux. When another arrow came dangerously close to hitting her, it became apparent this was not the time to try and correct what was obviously a horrible mistake. Kinyan reached around to grab the reins of Dardus's gelding and tapped Grinaglet with her spurs. The huge stallion lunged forward in a reckless race for safety.

"Hang on, Dardus!" Kinyan yelled. "We've got to run for it!"

Fear catapulted Kinyan across the grassy plains, with Dardus Penrod in tow. She glanced over her shoulder occasionally, but didn't slow her hazardous pace even when she saw no signs of pursuit. Gradually, she became aware of Gringalet's bellowed breathing and lathered withers, and her consideration for her horse brought a return of sensibility. Kinyan had known for some time she wasn't being followed, but it was as though by running from this one danger she could escape from all her fears—first Ritter, then rustlers, and now renegade Indians!

Kinyan pulled Gringalet to a walk and glanced over her shoulder to make sure Dardus still held on to his mount. He lay there unmoving, head bowed low and bobbing beside the neck of his dun, the arrow in his back a grim ultimatum. Kinyan didn't remember breaking off the arrow in her arm, but only a small piece of the shaft protruded from the bloody hole in her cotton blouse. The pain throbbed mercilessly. She refused to cry! Kinyan rubbed the back of her hand across her blurry eyes and groaned aloud in agony when she realized she'd used her wounded left arm.

Kinyan felt trapped, like a longhorn snarled up in cruel barbed wire, like a wild horse fettered on a too short tether. She could feel the panic rising in her. She hadn't realized the extent of the burden John had left behind. Now she wouldn't even have a foreman! How was she supposed to learn what to do?

Ritter's handsome mask loomed before her mocking, *"Fool! Fool! Fool!"* She squeezed her eyes shut, but the wickedly handsome face merely smiled in triumph. Kinyan's eyes flashed open on the barren plains that belonged to her, but that she would now be obliged to pass to a husband's control. Her hopes of the morning had been dashed so impossibly fast! She burned. She raged. She gnashed her teeth in helpless fury.

"I'm coming, I'm coming."

Dorothea Holloway quickly tucked a stray silvery-gray hair into the thick bun at the base of her neck. Then she finished wiping the flour from her hands onto the apron that surrounded her ample girth and protected her best Sunday dress before she grabbed the shiny brass doorknob to answer the persistent knock at the front door. The black bombazine hadn't stopped swishing around her ankles before she found herself face-to-face with her visitor.

"Hello there," Dorothea said.

After sixty-nine years of frontier living, nothing much surprised Dorothea Holloway anymore, not even the appearance of a total stranger, hat in hand, at her front door early on a morning that had promised since sunrise the kind of scorching August heat that left one prostrate by midafternoon.

"I'm looking for Mrs. Holloway."

"Well, you've found her. What can I do for you?" Dorothea inquired matter-of-factly. The elderly woman dabbed at the rivulet of perspiration on her left temple with the edge of her voluminous white apron. She observed the slight widening of the dark blue eyes in the scarred face across from her, which otherwise retained a strict guise of indifference. Dorothea allowed the man to stare at her without speaking for some moments more before she repeated, "Was there some reason you were looking for me?"

Frankly, Colter was so disconcerted to find this stout, grandmotherly figure dressed in mourning clothes, rather than the feisty young woman he'd held in his arms the previous day, that he'd been rendered speechless.

"Yes," he managed to say. "Is this John Holloway's ranch, the Triple Fork?"

The heavyset woman's light gray eyes misted, and a mask of sorrow dropped into place. Her heavy jowls sagged, her prim lips became pinched, and wrinkles appeared in her otherwise smooth forehead. Her grief was a tangible thing that reached out to Colter across the threshold. He opened his mouth to express his sympathy but was cut off by the woman's voice. Startled, Colter realized the evidence of grief had vanished as quickly as it had come.

"If the Triple Fork is what you're seeking, that's what you've found," she confirmed. Dorothea squinted at the stranger. "I don't know you, do I?"

Dorothea had forgotten enough familiar faces lately to doubt her senses. However, she hadn't yet had so many lapses that she felt self-conscious about admitting to her failing memory.

"No," Colter said with an easy grin that revealed how much he immediately admired this unpretentious woman. "My name is Benjamin Colter. I'm up from Texas. Nice to meet you, Mrs. Holloway."

Dorothea Holloway had made her evaluation of the kind of man who stood before her the moment she opened the door. One didn't survive long in this wilderness without being a pretty good judge of character. She'd taken in the honest, clean-shaven face, the mended, freshly laundered black shirt, and the polished black boots in a glance. There was nothing the cowboy could do about the small rips and tears in the rawhide chaps, but he'd attempted—not too successfully, Dorothea thought—to shed some of the trail dust they bore. The hat he held politely in his hands was a disaster, but that only proved to Dorothea that the man before her had used it for the many purposes a cowboy's hat was intended to serve, including pillow at night, bucket for water, and shade from the sun.

Dorothea barely noticed the slash on the cowboy's face except in passing. In a land of bodies torn by grizzlies, fingers lost to frostbite, and heads that had survived a scalping, a scar here or there was to be expected. At the same time, Dorothea recognized from his loose-limbed, ready stance and searching eyes, not to mention the .44 Colt strapped to his hip, that this was a man expecting trouble. So she waited to see just what he wanted before she brought him into her home.

"Something I can do for you, Mr. Colter?"

"Yes, ma'am. I, uh . . ."

Colter found himself suddenly tongue-tied. It seemed indelicate to make an offer for the ranch with the two of them standing in the doorway to the widow's home. On the other hand, he couldn't very well invite himself in, could he? Colter looked away toward the stream of gray smoke rising from the cookshack, which was attached to a bunkhouse made of cottonwood logs by a roofed breezeway slung with saddles, bridles, and ropes. Colter knew, without being able to see them, that several scroungy dogs probably lolled in the shade of the breezeway. There wasn't a sign of the cowboys he suspected were sleeping off their Saturday night revels in the long, chinked-log bunkhouse. He thought back to his first picture of the ranch as he'd crested a small rise.

Colter had admired the contrast of the forest-green shutters against the stark white of the rest of the two-story wooden house. The outline of frilly curtains showed through the four sets of glass windowpanes he could see, and pink roses bloomed in profusion along either side of the three steps in front. The wide covered porch held up by thick round columns ran the length of the house and gave it a solid look reminiscent of a fine old Southern home. A wooden swing painted white hung from thick hemp tied to the porch rafters. He approved the two gray stone chimneys at either end of the house. He'd heard stories of the interminably long, frigid winters in the Territory, and he looked forward to staying warm.

Colter hadn't confined his perusal to the house but had

65

taken in the large, weathered gray barn, fresh-mown hay visible from the open loft doors. A good-looking grulla, two buckskins, and a bay wandered in the split-rail corral that hemmed the barn. He'd noticed that sparkling water ran fresh and clear in the creek at the bottom of the hill beyond the house. Cottonwoods along the creek provided shade that wasn't close enough for hostile Indians to use it for cover, but was close enough to enjoy if one cared to stroll there in the evening after supper.

And the grass! Vast seas of tall needlegrass and bluestem and a wealth of shorter buffalo grass, blue grama, June grass, and wheatgrass spread like a verdant blanket across the land. Colter's respect for John Holloway had taken firm root when he realized how carefully chosen the location of the ranch was and how conscientiously the man had kept the place. Remembering his first, highly favorable impressions gave Colter the impetus to broach the purchase of this land, despite his consideration for the widow's feelings. He shifted his gaze back to Mrs. Holloway.

"I understand the Triple Fork is for sale. I'd like to buy it."

There was no mistaking the shocked look on the elderly woman's face, which was replaced by rage, then desperation, and finally a look of stubborn determination. All of that passed in the flicker of an eyelash, yet Colter missed nothing. Not one of those expressions boded well for his purchase of the land, and it was only when Colter felt the sinking feeling in the pit of his stomach that he realized just how badly he wanted to settle down here.

"That girl!" Dorothea muttered under her breath. Then, brusquely, "Well, don't just stand there. Come on in and sit a spell."

Dorothea turned with all the dignity of a matriarch and marched into the parlor with a reluctant Colter following uncomfortably on her heels. As he pulled the front door closed behind him, Colter saw that a hall split the house in two. A set of wide stairs just inside the front door led upward to the second floor. To the left, he could see the stone fireplace in a dining room full of sturdy pine furniture, and beyond that, through an open doorway, the kitchen. The right side of the house was entirely taken up by the parlor. It was there Dorothea led him.

Colter admired the neat, clean appearance of the rose wallpapered room, with its polished wooden floors, crisply starched, crocheted doilies on the pine end tables, and simply framed family photographs displayed on the dust-free pine mantel over the fireplace. The whitened skull of a longhorn steer, with at least a nine-foot spread of pearly horns tipped in black, dominated the space above the mantel. The room had apparently also served as John Holloway's study, for books lined a floor-to-ceiling case that took up one side wall, and a massive oak rolltop desk sat majestically under the window at the far end of the room, overlooking the creek. The desire to make this place his home grew by leaps and bounds, and Colter cautioned himself not to become too excited by what might be out of his reach.

"Have a seat, Mr. Colter."

It was a demand, not a request. Nevertheless, Colter moved to the leather chair Dorothea indicated while she seated herself at the edge of the smaller chair situated next to it. He fit the leather chair, and it fit him. He felt as though he belonged there. Dorothea noticed it too, and it caused her next question to come out more sharply than she'd intended.

"Now, where did you get the idea this ranch is for sale, Mr. Colter?"

"I'm sorry if I caught you by surprise, Mrs. Holloway, but I heard in Cheyenne last night that John Holloway had been killed recently in an accident and you were losing stock to rustlers. I was told you might want to sell out."

"Sell out!" Dorothea spat.

Colter winced at the vehemence of the words Dorothea pronounced as though they were some vile disease.

"I'm prepared to pay you a fair price."

"I knew that girl felt no kinship for the land, but I never thought she'd go so far as this. Mr. Colter, I—"

The front door slammed open with a crash to reveal a tiny female form that Colter recognized instantly. Colter's brows came up in astonishment. She was wearing jeans!

"Come quick! It's Dardus! He's been hurt bad!"

Both Dorothea and Colter shot from their chairs after the retreating figure. Kinyan had come in by way of the barn, and several cowhands were already gathered around Dardus, easing him off his dun.

"Take him upstairs to the extra bedroom, Petey. It's the

last door on the left at the end of the hall," Dorothea directed. "It'll be easier for me to take care of him there. Now, girl, you . . ."

Dorothea started to give Kinyan a job and realized as she turned to look at the young woman that Kinyan was on the verge of fainting. In fact, as Dorothea watched, Kinyan's knees buckled.

Kinyan felt strong arms catch her at the shoulders and under the knees, lifting her up and bracing her against the solid wall of a chest. Kinyan closed her eyes on the concerned face that looked down upon her and gave herself up into the cowboy's care.

"It's just a flesh wound," Dorothea said as she quickly examined Kinyan's bloody arm. "She's not feeling any pain right now. I'll show you where to put her until I can take care of her."

Dorothea didn't even wait to see if Colter followed. She merely marched up the carpeted stairs to the second floor, turned right down the hall, and threw open the door to Kinyan's room. Dorothea unbuckled Kinyan's spurs and set them on the braided rug near the chest, then pulled down the decorative red-and-white ribbon-patterned quilt on the four-poster bed, exposing the clean white sheets beneath.

"Lay her on the bed. If you want to be some help, you can go down to the kitchen and start some hot water boiling. If you don't want to help, get back downstairs and stay out of the way."

Dorothea left Colter standing uncertainly in the room with Kinyan and bustled down the narrow hall to the room at the opposite end. She ran into Petey Watkins and Frank Little-john on their way out the door.

"Is Dardus gonna be all right, Miz Holloway?" Petey asked, swallowing so hard his Adam's apple bobbed up and down. His dark brown eyes were wide with fright.

"I'll do my best to help him, Petey," Dorothea reassured the youthful cowboy, whom Dardus had taken under his wing when he'd arrived at the ranch a year ago last spring, "but I can't promise anything. I'll know more after I take a closer look."

Colter hadn't yet left Kinyan's room. Knowing that staying busy would keep Petey from worrying, Dorothea said kindly, "It would be a big help if you could start some water to boil down in the kitchen. When it's ready, bring it on up."

"Yes, ma'am," Petey replied. The anxious youngster disappeared down the stairs with Frank following after him.

Dorothea crossed and leaned over to check on Dardus, who lay face down on the bed. She didn't like the spot where the arrow had lodged. It was too close to organs that didn't heal well. She tenderly smoothed the wiry gray hair on the back of Dardus's head.

"He's probably not going to make it."

Startled by the sound of a male voice when she'd thought she was alone, Dorothea whirled to find Colter standing just behind her shoulder.

"I've seen too many wounds like that. Too bad. He'll likely live awhile and be in a lot of pain."

Dorothea had come to just about the same conclusion herself, but hearing Colter say the words aloud seemed heartless somehow. This wasn't just another wounded cowboy, it was Dardus, who had been John's best friend, and her friend too, for more years than she cared to remember.

"I told you if you don't want to help, you can leave," she said tartly.

"I'll cut the arrow out of the girl's arm. Better to do it now while she's unconscious," Colter replied, unperturbed by the irritation in Dorothea's voice, accurately guessing the reason for it.

"Well, what are you waiting for?"

Colter grinned. Dorothea Holloway was a straightforward woman all right. "Nothing. Have you got some whiskey I can use to clean my knife?"

"There's some in the decanter on the mantel in the bedroom where the girl is."

Colter turned to leave, but stopped when Dorothea spoke.

"Mr. Colter . . ."

"Yes, ma'am?"

"Thank you."

When he returned to the room, the woman was awake. It was too bad she had regained consciousness. It would make his job tougher, and it wasn't going to be very pleasant for her either. Her eyes followed him like he was some creature slunk from a dark cave. For someone who made it a habit not to get involved in other people's business, Colter thought with a twinge of irritation at her continued blunt stare, he seemed to be interfering a great deal in this woman's life.

The sight of the cowboy she'd met the previous day led Kinyan to doubt her senses momentarily. She shook her head as though to clear it, but the vision didn't disappear. And that made her glad. She hadn't been willing to admit to herself how much she wanted to see the cowboy again, and after the events of the day, it seemed like a dream come true. But that didn't explain how her innermost wish had been granted.

"What are you doing here?" Kinyan demanded as she tried to sit up.

"I'm going to cut that arrow out of your arm," Colter replied, pushing her back down again.

"I mean how did you get here?" Kinyan persisted.

"On my horse," Colter said dryly.

"That's not funny. Who are you?"

"My name's Benjamin Colter." Colter hesitated before he asked, "What's yours?"

"Kinyan Holloway."

She must be Holloway's daughter, he thought. She looked even smaller lying on the big bed.

He looked younger, Kinyan thought, without the beard. Absent his hat, the black curls drifted down to dust his forehead. The blue eyes looked worried, and Kinyan wondered what troubled him.

"And you just happened to be riding by?" Kinyan asked, still trying to figure out how he had ended up in her bedroom.

"I was . . . look, how about if I cut that arrow out first and then you can ask me all the questions you want."

Colter moved to the fireplace. As he walked, he pulled his knife from the hidden sheath in his boot. He located the crystal decanter, half full of whiskey, and the delicate crystal glasses beside it. He poured himself a generous drink and swallowed it in a single gulp. It was good whiskey and a shame to drink it so irreverently, but by God, he needed it! How had she managed to get attacked by Indians? She was part Indian herself!

When he started to pour more whiskey, Kinyan said, "If you're going to be cutting on me, I'd rather you didn't get drunk."

"This one's for you." He brought the drink and the bottle over to Kinyan. "I thought you might need it."

"I don't drink. That was my husband's favorite whiskey."

"Then I guess we shouldn't waste it." Colter downed the second glass of whiskey and set the bottle on the table next to the bed.

Kinyan's eyes lit with anger, but Colter ignored her as he crossed over to the dry sink to remove the flowered water pitcher from the matching bowl in which it sat. After pouring some water from the pitcher into the bowl, he carried the bowl with him over to set it beside the whiskey bottle.

"Scoot over. I'll need some room to work."

Kinyan raised her brows and looked at the ceiling in an exaggerated expression of disbelief, but complied with the cowboy's demand, making a space for him at the edge of the bed.

Colter sat down to cut the bloodied sleeve away at the shoulder with his knife. He was careful, but even the slight movement of the material around the wound sent the blood from Kinyan's face.

"Steady," Colter said with a taut smile. "You'll ruin my reputation for painless surgery."

At the reference to surgery, Kinyan's brows rose again. His gentle touch bespoke a tenderness in stark contrast to the strength of the callused hands that ministered to her. Kinyan sought the drifter's eyes. At first, she thought she perceived that same tenderness in his gaze, but when he caught her so boldly watching him, a mocking laughter replaced it. Before Kinyan could take umbrage, Colter stripped the case off one of the pillows and began tearing it into small pieces.

"What are you doing?"

"I need something to use to clean your wound and for bandages."

"That was a perfectly good pillowcase!"

"Yes, it was," he agreed with a grin. "Just right for the job." Colter took a strip of the cloth and soaked it in whiskey.

Kinyan gasped when Colter touched the skin close by the

71

arrowhead as he cleansed it with the whiskey-soaked rag, and she bit her lower lip. Her father would have censured her had he heard her cry out in pain. But it had been too long since she had needed to be stoic. It no longer came naturally.

Colter pulled one of his buckskin riding gloves from the waist of his Levi's.

"If you want something to chew on, try this. I have some personal experience with those teeth and they can be deadly."

Despite her wish not to be charmed by the drifter, Kinyan laughed, a gentle sound that sent Colter's heart to his throat. She took the glove and put a corner of it between her teeth.

Before Kinyan really had a chance to anticipate the pain, Colter grasped her arm to keep her from moving it and made a quick, shallow cut with his knife.

Although beads of sweat broke out on her forehead, Kinyan remained absolutely still. She needn't stay quiet as a Sioux, she told herself, but there was no excuse for feminine hysterics either. When Colter was done, Kinyan yanked the glove from her mouth and exclaimed, "That hurt!"

A wry smile bent Colter's mouth at the way the woman had chosen to express her pain: no tears, no whining, no crying, just a simple statement of fact. He warned himself not to admire her fortitude too soon. The arrow wasn't out, and she hadn't been stitched yet.

"Now, are you going to tell me what you're doing here!" Kinyan demanded.

"I came here to buy the Triple Fork," Colter admitted, hoping that if he answered her, she would shut up so he could finish.

"It's not for sale!"

Kinyan sat bolt upright in bed as a sudden irrational fear took hold of her. Had John made any promises before his death? Had Dorothea agreed to such a thing? Kinyan rejected both possibilities almost as soon as they occurred to her. Yet the idea of being able to make her own choices was still too new to be familiar.

"Lie down," Colter demanded.

Kinyan glared at him, confidence rising as it dawned on her that if she didn't choose to sell the Triple Fork, then it wasn't for sale!

72

"Nobody tells me what to do anymore," she announced, slipping under Colter's arm and off the bed.

"What the hell are you doing? You're going to hurt yourself!" Colter tried to grab Kinyan as she scooted past him.

Kinyan jerked out of his grasp, crying out when she did in fact hurt herself trying to escape him.

"It's not for sale, I tell you!"

"It is if John Holloway's widow says it is!" Colter roared. "Now get back in bed!"

"Well, I'm his widow, and I say it's not!"

"If you're John Holloway's widow, then who's the lady in black down the hall?!"

"John's mother!"

That shut Colter's mouth but didn't still the confusion raging in his mind.

"Look," he said reasonably. "I've got just one more cut to finish this job. Let me get that arrow out and then we can discuss this sensibly. You're bleeding while we argue," he pointed out.

Disoriented by her activity, Kinyan glanced down at the stream of warm blood that trailed down her arm to her wrist, but couldn't seem to accept it as part of her own body. She bent her arm at the elbow and the blood streamed back the other way.

"There's nothing to discuss. The Triple Fork isn't for sale!"

"Lady, you lie back down on that bed and let me finish or I'm going to hogtie you down!"

Finding an enraged man more than she could cope with right now and feeling a little dizzy anyway, Kinyan hurriedly took two steps. When the back of her knees hit the bed, she sat down. Colter put a surprisingly gentle hand on her shoulder and pressed her back on the bed.

"I—"

"Shut up and bite down!" Colter said brusquely, flinging his other buckskin glove into her hand.

Colter poised his knife above the arrow, trying to determine the best way to make the second cut so he could get the barb out with the least damage.

Kinyan braced herself for the pain, closing her eyes

73

because she couldn't bear the agony on Colter's face as he worked.

Colter put a hand on Kinyan's shoulder and set the tip of the knife against her skin but was interrupted by an angry voice at the door.

"Get your hands off my ma!"

CHAPTER 6

JOSH AND JEREMY had spent the morning clustered with a bunch of young cowboys around the stove in the center of the bunkhouse, the traditional meeting place, summer or winter, listening to stories of the previous night's adventures in Cheyenne. The whitewashed interior of the bunkhouse looked as if a tornado had hit it, yet woe be unto the "idjit" who moved a single item from the spot on the wooden floor or trunk or iron bed where it had been carefully dropped by a cowboy so it wouldn't get lost. The roomful of men had its own peculiar fragrance, a conglomeration of smells derived from boots decorated with cow dung, the licorice in chewing tobaccos, the kerosene in the lamps, and, of course, the wide variety of personal bouquets that emanated from the none-too-clean occupants of that abode.

"It's him!"

Frank Littlejohn's exclamation as he crossed the threshold of the bunkhouse was so loud, it stopped the conversation at the middle of the room and all eyes turned to see what the commotion was about. Frank was an anomaly, a heavy-set cowboy who managed to survive in a world where everyone else was downright lean. To his credit, he was a gossipy, cheerful fellow with bright greenish-gray eyes and ruddy cheeks. He'd risen to his present position, second to Dardus, because he was reliable in a pinch and he could land his rope on anything he threw it at.

"I tell ya it's him! The one that drew on Ritter and beat him! Shot the gun right outta Ritter's hand in the blink of an eye!" Frank insisted, snapping his fingers to show how quickly it had all happened.

"Naw, couldn't be him. Nobody'd be dumb enough to leave Rosie this early in the mornin'. But if it is, what's he doin' here?" P. J. Gresham asked.

"He kept talkin' 'bout buyin' some land, and Willis Smithson mentioned the Triple Fork. Made Ritter mad as hell, but Colter picked right up on it. Cain't say as I'd wanta ride herd for some gunslinger, but Miz Holloway already let that Colter feller in the house. What d'ya s'pose that means?"

"I dunno," P.J. said, shaking his head. "But when ya figger Dardus is outta the saddle, maybe permanent like, Miz Holloway'd be crazy not to take 'im up on any offer he makes. I'd sure rather work for just 'bout anybody 'cept that Ritter Gordon. Don't like that smooth-talkin' rattler."

"What's wrong with Dardus?" Josh asked.

"Lordy mercy! Him and yer ma got shot up by Injuns. Didn't nobody come tell you boys?"

The twins were gone before Frank finished his sentence, Josh barking instructions to Jeremy as the two raced for the house.

"You go around the back way and see what's happenin' in the kitchen. That's where Grandma Thea prob'ly is."

"What're you gonna do?" Jeremy hurled back. He was not really contesting Josh's order, merely curious. Somehow that extra five minutes of life gave Josh a natural position of authority between them, and Jeremy had always been content to follow his brother's lead. If he followed Josh a little cautiously on occasion, it was only due to his own need to take time to consider the pitfalls in a given course of action, which Josh's headlong rush seldom allowed.

"I'm goin' upstairs and check on Ma. You join me soon's you can."

Halfway up the stairs, Josh had recognized his ma's voice raised to a level he'd not heard the likes of since his pa had died, and a strange man's voice was shouting back just as loud. He'd galloped down the hall to her doorway and stood stunned at the sight of the cowboy they'd met the previous day with a knife poised over his mother's arm. Josh had naturally ordered the cowboy to take his hands off his ma, but he was horrified when he heard the cowboy's response.

"Sure," Colter replied agreeably, although a grim look remained around his mouth. "You can take over for me. This arrow needs to be cut out of your ma's arm."

Colter extended the handle of the bloodied knife toward Josh.

"I can't. I mean . . ." Josh's face paled, and he stuck his hands in a knot behind his back.

Colter waited patiently for Josh to take the knife, and the silence became uncomfortable.

"Where's Grandma Thea?" Josh demanded.

"She's taking care of Dardus."

The silence lengthened again.

"Just don't hurt her," Josh mumbled at last, his eyes on the scuffed toes of his boots.

"Don't worry," Colter said, expelling a lungful of air he wasn't aware he'd been holding. "I won't hurt her any more than I have to."

Kinyan breathed a sigh of relief at almost the same time as Colter. How had the cowboy managed to defuse Josh's anger so quickly and efficiently? He'd done it without raising his voice, as she knew John would have. He'd done it without humiliating the boy, as she feared Ritter would have.

When Colter turned back to Kinyan, he found her studying him intently. When her eyes skipped to a point behind him, Colter realized the boy hadn't moved.

"If you're going to stay, you can be a help to me. Come over here."

Josh gulped before he took the few steps that put him at his mother's side.

"I'm only doin' what you say to help my ma," Josh said to make sure the reason for his obedience was clear to the cowboy.

"Then sit here beside your ma and hold her arm still for me," Colter directed.

Josh obeyed, grasping his mother's arm at the elbow.

Colter was good with Josh, Kinyan thought as she watched the two of them working together to mend her arm. She listened while Colter instructed Josh on the importance of making a clean cut rather than forcing the arrowhead and ripping the skin. A clean cut, he explained, could be stitched more easily and would heal more rapidly. Colter's sense of

77

calm had transmitted itself to Josh, and Kinyan was grateful the fear had disappeared from her son's eyes. Kinyan had already observed that the pain she endured was reflected on Colter's face. His influence on Josh was so complete that what she saw now were two agonized faces instead of one.

Kinyan tried to imagine the same scene with Ritter and found it a dismal disappointment. In the first place, she couldn't imagine how Ritter would have managed to get her upstairs. Colter's black shirt bore dark bloodstains where he'd cradled her body in his arms. Would Ritter have been willing to sacrifice one of his immaculate blue shirts? In the second place, she feared he and Josh would have come to blows. Their words of war hadn't been as discreet as either supposed. Given a choice between the two men as fathers, Kinyan found the decision amazingly simple.

Once the idea of Colter as a father for her children took hold, Kinyan found it hard to shake. Colter wanted the Triple Fork. She wanted someone to teach her how to manage the ranch and be a father to her children. Why not offer Colter what he wanted in exchange for what she wanted? Kinyan found it appalling that she was seriously considering marriage to a veritable stranger. On the other hand, when she had married John he'd been a perfect stranger and that hadn't turned out so badly. . . .

The more Kinyan thought about it, the more the idea appealed to her. Of course she'd have to make sure Colter wasn't as averse to the idea of a woman managing a ranch as Ritter had been. But once he accepted the idea, and with a few rules to guide them, they should do just fine.

The first rule would address how they lived together as man and wife. Because she was so recently widowed, it shouldn't be difficult to convince Colter to keep their relationship strictly business. It wasn't that she didn't find Colter physically attractive. Much as it chagrined her to admit it, she did. But she'd already had the experience of one dominant though benevolent husband who'd kept her in total ignorance. If she wanted to learn how to run the ranch, it was important that Colter treat her as a business partner rather than as a woman.

Kinyan refused to further analyze her feelings about Colter as a man with whom to spend her life. After all, she wasn't looking for a husband in the true sense of the word. He was not being judged as a lover or companion. She simply found Colter better suited than Ritter for the roles of teacher and father. There were simply too many good reasons for her to become Colter's wife not to at least suggest the arrangement to the cowboy.

"Hold tight," Colter warned, interrupting Kinyan's thoughts. "I'll be freeing that arrowhead now."

The words were ostensibly for Josh, but Colter knew from his previous experience that Kinyan would likely hold herself still if she had fair warning. Josh took the warning to heart and gripped his mother's elbow tightly with both hands.

Colter made one more cut at the back of Kinyan's upper arm, at the very edge, where the grayish bulge of the arrowhead was plainly visible. Because the shaft had been broken off so close to the skin on the other side, there was no way he could use it to push the arrow all the way through, so Colter had needed to make the cuts in order to allow him to grasp the arrowhead with his fingers and pull it out.

Although Colter worked quickly, the excruciating pain forced an anguished groan from Kinyan's throat. She bit hard into the buckskin glove, tasting Colter's salty sweat and then her own blood, but she managed to stifle the scream growing in her chest. Her Sioux father would have been proud. Only a low moan got past her lips before she fainted.

"Ma!"

Colter dropped the chipped stone arrowhead into the flowered bowl of water and rinsed his hands.

"If we work fast now, we can be done before she wakes up. Do you know where your ma keeps her needles and thread?"

Josh nodded without speaking, staring at his unconscious mother.

"Then go thread a needle for me and bring it here quick while I get her ready to be stitched up."

Colter put a reassuring hand on Josh's trembling shoulder, and the boy opened his mouth to speak. Instead, he jerked away and stumbled out of the room.

Josh had wanted to say he'd never threaded a needle before, but if this strange cowboy expected him to know how to do it, then he wasn't going to show his ignorance.

When Josh found the needles and thread in the hall chest, it didn't take him very long to figure out that the needle had a hole in it and that the thread obviously went through the hole—if you had a steady enough hand to do it. Unfortunately, Josh's hand was shaking something terrible.

Just when Josh thought he was going to have to let the cowboy know he was so scared his fumbling fingers wouldn't stay still enough for the job at hand, Jeremy showed up.

"Here," Josh said authoritatively. "Thread this needle."

Josh thrust the needle and a long string of black thread into a perplexed Jeremy's hands.

"Just put the thread in the hole," Josh instructed with the confidence of his five minutes' prior contact with the needle and thread. "What'd you find down in the kitchen?"

"Petey's boilin' some water. I'm supposed to go back down and get some for Grandma Thea in a minute. Here," Jeremy said as he handed the threaded needle back to Josh. "What's it for?"

"Follow me," Josh ordered. He marched back to his mother's bedroom, his self-confidence somewhat restored at the successful accomplishment of this task.

Meanwhile, Colter cleansed the wound with whiskey and tied it with a strip of pillowcase to stem the bleeding. Then, when Josh still hadn't returned, he dipped a piece of the pillowcase into the clean water in the flowered pitcher and wrung it out. With awkward tenderness, he used the dampened cloth to wipe the dewdrops of perspiration from Kinyan's forehead and from the space above her upper lip. Colter's stomach muscles tightened as his knuckles brushed the smooth skin of Kinyan's flushed cheeks. Where this woman was concerned, all his well-laid plans not to get involved seemed to go out the window.

Colter fought the urge to kiss away the hurt as he dabbed at the drop of blood on Kinyan's full lower lip where she had bitten herself trying not to cry out. Yes, he desired her, Colter told himself, but that was a physical thing, and once he had her, it would go away. The hell of it was, he admitted, you couldn't just go around satisfying your lustful urges with respectable women without paying the consequences. If he were smart, he'd get himself out of here before he did something stupid.

Kinyan's eyelashes fluttered. Then her eyes opened and she stared, unspeaking, into a face rampant with conflicting emotions—concern, desire, irritation, and finally, anger.

"Hellfire, woman! If you'd just stay unconscious, you'd save us both a lot of pain!"

Kinyan smiled at the absurdity of the irate man's request.

"I assure you, I'm not trying to make your job more difficult," she responded with a shaky laugh.

At that moment the two boys burst into the room.

"I got the needle and thread," Josh announced. "Do it quick before . . ."

When Josh realized his mother was awake and smiling at the cowboy, he shot a resentful glance at Colter. Then Josh remembered his mother had argued with the cowboy too, just like with Pa. Josh wished he could sew his ma's arm up himself so he could send Colter away. But he knew he couldn't.

"Are you going to help?" Colter asked.

Josh gave Colter his special evil eye because he knew he was going to be sick if he stayed around to watch those stitches being put in.

"Me an' Jeremy gotta go get Grandma Thea some hot water. Here." Josh thrust the needle forward, accidentally stabbing Colter.

"Thanks, Josh. You've been a big help," Colter said as he sucked on the rising spot of blood left by the needle. At least Josh had put this new wound on the same hand Kinyan had bitten, Colter mused wryly.

Josh bit the inside of his cheek until it hurt and used the pain to harden his voice, and his heart. He wasn't going to let any man take his pa's place, no matter how nice he acted.

"I did it for my ma," Josh replied coldly. "Come on, Jeremy. Let's get outta here."

Josh turned and stalked from the room, but Jeremy stopped at the doorway.

"Thanks for helpin' Ma, Mr. Colter," Jeremy said. "Frank said you beat Ritter to the draw. He said you shot the gun right outta his hand! Me an' Josh would've loved to see Ritter laid low. I bet that was really somethin'!"

Colter had no chance to respond before Jeremy pivoted and raced down the hall after Josh.

"You shot Ritter Gordon!" Kinyan gasped as she rose to a sitting position on the bed. "Why?"

Colter felt an unreasonable jealousy wash over him at Kinyan's apparent concern for the good-looking Ritter. When he examined her face more closely, however, he thought she appeared more surprised than frightened or angry. Still, he tested her concern for Ritter with his next words.

"We fought over a woman."

Kinyan blanched.

Colter swore under his breath. She did care for Ritter! Why else would she be so distraught about Ritter's involvement with another woman?

Kinyan was concerned all right, but it was Colter's involvement with another woman that had distressed her. She turned her face away from Colter, afraid her feelings were written there. It had come as a shock to her that she could feel jealousy over Colter's relationship with another woman. A Sioux wife shared her husband with as many wives as he could afford to keep. If she had married Rides-the-Wind eleven years ago, she probably would have shared him with several women. But John had made it clear he desired no other woman, even though he could certainly have supported several more. She had come to understand the white custom of taking only one wife.

At first she'd thought it silly. She and Dorothea could have used the help in the house that would have come if John had taken another wife. But as time went on, she saw that John turned to her at all times, and she admitted there were indeed some advantages to having a man all to yourself. And, she realized, she wanted Colter to herself. That would have to be rule number two.

Colter ignored the tight feeling in his chest. So she felt something for Ritter. So what? He wasn't going to get involved with the woman himself, so what did it matter? Only, it did. He wanted to see her face full of concern for him. He shrugged off the yearning deep in his soul.

"Doesn't sound like your kids care much for Ritter," Colter observed, finding some solace in that fact.

"They miss their father."

"I know."

Colter's perceptive answer startled Kinyan, but then

Josh's feelings were pretty transparent. "It's the reason I don't want to sell the ranch. It's all they have left of John."

"Your boys won't likely consider steers and grass to be a fair substitute for their pa," Colter replied.

"No, you're right. They don't think losing their father was fair at all. And there is no substitute for John."

That last was a lie. John could be replaced. In fact, barely three months after his death, she was about to take another husband. And that led Kinyan to rule number three. Colter would have to teach her whatever she wanted to know about managing the ranch. If she had a question, then it would be his responsibility to answer it. If she wanted to learn something, then he would have to give her lessons. She would never let herself be put in the position of needing a husband to keep what was hers. And if Ritter Gordon couldn't take her decision to marry Colter gracefully, well, hadn't Colter already proved he could handle Ritter?

Kinyan felt the weight of warm gold at her throat, felt the tickle of the eagle feather on the rawhide cord. Surely a woman with the inborn cunning of a Sioux and the cleverness cultivated over eleven years among the whites could manage a lone, unsuspecting cowboy. Her decision made, there was nothing left but for Kinyan to take action.

Kinyan rose and tucked her slender, jean-clad legs under her slim body. She braced her right palm flat against her knee while her left arm dangled uselessly at her side. When her shoulders straightened, her breasts jutted from the remnants of the cotton blouse. She shook her head, flinging thick black tresses out of her way. Determination grew in Kinyan's eyes, until the woman who faced Colter was the tempestuous she-cat of their first meeting.

"How badly do you want the Triple Fork?" Kinyan challenged.

"I want it," Colter admitted, his eyes narrowing as he pondered what had caused this abrupt transformation.

"I'll be frank with you, Mr. Colter. I don't want to sell, but I can't manage the Triple Fork alone. I need a husband, and my children need a father." When Colter opened his mouth to respond, she ordered, "Don't interrupt. Hear me out first.

"There are over three hundred thousand acres of Triple Fork range, but almost all of it is government land, which I can keep only so long as I can enforce my claim against all comers. With my husband dead, every rancher close enough to grab a piece of the Triple Fork will be bound to do so. Furthermore, the Triple Fork is plagued by rustlers, and squatters have planted themselves on the land as well. Now that you know all that, if you still want the Triple Fork, it's yours."

Kinyan paused for effect.

"But you'll have to marry me to get it."

Colter stared at Kinyan for a moment. Then he stalked to one of the windows and peered out through the swagged curtains. Smoke still rose from the cookhouse. From here, he could see the two scroungy mutts he'd only supposed lolled in the breezeway. A cooling zephyr carried the smells from the cookshack, and he knew the cowhands could expect sonofabitch stew and biscuits for dinner.

He wanted this land!

But her price was marriage!

He'd sworn he would never marry again.

But he needn't let his heart get involved. It'd just be a marriage of convenience for both of them.

Her sons didn't want another father.

But they were fine boys and would grow into good men with the right kind of guidance.

He was asking for trouble from Ritter.

But the Triple Fork was worth fighting for.

Colter's decision was made in the moment he turned back to Kinyan. He would take her land, because she offered it. He would take her body, because that appeared to be part of the bargain as well. Besides, he wanted it. Hellfire! He *needed* it! In exchange, he'd keep the Triple Fork whole, as a heritage for her sons. He'd give her boys a father, because they deserved one. But he wouldn't entrust the woman with his heart, nor would he seek to gain hers.

"I'm willing to marry you and be a father to your sons," he said. "And I'll keep the Triple Fork in one piece," he added solemnly. "You have my word on that."

Kinyan would have sighed with relief, except that Colter's simple acceptance of her proposal was useless to her unless he also agreed to abide by the rules she'd worked out: it would be a business arrangement; there would be no other female relationships outside the marriage; and he would teach her what she needed to know to run the ranch. She decided it was best to tackle them one at a time.

"Before you commit yourself, we need to get some things settled," Kinyan announced.

Colter eyed her cynically. "What more do you want?"

"I want you to teach me everything I need to know to run the Triple Fork by myself."

Colter couldn't control the incredulous snort that erupted from his chest.

"That's all?"

"I'm serious," Kinyan hissed.

Colter had the distinct impression of sharp claws slipping from soft sheaths. He perused the stormy-eyed wanton who sat facing him on the big four-poster in a torn, bloodied blouse and Levi's jeans. She was serious. Why on earth did she want to learn how to do something for which she was so ill suited? She was too tiny to be roping cattle. She was too fragile to spend her days in the hot sun and the icy cold. The kick of a Winchester would likely knock her over. Dehorning, castrating, and branding calves was unpleasant and exhausting even for cowboys inured to it. Why would she want to subject herself to the stench of burning hair and flesh and the bawling of the frightened animals?

"Why?" he asked finally, voicing his thoughts.

"Because if something happens to you, I don't want to be at the mercy of the next man who thinks he'll make me a good husband!"

That brought Colter's head around with a snap.

"Just what exactly do you expect to happen to me?" he asked suspiciously.

"Nothing," she answered. "But then I expected John to live a lot longer than he did too. Do we have a deal?"

Colter paused a moment before responding, and Kinyan's heart sank to her stomach and rumbled there in agitation. He was going to refuse. He probably thought she was crazy. She would have to marry Ritter after all. Before she had a chance to further despair, Colter spoke.

"I'll teach you what you want to know, but it'll have to be on my terms."

"Which are?"

"You obey me instantly when we're on the range. The first time you're not willing to handle the job you're assigned, that's it. School is out. Agreed?"

Kinyan bristled at the conditions Colter snapped out, and it was on the tip of her tongue to refuse when she realized what he'd asked wasn't so unreasonable. He would have asked no less of any cowhand he hired. And she was at least as capable as the lowliest cowboy who rode the Triple Fork line.

"I agree," Kinyan said.

He was willing to teach her, but Colter didn't think the lessons would last long. At the first blister, at the first burning hide, when the first pair of calf testicles fell on the bloody grass, he expected her to concede the issue. He could put up with the nuisance of having her along for the day or two it would take to make his point.

"Shall we shake on it?" Colter inquired with a grin. He couldn't hide his unbounded pleasure at the way things had turned out. He attributed his deliriously happy state to the fact he'd have the Triple Fork for his home. He put the thought of Kinyan as his wife aside in a cubbyhole for special things you didn't inspect too closely for fear they wouldn't be so perfect on second glance.

"Yes, let's shake on it." Kinyan was willing to accept Colter's hand as his word because John had sworn a cowboy stood by his handshake, and John had rarely been wrong. Kinyan slipped off the bed and stepped forward.

"No claws," Colter murmured sardonically as he encompassed her outstretched hand in his slender fingers.

"What?"

"Never mind," Colter said, his grin widening. "One other thing," he added while he held her in his grasp, "while we're getting things settled. I need to have possession of the Triple Fork before the Laramie County Stock Association meeting on Wednesday to ensure confirmation of my membership. Also, I have some longhorns in the Denver stockyards and I want to make arrangements to have them shipped north. I can't do that before I'm sure I have land on which to graze them when they arrive, so the sooner we're married, the better."

Colter's words had been about the Association and cattle, but his avid look made Kinyan blush. She hesitated only momentarily before she said, "Then it'll be best if we get married today."

"That's fine with me," Colter said, a brow arching roguishly. "But that means riding into Cheyenne to find the preacher this afternoon. Do you think you're up to it?"

"That won't be necessary. Our minister, Hiram Goforth, has dinner with us the last Sunday of every month."

Colter's face remained blank for a moment until he realized that today was the last Sunday in August. A smirk twitched the corners of his mouth.

"Then I await your pleasure, ma'am."

For Kinyan, the immediacy of the marriage brought to mind the two other matters on which they hadn't spoken.

"Mr. Colter . . ."

"Plain Colter will be fine, Kinyan," he said gently, acknowledging their new relationship.

Kinyan could feel the red flush begin at her bosom and rise steadily up her neck until the warmth in her cheeks declared her self-consciousness. Kinyan wished Colter were not still holding her hand.

"This . . . this will be a . . . a business arrangement, Colter, nothing more, but . . . but I expect you to respect the marriage vows, and . . . and there'll be no other women while you're married to me."

Colter's lips narrowed to an invisible line. His eyes became crystal slits. His face flushed so the slashing scar stood out like a bolt of lightning on his livid face. His fingers tightened around Kinyan's until she cried out, "You're hurting me!"

Colter released her hand. His fist clenched and unclenched once before he turned his back on Kinyan and stalked over to stare out the window that overlooked the creek. Colter traced the scar along his cheek with his forefinger, then ran his hand behind his neck to soothe the tension there. A fly buzzed by his ear and he slapped at it with an oath.

Oh, she was so clever, Colter thought furiously, to suck him in and then to spit him out. Well, he would have it all or he would have nothing. The woman would be his. He had already accepted the offer of marriage. It was too late for her to back out.

It was frightening, Kinyan thought, that taut, sinewy back

that shut her out. His unguarded response had surprised her. She'd expected him to accept this part of the bargain without contesting it. Which was, she realized now, not very realistic considering he hadn't exactly been receptive to her first suggestion.

When he turned and spoke, his voice, hardened and cold as ice, brooked no denial.

"If I marry you, there'll be no need for other women, because we'll live as husband and wife. I am not, by God, going to spend my nights taking cold dips in the creek to keep from raping you. I don't love you, and I don't expect you to love me. If that's what you mean by keeping this a *business arrangement,* then to *that* I am amenable."

Colter realized the risk he took in demanding his marital rights. She could say no. He could lose the Triple Fork. It was irritating to admit he wanted the woman so badly he'd insisted on his right to bed her. That only made him more furious with himself, and with her, for eliciting these uncontrollable feelings.

"Well?" Colter asked brusquely. "Do you agree?"

So much for manipulating the unsuspecting cowboy!

What he'd suggested was so . . . heartless. But no more so than what she'd suggested. A marriage without loving. A marriage without love. What was the difference? They made too good a match, she thought bitterly. Kinyan had spent too much of her life fighting not to know when to cut her losses and run. But she had Colter's word that he'd teach her to run the Triple Fork, and he'd said there would be no other women. Two out of three wasn't bad.

"Yes," Kinyan retorted. "I agree."

Colter's hot eyes roved the body of the woman who would be his wife before the day was out. Dangerously bright blue eyes met his sensual gaze without flinching.

"Now, I think it's long past time I finish sewing you up," Colter said.

Colter crossed swiftly and surprised Kinyan by sweeping her up into his arms. Kinyan laid a hand against his chest to steady herself, and in the moment before he laid her down, she felt his heart thrumming crazily under her palm. He was as nervous as she was! A sad smile played at the corners of Kinyan's mouth, and she began to plan what must be done to bring this marriage to fruition.

Kinyan couldn't help thinking John would not have begrudged her this new husband. Although John had loved her, he'd hinted often enough that he regretted stealing her youth to make her an old man's wife. How many years lay between them? Twenty-six, she thought. No, it was twenty-seven. John had been fifty-two when he died. Funny, she'd never thought of him as old. She'd been with no man before John, and he'd kept her too well satisfied to seek pleasure elsewhere.

Kinyan couldn't explain it, but with Colter she felt . . . different. The sudden flashes of overwhelming desire, the tingling deep inside whenever she thought of being touched by Colter, were new to her, a woman married eleven years. Her eyes rose to Colter's fine-boned face. She wanted to touch him, to have him touch her. Colter excited her. He titillated her senses with the promise of untold pleasure.

She didn't delude herself that for either of them love played any part of this arranged marriage. How could it? They'd only just met. If Colter's attitude was any indication, it never would. Yet because Kinyan had been loved by John, she knew how much she would miss the sense of belonging, of being cared for, that she had enjoyed with her first husband.

Colter settled Kinyan comfortably upon the bed, then sat down beside her. He removed the temporary bandage, and after daubing her wound one more time with stinging whiskey, he retrieved the needle and began methodically stitching Kinyan's arm. Kinyan was determined to stay quiet while Colter worked, the needle jabbing as it went in, the thread burning as it pulled through. So she sent her thoughts back to the first time she had been stitched, when she was seven years old.

She and Rides-the-Wind had been out riding. He'd been showing off for her, slipping to the side of his pony and clinging by his heel to a rope around the neck of the galloping horse. Kinyan had shouted, "That looks easy!" and promptly slid off her horse as well. Only her heel hadn't caught on the rope at the horse's neck, and she'd landed in a pile on the ground. Her face, her hand, and her leg had all been scraped raw by the friction of the fall, and her right knee had come down on a sharp rock and been badly cut.

Rides-the-Wind had shoved her back on her pony and

they'd raced back to her tepee. Soaring Eagle had been there, and when he'd found out what she'd been doing, he'd said, "Well, my little brave, if you will take the chances of a warrior, then you must bear the consequences."

Her father had lifted her off her pony and carried her inside the tepee, where Wheat Woman had collected a bone needle and some gut. Kinyan's eyes had rounded hugely at the sight of the needle and she'd turned to Soaring Eagle and buried her face in his shoulder for protection.

"What must be done must be done," he'd said, laying her down on a buffalo robe. He'd adjusted her head on a stuffed foxskin pillow, then sat cross-legged next to her head and held her hand while her mother had cleaned the wound. When she'd whimpered once, he'd simply shaken his head, and she'd known then what he expected of her. She had the example of her father, who had not made a sound when he'd had his war wounds tended. And hadn't her father called her his little brave?

She had wanted to please him so badly, she hadn't made a sound. She hadn't shed a tear. And Soaring Eagle had been so *proud*. She'd often pleased him in other ways in later years, but never had she been so sure of his approval as she had been that first time, when he'd smiled at her and said, "A father could not wish to have a more courageous child."

She hadn't realized then what courageous acts he would ask of her. She hadn't dreamed then of being asked to leave her father and mother, of being asked to leave Rides-the-Wind and her people and go among the white man to live. She hadn't realized then that one day her father would shut her off from all she loved and expect her to survive the calamity. But she had. And she would.

Colter admired the strength of will that allowed Kinyan to lie motionless under his ministrations. As he glanced at his wife, for he could think of her in no other way now, a single tear slid from the corner of Kinyan's eye down the side of her face.

Colter was helpless to resist his next impulse. He leaned over and kissed the teardrop where it had stopped at her temple. His tongue dipped out to taste the salty liquid.

Kinyan's eyes closed at the endearment. She could not bear it. How could she marry another man when grass had barely grown over John's grave? *How could she not?* she thought bitterly. The marriage was necessary, and because Colter had made it part of the bargain, it would be necessary to lie with him.

Kinyan thought ahead to the night when their naked bodies would lie entwined. Even now she felt the blood surge to her loins, felt the moistness ready her sheath for his thrusting shaft. Violent tremors shook Kinyan's body, and she gasped at the enormity of the need that held her in thrall. What spell had he cast to make her desire him? She had loved her husband, and she loved him still. How could she willingly give herself so soon to another man? How would she endure the intimacy of the night ahead?

CHAPTER 7

By the time Dorothea showed up at the door again, Colter had nearly finished.

"Just checking to see how things are coming along," she said as she closed the distance to where Colter sat on the bed sewing. "I heard some noise down here a while ago, but couldn't come at the time. Everything seems settled down now."

"Yes, ma'am," Colter said, his eyes meeting Kinyan's and coaxing a wan smile from her.

Dorothea didn't miss the intimate look, but neither did she remark upon it. Instead, she said, "That's good work. It won't leave much of a scar. Where'd you learn that kind of fancy stitching?"

"Picked it up from a friend a long time ago," Colter replied. "Haven't used the skill much since then except, of course, on my shirts."

An image of bloodied bodies, of surgery in the filth and mud of a Yankee prison, flashed before Colter's eyes and he closed his eyes to rid himself of the picture, then opened them again and tied off the last stitch.

"How's Dardus?" Kinyan asked.

"It doesn't look good, I'm afraid," Dorothea said. "If he survives, he's going to be laid up for some time. We're going to need some help running this place—that is, assuming you don't plan to sell it to Mr. Colter. He came here this morning to offer to buy the Triple Fork," Dorothea said archly, her disapproval plainly evident.

"Mrs. Holloway has decided not to sell," Colter announced.

"I assume then, Kinyan, you have a plan for how we're going to manage without Dardus," Dorothea said.

"She's going to get married."

"Yes, I know about Ritter Gordon's offer of marriage. That's certainly one solution," Dorothea admitted, her lips pursed in distaste.

Colter's brow shot up and he flashed a frown at Kinyan, who blushed guiltily.

"She's not . . ."

Colter paused as a little girl appeared in the doorway. The sleepy child wore a sleeveless, round-necked blue nightgown that came within an inch of the floor. Colter hadn't known that Kinyan had a daughter, but the girl was a perfect miniature of her mother. She possessed the same silky black hair, naturally arched black brows over wide, sky-blue eyes, bowed lips, a delicate nose that turned up at the tip, prominent cheekbones, and that complexion of soft honey-gold. Colter watched, entranced, as the sprite slung a small ragged red calico blanket up over her left shoulder so one corner barely touched the floor behind her. She lowered her chin to her chest and looked coyly upward through her lowered lashes at Colter.

When Colter's glazed expression didn't change, the little girl glanced inquiringly at her grandmother and then to where her mother lay fully dressed on the bed. Seeing the ugly black stitches on her mother's arm and the bloodstains on the sheets and on her mother's torn blouse, the now-wide-eyed urchin padded over to confront Colter.

"Is my mama gonna die?"

Colter couldn't breathe. He tried to take a breath, but the air wouldn't come. Tight bands constricted his chest, crushing him. Once before in his life he'd needed to answer the same frightened question. The vision of a little girl about the same age, with the same blue eyes and black hair, overtook Colter, blinding him to his surroundings and sending him back to the past. There was blood on the little girl and pooling in a dark circle around her. He lay on the floor across from the child, but couldn't move to reach her. The girl's mother lay sprawled on the rumpled bed nearby, bright red blood flowing freely from slashes on her arms and chest

93

and abdomen. Colter shrank from the intense pain of the memory, forcing himself back to the present.

When his eyes refocused, only a few seconds had passed and the little girl was still standing before him. Colter raged inwardly at the fate that had thrust this child in his path as a living reminder of a nightmare he was trying to put behind him. He didn't know what force kept him from fleeing the room. Perhaps it was simply that he'd decided to stop running. Perhaps it was because for the first time in eight years he had a place to call his own again. His ragged breathing told him it wasn't going to be easy to cope with this tiny girl who reminded him so much of his own daughter.

Drawing the wrong conclusion from the tall man's raspy breathing and his intent stare, Lizbeth broke into tears.

"There now, Lizbeth," Grandma Thea consoled, drawing the child close. "Your mama's just fine."

"I'm fine, Lizbeth," Kinyan soothed, sitting up and taking the little girl as Dorothea ushered her into her mother's arms. "I'm not going to die. I just hurt my arm. I'll be good as new in a few days."

"I'll go unsaddle Hoss and put him in the barn," Colter said abruptly.

"Mr. Colter and I . . . I invited Mr. Colter to stay for dinner," Kinyan hurriedly explained to a quizzical Dorothea. Kinyan didn't know why she put off telling Dorothea about her marriage plans, except Dorothea was, after all, John's mother. Could she truly be accepting of any man Kinyan chose to replace John?

"Why, it'll be right nice to have Mr. Colter as a guest for dinner," Dorothea said. "Reverend Goforth will be here as well."

"Yes, ma'am, I know," Colter said. He shot Kinyan a look somewhere between a grimace and a grin. He'd noticed her reluctance to tell Dorothea about their marriage but decided to let her take things at her own pace. Dorothea would find out the truth soon enough.

"Oh my goodness!" Dorothea exclaimed. "I just remembered I was right in the middle of fixing a dried-apple pie when you came to the door."

"I surely do like apple pie," Colter said, regaining some of his equanimity.

"Lizbeth, you come with me and get dressed. Then you can help me with that pie." Dorothea picked the girl up from her mother's arms and set her on the floor.

"Can I roll out the dough?" Lizbeth begged, tugging on her grandmother's skirt.

Dorothea shooed Lizbeth through the door ahead of her. "If you promise not to eat too much!"

Colter's face had paled again as he watched the exchange between the enchanting little girl and the older woman. When they were gone, he ran his fingertips agitatedly through his black hair.

"What's the matter?" Kinyan asked.

"Nothing," Colter hedged. "It just surprised me to find out you had a daughter, that's all."

"Lizbeth is a very loving child. I know she'll take to you, since—"

"I've got to take care of Hoss," Colter interrupted. "Then I think I'll go talk to the hands in the bunkhouse."

"Yes, that would be a good idea," Kinyan agreed. "That will give me a chance to speak with Josh and Jeremy. If you see them, would you send them up here please?"

"Sure. Call me when the reverend arrives. I want some time to clean up before the ceremony."

Kinyan caught the untamed passion in Colter's eyes before he quickly left the room, and both dread and desire began to war within her breast. However, at that moment the twins arrived at the doorway, their shoulders pressing the doorjamb as they both attempted to enter at the same time. The humor of their predicament left Kinyan free to face her sons with, if not peace of mind, then at least a healthy imitation of it.

"Mr. Colter said you wanted to see us. Is something wrong?" Josh asked.

"No, no, everything's fine," Kinyan reassured Josh. "I wanted to tell you some good news."

"Dardus is going to be okay," Jeremy said, deducing that was the most likely source of good tidings.

"As a matter of fact, Dardus is probably not going to be all right. That's why I wanted to talk to you."

There was no best way to say what had to be said, so Kinyan just said it.

"Mr. Colter and I are getting married. Today."

95

"Bullshit!"

"Joshua Holloway, do you want me to wash your mouth out with soap right now!"

"Ma, you can't do this to me!"

"I'm not doing anything *to* you. I'm doing this *for* you."

"You're marrying a no-'count drifter for *me?*"

"To save the Triple Fork for you and Jeremy and Lizbeth I'd even have married Ritter Gordon! But Colter's a better choice, so I'm marrying him!"

" 'Cause you love him, Ma?"

Jeremy's astute query stopped Kinyan cold. Love had never entered into the decision. She was marrying Colter because she needed him as a teacher and a father for her children. Her feelings for Colter did not extend to caring, and he had made it plain he wouldn't mind if they never did.

"There are reasons why Mr. Colter is a better choice," Kinyan explained. "He'll make a good pa for—"

If Kinyan had been less exhausted from the trials of the morning, she would have been more cautious than to use the term *pa* in relation to Colter. It was the flame that set off an already explosive situation.

"He won't be my pa! He won't be nothin' to us! My pa is *dead!*"

The shame of the tears he couldn't keep from spilling down his tanned cheeks and the uncontrollable quivering of his stubborn chin sent Josh spinning out of the room. Kinyan could hear him slamming down the stairs two at a time.

Kinyan was heartsick at her son's reaction. Josh's tears had caused Jeremy to cry as well, and his tear-streaked freckled face met Kinyan's with a look of utter hopelessness.

"He says Pa's dead, but he ain't never gonna let Pa die, not really."

Kinyan beckoned and Jeremy flew into her embrace. She let him cry for a while before she could calm her own voice enough to speak. She wished for Wheat Woman's understanding. She wished for Dorothea's wisdom.

"I'd never want you boys to forget your pa. His spirit will always live in our hearts, and we'll never stop loving him. But he wouldn't want us to stop living because he's not here with us."

The speech was a plea to Josh, who hadn't stayed to hear

it. Yet when Jeremy's head came up from his mother's breast, where he had laid it, the hopelessness was gone from his cherubic face.

"Pa would understand why you gotta marry Mr. Colter, wouldn't he?"

"Yes, Jeremy, I believe he would."

"What does Grandma Thea think?"

"I think . . . it's a fine . . . idea," Dorothea wheezed, out of breath from her quick climb up the stairs. Josh's incoherent railing had sent her racing upstairs to hear the truth of the matter for herself. She was a little too old to be racing, Dorothea thought ruefully, but it had been worth the trip to overhear Kinyan's words to her son.

"Why don't you go find Josh and tell him not to go far. It'll be dinner time soon," Kinyan urged Jeremy. She wanted a moment alone with Dorothea.

"Sure, Ma," Jeremy said. "Is Reverend Goforth gonna marry you to Mr. Colter?" When Kinyan nodded, Jeremy continued, "Before dinner or after dinner?"

"What difference does it make?"

"I just wanta know how soon me and Josh are gonna have to do what Mr. Colter says."

"I'll think about it," Kinyan answered with a smile. "Now get on outside and find Josh."

Dorothea was quite satisfied with Kinyan's decision. She liked the cowboy. She liked his forthright manner, the way he took charge, his easy way with the boys, and the way Kinyan's eyes lit up when she saw the man. The only thing Dorothea didn't like was this latest incident with Lizbeth. There was something haunting the scarred man, and she didn't want it throwing a shadow on her family. Well, it would be a simple matter to keep a close eye on things. If the situation continued, she'd just ask Colter point-blank about the problem. Once she knew what it was, Dorothea was sure there'd be some simple solution. There usually was. Right now it was time to make plans for a wedding.

"I have something special I hope you'll want to wear today," Dorothea said. "It's a dress I was making as a surprise for your anniversary party with John. Perhaps it will bring as much happiness on this day as it would have then."

"You don't mind, then—my marrying Colter, I mean."

"It's a sight better than the alternative of marrying Ritter," Dorothea responded. "John hated Ritter," she said, as though that explained everything. And as far as Dorothea was concerned, it did. "Now you just rest and I'll go back down to the kitchen and prepare a feast fit for a wedding celebration."

Kinyan leaned back and closed her eyes. Then, while all around her scurried and worried, Kinyan slept.

Reverend Hiram Goforth stood piously on a square of flagstone before the gray stone fireplace in the Holloway parlor as though he were on the dais of his pulpit. He ran his chubby finger around the stiffly starched collar of his white shirt, which was a sore trial and a tribulation to him in light of the midafternoon August heat, then brought his left hand back down to balance the large gold-inscribed leather-bound black Bible that kept threatening to slip from his sweaty right palm. Hiram suspected God had planned this day to test the truly faithful, and Hiram was flunking the exam.

Hiram's upset stomach gurgled once to remind him he'd overindulged in Dorothea's excellent pot roast. Overeating was a way of life for Hiram, and as was his habit, he'd surreptitiously unbuttoned the top button of his pants and let out his belt a notch to accommodate his gluttony at the table. Everything had been just fine until Dorothea served her flaky-crusted, dried-apple pie, with homemade cheese on top. Hiram was just finishing his second slice when Kinyan had announced she wanted him to perform a wedding ceremony. When he'd inquired as to who the happy couple could be, Kinyan had announced, "Mr. Colter and I would like to be married."

Hiram had been absolutely flabbergasted. Kinyan Holloway wanted to marry the guest she had introduced to him when he'd arrived—a complete and total stranger! An ordinary cowboy! A drifter!

"Mrs. Holloway, shouldn't you think about this a little more?" he'd suggested, chewing one last spoonful of apples.

"The lady's mind is made up. If you're not willing to perform the marriage, we'll find someone who will," the tall cowboy had said in an intimidating voice.

"Kinyan Holloway is a member of my flock," Hiram had replied huffily as he'd stuffed a piece of cheese in sideways.

"Never let it be said that Hiram Goforth refused to minister to one of his lambs!"

That earlier discussion had left his digestion in a shambles because Hiram knew, as sure as he knew the Psalms, that Ritter Gordon wasn't going to like this at all. Ritter had staked his claim on Kinyan Holloway at the last Association meeting, and when Ritter found out Hiram had performed this wedding ceremony, all hell was going to break loose!

Now Hiram cleared his throat loudly and swallowed the bile that rose and threatened to choke him.

"Uh, where is the bride, Mr. Colter?"

"I think she's changing her clothes," Colter answered with a careless shrug.

Colter had changed into black pants and a clean white shirt and added a string tie before the reverend arrived. He'd put back on his black leather vest and black boots, but he'd left his holster and gun in the barn. He felt naked without them. The waiting was making him nervous, and he could tell his nervousness was making the reverend nervous. They should have had the ceremony before dinner, Colter thought. His food lay in his stomach like a lead weight.

"I just helped Kinyan button up her dress, so she should be down in a moment," Dorothea announced as she entered the parlor. Her stomach growled noisily, and she laughed self-consciously at the sound. She hadn't been able to eat a thing at dinner.

Jeremy was regretting the impulse that had caused him to urge his ma to delay the wedding until after dinner. He'd been so excited, he hadn't been able to sit still for dessert. When he'd found out later that Grandma Thea had promised all the leftover pie to Reverend Goforth, he'd run to the kitchen and gulped a whole slice down in just four whopping bites. Now it was threatening to come back up.

Lizbeth was confused. Josh had told her she was *not* to call Mr. Colter Pa. When she had asked him why not, he had just said, "Because he ain't your pa. Your pa is dead." But Mr. Colter was marrying Ma, so why wasn't he gonna be her pa? She wished she could ask somebody grown up, but Mr. Colter frowned at her every time she looked at him, and when she'd mentioned she had a question about Mr. Colter, Grandma Thea had said to ask Mama, but not right now because she had to rest. Lizbeth felt a little queasy, but it

99

was probably just all that pie dough she'd eaten before dinner.

Josh thought he was going to be sick to his stomach any minute. His mother had insisted he come to the dinner table, invoking his pa's name. "Pa would expect you to accept this like a man," she'd said. If he were really a man, he thought miserably, his ma wouldn't have to marry this drifter.

"Josh."

Josh sat up with a start when he heard his mother softly call his name. She stood at the open doorway of the parlor, and Josh gaped because he'd never seen his ma look quite so pretty.

"As the eldest male relative present, I believe you must give away the bride," Dorothea said, nudging Josh in the direction of his mother.

Colter's heart lurched when Kinyan smiled at her son. Her face was flushed—probably from the August heat, Colter thought, but it didn't make her look any less wonderful. Her ebony tresses swirled down softly over her shoulders, and he found himself wanting to wrap the silky stuff around his fingers and run it across his face and his chest and . . . other places.

"Mama, you're so pretty," Lizbeth said, beaming.

"Yeah, Ma, you look great!" Jeremy agreed with a grin.

Tears rose in Dorothea's eyes. She was glad she had finished the dress after John's death. Kinyan made such a lovely bride. Dorothea knew John would have approved.

Kinyan trembled with excitement. It was all happening so fast! She hadn't eaten any breakfast, nor had she been able to swallow much food at dinner. She attributed the fluttery feeling in her stomach to hunger—and the snug fit of the gown Dorothea had made for her.

Kinyan loved the gown of pale blue silk, the bodice of which was trimmed with white lace and dotted with clusters of seed pearls. She had been a bit embarrassed at the way her breasts rose in gentle swells above the heart-shaped décolletage of the fitted bodice, but Dorothea had assured her it would please Colter.

For the first time in her memory, Kinyan had removed her amulet. The eagle feather hadn't looked right with the elegant silk gown, and the gold heart alone seemed out of place on the rawhide thong. Kinyan felt odd without the necklace. But then nothing she'd done lately had been very ordinary.

The long sleeves of the gown were fitted from the shoulder, covering the ugly stitches, and buttoned from the elbow down to her wrists. The skirt was draped in back and fell in graceful swagged folds to a ruffled trim at the bottom. The silk gown rustled in the quiet of the room as Kinyan marched steadily toward Colter on Josh's arm.

Colter couldn't help thinking of the first woman who had come to him this way. He had been a boy of seventeen, anxious to marry his sweetheart before he left to fight for the Confederate cause. Sixteen-year-old Sarah, with her sable hair and gray eyes, hadn't been so beautiful, but she had been a gentle girl and he had idolized her. They'd had only a week together before he'd gone to war, but their daughter, Hope, had been conceived in that short time. He had been in a Yankee prison, assisting the camp surgeon, when he heard the news of his daughter's birth. It had given him the courage to eat the maggoty food and to drink the fetid water, and he had survived until the war ended.

What a joyous homecoming it had been! He'd determined to make up that lost time with Sarah and with Hope, and he'd given them all the love he'd saved up those two long years he'd been a prisoner of war. And then, when everything was going so well, when he had branded enough Texas mavericks to know the Circle C would one day have a fine herd, tragedy had struck.

Three ragtag men in worn-out Confederate uniforms had come seeking a roof and a meal. The war had been over more than a year, but because they were fellow soldiers in a lost cause, he had invited them into his home. They had repaid his kindness by raping and butchering his wife, murdering his child, and leaving him for dead. Then they had stolen his fine herd of branded mavericks and run.

He had stalked and killed two of the three men who had murdered his wife and child. They had not died easily. He had searched eight years but had never found the third man. The bastard had disappeared into thin air! Finally, this past spring he had admitted he was never going to find that third soldier. So he had laid his vengeance to rest and come to the Wyoming Territory to begin his life anew. He would not love

101

again. He would not lay himself open to the kind of pain he'd suffered when he lost Sarah and Hope.

When she first crossed the threshold, Kinyan had dared a glance at Colter to see if he approved of the gown. At first, Colter's face had reflected the kind of admiration every bride hopes to see in her husband's eyes. But slowly and surely, his expression had become more and more distressed, until finally he stood waiting by the reverend with a scowl on his face.

Kinyan's pride was hurt, and she said testily, "If you have any doubts about this, you can back out now."

Kinyan's outburst brought Colter's mind back to the present.

"What the hell?"

"I said if you've changed your mind, we don't have to go through with this!"

Kinyan's eyes shot fire at Colter, rousing the flickering desire he'd only barely managed to keep banked through dinner. Standing spread-legged, Colter's hands went to his hips in exasperation.

"Get over here, and stop being ridiculous. We have an agreement, and I intend to abide by it."

"An agreement?" Hiram questioned, his curiosity overcoming his fear of the two strong-willed souls clashing before him.

"Stay out of this!" Colter snapped.

"Ma, have you got an agreement with Mr. Colter?" Josh asked.

"It's just an understanding, Josh," Kinyan said, attempting to placate the suspicious youth.

"Is it in writing?" the ever-practical Jeremy demanded.

"No, it's—"

"Why not?" Dorothea interrupted. "Mr. Colter, I don't mean to interfere, but it seems to me that on such short acquaintance Kinyan is entitled to some guarantee that when you're her husband you'll not sell the Triple Fork out from under her."

"She has my word!"

"Surely it wouldn't be asking too much to put it in writing," Dorothea said smoothly, moving to the desk under the window to collect paper and pen.

Colter looked from expectant face to expectant face. When he caught sight of Lizbeth's innocently trusting features, he marched over to take the pen from Dorothea's hand.

He scribbled busily on the paper for a few moments, then crossed back to thrust the parchment into Kinyan's hand.

"Read it! See if it doesn't spell out our agreement to your satisfaction."

Kinyan stared stupidly at the paper before she admitted in a small voice, "I can't read."

"Hellfire and damnation!"

Hiram winced, but wisely kept silent.

Colter snatched the paper from Kinyan, scribbled something on the bottom, and then held it out again, demanding, "Can anybody here read?"

"I can!"

"Me too!"

Colter's brow furrowed. How was it the sons could read but not the mother?

Josh stepped boldly forward, holding out his hand for the contract. Colter put the paper in Josh's outstretched palm and Josh read in a loud, steady voice:

I, Benjamin Colter, upon my marriage hereby cede to Kinyan Colter, my wife, the absolute and final right of disposition of the Triple Fork ranch; except that I, along with my heirs, if any, shall retain the right to use Triple Fork range to graze cattle. In consideration for such grazing rights, I agree to teach Kinyan Colter the necessary skills to manage the Triple Fork ranch—*including how to read!*

Benjamin Colter
August 29, 1875

"Sounds good to me," Dorothea said, taking the missive from Josh's hands. "Shall we get on with the ceremony?"

The parties lined up before Hiram, with Colter to his left, then Josh, Kinyan, Jeremy, Dorothea, and Lizbeth.

"Really, I think . . ."

When he met Colter's savage stare, Hiram shut his mouth. Well, if they wanted to get married under such circumstances, Hiram thought petulantly, that was their business.

"Dearly beloved . . ."

Hiram droned on until he got to "Who gives this woman unto this man?"

"I do, but not until I have my say," Josh snarled. He repeated to Colter the litany he'd been telling himself all day.

"You ain't gonna be my pa no matter how long you're married to my ma, and no drifter is ever gonna be the one to tell me what to do!"

Then he turned to his mother. The seething resentment in his voice became the panic-stricken agony of a lost child who feels himself abandoned.

"You never loved Pa! You didn't care for him at all! Otherwise you wouldn't be in such a hurry to get married again!"

Kinyan had slapped Josh's cheek before she was aware of what she was doing.

"I hate you."

It was a cold, flat statement of fact made by Josh to Colter. Then Josh whirled and bolted from the room.

"Joshua!"

Kinyan's anguished cry followed Josh, but Colter grabbed her hand in his and turned her back to the minister.

"We're not finished," Colter said harshly. His fierce look quelled Lizbeth's whimper, and when he nodded, Hiram Goforth began to read the beautiful vows in a rapid staccato that stripped the meaning from the words. He skimmed through "love, honor, and cherish" as though they wouldn't be a part of these two lives and got on to the business of pledging troths.

Kinyan heard only vaguely the husky "I do" spoken by Colter and was scarcely aware when she repeated the words. She hardly knew when Colter removed John's ring and pressed upon her finger the thin gold band that had been Sarah's.

"I now pronounce you man and wife. You may kiss the bride."

Colter put a finger under Kinyan's chin and lifted her face up to his. Oh, how he yearned to take the unutterable sadness from her eyes! Colter leaned down to press a chaste kiss upon his wife's cold lips.

At that moment Lizbeth did what everyone in the room had been yearning to do for the past half hour. She up-chucked the entire contents of her stomach on the polished wooden floor.

Kinyan rushed to comfort the crying child, and Dorothea sent Jeremy for a rag to clean up the mess.

"I'll be taking my leave now," Hiram said abruptly. The Lord had certainly seen fit to end this ceremony in a most unpropitious manner.

"Here's a small token of our appreciation," Colter said as he slipped a coin into Hiram's ready hand.

"We want to spread the word of our happy union our-selves at the Association meeting on Wednesday, Reverend. We want to see for ourselves how the news thrills our neighbors. Do we understand each other?"

Hiram looked down at the generous contribution in his pudgy palm.

"I understand your feelings perfectly, Mr. Colter. I'll leave the telling to you. Now I really must be on my way. I'll see you after the roundup in September, then, on my next visit?"

Hiram was not quite sure of his future welcome at the ranch.

Kinyan had paled and was dangerously close to collapsing when Dorothea caught Colter's attention.

Colter grasped the situation in a glance and, despite Kinyan's vigorous verbal protest, picked up his wife in his arms.

"If you'll excuse me please, Reverend, Mrs. Colter was attacked by Indians this morning and isn't feeling well."

"Attacked by Indians? But I thought it was Dardus who was attacked by Indians!"

Colter crossed the parlor in bold strides while Hiram, his eyes bugged out so they nearly left his rounded face, skip-hopped along behind him.

Colter quirked a brow at Hiram when he reached the foot of the stairs that plainly said he needed no further escort. Then Colter carried his bride up the stairs.

"In broad daylight!" Hiram gasped aloud.

"As you can see, Hiram, Kinyan is in capable hands. We'll see you in September, after the roundup," Dorothea said as she ushered the reverend to the front door.

As he stepped into his buggy and aimed his horse toward Cheyenne, the Reverend Hiram Goforth heaved a great sigh of relief for his continued welcome at the Holloway—that is, the *Colter* ranch. After all, Dorothea Holloway baked the best dried-apple pie in the county. However, he was going to be chewing on something even more appetizing than Dorothea's apple pie until Wednesday: delicious, tantalizing, savory, succulent, full-bodied, absolutely exquisite *gossip!* How was he ever going to bite his tongue on the fascinating events of the afternoon until then?

CHAPTER 8

THERE WERE DISADVANTAGES, Colter thought wryly as he laid Kinyan down on the four-poster, to marrying in the middle of the day. He still had the afternoon and supper to get through before he'd have Kinyan to himself. Even then, Kinyan might not be well enough to fulfill his urgent need. She'd done much better coping with the pain of her wound than with the accusations Josh had hurled. The boy's cutting words had laid her low where arrow and knife and needle had failed. Hellfire! He didn't feel so great himself. Josh hadn't made this day easy for either of them.

"Do you need any help getting out of your dress?"

Kinyan's eyes were closed and she debated whether to answer Colter. Thinking he would just leave her alone if he thought her unconscious, she played possum. Kinyan heard Colter grunt once and then mutter under his breath. She forced herself to breathe evenly, though she became anxious when she didn't hear her new husband depart.

Colter couldn't make up his mind whether to just leave Kinyan in the dress or try to take it off. After all, they'd only been married a few minutes, and while he'd disrobed plenty of women in the past, none of them had been respectable. He'd never undressed Sarah because she'd been too shy. Of course he'd learned some things since then to overcome a woman's shyness. He sighed, then let practicality decide the matter. The silk gown couldn't be comfortable in the August heat.

"Kinyan."

Colter's voice was husky and low and his soft mouth grazed Kinyan's ear, sending shivers down her spine.

When Kinyan didn't rouse, Colter rolled her onto her right side, lifted her raven tresses aside, and leaned over to attack the immense line of tiny pearl buttons down the back of the gown. It was a good thing, he thought with a chuckle, that he didn't have anything else to do this afternoon.

"I'm awake," Kinyan said when she realized Colter intended to undress her.

"Good, then you can give me some help when the time comes."

Kinyan quickly sat up with her back to Colter.

"I'll get Dorothea to do this," she said without turning to meet the hot eyes she could feel focused upon her.

"Dorothea is taking care of Lizbeth."

"Then I'll take care of myself."

"Kinyan, you can't undo these buttons one-handed. Besides, there must be thousands of them," Colter countered, shaking his head.

"Thirty-six down the back and sixteen on each sleeve."

"What?"

"There are only thirty-six buttons down the back of this dress and sixteen on each sleeve," Kinyan answered. She knew it might as well be a thousand. Colter was right. There was no way she could unbutton all those buttons without using her left arm, and while it didn't bother her much while she kept it still, any movement resulted in an immediate protest from the tender flesh. Stretching her wounded arm to reach buttons was out of the question.

"All right," Kinyan conceded without grace. "I need your help."

"It's my pleasure." The words could have been taunting, but they weren't. Instead, Kinyan felt Colter's caressing tone waft over her like a protective net that kept her secure but left her free to move without restraint. Colter put a knee on the soft mattress, then leaned over and kissed the back of Kinyan's neck, where he'd already unbuttoned the first four buttons.

"Don't!" Kinyan gasped, twisting away.

"Why not?"

"I don't know you."

"I'm your husband."

Colter put a hand on either side of Kinyan's waist. His hands were large. Her waist was small. She wore no corset. His thumbs met in the center of her back, and he massaged the tense muscles on either side of her spine. He felt several clusters of tiny pearls as his fingertips slipped up from her waist to rest just under her breasts. He ached to reach up and cup her fullness, to feel the budding tips harden under his caress.

"Please."

Kinyan whispered the word so softly Colter barely heard her. Did she want him to go on? Or did she want him to stop?

Colter put his other knee on the bed as well and shifted Kinyan so she sat between his thighs with her back resting against his chest. Then, when he had her within his embrace, he carefully lifted her left arm and began to unbutton the sleeve, beginning at the wrist and working upward.

Kinyan closed her eyes and let her head fall back against Colter's shoulder. She could feel his breath, warm and moist on her ear. Colter set her left hand down, then lifted the right. He trailed his forefinger up her arm as he unbuttoned the pearl studs, and a tingling began at her wrist and followed the path he traced, ending far from its source, in the depths of her being. Then Colter put a hand on Kinyan's back to bend her forward.

It felt so . . . right . . . so good.

Kinyan's body obeyed Colter's command without contest. Colter lifted her hair and gave in to the desire to sift a skein of the silky strands through his fingers as he moved it out of his way. He began to count the buttons as he released them, as a way of keeping control over his fractious emotions.

"Seven, eight . . . fourteen, fifteen . . . eighteen, nineteen . . ."

Kinyan heard the numbers, and a bleak smile crossed her face. Soon. Soon, she would be bared to her husband's touch that so insidiously robbed her of her will.

"Thirty-one, thirty-two . . ."

Kinyan knew when Colter reached the last button, because his breathing stopped. She waited for the gentle eddy to begin again. Finally, a ragged rush of air swept past her ear and brushed her cheek. Colter put the palm of his left hand in the center of Kinyan's back and spread his fingertips so they reached her nape and her shoulder blades. The hand slipped upward, curling around Kinyan's willowy neck and along the ridge of her jaw. It spread down her velvety throat, lower, then skimmed her breasts and came to rest on the taut plane of her stomach.

"Kinyan."

It was a bold plea. It was a starry-eyed wish. It was an invitation to delights beyond her imagination.

Kinyan sucked a breath of air into her lungs and held it.

"Please . . ." she whispered, lungs bursting.

At the word, Colter's hand slipped down even farther to cup the warmth of her through the layers of satin.

"Not . . . yet," she exhaled in a mournful cry.

Abruptly, Colter left Kinyan bereft as he crossed to the door and waited there.

Kinyan knew he was waiting for her to call him back, but she couldn't make the words come out. Finally, he spoke.

"Later, then," he said. "Tonight."

It was a promise.

"You can finish undressing yourself. I want to talk with Josh." Colter left the room, closing the door firmly behind him.

Kinyan moaned. Then it dawned on her what Colter had said. *He was going to talk with Josh!* Just because he'd never raised a hand to Josh before they were married didn't mean he wouldn't now. If she'd been provoked to hit her own son, how could she expect Colter to keep his temper? She had to be there when Colter found Josh!

The blue silk slipped off her shoulders and down past her hips, followed by the stiff petticoat Dorothea had made to go with it. Kinyan unhooked her buff high-heeled pumps and kicked them off. She rolled down her stockings and grabbed a pair of heavy socks from the chest that would cushion her boots better. Being careful of her arm, she buttoned on a long-sleeved red gingham blouse over her chemise, yanked Jeremy's jeans up over her pantalets, and slid into her boots in a third of the time it had taken Colter to unbutton the blue silk gown.

Of course Colter hadn't been in a hurry, she thought. He'd been taking his own sweet time. Kinyan shook her head in chagrin. It had already been a very long day, and Colter had warned it was going to be an even longer evening. She would have to worry about that when the time came. Right now she had to find Josh.

It startled Dorothea to see Kinyan skidding down the stairs only moments after Colter had gone, grim-faced, out the front door.

"What in the world is going on?" Dorothea asked.

"I'll tell you about it later. Where's Josh?"

"Your guess is as good as mine. I told Colter to try down by the creek. There's a willow down there that Josh hides under when he's brooding."

"You told Colter where to find Josh?!"

"Why shouldn't I?"

"Never mind," Kinyan replied. As Kinyan headed for the front door, an amazingly strong but tiny arm wrapped itself around her thigh and held on. Kinyan had walked two steps with the added appendage before Lizbeth's weight slowed her down.

"Mama," Lizbeth said insistently.

"I'm in a hurry, Lizbeth. Let me go."

"Mama, I have a question."

"Not now, Lizbeth." Kinyan untangled Lizbeth's grasping hands and took the child's face in her palms. "Are you feeling better?"

Lizbeth nodded.

"Good. I'll talk to you as soon as I get back." Then Kinyan brushed past Lizbeth and yanked open the front door. The panes rattled when she slammed it behind her.

"Grandma Thea?" Lizbeth said, tugging on her grandmother's skirt.

"Yes, Lizbeth." Dorothea walked with Lizbeth into the parlor and sat down in Kinyan's chair. She pulled the little girl into her lap and held her there. Once upon a time she would just have squatted down to Lizbeth's level, but these days it wasn't that easy to get back up again.

"Why isn't Mr. Colter my pa now?"

"Who said he isn't?"

"Josh did."

"What do you remember most about your pa, Lizbeth?"

Lizbeth answered instantly.

"Pa had scratchy whiskers, and when he kissed me good night, he called me his special girl. I was his only princess," she remembered with a wistful smile.

It seemed to dawn on Lizbeth then that she was not Mr. Colter's special girl. Nor was she likely to be his only princess.

Dorothea saw the light of understanding brighten Lizbeth's eyes. Grown-ups too often underestimated a child's capability for grasping realities, she thought.

"Oh," Lizbeth said aloud. "I see."

"What made your pa special was the way he felt about you and your brothers and your mama and the way you all felt about him. You loved each other. Right now Mr. Colter is a stranger. He'll be sitting in your pa's chair and doing the work your pa left to be done, and he'll be your mama's husband. Part of being your mama's husband is being your pa, even if he isn't very good at it at first. He'll learn, though, if we're just patient with him and teach him how to be the kind of pa we'd like to have."

"Are you gonna teach him, Grandma Thea?" Lizbeth asked in an awed voice.

"I'm going to give it a try," Dorothea said. "But you're a more important teacher than I am."

"I am?"

"You sure are. Who else can teach him what it means to have a special girl who's his only princess?"

A radiant smile lit Lizbeth's face.

"Grandma Thea . . ."

"Yes, Lizbeth?"

"Can we start tonight?"

It took Kinyan just three minutes to reach Lodgepole Creek. It took one more minute to get to the willow that hung low over the creek, actually dipping its branches into the rushing water. She could hear voices from within the silvery green canopy, but to her surprise, they were not raised in anger. Kinyan slowed her approach until she stood just at the fringe of the gently swaying refuge.

Colter, Josh, and Jeremy were sitting cross-legged, Indian style, in a circle within the hovering branches of the willow.

"I never had any sons," Colter said.

"Did you ever want a son?" Jeremy asked.

"Every man wants to have sons to carry on after him. A man can build an empire, and if he has no sons, it dies with him. With sons, he knows what he's built has permanence. I suppose none of us thinks much about dying, but having sons gives a man a little immortality. Your pa knew someday you boys would carry on the Triple Fork after him."

"Only you got the Triple Fork instead of us," Josh raged bitterly.

"Your pa didn't count on dying before you boys were old enough to manage the ranch by yourselves. I plan to make sure the Triple Fork's still all in one piece when you're both grown."

"What about your promise to teach Ma how to run the ranch?" Jeremy questioned.

"That's between your ma and me. It doesn't concern you boys."

"Once Ma knows how to run the Triple Fork, we won't need you around here anymore!" Josh blurted.

"I promised to try and teach your ma. There were no guarantees how much she'd learn," Colter said sardonically. "I wouldn't put all my eggs in that basket, Josh," Colter warned.

"I ain't gonna call you Pa!" Josh ranted.

"Neither of us would be comfortable if you did that. Colter will be fine."

"Colter," Jeremy said, tentatively trying the name out, "would you teach me and Josh the same things you're gonna teach Ma?"

"I'd be pleased to, except I'll give you the same rules I gave her."

"What rules?" Josh asked.

"When we're on the range, what I say goes. First job you won't try to handle, we're quits."

"I can live with that," Jeremy replied, excited by the prospect of working with Colter. "How 'bout you, Josh?"

"All right, *Colter,* that suits me fine."

The way Josh said the name, it was an insult, and despite his vow not to let the boy get under his skin, Colter bristled.

"One other thing," Colter said between gritted teeth.

"What's that, *Colter?*" Josh asked insolently.

"It's about your ma."

Josh and Jeremy perked up.

113

"There will be no more disrespectful remarks to your ma about her relationship with me. She and I will be living together as man and wife. If you think any less of her for that, then keep it to yourself. Or take it up with me. Do we understand each other?"

He didn't bother to threaten, Jeremy noted, but the challenge was there.

"I understand you fine," Jeremy admitted.

Josh's face flushed scarlet, but he didn't pick up the gauntlet Colter had thrown.

"Josh?" Colter queried, demanding an answer.

"I understand you." Josh's voice broke, and he cleared his throat as though that had caused the problem.

"Now, I need to give some instructions to the hands about what I want done tomorrow. You're welcome to join me."

That was as much of an invitation as Colter could bring himself to give. This was much, much harder than he'd thought it was going to be. It would be easier to ignore the boys, he thought, than to bear Josh's animosity and Jeremy's eagerness. Their behavior was proof of just how much they missed their father.

Colter rose languidly, his head reaching up to the lowest of the willow's limbs.

"Well, are you coming?"

The boys scrambled to their feet, like two hungry cubs ready for their first hunting lesson.

Colter spread the weeping limbs and stepped out into the stark sunshine, the twins tumbling after him.

As they left the shadowy hideaway, Kinyan stepped inside behind them. It was cool and quiet, the peace broken only by the burbling of the creek, an occasional bluebird, and the slap of the cottonwood leaves as the breeze blew them against one another.

She needn't have worried. Colter was much better with her sons than she'd had a right to hope. She'd almost choked, though, keeping quiet when Colter had intimated he would try to teach her but he couldn't guarantee she'd learn! The proof was in the pudding, she thought. Colter didn't know it yet, but she was a damn fine cook! Speaking of which, she'd better help Dorothea get supper started.

On her way back up the hill, Kinyan remembered she'd

left Lizbeth's urgent question unanswered, so when she reached the house she searched out her daughter. She found her in a most predictable place.

"I'm ready to answer your question now, Lizbeth," Kinyan said, sitting down on the back steps.

"Grandma Thea already answered it," Lizbeth replied without looking up from the white-booted black kitten in her lap. The sharp-toothed kitten chewed industriously on Lizbeth's fingers, its paws wrapped around the girl's slender wrist.

"Is there anything else you'd like to ask me?" Kinyan prodded.

"No."

Kinyan sighed in exasperation. "Well, what did Grandma Thea have to say?"

"Nothin' much. Ouch! Bad kitty!" Lizbeth yelped when the kitten's playfulness resulted in a scratch. The kitten fell away from Lizbeth's arm and took off toward the barnyard with Lizbeth in hot pursuit.

"Lizbeth!"

Lizbeth was too caught up in the chase to respond to her mother's cry.

The door opened and Dorothea stepped onto the back porch. "I thought I heard you out here."

"I was just asking Lizbeth about her question. She said you'd already answered it."

"She wanted to know why Colter wasn't her pa now that you're married to him."

"Oh."

"I told her Colter would have to learn how to be her pa, and she'd have to help teach him. That seemed to satisfy her."

Kinyan reached up to take Dorothea's gnarled, work-reddened hand, then held it against her smooth cheek.

"It's easy to see why John was such a good father."

"We'd better get supper started," Dorothea said. Kinyan's confidence kept her from feeling her sixty-nine years, but she'd get a swelled head if she let the girl go on this way, so she gently pulled her hand from Kinyan's trusting grasp.

"Why don't you go peel some potatoes to fry with the chicken that's about to volunteer to be our supper. I've had

115

my eye on one of those speckled hens that attacks my ankles every morning when I spread feed," Dorothea said with a predatory laugh.

The two women worked together expeditiously and within the next two hours a pesky hen's neck had been wrung and it was gutted, plucked, floured, and fried, ready for the hungry horde that descended when Kinyan took up the metal rod and circled the inside of the triangle to signal supper.

Kinyan seated Colter at the head of the pine trestle table, with Josh to his right and Dorothea next to Josh. Jeremy sat on Colter's left, next to Lizbeth. Kinyan seated herself at the opposite end of the table.

Colter had rinsed off before coming to the table, and the hair he'd brushed back with his fingers was still damp. A drop of water clung to one eyelash. A shadow of beard covered the lower half of his face and the space above his upper lip, and Kinyan wondered if he would shave before coming to bed. Colter hardly looked threatening, Kinyan thought, so why did she perceive the coming darkness with such dread?

Kinyan busied herself with the table to take her mind off the events to come. She had put an embroidered tablecloth on the table and used her good pewter dishes and utensils. She had set two candles at the center of the table in the wooden holders John had carved, more because she liked their bayberry smell as they burned than because the room needed light. She was determined to see that this first meal together as a family would be a memory to cherish.

Neither Dorothea nor Kinyan had counted on Colter's appetite. The small portions he'd eaten at dinner were obviously not indicative of his capacity for food, and as Colter heaped his plate, the two women realized they'd sorely miscalculated the amount of chicken they'd need to feed everyone at the table.

Colter was hungry, and he'd taken a breast, thigh, leg, and wing, which was what his eyes told his stomach it needed to be full, before he became aware of the gaping stares from around the table. He followed their gaze to what remained on the platter and realized he'd taken nearly half the chicken. He could feel his face begin to flush. He returned a thigh, leg, and wing to the platter.

"Guess I'll fill up on beans and potatoes," he said with an embarrassed laugh.

"I'll know better next time," Kinyan hurried to reassure Colter.

"You can have my piece," Lizbeth offered.

"Mine too," Jeremy quipped.

"Well, you can't have mine," Josh said, spearing a leg and a wing. "I'm hungry."

"Thank you, Lizbeth and Jeremy, for your generosity," Colter replied. "But I'll be just fine with what I have."

"You're welcome, Pa," Lizbeth said.

"Who told you to call me Pa?" Colter asked.

Lizbeth saw the fierceness in Colter's eyes, recognized the tautness of his jaw, and paused uncertainly before she answered, "I just—"

"Well don't!"

Colter was sorry as soon as the words were out of his mouth, and he tried to make amends immediately by saying, "Call me Colter, same as Josh and Jeremy."

Lizbeth's face puckered and her eyes filled with tears. She stared at her empty plate without seeing it. Then she looked back up at Colter through long, wet lashes, her chin trembling as she spoke.

"Aren't you gonna be my pa?"

Colter threw his fork down and glared at Kinyan. "What have you been telling this child?"

He tried to put the blame on Kinyan for his own inability to deal with Lizbeth, but she was having no part of it.

"She's just a baby!" Kinyan shrieked, jumping up from her chair in maternal fury. "You could have a little more consideration for her feelings!"

Unfortunately, she'd said it all in Sioux.

Josh graciously translated, embellishing freely on his mother's words.

"What about my feelings?" Colter shouted back at Kinyan, standing up so fast his chair flipped over behind him. "Half your kids don't want anything to do with me, and the other half want me to step right into your dead husband's boots!"

"How dare you bring up John's death!"

"I never said . . ."

Four sets of eyes pinned Colter accusingly, only Dorothea bypassing the opportunity by keeping her face averted.

"Hellfire!" he muttered in frustration.

Colter righted the chair behind him and sat down once more at the table. He viciously stabbed some potatoes with his fork and stuffed them in his mouth, forcing himself to chew and then swallow over the horrible lump that had risen in his throat.

Kinyan choked down the crunchy chicken thigh on her plate, her swallowing made difficult by the rebellious upward thrust of her chin. She'd skipped breakfast and skimped on dinner, and if Colter's temper at the table was any indication, she was going to need all her strength for the evening ahead. Once she got the first bite down, however, her hunger took over and before long there was nothing left on her plate except a well-picked thighbone.

By the time they'd finished eating supper, night had fallen in earnest and Dorothea lit several lanterns to brighten the room.

"You boys best get to bed early. We have a big day tomorrow," Colter suggested gruffly.

"I'll take care of the dishes and then check on Dardus," Dorothea announced.

Kinyan rose from her place at the table. "Come along, Lizbeth," she said. "Time for bed."

"Are you coming, Colter?" Lizbeth asked.

Colter looked surprised at Lizbeth's question. "I'll be up later."

"Will you come say good night to me?"

"You'll probably be asleep by the time I get there," Colter said, grasping at any excuse to avoid having to spend time with the little girl who was such a painful reminder of his own.

The child waited expectantly for him to say he'd come anyway.

"Go on to bed, Lizbeth," Colter said finally, his voice brusque and irritable.

"Josh, Jeremy, come along with me. It's time for bed," Kinyan ordered, her anger at Colter's cruel disinterest in Lizbeth simmering on the surface. How could he be so considerate of the boys and so callous toward Lizbeth?

Aware of their mother's all-too-human tendency to lash

118

out at the closest object when pushed beyond her limit of patience, the two boys hopped up the stairs. Lizbeth gave Colter one last sad, wistful glance before she followed after them. Kinyan lanced Colter with a blistering look as she purposefully turned her back on him and followed her children up the stairs.

The sparks flying from Kinyan's eyes told Colter what she thought of his excuse, but it was the perceptive understanding in Dorothea's eyes that finally sent him from the room.

"I need to check on Hoss," Colter growled as he headed for the front door. It was the coward's way out, and only a brief respite at that—and he knew it even as he touched the shiny brass doorknob. All too soon he'd have to come back and face Kinyan and the fact he was now the father of that little girl. He yanked the front door open and hurled profane epithets at the dark night and the dark past that had left him so miserably scarred, body and soul. He headed for the familiar comfort of his horse, which wouldn't judge, or answer back, or flash sad, wistful looks that tore his guts inside out and left him feeling empty.

CHAPTER 9

COLTER HESITATED BEFORE the door to Kinyan's bedroom, unsure whether to knock or just walk in. He'd dallied in the barn so long that the rest of the upstairs was dark and quiet. He didn't want to announce his presence to the entire upstairs population by knocking, yet neither did he want to deny Kinyan that small courtesy on their wedding night. He decided with a rueful grin that a soft rap with his knuckles at the same time he opened the door was a fair compromise for both of them.

Kinyan was ready when she heard the tap on the door and it swung open to reveal Colter. She stood across from him next to the four-poster dressed in a white flannel nightgown better suited to midwinter. The high collar of the gathered neck was tied with a simple piece of white yarn. The long sleeves were gathered and tied with bows of the same white yarn at the wrists. It fell long to the floor so that only her bare toes showed at the ruffled hem. Even with nothing on beneath it, the gown was miserably hot, but it was the least attractive, most unrevealing nightdress she owned. Kinyan could already feel a rivulet of sweat gaining momentum on its journey down the valley between her breasts.

Colter had never seen Kinyan look more enticing. On her face was an expression of composed serenity that he found beguiling. The innocence of the prim white gown contrasted with the facts he knew about his wife. She was no virgin bride, but a woman who had conceived three children, then labored and delivered them into the arms of their sire. The flannel clung to full, rounded breasts that had nursed three babes. The scant light of the single lantern behind her was not enough to outline Kinyan's form beneath the soft gown, but Colter remembered well the strong tapering legs in the pair of tight jeans. Kinyan's legs had gripped her stallion with sufficient strength to move as one with the animal at a full gallop, and he'd been waiting all day to have her thighs and calves wrapped around him with the same strength in a moment of fierce ardor.

He was intrigued by what he could not see, and she had covered nearly everything. The toe that peeked at him from under the gown brought a smile that flashed white against his tanned, newly shaven skin, and without realizing he did so, Colter closed the distance between them.

Kinyan searched Colter's face, trying to gauge what kind of man she'd married. Her earlier anger with him had dissipated once she discovered Lizbeth was less troubled by Colter's actions at the supper table than she had been. When she thought how good he was with Josh and Jeremy, she willingly forgave him for the isolated incident with Lizbeth. It really had been a very long day. Yet it was not his relationship with her children that concerned her now. She wanted to know what her hours alone with this man held in store for her.

"You look lovely," Colter said. "Good enough to eat."

"I knew I should have fed you more chicken at supper," Kinyan muttered.

"I'm partial to breasts and legs," he quipped with a roguish grin. "Yours look especially tempting."

Colter was not making it very hard for her to guess his plans for the evening. She had put on this uncomfortable nightgown hoping to stem his ravenous appetite and had ended up causing exactly the opposite effect. He made no effort to hide the wolfish hunger that smoldered in his eyes. She wet her lips with her tongue unconsciously and saw the quick flicker of lust that challenged his civilized constraint.

"I'm not sure I can go through with this," Kinyan admitted, backing away from Colter. "It feels strange to be alone with another man in the room John and I shared for so many years. There are so many memories . . ."

"Having second thoughts?"

"We hardly know each other."

"What would you like to know about me?"

Kinyan thought of a hundred questions at once, but before she could ask the first one, Colter stepped forward and gently tipped her chin up with his finger.

"You're very beautiful," he murmured. Without warning, Colter leaned down and his lips brushed Kinyan's. In that fraction of a second, his tongue gently tasted her, sipping only enough nectar to whet his appetite. He kissed the left edge of Kinyan's mouth, then the right. His hunger grew. Colter's fingers threaded through his wife's raven tresses, until the callused pads of his fingers captured her nape and his thumbs caressed the racing pulse points at her throat.

Knowing that in a few moments she wouldn't have the will to speak at all, Kinyan blurted, "Where are you from?"

"Texas," Colter drawled, his hands doing dangerous things to Kinyan's pulse as his fingertips massaged the tense muscles at the base of her neck.

"I guessed that."

"You did?" he said with a lazy smile. "How?"

"Your hat, the star on your vest, the double cinch on your saddle, your voice . . ." she recited.

"My voice?"

His words were a seductive caress, and Kinyan's eyes closed and her palms came up involuntarily to rest on Colter's hard chest as she answered, "It reminds me of a man who came here from Texas a long time ago, right after the war."

Kinyan's eyes snapped open when Colter's hold on her throat tightened abruptly. The expression on his face was cold. Savage. Merciless. Kinyan's hands groped at his wrists, as though her insignificant strength could protect her, and she tried to pull away.

"Don't," he warned. "Tell me what you remember about the man from Texas."

"Nothing really. He—"

"Think!" Colter demanded, his ferocious grasp tightening painfully.

Kinyan stared at him wild-eyed. She had married a madman. He could break her neck with a single twist, and from the look on his face, he would do it if she didn't tell him what he wanted to know. But what did he want to know? Why on earth should he care about some cowboy from Texas?

The look of terror on Kinyan's face finally penetrated Colter's red haze and with a cry of anguish he pulled her into his embrace and buried his face in her hair.

"Oh God, I'm sorry!"

He'd been interrogating her, needing to know if the long-ago Texan was the third man who had wreaked havoc on his life. He hadn't left it all behind. It had all come to Wyoming with him—the pain, the horror, the drive for revenge. Please, please, God, he begged. Let it be over! Let me forget! Unaware he did so, Colter groaned aloud.

Kinyan could feel his suffering. The arms that bound her now were desperate, urgent, but no longer threatening. She reached out to comfort Colter as though he were one of her children who'd awakened in the night, frightened by imagined devils in the dark. Her own fear forgotten, she touched him. She combed her hands through his thick hair and skimmed soothing fingertips over taut shoulders, down the hard slope of his spine, then back up again all the way to his nape, where they worked to ease the tension there.

Colter gradually became aware of Kinyan's velvet touch that cushioned his pain. He sought to return the peace she brought him, and his own hands roamed reassuringly over her soft shoulders, down each knobby bone of her spine, all the way to the curve of her buttocks. His lips found the steady pulse at her throat, hardly noticing that it leaped at his touch.

So totally involved were the two lonely people in comforting each other that they failed to recognize the subtle changes wrought by their enforced contact. The first time Kinyan's hand accidentally brushed Colter's nipple, he felt a sensation of pleasure, but she was ignorant of it. The second time her consoling touch crossed his chest, the nipple had become a hard bud, and when she brushed it, her awareness of his arousal caused a similar response in the tips of her own breasts. Colter felt the pebbled tips of Kinyan's breasts against his chest through her gown and his own cotton shirt, and the heat spread to his loins. His hold on Kinyan's buttocks firmed and he brought her center hard against his own.

The instant she perceived Colter's hard masculinity, Kinyan shoved against his chest to be free.

"Colter, stop!"

None of her questions had been answered, and her one attempt to learn about Colter had ended disastrously. If she hadn't married a madman, then she'd surely married a man of potential violence. Until she knew more about him, she feared to give herself wholly to him.

"Please, can we talk?"

The desperation in Kinyan's voice reached Colter and he released her abruptly.

"I said I was sorry," he snapped defensively when a closer look revealed the fear in Kinyan's eyes.

"I know. I know you are," she said, attempting to placate the fierce-looking man. "But couldn't we just talk for a little while before . . . before . . ."

Ashamed, irritated with her understanding, wanting her more than he would admit, Cotler brushed both hands through his hair and turned away from Kinyan, crossing to stare out the window on the moon-kissed darkness.

Kinyan crawled up onto the foot of the bed, hugging one of the corner posts for security.

"Can you tell me what happened?" Kinyan asked.

Colter sighed. She deserved an explanation, no matter how hard it would be to give it. How much should he tell her? Not everything. He couldn't bear to tell her everything.

"I swore vengeance on three men who hurt me and my family a long time ago," he began. "Two of them have paid with their lives. I never found the third man. I decided this past spring to stop looking, so I came here to the Territory to start my life again. When you mentioned the man from Texas, I . . . I'm trying to forget," he admitted, turning back to face Kinyan, "but I'm not always successful."

Colter's explanation raised as many questions as it answered. Kinyan wanted to know what had happened to his family.

"Did you leave anyone special behind in Texas?"

The way Colter's body stiffened, Kinyan was certain he must have, and a lump caught in her throat and stayed. Since her eyes were focused there, Kinyan perceived the whiteness around Colter's mouth as he answered, "There's no reason for me ever to go back, if that's what you're asking."

It wasn't a totally satisfactory answer, but it was all he offered, so Kinyan accepted it.

"What about you?" Colter surprised Kinyan by asking. "Are you really part Sioux?"

"My father, Soaring Eagle, was a great warrior. He captured my mother, Wheat Woman, on a raid of a wagon train headed for California."

"Did your mother teach you to speak English?" Colter asked as he moved closer to Kinyan.

"Yes."

"But not how to read or write?"

"How could she teach me what she could not do herself? Besides, there were no books to read, no reason to write."

Colter stood beside Kinyan now, leaning against the same post she hugged.

"Do you visit your family often?"

"Every summer. But no one knows I'm part Sioux, so it must be done in secret."

At Colter's questioning look, Kinyan explained, "It was John's wish. He feared his friends wouldn't accord me respect if it were known I'm part Indian." In a brittle voice, she added, "He was right."

"You sound very sure."

"I've been to Fort Laramie. I've been to the Red Cloud Agency. My people are treated as animals. No, not so well as animals, for I feed my horse when he is hungry and I care for him when he is ill. I would not take my children to starve and die among the Sioux! I would have married the devil himself if it had been necessary to save . . ."

When Colter stiffened, Kinyan realized the implication of her vehement cry—that marriage to Colter was only a slightly less horrible alternative than the life she'd described. Kinyan covered her mouth with her hand, but it was too late to contain the words that had already spilled. Her rash, rash tongue! It would be the end of her yet! And soon, she thought, as she watched Colter's body assume an unnatural rigidity.

"Perhaps you have bargained with the devil," Colter taunted. "Because, like the devil, I will have my due."

Colter freed Kinyan's arms from around the bedpost and drew her off the bed to stand before him. Despite his threatening voice, Colter's touch was decidedly gentle. Kinyan was helpless to move, either toward her husband or away from him. She had made the bargain, fully realizing how difficult it would be to keep. She remembered the paralyzing grip with which he'd held her throat and knew it was fruitless to fight his strength. If he wanted her, he would have her. No matter how unwilling, she must submit.

Colter leaned down to take her mouth with his own, his tongue tracing the outline of her lips. His hands reached out to cup the budding breasts he had yearned to touch, and Kinyan's body betrayed her. She was not unwilling. She was all too willing!

Colter's mouth sought Kinyan's forehead, her eyelids, her cheeks, her throat. He was starving and must be fed. His mouth found a nipple through the flannel, and sparks of desire shot from Kinyan's breasts to her loins. She was on fire!

Kinyan didn't understand why Colter's nearness heightened her senses and stole her will. Perhaps he *was* a devil. Else, how had he so completely captured her spirit? Colter's kiss had left her unfulfilled and yearning to taste him more fully. When his lips finally sought hers again, Kinyan opened her mouth to him.

It was all the invitation Colter needed. He gave rein to the passion he had curbed since he'd first held Kinyan in his arms. Savagely he plundered the deep, moist recesses that had been forbidden, taking what he needed. Abruptly, he forced himself to slow his ardor. He must be gentle. He must give as well as take. This was no woman for one night. This was his wife.

"I wanted you yesterday," he murmured against her lips.

"I could tell."

"I want you now."

He pulled Kinyan against the full, hard length of him.

"I can tell," she whispered with a rumble of healthy, husky laughter. This was not submission. It was full, unequivocal acknowledgment of the pleasure they could give one another.

Kinyan put her hands on Colter's hips and moved them down his flanks and around to his taut buttocks. There was sinewy muscle there, rock-hard and firm, *not so different from John*. Kinyan cursed herself for the mental comparison

126

she'd just made and immediately tried to extricate herself from Colter's grasp.

"Colter, I—"

Colter cut her off with a teasing thrust of his tongue. At the same time he wrapped his arms around her so his fingertips just brushed the undercurves of her breasts and lifted her so her body met his where it would do the most good. Kinyan arched into him instinctively. Her left arm dangled safely out of the way while her right grasped at Colter's silky hair and neck and shoulders, anything she could reach to bring his body into closer contact with her own.

Colter took Kinyan's entire weight in one arm and sent the other hand down to cup her firm buttocks and help them match the slow, seductive rhythm of his tilting hips. With her thighs pressed hard to Colter's, the fullness of his need was unmistakable. Kinyan felt the straining muscles through the layers of cloth, and a warmth spread across her loins. Colter's thrusts became more urgent and he captured her mouth with his own with an abandon that drove Kinyan wild.

Their tongues dueled feverishly, two ravening bodies, two famished souls, consuming each other in a frenzied attempt to sate an insatiable hunger, to slake an unslakable thirst.

It was not until the door crashed open that either of them realized someone must have been pounding on it for a considerable time. Kinyan had assumed it was her heart. Colter had been sure it was his.

Josh stared thunderstruck at the sight of his mother standing there in her nightgown, clutched tightly in Colter's amorous embrace. Both of them were breathing raggedly. His mother's face was hidden from him where it lay against Colter's chest.

"What do you want?" Colter asked with feral challenge, his heavy-lidded eyes glazed with passion, his interrupted body throbbing for release.

"I . . . I just wanted to make sure Ma was all right. She didn't answer the door. I . . . I didn't hear you come in," Josh stuttered. He was gone an instant later, and they could hear her door quietly click shut down the hall.

Colter felt Kinyan grip his arm and then push against his chest to be freed. Reluctantly, he released her.

"I'll put a lock on the door tomorrow," Colter said, running a hand through his hair. He thought he knew what Kinyan must be feeling, but didn't think he was the one who should be apologizing for what Josh had seen.

"You won't be needing it," Kinyan whispered.

"What did you say?"

"There won't be any need for a lock on the door."

"You may be willing to take the chance of one of your children walking in on us again, but I'm not!"

"I can't do this, Colter," Kinyan pleaded. "Not yet. It's too soon."

"It wasn't too soon a moment ago," he countered, not hiding his anger and frustration at Josh's intrusion. Colter pulled Kinyan into his arms and kissed her fiercely, greedily. Kinyan fought the rising tide of passion only a moment before she succumbed to her need and hungrily returned the devouring kiss.

Colter broke the embrace and stared triumphantly down into the limpid blue pools of Kinyan's eyes, daring her to deny her desire.

"I touch you and I think of John."

Colter's sharp intake of breath told Kinyan her point had struck home. She couldn't have said anything more calculated to incense or repulse the man who held her in his arms. Colter became rigid against her, and his eyes narrowed in fury. He pushed Kinyan away from him, only barely managing to control his strength so she landed against the corner of the bed instead of being thrown completely over it.

Kinyan hadn't intended to hurt Colter. She'd only said the first thing that came into her head to retaliate because he'd been right about her inexplicable weakness for him. Oh, her quick, barbed tongue! How she regretted its prick when she saw the blood it drew!

"How do I measure up?" Colter demanded coldly.

"I wasn't comparing you! I tried to tell you I couldn't do this, but you forced me into it," she accused. "You insisted on coming to my bed!"

The thought of being a substitute for another man turned Colter's face pale with fury. Was that why this respectable woman had responded so wholeheartedly to him? He almost groaned aloud, but his pride kept him silent.

"I just need time to adjust," Kinyan rushed to explain.

"How much time?" Colter grated out.

Now that Colter seemed willing to concede her a respite from his advances, how much time did she dare ask for? Kinyan wondered.

"Six months," she bargained.

"One."

"Three months."

"Six weeks," he said flatly. "That's all. Then this marriage will be consummated, *and there will be no thoughts of John Holloway!*"

Colter recognized the absurdity of the demand as soon as he had voiced it. He, of all people, knew the difficulty of keeping beloved memories in the past, where they belonged. Yet his need to be foremost with this woman was such that he had not been able to curb his speech. How had lust become a craving to be the only man in this woman's life? It simply didn't make sense to him.

Kinyan saw the demon Colter fought, but she couldn't help him. She hadn't yet come to grips with her own feelings, which were confused. How could she possibly keep the memory of John from rising when she was in Colter's arms? Only she hadn't thought of John, she realized with surprise. She hadn't thought of John after the first moment Colter had taken her in his rapacious embrace.

She still cared for John. The love of him flowed through her. Yet she felt something unique for Colter as well. She couldn't call it love. With John, love hadn't come for months—not until she'd learned what kind of compassionate, caring man he was. With Colter, the feelings were lightning and thunder, a sudden flood, a tornado, all wild and uncontrollable, violent and destructive forces that reshaped the land over which they passed. She had to be cautious—if not for her own sake, then for the sake of those who depended on her.

"What do we do now?" Kinyan asked, her trepidation plain on her face.

"Now, my dear wife, I suggest we go to bed. We have a lot to do tomorrow."

"Surely you don't intend to sleep here?" Kinyan sputtered, aghast.

"Where else would I sleep?"

"But you just agreed—"

"I just agreed not to consummate this marriage for six weeks. I didn't agree to give up my bed. Don't worry." He laughed raggedly. "I wouldn't touch you right now if you begged me to. When I make love to you, I intend to be the only man in your arms. I'm not taking a ghost to bed with me!"

Then Colter hauled Kinyan up into his arms, laid her on the bed, taking care not to further injure her arm, and headed out the door.

"I'll be back," Colter announced, giving Kinyan one last thorough appraisal.

"Where are you going?" a startled Kinyan asked.

"I'm going down to take a dip in that damn creek!"

CHAPTER 10

MORNING CAME SOONER than either of them wished. In the shrouded mystery of sleep, it was easier to hide from feelings neither could understand or accept.

Colter had returned from the creek and, grateful that Kinyan was asleep, stripped in the dark. He knew women found the scar that could be seen at his throat enticing, but he'd learned from painful experience the revulsion that followed when he removed his shirt and those same women saw how his flesh had been scarred by the slashing sword of the third man. Colter hadn't really figured out how he was going to keep his wife from seeing him when he planned to sleep with her. He only knew he couldn't face the same look of pity and disgust in her eyes that he'd seen from those first few whores.

Because of the heat, both Kinyan and Colter had thrown off the covers during the night, and Kinyan's flannel gown had worked its way up to her waist. Her body, on the other hand, naturally reached out for the touch of warm flesh nearby. Consequently, when his fear of exposure brought him awake at first light, a naked Colter found Kinyan's half-naked body lying sprawled across his own. Her smooth thigh rested on his hairy one, and her wounded left arm was wrapped securely across his flat stomach. The smile on his face quickly became a scowl when he realized the restrictions he'd placed on himself. How was he ever going to last six long weeks without having her?

"Wake up!" he growled at Kinyan.

"John?" she mumbled.

"Hellfire!"

If she kept mistaking him for John Holloway, he wasn't going to have any trouble at all leaving her alone, Colter thought angrily. He reached over to shake Kinyan awake but stopped when he realized that his scarred body lay visible to her in the shadowy light. He carefully pulled himself from her grasp and slipped on his Levi's and shirt. Then he lay back down on the bed next to Kinyan and watched her sleep. He wrapped his fingers around a lock of hair and brought it first to his cheek, then to his jaw, then to his chin. He held it beneath his nose and breathed the scent he was coming to identify as Kinyan's.

Kinyan rolled over in her sleep and her hair was yanked from Colter's grasp. She awoke with a start to find herself under Colter's sensual scrutiny. When his eyes shifted to her navel and his brow quirked in speculation, Kinyan looked down to see what was so interesting, only to discover her nudity.

"Aaargh!"

Kinyan yanked the gown down as she came flying out of bed.

Colter raised his eyebrows in a comical leer and lunged for his wife. A shriek of girlish laughter escaped Kinyan as she dashed around a corner of the four-poster. Colter cut her off, backing her up, step by breathless step, into the corner of the room. He braced one palm on the wall on either side of Kinyan's head and brought his mouth down to within an inch of hers. Kinyan watched his gaze roam over her face, her throat, her breasts, her hips and back again as he ate her with his eyes.

"How's your arm this morning?"

After the look Colter had just given her, the question caught her off guard. She tested the arm. It was stiff and the movement caused pain, but it was by no means unbearable.

"It's sore."

"Do you want to take a day to rest before we start your lessons?" he asked lazily, his eyes on Kinyan's mouth.

Kinyan licked her lips. "I'm ready now," she said unsteadily.

"Yes, I guess you are."

Colter's mouth slowly descended toward Kinyan's, and her pulse began to leap in anticipation.

"Lest there be any mistake," he murmured, "this is Benjamin Colter kissing his wife, Kinyan, good morning."

Colter brushed Kinyan's lips so lightly she wondered if he'd touched them at all. Her fingers reached out to chart the jagged scar on his jaw, then slipped behind his head to pull his mouth down to her own in a more satisfactory meeting. When her tongue came out to trace Colter's lips, he jerked himself from her grasp.

"Have you changed your mind?" He wanted her. Oh, God, how he wanted her.

Kinyan recognized the fire in Colter's eyes and snapped a quick, defensive, "Of course not!"

"Teasing witch!"

"You touched me first!"

The fact she was right only made him angrier. She was Circe, the Sirens, every lovely, dangerously seductive female from history he'd ever heard of rolled into one, and he'd be damned if he'd fall under her spell again!

Colter left Kinyan standing in the corner and went to get clean socks from John's wardrobe, where he'd put them when he'd unpacked his few possessions.

"Get dressed," he ordered.

Unwilling to test Colter's willpower, Kinyan put up with the struggle of donning her chemise and pantalets underneath the gown before she took it off. By the time she was done, she was sweating profusely and fit to be tied. When she finally got a blouse on, she undid the tie on the gown, opened the neck, and let it slip down over her hips. Colter appeared to remain totally oblivious to Kinyan's predicament until, standing in her pantalets and hopping on one foot, she started to slip Jeremy's jeans up over her legs.

Colter crossed the room and snatched the Levi's out of Kinyan's hands.

"What do you think you're doing?"

"Getting dressed."

"No wife of mine is wearing an outfit that shows off every curve of her body to any cowboy who cares to look," he said. "Find something better to wear." In truth, it wasn't the cowboys he worried about so much as his own peace of mind.

"If you expect me to be able to handle the same jobs as any other cowhand, there isn't anything better to wear!"

133

Colter thought about that a minute. He was sorry he'd agreed to teach her, but the fact was, he had. Still convinced, however, that it was only going to be a matter of a day or two before she retired as a cowboy, he conceded the jeans weren't a bad idea.

"All right," he agreed gruffly. "Have you got some chaps too?"

"No, I—"

"Borrow some."

Neither spoke as they finished dressing, and Dorothea's breakfast of eggs, beef, biscuits, and coffee was a quiet affair as well, with Lizbeth still in bed and Josh noticeably absent from the table.

"How's Dardus?" Kinyan asked Dorothea.

"Still holding his own. No better, no worse. He was awake for a few moments this morning, but in a lot of pain."

Dorothea looked at Colter, remembering his prediction. Colter remembered it too. He shrugged away his sympathy. John's death and the attack on the foreman had left him with work to do, and it was time he started doing it.

"Jeremy, I want you to go with Frank today. He'll be treating cattle for blowflies," Colter ordered.

"But, I wanted to go with—"

"No buts! You have your orders. Obey them."

This was an entirely different Colter from the polite, considerate cowboy of the previous day. His aura of authority was unmistakable, his lithe, powerful body, a banner of command.

" 'Scuse me," Jeremy mumbled. He shoved his chair back and quickly left the room.

"I forgot to send for more turpentine!" Kinyan blurted, remembering her unfulfilled promise to Dardus.

"I sent Petey into Cheyenne to get some yesterday, after I talked with Frank," Colter said chidingly. "First lesson, Kinyan: the ranch comes first, before anything personal."

Kinyan's face reddened in humiliation. How could he? He knew perfectly well there was no time yesterday she could have taken care of that detail. Yet, she admitted grudgingly, he had found time.

She tipped her chin up, undeterred. She was *not* stupid; only a mite ignorant, perhaps. And if he thought she couldn't take a little criticism, well he was wrong!

134

"I won't forget," Kinyan said evenly, meeting Colter's assessing gaze. "The ranch comes first."

"Where's Josh?" Colter asked Dorothea.

"He left early with the men you sent to move the cattle down from the mountains. He took a bedroll and said he'd stay with the hands until the job was done."

Colter chanced a look at Kinyan, who was staring back at him accusingly. Hellfire! It wasn't his fault the boy had walked in on them last night!

"Good," he replied, daring Kinyan to say anything.

Kinyan wouldn't have known what to say. She was worried about Josh. Surely he would learn to accept Colter. Surely the two of them would find a way to make peace. She refused to dwell on the result if they didn't, but the prospect of Josh feeling unwelcome in his own home haunted her.

Dorothea saw Kinyan's distress and whisked Colter's coffee cup from him, commenting, "I can't sit here all day. I've got things to do."

Colter swallowed the coffee in his mouth, which was suddenly very bitter, then said to Kinyan, "Let's go. Day's wasting."

Kinyan followed Colter from the room, running to keep up with his long strides as he headed for the barn. They saddled up and rode northeast. It was a long two hours before Kinyan's curiosity finally got the better of her, and she broke the silence that had reigned between them since they'd left the house.

"Where are we going?"

"Frank said squatters have been perched out on the edge of the ranch for about a week. I just want to take a look for myself."

"What are you going to do if they are there?"

"I won't know that until I meet them," Colter said grimly.

"Colter, you won't have to kill anyone, will you?"

Kinyan shuddered at the icy look in his eyes when he turned to her.

"They're on Triple Fork land. I intend to ask them to leave. The rest is up to them."

"But surely you wouldn't just shoot them!"

"Second rule, Kinyan: you've got to be willing to fight for what's yours. Do you know how to fire a gun?"

135

"There was no reason to learn," Kinyan said defensively. "John and Dardus took care of everything."

"John is dead. Dardus will be soon."

"That was cruel," Kinyan said after she had recovered from the shock of his statement.

"That was the truth."

"Dardus isn't dead yet."

"Miracles have been known to happen," Colter admitted. "I even prayed for one myself once. If you plan to manage the Triple Fork, though, you'll need more than miracles. You'll need a Colt and a Winchester, an eagle eye, and a steady hand. We'll start with the handgun, then work with a rifle. You'll start carrying a gun as soon as you know how to use it."

"I don't want to carry a gun. I wouldn't be comfortable with one."

Colter stopped his horse. "Then I guess we better go on back now. I didn't think you'd last very long, but I was willing to give you the benefit of the doubt. Two hours in your company wasn't bad at all. You can go on home now and take care of Lizbeth."

"You can't be serious."

"Perfectly serious."

"That isn't fair!"

The childishness of that argument struck Kinyan at once. How many times had she told Josh or Jeremy that life was never fair.

"I thought you wanted to learn how to run the Triple Fork."

"I do, but . . ."

Colter quirked his brow and started to turn Hoss around.

"I'll learn to shoot," Kinyan blurted.

"And carry a gun," Colter added, eyeing Kinyan speculatively.

"And carry a gun," she said from between clenched teeth.

Colter headed Hoss northeast and kicked him into a distance-eating lope. Muttering her displeasure, Kinyan spurred Gringalet and followed him. All she'd really had in mind when she'd made her bargain with Colter was that he'd teach her what she wanted to learn. Colter had amended that slightly to include teaching her what he thought she ought to know. She would have argued further with him, she told herself, except that he was right. It wasn't such a bad idea for her to know how to shoot a gun. She simply couldn't imagine herself wearing one.

Another thirty minutes brought them within sight of a heavy covered wagon, which was all the shelter the squatters had. They were camped along Little Bear Creek, which provided water, and there were a few cottonwoods for shade. Colter noticed three horses and two mules hobbled a short distance away.

"I don't plan to do anything but talk right now," Colter warned Kinyan. "I want you to stay back behind me. Keep your mouth shut and listen."

"Howdy," Colter called as they approached.

Two rough-looking men stood at either end of the wagon. One held a Winchester, the other a shotgun. Both also wore low-slung holsters with Colts in them. The younger of the two had a pinched nose and dirty brown eyes set too close together. He kept dragging his hand through his shaggy blond hair to keep it off his face as the wind ruffled it. He wore Levi's, rather than coveralls, and his boots were suited to riding, not working the land. He shifted the rifle comfortably in his hands, like he'd been born holding one.

Colter's glance flicked to the older man, whose black hair had grayed in streaks and whose jutting black brows masked deepset eyes that glittered with malice. He hadn't shaved for a while and the stubble on his face was mostly gray, with traces of tobacco spittle staining it brown around his frowning mouth. He had on a filthy red long-john shirt with a hole near his bulging belly and Levi's that hung so low on the narrow hips under his stomach that they threatened to slide on down. The bore of the shotgun he held in his grimy hands was aimed at Colter's chest, and the man didn't bother to lower it when he spoke.

"Don't come any closer, less'n you want your heads blowed off," the older man said.

Colter stopped Hoss and kept his hands in plain sight, resting on the horn of his saddle.

"You folks just passing through?"

The two rough-looking men eyed each other, and when one shifted his gaze to the wagon for just a second, Colter realized a third man must be hiding there.

"No, we kinda like it here," the younger man said with an

insolent grin. "We'd like it even better if that little girlie with you would get down off her horse and make us feel welcome."

"Shut up, Dobie. I'll do the talkin'."

"Aw crap, Cletus. You always do the talkin'," Dobie whined. "How 'bout it, girlie? You gonna make ole Dobie feel real good?" Dobie grabbed his crotch in an obscene gesture.

Dobie's eyes were glued on Kinyan, so he missed the slight narrowing of Colter's eyes and the tic in his jaw muscle that caused Cletus to take a tighter grip on his shotgun.

"You'd have me howling in no time, wouldn't ya, bitch?" Dobie said with a raucous laugh.

Colter heard Kinyan's gasp behind him, and he hardly recognized his own voice when he said, "This is Triple Fork land. I suggest you clear out."

"I tole you to shut up, Dobie," Cletus barked.

"I ain't gonna—"

Dobie shut his mouth when he realized what was causing Cletus's anxiety. Colter had his .44 out and aimed at Dobie's face, while Dobie's rifle still lay cradled in his arms.

"Don't try it," Colter said menacingly to Cletus, who'd shifted the barrel of the shotgun slightly. "You'd be a dead man. Put your guns down."

With a snarl on his face, Cletus nodded to Dobie, who laid his gun down, and then he himself complied. They eased their Colts from their holsters and pitched them on the ground as well.

"Now, tell whoever is in the wagon to leave his weapon on the floor and come on out here."

"There ain't nobody—"

Colter cocked the .44.

"I'm comin' out," a scared voice whimpered. "Don't shoot."

The third man came out of the wagon with his hands held high in the air. He had the same pinched nose and close-set eyes as Dobie, but his hair was muddy brown, and despite the fact he was younger than Dobie, he was missing most of his front teeth.

"You wasn't ever much good for nothin', Jimmie," Cletus said in disgust.

"I want to know what you're doing here," Colter demanded.

"Why, we was homesteadin', o' course," Cletus replied with a smirk.

Colter noted the well-oiled guns and the absence of amenities for farming or ranching, not even a running iron such as rustlers used to change brands. These were outlaws of the worst ilk, amoral and vicious, and somebody had put them here for a reason.

"I want to know who sent you here."

"Cain't rightly remember," Cletus said, scratching his ear in feigned forgetfulness.

Colter shot the rowel off Cletus's right spur.

"It were that Ritter fella," Jimmie screamed in fear. "He tole us if we'd stay here he'd pay us good."

"He's lying!" Kinyan exclaimed, nudging Gringalet up beside Colter's horse. "Ritter wouldn't . . ."

Colter took his eyes off the three men when Kinyan yelled, and Cletus and Dobie scrambled for their guns.

Colter cursed Kinyan, cursed his own carelessness, cursed Dobie and Cletus, but when he was done shooting, Cletus had a bullet in his thigh and Dobie had one in his arm and Jimmie was curled up in a ball on the ground crying.

Colter swung down off Hoss. He calmly walked over to pick up the weapons strewn on the ground around the wagon and threw them into the stream.

Kinyan stared aghast at the carnage before her. Colter had been so controlled and the devastation so complete that it took a moment for her to accept what her eyes told her had happened. It must take a great deal of practice to react so incredibly fast. Kinyan wondered with horrified admiration just what kind of man she'd married. Colter's icy voice finally penetrated her haze.

"I said get down from there. I need your help."

Kinyan dismounted and walked unsteadily over to Colter.

"Have you ever hitched a team?"

"Yes," Kinyan whispered.

"Go get those mules and hitch them to this wagon."

When Kinyan didn't move, Colter grabbed her chin in his hand and caught her eyes with his own. "Did you hear what I said?"

Kinyan nodded.

"Then get to it."

Colter tied off the wound in Cletus's leg and then picked up the unconscious man and threw him over his shoulder to carry him to the back of the wagon.

"Jimmie," he called. "Come here."

The sobbing boy came up off the ground like a whipped dog and slunk toward Colter.

"Get up in the wagon and catch his head and shoulders when I hand him over."

Jimmie did as he was told, then climbed into the front seat of the wagon to drive.

Dobie tied his arm with the filthy yellow scarf from around his neck, keeping his eye on Colter and staying a safe distance from the angry cowboy at all times.

After Colter dropped Cletus in the back of the wagon, he helped Kinyan finish harnessing the mules.

"Get in the wagon, Dobie," Colter ordered when they were done. "Get off Triple Fork land and don't come back, or you won't be leaving at all next time."

Jimmie *chked* to the mules and the wagon lurched forward, drawing a muffled curse from Dobie when his arm slammed against a rail. When the wagon was well away, Colter turned to Kinyan.

"Get on your horse."

Kinyan responded to the suppressed fury in Colter's voice and quickly remounted Gringalet.

They were halfway back to the ranch before Colter spoke. It had taken him that long to stop shaking. Despite outward appearances, he'd been out of control during the entire episode with Dobie. He'd wanted to strangle the rude sonofabitch for his lurid words and actions toward Kinyan, and it was the fear of injury to Kinyan that had caused him to shoot at flesh rather than the ground beneath the three outlaws' feet. His fury and fear had been irrational, he knew, and it irritated him that his feelings for Kinyan could so rattle him. At long last, when he'd contained his fear and managed his anger, he was ready to confront Kinyan.

"When I give you an order, I expect you to obey it. You could have gotten us both killed."

Kinyan had been expecting some form of chastisement and had worked up a great deal of righteous indignation waiting for Colter to speak.

"I wasn't the one who pulled a gun on those men! You were just going to talk. Do you always let your gun do your talking for you?" she asked sarcastically. "At least you didn't murder those men, though I don't imagine you spared them on purpose. What's the matter, was your aim off?"

Murder? Murder! Colter marveled at Kinyan's naiveté. She apparently had no idea Dobie and Cletus weren't genuine squatters. She apparently had no idea the real danger they'd been in.

"If I'd wanted to kill them, they'd be dead. I wouldn't have had to fire at all if you'd stayed quiet like I told you to do!"

"But that man Dobie must have been lying! Ritter offered to help me move those squatters off Triple Fork land himself!"

"Did he?" Colter said cynically. "How convenient."

Kinyan was hot and tired and emotionally drained, and her shoulders slumped as she realized the futility of trying to argue with Colter. She just wished he'd give her opinion a little respect. So far, their relationship hadn't exactly been her idea of a partnership.

"Ready to quit now?" he asked.

Kinyan turned to Colter and it suddenly dawned on her that he'd known something like this might happen when he'd asked her to ride with him. Maybe he'd even wanted it to happen, just so she would give up on the idea of managing the ranch.

"You're not getting rid of me that easily," Kinyan said in a steely voice. "I'm as willing to fight for the Triple Fork as you are."

"I'm glad to hear it," Colter replied, a little surprised to realize that he meant it. "Because tomorrow you start working with a Colt."

CHAPTER 11

"THIS LOOKS LIKE a good spot."

Colter "whoaed" Hoss to a stop, swung his leg over Hoss's rump, and stepped down from the saddle into the shin-high grass. Kinyan slipped off Gringalet and led the stallion to the nearby creek for a drink. Colter fumbled through his saddlebag for a moment, drawing forth a .44 Colt with a scarred walnut butt.

Kinyan took advantage of Colter's preoccupation to examine their surroundings. He had brought them to a sheltered spot on Little Horse Creek. A heavy growth of cottonwood created sufficient shade to keep the early afternoon sun from searing them, but the heat shimmered off the undulating grass as far as the eye could see.

Kinyan was already exhausted and ready for a nap, not the target practice Colter had planned for her afternoon. He'd insisted they ride the west perimeter of the Triple Fork all morning, and they'd moved several bunches of cattle because Colter considered the animals had eaten the grass down low enough where they were. Kinyan's back ached, her hands, buttocks, and thighs were sore, and she had a splitting headache from squinting in the sun. But she hadn't refused a single order from Colter and she wasn't about to start now. On the other hand, wasn't she at least entitled to get a break to eat?

"Colter?"

"Uh-huh."

"I'm hungry," Kinyan announced.

"I want to get in a few rounds of target practice first. Then we'll eat."

As he loaded the .44 Colt single-action army revolver, Colter surreptitiously watched Kinyan gently massage her buttocks and inner thighs, a curiously tight feeling growing within him. Then she flexed her shoulders back, pulling her gingham blouse tight over her rounded breasts. She stripped the bandanna from her neck and unbuttoned her blouse halfway, dipping low with the triangle of cloth to swipe at the dripping sweat. She leaned forward and waved the gingham away from her body a couple of times, trying to catch the breeze and giving Colter a heady view of ripe fruit waiting to be plucked. Then she threw her head back and splayed her fingers through her raven hair, the wind whipping it away from her face and at the same time evaporating the droplets of perspiration at her temples and above her upper lip.

It seemed impossible Kinyan could not know the effect her actions were having on Colter, yet such was the case. After long years spent with John, she had slipped into the familiar complacency of married life, where arousal often gave way to the exigencies of the moment, with the sure knowledge that satisfaction would be forthcoming at a later time. For Colter, there was only now.

"I'm ready if . . . you are," Kinyan said. The sentence ended in a whisper. It was apparent Colter was more than ready. The telltale ridge along his Levi's would have given him away if she had looked, but Kinyan never got beyond his eyes, which were hooded, dark with desire, and focused unerringly on her throat and the soft mounds of flesh that rose above her unbuttoned blouse.

Kinyan's attention shifted to the .44 revolver Colter held extended in his outstretched palm.

"Where did you get that?" Kinyan asked when she recognized John's gun.

"Dorothea gave it to me when I mentioned getting a weapon for you. This one will do very well."

The barrel of the gun was seven and a half inches long, and when Colter laid it in Kinyan's hand, she was surprised by its over two-pound weight.

"Just hold it for a moment. Get the feel of it. Wrap your fingers around the butt."

"It's heavy!" Kinyan exclaimed, shifting the gun in her hand. Kinyan did as Colter bade her but couldn't seem to find a comfortable way to hold the gun.

Colter stepped closer to Kinyan and cupped his hand under hers to help support the Colt as he showed her how to adjust the cylinder to load the six bullets. He rolled the cylinder around once with his thumb and asked, "Got it?" before he left Kinyan once again with the entire weight of the weapon.

"Straighten your arm. Let the gun be an extension of your hand."

Kinyan extended her arm and promptly let it drop back to her side.

"Don't you have something a little smaller and lighter?"

"A forty-four is called the Peacemaker for a reason, Kinyan. It can end an argument before it gets out of hand."

Colter was left-handed, Kinyan right-handed, and as they worked together it was necessary for Colter to wrap his arms around Kinyan in order to be able to manipulate her right hand with his left. He put himself behind her and helped her hold the Colt with her arm extended. Kinyan fidgeted, and her buttocks scraped Colter's groin twice before he finally admitted he was the one coming away the worse for wear in this encounter. It was definitely time for a break.

"Just aim at that cottonwood across the creek and fire," he ordered.

Kinyan carefully lifted the gun, aimed, and pulled the trigger. To her delight and Colter's surprise, she hit the tree.

"I did it!"

She shot until all six bullets were spent, and hit the tree every other time.

"Not bad," Colter said noncommittally, although she'd performed better than most men in the same situation. "Let's eat."

A slow smile formed on Kinyan's lips. That was more of a compliment than she'd expected considering Colter had hinted all morning she would probably be scared silly by the noise and the .44's hefty kick.

144

"Actually, I thought I did pretty well," Kinyan said as she divided the beef and biscuits they had brought along.

"If your target was a barn, yes, I'd agree you could hit it," he replied sardonically. "It's rare, however, that a barn attacks you."

Kinyan laughed, acknowledging the ridiculousness of his comment, as though Colter had made some very clever joke.

Her refusal to be piqued by his sarcasm left Colter in a worse mood than before. How was he going to keep from throwing her to the ground and ravaging her if she kept on being this delightful pleasure to his eyes and ears? Colter remained silent during lunch while Kinyan regaled him with her dreams about running the ranch. Colter didn't tell her he thought her dreams unrealistic, but he decided to show her they were. He had been easy on her so far, not pushing her beyond what he thought she could handle. Now the woman had actually begun to believe she could accomplish what she'd set out to do. Well, today he would let her prove to herself that she hadn't the physical or emotional stamina to handle the job. Then she would stay home and he wouldn't spend the entire day wanting her like this.

"Are you finished?" he asked curtly.

"I was just waiting for you," she replied agreeably.

Colter had Kinyan stand, feet apart, extend the .44 at arm's length, and fire at a small target far more distant than she was ever likely to use the Colt to hit. He kept her that way for an hour. It was necessary, occasionally, for him to put his arms around her to correct her aim.

"Squeeze, don't pull."

"I am squeezing."

"Like this."

"Oh, I see."

His aroused body began to ache from the constant contact with her, until he thought he'd have to give in to her stubbornness. But he didn't. By the end of the hour, although her arm muscles trembled from the strain, she was hitting the target with regularity.

Colter cursed. She'd mastered the task he'd set and hadn't cried uncle. But she would—before he did.

"Hitting a target when you have plenty of time is no

problem," he said casually. "But how would you do if you had to hurry?"

Kinyan shot Colter a persecuted look that spoke louder than words. But she didn't ask to quit.

He spent the next hour having her draw the gun and fire in a single smooth step. She used a different set of muscles, and though the fatigue showed on her face, she stuck it out. He stood at her shoulder, her buttocks pressed against his thighs, so he could teach her the necessary fluid motion.

"Slow and easy."

"I am going slow."

"Slower. Smoother."

"Oh, I see."

He had gritted his teeth at his constant state of tumescence. But he didn't give in. Neither did she. By the end of the hour, she was hitting the target with regularity.

Colter cursed again.

"Hitting a standing target is no problem," he said casually. "But how would you do if the target moved?"

Kinyan shot Colter a pained glance that spoke louder than words. But she didn't ask to quit.

Colter picked up several good-sized stones and hefted them in his palm.

"You don't expect me to hit something as tiny as that?" Kinyan asked incredulously.

"A man's heart isn't a very large target."

"No, I suspect yours is pretty small indeed," she replied dryly.

She had hit her mark with that comment better than she knew, because right now Colter felt about waist high to a piss-ant for pushing Kinyan so hard. He spent the next hour pitching the rocks fast and high. Every time she aimed, Kinyan extended her arm above her breast, lifting the jutting tip just slightly and sending a curious spiraling sensation to Colter's loins.

Kinyan used a different set of muscles for this trial, together with all the other worn-out ones. Sweat streamed from her temples and dotted the space above her upper lip as she concentrated on the rocks and tried to forget the aching muscles in her hand, her arm, her shoulder, her ribs, her back, and her neck. Was there anything else? Oh yes, her aching feet.

146

"Look before you shoot."

"I can't see the rock. It's too small."

"Follow it with your eyes."

"Oh, I see."

Colter watched the line of sweat widen and make Kinyan's shirt stick to the center of her back until he could actually see her skin through the thin material. Her armpits were wet too. He imagined how salty she must taste. He groaned. Kinyan did too. By the end of the hour, she was hitting the target with regularity.

Colter cursed.

"Hitting a moving target without the sun in your eyes is no problem," he said casually. "But how would you do if you had to cope with the glare?"

Kinyan shot Colter an aggrieved glower that spoke louder than words. But she didn't ask to quit.

Colter sent Kinyan into the three o'clock sun. He stayed in the shade. The sun glistened on her skin. Even with her hat on, she squinted her eyes in the harsh glare. Good, Colter thought. No one likes a woman with squinty eyes. Only he remembered those azure eyes languid with passion. His body hardened, and he closed his eyelids on the aching pain.

"Are you all right?" Kinyan asked worriedly, coming back to his side. She put her hand on his shirt and his nipples peaked.

"I'm fine," he gritted out. "Get back out there."

"If you're sure there's nothing I can do for you," Kinyan replied concernedly, brushing a lock of hair behind his ear.

Colter growled low in his chest. Kinyan strolled back out into the sunshine, her jean-clad buttocks swaying seductively from side to side with each step.

Colter swallowed hard. He'd never seen Kinyan walk like that. Ever. Then he laughed out loud. Beguiling minx! She knew exactly what she was doing!

Kinyan turned and smiled at Colter. Now all the cards were on the table.

Colter pitched the stones so Kinyan had to compensate for the sun's brightness.

"Don't squint."

Kinyan snickered.

"Focus on the shade."

"Oh, I see."

She was tired. So was he. By the end of the hour, she was hitting the target with regularity.

Colter cursed.

The sun was coming down. They were far enough from the ranch that they should stop if they wanted to get back in time for supper.

"Hitting a moving target, even with the sun in your eyes is easy," Colter said casually. "But how would you do if the target was shooting back?"

Kinyan's eyes widened in fright. Surely he didn't plan to shoot at her! Or for her to shoot at him!

Kinyan shot Colter a searching side glance that spoke louder than words. But she didn't ask to quit.

Colter stared at Kinyan a moment before it dawned on him she was ready to go as far as he asked. He couldn't see any higher than the piss-ant's knees and he realized he was in trouble.

"Hellfire and damnation!"

He stomped over to Hoss and pulled John's holster from the saddlebag. He crossed back to Kinyan, reached around her with the holster, and brought the two sides together in front to buckle it on her womanly hips. He took the Colt from her blistered hand, shoved it down into the holster, and snapped, "Wear it every day from now on until I tell you to take it off!"

He had to help her into the saddle. She groaned audibly on the ride back to the house. He did too. How could he have been so pigheaded? How could she have been so pigheaded? He supposed they deserved each other.

When they got home, Colter carried Kinyan upstairs and laid her on the four-poster. He asked Dorothea for some cool water from the creek and some warm soup from the kitchen. He asked Jeremy to fill the tub with bathwater. On Jeremy's fifth trip upstairs, Lizbeth came with him.

"Can I help?" Lizbeth asked.

"No," Colter answered too quickly. When Lizbeth waited for an explanation, he added, "You're too small, Lizbeth. Go back downstairs and help your grandmother."

Lizbeth stuck her hand into the stream of water as Jeremy emptied the pail, giggling delightedly when it splashed out onto her pinafore.

Colter's face turned ashen. He saw Hope, playing while he poured water for Sarah's bath.

"Hellfire!" he roared.

Startled, Lizbeth leaped backward into Jeremy, who dropped the bucket, splashing the rest of the water over the floor.

Colter turned accusing eyes on Lizbeth.

"Now look what you've done! Get out!"

Jeremy's brow had narrowed in confusion and something else that Colter finally recognized as disappointment.

Jeremy put a reassuring arm around a tearful Lizbeth's shoulder and said, "I'll take her downstairs. That ought to be plenty of water for Ma's bath."

Colter turned and found Kinyan's face equally confused . . . and disappointed. When Kinyan opened her mouth to speak, Colter snapped, "I'll get something to clean up that mess." He was thankful when Kinyan didn't press the issue, and he kept himself busy mopping up the water on the floor while a stern-faced Dorothea delivered the soup, followed by Jeremy, alone, with the bowl of cold water he'd asked for. After they had deposited their burdens and left, Colter closed the door and bolted it.

Neither of them spoke while Colter soaked the blisters on Kinyan's gun hand in the cool water Dorothea had brought. He damned his obstinacy when he saw Kinyan flinch and then bravely bite her lower lip to keep from crying out. He felt so low he couldn't see over the piss-ant's ankles, but then, what could you expect from a heel?

All day long Kinyan had done exactly as Colter requested. Not once had she said him nay, until, when he'd finished soaking her gun hand, he put his fingertips to the buttons of her gingham blouse, with the evident intention of removing it.

"No."

"Let me help you," he said, removing her hand gently from its position guarding the top button from his touch. "I haven't forgotten our agreement. I know you're tired. This will be the fastest way to get you bathed and in bed to rest."

Kinyan lifted her eyes to Colter's and saw the unspoken plea for forgiveness there. He'd pushed her hard, harder than she'd thought possible for her to endure. And to be honest, she wasn't sure she could lift her arm to unbutton her blouse. The sexual battle they'd fought all day had been wearing for her as well. The trust she placed in him to abide by their agreement was in her azure eyes when she let her hand drop hesitantly to her lap.

Colter stripped her, handling her body as impersonally as though she were a small child. He dropped her clothes in a pile on the braided rug and slung the gunbelt on the bedpost at the head of her side of the bed.

Kinyan could feel the hot blush that covered the entire upper half of her body when she stood naked to Colter's gaze. Her breathing quickened as her large areolas, the rich, warm brown of clover honey, puckered, and her nipples formed small, hard nubs. She prayed that Colter was stronger than she.

Colter recognized Kinyan's arousal but fought to ignore it as he bent and lifted her easily into his arms. Her wide, anxious eyes speared him as he held her close, and he knew she waited for him to prove himself a liar. He feared she would feel his thundering heartbeat as he carried her the few steps to the tub. He released his hold under her knees, and when her feet were steady in the cool water, he stepped back quickly from her, then waited, paralyzed with indecision.

He'd thought he could do this for her. He'd thought he could just touch her and not feel anything. His raging body told him he was wrong. And then she sat down slowly, until all he could see was her lambent eyes and the honeyed flesh of her neck and shoulders. The promise of all the rest remained only as a reflection in the rippling water. And then she smiled. A small, trusting smile. He dropped to one knee beside the tub and took up a washcloth and soap.

Kinyan shivered at his first gentle touch.

"Are you cold?"

"Hardly." She laughed in a low, husky voice.

"Neither am I," he agreed with a chuckle.

With those few words the tension was broken, and he began to repair the damage he had wreaked.

Colter's fingertips worked the tension from Kinyan's neck and shoulders. He laved her gun arm with soap and gently massaged the sore muscles under her right armpit. She thought she must have imagined the imperceptible hesitation as his fingers slid along the ribs under her right breast, because the touch of his hands during the rest of the bath, though gentle, was brisk.

When he'd finished bathing Kinyan, Colter tenderly dried her. He dressed her in a simple pink nightgown, then pulled down the spread and laid her on the cool, crisp white sheets. She sighed. He sighed too. He fed her Dorothea's soup a spoonful at a time, and this time, exhausted beyond caring, she unresistingly accepted his service. When she was done eating, Kinyan laid her head back on the pillow and almost instantly fell asleep.

Colter used the bathwater himself, trying to wash that uncomfortable feeling away. She should have quit sooner, he thought. But she hadn't. She should have melted in the heat or broken under the strain. But she hadn't. He gazed at his wife, sleeping angelically. How could such a seemingly frail creature endure so much? He would teach her what she wanted to learn, but he wouldn't push her again because, he admitted, he couldn't bear to see that wonderfully defiant spirit broken.

He slept then, in the same bed with his wife. Even though Colter was very careful not to touch her, he found Kinyan clinging to him again, like ivy on a scarred crag, when he awoke in the morning. He freed himself and dressed, except for his boots. Then he lay back down beside his wife, waiting for her to wake, anxious to spend the day with her, wanting her by his side.

When she awoke, Kinyan stirred and stretched, and Colter's guilt resurged when he saw the winces of pain as her sore muscles fought the day. She slipped on pantalets and a chemise under her nightgown, unwilling to test Colter's willpower, or her own, now that fatigue no longer plagued either of them. Then she let the gown slip to the floor. She added a petticoat and it became apparent she intended to wear a dress. She picked a prim dark green calico that buttoned up the front all the way to her throat, with three-quarter-length sleeves trimmed in lace.

"A dress?"

"It's Wednesday. I assume you want me to wear a dress today, since we have to attend the Association meeting in Cheyenne. But if you don't . . ." When Colter didn't answer right away, Kinyan began to unbutton the dress again.

Of course he didn't want Kinyan parading around Cheyenne in men's pants. What kind of husband did she think he was? He didn't really want an answer to that.

"What you have on is fine," he agreed.

Kinyan buttoned the dress up again, then walked over to the bedstead, picked up the heavy Colt in its holster, and nonchalantly buckled it around the fitted waist of the dress.

She looked ridiculous.

At that moment Colter didn't know whether to kiss Kinyan or throttle her. He saw the mischievous glint in her eyes and knew she was daring him to say anything. After all, he'd *ordered* her to wear the gun every day from now on until he told her to take it off.

Kinyan continued with her toilette. She brushed her long black tresses, then separated the hair in thirds and braided it into a single plait.

Colter noticed how a few tendrils broke free and softened the edges of her heart-shaped face. He would be a laughingstock if his tiny wife showed up at the Association meeting wearing a .44 Colt. And she knew it. Hellfire and damnation! She had him over a barrel, and he'd helped her to put him there!

A bubble of laughter rose in Colter's chest at the way his wife had subtly bested him. With a bursting guffaw, he grinned and admitted, "You win! Take it off!"

Kinyan giggled delightedly. She unbuckled the belt and wrapped it back around the bedpost. She turned to Colter and gave him a smile of triumph.

Colter's heart did flipflops at the enchanting, childlike innocence of her joy at having forced his capitulation, and he felt a warm glow of happiness at having so easily pleased his wife.

"Let's go, wife," he commanded. "We have business in Cheyenne today."

Kinyan nodded meekly and followed her husband out the door.

CHAPTER 12

"I'D LIKE TO SEND a telegram."

"Yessir," the youthful telegrapher said, so intent on transcribing an incoming message that he handed Colter a piece of paper and a pencil without looking up. "Just write your message down how you want it sent."

Colter took pencil in hand and wrote:

Have grassland. Ship cattle and winter feed to Cheyenne next available train. Send word to Triple Fork when you arrive.

Colter

"Send that to Boley Snow at the Broadwell House in Denver."

Colter turned to Kinyan, who waited patiently by the door of the Cheyenne telegraph office.

"Pardon me, sir," the telegrapher called out to stop the scarred man dressed entirely in black. "This says send word to the Triple Fork."

"Yes?"

"That's the Holloway ranch."

Then the telegrapher saw Kinyan standing behind Colter.

"Oh good afternoon, Mrs. Holloway. I didn't see you. I didn't know you had a guest at the ranch."

"Andy, I'd like you to meet my husband, Benjamin Colter. This is Andy MacDougall. His father runs the Bar 7, which borders the Triple Fork on the south. Will your mother be at the Association meeting this afternoon?"

The redheaded youth's hazel eyes had widened in his astonished, ginger-freckled face.

"Yes, she will . . . but, holy smokes! Last meeting Ritter Gordon said you and he were . . . holy smokes! . . . engaged!"

"I'm pleased to meet you," Colter said, to rescue the floundering youth. He extended his hand to Andy with a smile. "I'm looking forward to having you as a neighbor."

Andy jumped up to shake hands. "Yes, sir. Well, I better get this telegraph off so I'm not late to the meeting." Andy plopped down and set the key to clacking.

Walking arm in arm, Colter and Kinyan headed for Hoot Beaumont's house at the very end of Main Street, where the Association was holding its meeting.

Kinyan smiled inwardly, remembering Andy's reaction to her announcement. There were going to be a lot more surprised faces before the afternoon was over. She only hoped the rest of the responses she received to the news of her marriage to Benjamin Colter were as innocuous as Andy's "holy smokes." Actually, there was only one person she was really worried about.

"Ritter's liable to be spitting mad when he finds out we're married. Are you sure I'm not going to need my Colt this afternoon?" Kinyan said, only half teasing.

Colter's lips quirked, but he bit down on the smile that threatened. It was liable to make her impossible to live with if he acknowledged again how well she'd cornered him on that point this morning.

"Don't worry," he replied. "I'll take care of Ritter."

After her initial gibe, Kinyan didn't speak again during the walk, allowing Colter's gentle massage of her blistered palm to speak for him. They arrived just a few minutes before the meeting was scheduled to begin. Colter ushered Kinyan inside the elegant foyer of the Beaumont house, with its polished oak floors overlaid with muted Aubusson rugs. A collection of Matthew Brady photographs of the Civil War hung in the hallway, and Colter experienced a surge of renewed sorrow at the wounded his inadequate surgery had been unable to save when he glimpsed one particularly poignant scene of youthful bodies sprawled in death.

Ritter Gordon stood at the end of the hall greeting members as they arrived, but not shaking hands, since his bandaged right hand rested dramatically in a sling. Kinyan was caught in the growing crowd at the doorway, and she and Colter became separated.

"Welcome, Mrs. Holloway. What a surprise to see you here."

Ritter fought not to smile too broadly. Using the renegade Indians to take care of Dardus had been an inspiration. He'd been pleased to learn they'd acted so quickly, but not so pleased to discover that Kinyan had almost become a victim as well.

"What brings you here this afternoon?" he whispered intimately in Kinyan's ear. "Have you decided to accept my proposal?"

"No. I—"

"She's with me."

Ritter stiffened when he recognized the slow drawl of his nemesis. His eyes flew to Colter's face.

"And what could you possibly have to do with my fiancée?" Ritter asked venomously.

"Your fiancée just happens to be my wife!"

"Colter and I were married on Sunday," Kinyan confirmed.

Ritter's face turned white with shock, then red with humiliation, then purple with fury.

"I'm certain when the members of the Association hear Colter has become my husband, they'll want to make him welcome," Kinyan said, her chin tipped up proudly, unintimidated by the rainbow of emotions on Ritter's face. "Please come with me, dear. There's Warren and Bessie MacDougall. I'd like you to meet them."

A stunned Colter found himself sailing past an enraged Ritter before either man could protest.

"You don't have to fight my battles for me," Colter hissed in Kinyan's ear as she introduced him to the third couple in as many minutes.

"I wouldn't think of it. After all, you're the one wearing

the Colt, not me," Kinyan quipped with an engaging smile that mellowed his temper until it turned out to be for the next couple they approached.

The Reverend Hiram Goforth had noticed Colter and Kinyan when they arrived and, grinning broadly, found himself a comfortable place near the refreshment table and sat back to watch the show.

Through the round of introductions to the members of the Association and their wives, the men remained openly leery, having heard of Colter's previous brouhaha with Ritter. They were cautious about befriending someone who had so hellaciously offended Ritter with this sudden marriage. Yet when Ritter remained charming despite Colter's presence, they began to relax and enjoy Colter, who was not without charm himself. The women openly admired the tall, somewhat forbidding man who had snatched Kinyan Holloway right from Ritter Gordon's grasp.

After a brief social period, the men planned to retire to Hoot Beaumont's study while the women would follow Wilhelmina Beaumont to the parlor. However, Colter protested his separation from Kinyan.

"I would feel more comfortable if my wife could join me," he said.

Kinyan recognized the opportunity Colter was offering her to see how the Association functioned, which would be important to her if she ever hoped to run the Triple Fork on her own, and she was grateful.

Before Ritter could veto Colter's suggestion, Wilhelmina piped up, "That sounds like a wonderful idea. I've often wondered what these gentlemen talk about when we're not around to listen." She took herself to a wingback chair near Hoot and sat down with her embroidery in her lap.

In close order, Bessie MacDougall found a chair near Warren and Andy, and Mandy Smithson sat down next to Willis on the peach-colored settee. When all the ladies were done crowding in, there were twenty-four people in the room. The close quarters and the presence of the women gave the meeting an air of holiday good humor that had Ritter Gordon grinding his teeth.

The first topic of conversation was Benjamin Colter's

application for membership to the Association. Ritter looked smugly to Willis Smithson for the agreed-upon motion to deny Colter membership in the organization. However, before Willis could speak, Mandy Smithson, who had intercepted Ritter's look, whispered loudly in Willis's ear. When she was done, Willis looked at Ritter and shrugged helplessly. Mandy, it appeared, approved of Colter's admission to the Association. It was all too clear who wore the pants in Willis's family.

Already resigned to losing the Triple Fork government lands to Ritter, the members of the association now found a certain perverse pleasure in seeing Colter steal the Triple Fork from under Ritter's nose. Ritter nearly choked when Warren MacDougall, with the smiling support of his wife, Bessie, introduced Colter and moved, in light of his marriage to Kinyan Holloway and the payment of his membership fee to Ritter, for unanimous approval of Colter's membership in the Association.

In the face of the murmurs of approval, Ritter panicked.

"Wait just a moment," he objected before a vote could be taken. "I'd like to know a little more about the man we're welcoming to our hearths and homes."

Not a rancher there wasn't aware that Ritter had a private ax to grind. Neither, however, was there anyone present willing to risk the abrasion it would take to stop the spin of the grindstone.

It was Colter who finally broke the tense silence.

"I'm from Texas," he began. "My family had a ranch there. I left it to fight for the South. When I came back, it was in pretty bad shape. A few years later, I gave up ranching and I've been drifting since then, planning and saving to settle down. I got tired of barbed wire and decided to come somewhere they haven't started fencing yet, which is what brought me to Wyoming. I'm having about two thousand head of longhorns shipped up from Denver, and I plan to implement a few ideas I've been mulling over on how to improve on open-range ranching."

"Fought for the South, did you?" Hoot Beaumont noted approvingly.

Colter nodded.

"I served under Lee myself," Hoot reminisced as he

puffed on a thick cigar. "Ritter rode for the Cause, and Warren too," he added. "New ideas, you say?"

"I'm planning to feed my cattle hay through the winter rather than let them forage for themselves."

"You aimin' to become a farmer?" Ritter sneered.

"Most cowboys won't set foot behind a plow," Hoot warned. "Who're you going to get to grow your feed?"

"I don't have to worry about that until next spring. I'm buying hay this first winter," Colter admitted.

"Most of us can't afford to do that," Warren confessed.

"Open-range ranching has been used for a long time around here quite successfully. What makes you think we need something new?" Ritter challenged.

"I heard most of you lost half your stock in the winter of seventy-three."

There were a few nervous coughs before Willis Smithson said, "That wasn't a typical winter. 'Sides, who could've gotten feed out in that kinda weather anyway?"

"It's being done," Colter confirmed. "I intend to do it."

"Well, we'll all be watching to see if it works," Hoot said, chewing idly on his cigar. "If nothing else, we can all learn from your mistakes."

"I've been thinking about growing feed myself," Warren admitted as an aside to Colter, who was sitting next to him. "And John had already started doing it. Just didn't want these fellows laughing through their teeth at me. You've got one ally, Colter, if you want one."

"I'll be glad to have company. Since our ranches border one another, perhaps we can work together."

"Aren't you being a little premature?" Ritter asked when he overheard Warren's comment. "Colter isn't a member of the Association yet."

"That can be easily remedied," Warren said breezily. "I call for the vote."

"I want another question answered first. I want to know how this drifter plans to pay assessments when they come due. Is he going to sell off Mrs. Holloway's cattle? Or will he just do some bank robbing on the side?"

Ritter let the members' thoughts dwell on the possibility that Colter was unscrupulous or an outlaw or both while he patted his wounded arm. It was something to consider. After all, Ritter was known to be a pretty fast gun, and Colter had been even faster.

Kinyan blanched, remembering how Colter had shot Cletus and Dobie. Then she let good sense take over. No common outlaw would have been so considerate of her or her children. Would he?

Ritter noticed the tightening of the cowboy's jaw muscle. He probably *was* wanted by the law, Ritter realized. Well, that was going to solve a lot of problems for him. Now that Colter had married Kinyan, he would have to die. It would serve his purposes very well if Colter could be shot legally. He'd contact Bart Jefferson to see what he could dig up on Benjamin Colter. Bounty hunters always knew who had a price on his head.

"I sold my ranch in Texas and invested the proceeds," Colter answered calmly. "I'd planned to deposit the balance of my earnings with the Association. I understand you've got a treasury."

"I'm the treasurer," Willis volunteered. "How much did you want to deposit?"

Colter handed a bank draft to Willis.

"This is for twenty thousand dollars!"

"Must have been some ranch," Hoot muttered. "Maybe you might have something with that feeding business."

Kinyan gasped. Would the surprises this man held in store for her never cease?

"There can't be any question now that Colter's a good candidate for membership," Warren said to Ritter.

It was amazing, Colter thought dryly, how much respect twenty thousand dollars could buy.

Ritter could see the futility of attempting to blackball Colter's membership. Besides, there were more effective, more permanent ways to get rid of Colter, and then he'd ensure that the Association made good use of Colter's twenty thousand dollars. He determined to send a telegram to Bart this afternoon.

"All right," Ritter conceded, his temper well in check, his charm carefully in place. "All those in favor of electing Benjamin Colter to membership in the Laramie County Stock Association signify by saying aye."

A chorus of eleven ayes resounded.

"All opposed?"

The deafening silence was broken by the congratulatory comments of Warren, Hoot, Willis, and the host of ranchers present. All except Ritter.

Warren slapped Colter companionably on the back. "You said you have more cattle coming?"

"I brought up some good breeding cows, some two- and three-year-old steers, and a longhorn bull I'm particularly pleased with," Colter revealed. "They should be here in the next week or so."

So Colter was proud of his longhorn bull, Ritter mused. That bull was one animal that wasn't going to make it all the way to Triple Fork grass. He could at least see to that, he thought pleasantly. Ritter's golden eyes came to rest on Kinyan. She felt his animosity and turned to face him.

Kinyan shivered at the virulent hatred in the unblinking, snakelike eyes. She had known Ritter would be angry about her marriage to Colter, but his menacing stare frightened her. She would have asked to leave if Colter hadn't been so animatedly involved in his discussion with the other ranchers.

Colter was caught up evaluating the relative merits of breeding bulls and then arguing the relative merits of fencing with barbed wire. He had a captive audience for the latter, since the idea of using twisted wire to contain cattle had become popular only a year or so earlier. Colter told the northern ranchers how the fencing of land in the South was beginning to interfere with the larger cattle drives. Although, he admitted to the assembled group, when you went out to search for fenced cattle you knew where to find them.

That, the other ranchers agreed with rueful chuckles, would be a pleasant advantage indeed. Unfenced cattle tended to drift with the wind and the weather, and the search for cattle often led many a rancher a merry chase.

With the introduction of the search for cattle, discussions of the upcoming roundup followed naturally.

"We'll begin next Monday," Warren explained to Colter. "We're meeting at Ritter's ranch house on the Lazy 6 to start. I'm foreman for the roundup, and we all work together. We sort cattle as we brand them, and an Association rep keeps tally. Any mavericks belong to the Association.

160

The cattle are shipped to market or sent back out on the range as each owner decides."

"We'll be there," Colter said.

"We?" Hoot questioned.

"My wife and I," Colter confirmed. At the quizzical looks on the faces of the ranchers and the furrowed brows of their wives, Colter explained patiently, "I enjoy having my wife at my side, and she's been kind enough to indulge me."

"A roundup is no place for a woman," Ritter argued.

"Nevertheless," Colter replied adamantly, "Kinyan will join me."

The web of tension settled once again on the room as though it had never been lifted. Various individuals shrugged their shoulders against it. Others fought it with a jab or punch of their neighbors. Some stretched necks and yawned it away. Kinyan finally lanced through it as she rose with purpose.

"We have a long ride ahead of us. Shall we go?"

Kinyan marveled at the way Colter had inveigled her attendance at the roundup. She wouldn't have minded shocking the ranchers and their wives with the knowledge that it was her idea that she go along, but Colter's argument had caused so many fewer problems she was content to let sleeping dogs lie.

Several other wives had also voiced requests to be escorted home. Warren moved to end the meeting, and since half the ladies had already left their seats, Ritter was left with little choice but to act on his motion. Before Kinyan could drag him away, however, Colter sought out Ritter.

"I'd like to speak to you in private."

"Hoot has a poker room off the study where we can be alone. Come with me," Ritter directed.

"Wait for me here," Colter said to Kinyan before he followed Ritter.

Concerned by the grim looks on their faces, Kinyan started to follow them despite Colter's admonition, but was prevented when Bessie MacDougall grabbed her by the arm to ask, "Where on earth did you find that thoroughly charming young man?"

The small, windowless poker room to which Ritter led Colter was poorly lit by a single brass sconce next to the door. It contained a circular oak table surrounded by five chairs. Ritter pulled out one of the heavy red velvet upholstered armchairs and seated himself like a king ready to hold court. His face was lit on one side by the sconce, but his lower chest remained in darkness. Colter moved to the opposite side of the table, disappearing into the shadows, his tone icy as he challenged Ritter's crown.

"Those three outlaws you hired are gone from Triple Fork land."

Shaken by Colter's announcement, Ritter responded with remarkable aplomb, "I don't know what you're talking about."

"The so-called squatters you put there. Who were they supposed to take care of? Dardus? A few of the hands? Or were they supposed to eliminate Kinyan and her sons?"

"You're barking up the wrong tree," Ritter said amiably. "What possible purpose could it serve for me to cause problems on the Triple Fork when I expected to marry Kinyan Holloway within the week?"

"Well, if you're not responsible for sending those squatters, it would be a waste of breath to warn you not to send anyone else onto Triple Fork property," Colter said with a steely voice. He turned abruptly and left the room.

Ritter hastily rose from the chair in which he'd been enthroned but found himself without a response or anyone to make it to. Colter hadn't warned, hadn't threatened, yet the warning was there, and the threat also.

Ritter seethed with fury. He would put that impudent drifter in his place yet! Colter was a dead man, and Kinyan Holloway, well, that bitch would pay for this afternoon's humiliation for the rest of her life!

When Ritter emerged from Hoot's poker room, he caught Andy MacDougall by the scruff of the neck before the lad could make his way out the door with his mother.

"Hold on just a moment," he ordered the hapless youth.

"Yes, sir, Mr. Gordon." Andy gulped. "Did you want something?"

"I'd like this telegram sent today, Andy."

"Yes, sir," Andy said. He was relieved Ritter had asked something so simple. He raced out the door before he glanced at the paper, but when he sat down at the telegraph key his relief turned out to have been premature. Holy smokes! Andy thought. Holy smokes! The telegram was sent to Bart Jefferson, Menger Hotel, San Antonio, Texas. Andy clacked out:

> Check Texas "Wanted" posters for Benjamin Colter. Six feet, black hair, blue eyes, lean, slashing scar on left jaw and at throat. Wears left-handed Colt. Respond immediately.
>
> Ritter

CHAPTER 13

THEY BURIED DARDUS PENROD early Thursday morning in
the same copse of cottonwoods where John had been laid to
rest. Kinyan was clearly agitated throughout the short service conducted by Reverend Goforth, but it was not a tearful
sadness that plagued her. She had never been close to
Dardus, but he had been one of the few remaining links to
John. Kinyan looked from the new cross made of cottonwood to the weathered one that stood at the head of John's
grave. Another connection to the past had been snapped.
When Kinyan raised her eyes, it was Colter's rugged features that greeted her.

"Day's wasting," he said.

The cowboys who had gathered for the service shoved
their hats back down on their heads and walked up the hill
toward their horses and the day's labor.

Colter felt a tug on his shirt and looked down to find
Lizbeth at his side. His eyes locked with those of the little
girl.

"Colter . . . "

"What?"

"Is Dardus with my pa in heaven now?"

Always an echo of the past! Colter reached out a hand as
though to touch the child's silky black hair in comfort, but
his fingers clenched into a fist before they reached their goal,
and he drew back his hand as though he'd been scorched.

Dorothea saw the situation and intervened to avoid another confrontation between the two. She put her own

gnarled hand on Lizbeth's raven tresses, her voice a soothing balm as she said, " 'Course he is, child. Now, you come with me. We've got to get back to the house and make sure Prissy's kitties have plenty of milk for their breakfast."

As she left the gravesite with Lizbeth, Josh, and Jeremy, Dorothea felt a growing grain of hope. At least this time Colter hadn't yelled at the child. With time . . . with time . . . perhaps whatever demons followed Colter would leave the cowboy in peace.

Through it all, Kinyan remained unaware of those around her. Colter studied his wife's detachment for a moment before he reached for her elbow to escort her back to the house.

"Don't touch me!"

Josh stopped his ascent up the hill when he heard his mother's cry.

Colter ignored Kinyan's words, responding instead to the need he saw in her eyes, drawing her into his arms. Then he stood stonily, arms wrapped around Kinyan, while she pounded her fists against his chest, venting her renewed anger, frustration, and grief over John's death.

When a gun cocked behind Colter, he froze. He slowly angled his head to perceive the danger to which Kinyan was oblivious.

Josh held a .44 aimed at Colter's back.

"Let her go," the boy said.

"Never aim a gun at a man unless you intend to use it," Colter responded, his voice frigid with fury.

"Let her go," Josh repeated, his voice breaking.

"No."

A flicker of fear skidded across the youthful face and lodged in the sky-blue eyes.

Kinyan had quieted in Colter's embrace, then struggled more fiercely to free herself to avoid the confrontation Josh was forcing.

"Let me go, Colter," she pleaded, now frantic with fear. Colter's arms remained around her like iron bands.

"Put the gun away, Josh," Colter ordered, "and go to your room. I'll be there to talk with you in a minute."

Josh's eyes widened in astonishment. He held a deadly weapon on Colter and the man acted as though it were some ten-year-old's toy.

"I'll use this thing if you don't let my ma go," Josh threatened shakily.

"I told you once that what happens between your ma and me is our business. At the time you claimed to understand the situation. Has something changed since then?"

Josh shifted his stance, the gun suddenly heavy in his hand. He looked to his mother's eyes and knew that the anguish and fear he saw there had nothing to do with Colter. Josh dropped his gun hand to his side, gave Colter his special evil eye, and then whirled and ran up the hill.

As soon as Josh was gone, Colter released Kinyan.

"Why didn't you let me go when Josh asked?" Kinyan snapped. "He might have killed you!" As soon as she said the words, Kinyan wanted to take them back. They intimated too great a care for the man who was a stranger and not enough concern for her own son. To Kinyan's relief, Colter hadn't recognized the words for what they were.

"Josh was just testing," Colter replied. "He wouldn't have shot at me."

"How can you be so sure?"

"He would never have taken the chance of hitting you," Colter said simply.

Kinyan closed her eyes and leaned her head back, pressing her hands together to stay calm in the face of Colter's idiotic reasoning.

"I think this would be a good day to start your lessons in reading and writing," Colter suggested. He told himself Kinyan would have too much time to think about John if they spent the day on horseback. He told himself he was only curious to see if she would be as quick to pick up reading and writing as she had been to pick up handling a Colt. He told himself his suggestion had nothing to do with needing to be close enough to touch her, and that he was totally in control where wanting Kinyan was concerned.

Kinyan found herself being dragged up the hill as Colter barked instructions at her.

"I'll meet you in the dining room after I speak with Josh. Tell Jeremy to stay with Frank again today."

"Colter," Kinyan cried, struggling to keep up with him. "What are you going to do to Josh?"

Colter stopped abruptly, towering over Kinyan from his

position uphill of her. "Something that should have been done a long time ago."

"I can make Josh behave! You don't have to punish him!"

"This is the second time he's warned me to stay away from you, Kinyan. The next time he's liable to shoot first and ask questions later. I'm going to settle this matter once and for all."

Colter's matter-of-factness frightened Kinyan.

"How? By beating a defenseless child?"

"Defenseless, hell! He was ready to shoot me in the back!"

His temper frightened her worse.

"But he didn't," Kinyan replied emphatically. "And he never would."

"So you say. I intend to make sure of it myself."

Kinyan should have trusted Colter. He had never given her any reason to believe Josh's punishment wouldn't be appropriate to his misdeed. Yet after a week of surviving one calamity after another, of having the rules she'd bargained for bent, if not broken, she was nearly hysterical at the power this near stranger had over her son.

"Colter, I'm warning you. I won't have you or any other man harming my children!"

Before Colter stood a she-wolf defending her cubs, teeth bared, neck hairs stiff, blue eyes dark with passionate fury. Colter stood in awe of his wife.

"You're *warning* me?"

Colter was appalled that Kinyan could believe him capable of violence toward any child. He was furious that she should think of him in such villainous terms. Then he thought of how he'd treated Lizbeth all week. But he couldn't help that!

"Just what teeth are there in your warning? Just what, exactly, will you do to me if I punish the boy the way he deserves?"

As much as she wished she could deny it, Kinyan needed Colter. She had been willing to bargain for his help. But the price he intended to exact now from Josh was too high!

Colter immediately regretted flaunting Kinyan's vulnerability when he saw the look of horror that rose in her eyes. He shook his head in disbelief at what he'd said.

"I'm sorry, Kinyan." Colter sighed. "I'm sorry." He rumpled his hair in agitation. "I don't know how I'm going to make my point with Josh, but if there's a way to do it without whipping the boy, I will."

Kinyan's face was white. As Colter moved to embrace her, she backed away from him down the hill.

"I don't think I want to be reminded how much I need you," she said in a low, trembling voice. "I'll go give Jeremy your orders and meet you in the house." With that, she stumbled up the hill past Colter as fast as her legs would carry her.

Kinyan had been the answer to an unspoken prayer, Colter mused as he followed her to the house. She was a rare flower of great beauty, as vibrant as Indian paintbrush in the sunshine, as contrary as the soft flowers on a prickly pear cactus, her temper as unpredictable as the Texas bluebonnets in spring. He yearned to hold the tender blossom close, but the thorns always seemed to get in the way. Josh was only one of them. Yet, Colter vowed, he would deal with the thorns one at a time. And then he would claim his rose.

Colter knocked, then entered the room Josh shared with Jeremy.

Josh straddled a ladderback chair facing the window, his chin pressed deep in his crisscrossing arms on the top rung of the chair.

Colter stayed near the door, letting the space between them temper the charged emotions both felt.

"I would never have shot you in the back," Josh admitted.

"I know. I would never have hurt your mother."

"I know. I mean," Josh added hastily, "you haven't done anything yet to . . ." Josh stopped. "I don't know what I mean," he amended. "I suppose you're gonna whup me now." Josh's voice trembled, and he stood up and pivoted to face Colter defiantly. "I'm ready."

Colter admired Josh's courage in the face of the expected punishment. He was such a strong-willed, fearless boy! Now, Colter thought, if he could just learn to curb his impulsive temper. How, Colter wondered, was he going to help Josh accomplish that? Kinyan was right, he decided. It couldn't be done with a strap. Definitely not with a strap.

"There'll be no lashing," Colter announced.

"What?"

Josh's eyebrows shot up with hope that died when Colter continued, "I have something a little more physical in mind."

Josh gulped. More physical? What could be more physical than a strapping?

"I want you to dig the post holes for the new corral."

"Dig post holes?"

Josh groaned in agony. Colter had just condemned him to a fate much worse than a mere whipping. No cowboy worth his salt would be caught dead doing manual labor that couldn't be done from the back of a horse. He would be the brunt of jokes from every cowhand who saw him lift the spade.

"It's honest work," Colter said, "and it'll give you some good practice controlling your temper." That was no understatement, Colter thought, well aware of the gibes that would be aimed at Josh. "I'll expect you to get started in five minutes."

Colter was gone before Josh could repent his sins and seek deliverance from the hell to which his own private devil had condemned him.

Colter searched John's rolltop desk for pencils and paper, then brought his supplies into the dining room, where Kinyan was already seated at the table.

"We'll start with the alphabet," Colter announced as though the entire incident with Josh hadn't occurred.

"Where's Josh?" Kinyan demanded.

"He'll be down in a few minutes. He's composing himself, coming to grips with his punishment." Colter anticipated Kinyan's concern and quickly added, "He's really not too excited about digging post holes."

Kinyan's eyes showed her relief. "Colter, I . . . I'm sorry for . . . thanks for understanding," she said solemnly. "About teaching me to read and write, I don't think I need to learn . . . I mean—"

Before Kinyan could finish, she was interrupted by a knock at the front door. When she started to rise, Colter put a hand on her shoulder.

"I'll get it." Colter crossed to the front door and opened it.

"Here's a telegram, boss," Petey said, handing Colter the message.

Colter felt a thrill of pride and satisfaction all the way to his toes at the title the young cowhand had accorded him.

"Thanks, Petey," he said, grinning.

Colter stepped back into the dining room and dropped the telegram in Kinyan's lap. "Here," he said. "What does it say?"

"You know I can't read!"

"What if this were a message warning of a drop in stock prices? What if it were a request to purchase a thousand head of cattle? What if this were a notice that the government planned to confiscate all cattle found on its land after a certain date?"

"Josh or Jeremy could read it to me."

"What if they weren't here?" Colter countered. "You're a cripple in any confrontation with someone who can read, Kinyan. You need to develop every asset you have if you hope to hang on to the Triple Fork. Third rule, Kinyan: if you have to fight, be sure to make use of all the ammunition at your disposal."

Kinyan began to have a sense of why she'd spent all that time batting her butterfly wings and getting nowhere. It wasn't enough to want to do something. You had to have the proper tools for the job. She reached down to run her fingers over the scarred walnut butt of the Colt strapped to her waist. A gun was one tool, and aggravating as it was to admit it, a pen was another.

"All right," Kinyan said. "Teach me to read."

They worked for two hours solid on the alphabet, and Kinyan thought if she drew another squiggly line she was going to go cross-eyed. Yet it was satisfying to be able to make the letters that spelled her name.

During the lesson, Kinyan had a reminder of how potent a physical effect she had on Colter. She'd gotten a pretty good idea during the shooting lessons that Colter became aroused when he was near her, but he'd kept his distance as much as he could since then. But now, Kinyan could hear his irregular breathing and there was the musky scent of aroused male. It was a heady feeling to know Colter desired her. John had never been so easy to excite, nor were his needs held so tightly in restraint, and Kinyan couldn't resist the temptation to see just how much titillation it would take before Colter lost the battle with his self-control.

For the next hour, the pencil simply failed to produce legible letters on the paper. In fact Colter had to guide her hand with his own to form many of the marks. Kinyan found it infinitely amusing to turn so Colter's arm brushed her breast or to lean into his hip with her own. As the lesson progressed, Kinyan noticed Colter had begun to flinch every time their skin came in contact.

"No, no, an S goes the other way," Colter admonished patiently.

"I just can't seem to get the hang of it. Could you please guide my hand again?" Kinyan implored.

Colter gritted his teeth and held Kinyan's soft hand in his own callused one. His skin burned where his forearm lay along hers.

"Like this," he advised, tracing the letter for her.

Their faces were side by side and Kinyan angled her head to peer up at Colter.

"How soon will I be writing?" she asked with a mischievous grin.

"You won't ever learn how unless you concentrate."

"I am concentrating," Kinyan protested, pouting.

Colter found the pouting lip more than he could resist. His head swooped the short distance to Kinyan's mouth and his teeth captured her lower lip before he realized what he'd done. His tongue found its way between her teeth, and the kiss deepened. Colter's hand grasped the back of Kinyan's neck to hold her mouth to his own.

Kinyan's teasing for the past hour had kept Colter in a state of readiness bordering on pain. His fingers went to the buttons on Kinyan's blouse, and when he couldn't manage them quickly enough, he simply ripped apart the garment, and the chemise beneath it, to bare her breasts to his hands and mouth. Kinyan gasped at Colter's savagery. His glazed eyes focused long enough to catch the momentary fear in her eyes, which put a quick halt to his passion.

"Hellfire!"

Colter jerked himself away from the table and paced the length of the room, coming back to stand, feet apart, hands on hips before Kinyan.

"You did that on purpose!"

"Did what on purpose?" Kinyan asked with a wounded look of innocence. She pulled together her ripped bodice as

171

best she could, but a great deal of flesh was left exposed. "You promised," she chastised, her eyes twinkling now with merriment, "that you wouldn't touch for six weeks, and it's only been four days."

"Four miserable days," Colter muttered, raking his hands through his hair.

Kinyan watched the way Colter's slender fingers left his hair in disarray. He did that whenever he was irritated, she had noticed, and since over the past four days he had often been irritated, he had a perpetual rakish appearance. Kinyan had thought only of ruffling Colter's smooth, confident feathers. She did not, she told herself, really want his attentions. The teasing had merely been a way, she told herself, to show him there were some areas of their relationship he did not control. It was also, she admitted, catching a glimpse of the angry fire in Colter's eyes, a very dangerous game to play.

"You never told me what was in the telegram," Kinyan said, neatly changing the subject.

Colter sighed. There was no sense staying angry. It was going to be a long six weeks, and he might as well face it now and try to make the best of a bad situation.

"My cattle arrive in Cheyenne tomorrow from Denver. I'll go in to meet the train and take some hands along with me to drive the cattle back here."

"A trail drive? I can't wait! How long will it take us?"

"Us? You're not going," Colter said flatly. He wasn't about to give up the respite the trip would provide him from the persistent ache he endured in his wife's presence.

"You promised to teach me everything—"

"You need to know to run the ranch," Colter finished. "You could manage the Triple Fork your whole life and never need to make a trail drive. No dice, Kinyan," Colter said with finality.

"You promised—"

"I know what I promised as well as you do!" Colter thrust his fingers through his hair, then tucked his thumbs into his Levi's on either side of his belt buckle.

Kinyan met his response with equal fervor. "It sounds to me like your word isn't worth much, Mr. Colter."

Kinyan watched Colter's face flush until the white scar on his cheek stood out as a livid white line on his flesh. The blue eyes darkened, but otherwise his features remained immobile as stone. His thumbs had stayed in his jeans, but his hands had become fists around them.

"I'm no liar," he said so softly Kinyan had to strain to hear. "I agreed to teach you, and I plan to stand by my word. But as you'll recall, there were certain other terms to our agreement. You agreed to obey my orders." Colter paused as though daring her to disagree. When she remained quiet, he continued, "And these are my orders. You can come to Cheyenne and watch the unloading of the herd at the station. But you can't come on the trail drive."

"How is this trail drive different from the roundup?" Kinyan demanded.

"We'll be out overnight. It's no place for a lady. So once the cattle are unloaded, Petey will take you home. Do you understand?"

As far as Kinyan was concerned, Colter had just abridged their agreement and that relieved her of the responsibility to obey his order. She was entitled to participate in the trail drive as in all other things she might someday need to know in order to manage the ranch alone. Besides, what did he mean, "no place for a lady"? Did he think she'd never spent a night out under the stars? She'd probably spent more nights on the prairie as a Sioux child than he had in his whole life. Well, if Colter wanted to draw lines, she would be glad to oblige him!

Kinyan's mouth formed a brittle smile, and her next words came out in a tone so subservient it etched a frown on Colter's stone-hard face.

"All right, Colter. When the cattle are unloaded, I'll head home."

Kinyan hadn't lied. She would never stoop so low. She did plan to head home after the cattle were unloaded. She simply wasn't going to make it all the way there. She would have to come up with some reason to stop. And then she could send Petey away. And then she would be free to . . .

CHAPTER 14

"BE CAREFUL OF that bull!" Colter shouted.

"Hell, Colter, I'm the one liable to get squished, not the damn ornery bull!" Boley Snow hurled back at him.

Colter laughed heartily at Boley's predicament. Colter's huge black-and-red-brindle longhorn bull, Hercules, had the long-limbed cowboy trapped in a niche between the railroad car and one of the rails that enclosed the ramp down out of the car and seemed disinclined to move and free Boley.

Beauregard Lee Snow was only a bit younger than Colter's thirty-one years, with blond hair, topaz eyes, and a frank, open face. He was tall and lithe, with a hardness around his mouth that didn't fit the rest of his features. Colter didn't know much about the man except he was a good cowboy, quick to laugh, slow to anger, and he was accurate with a .44. Colter knew Boley could shoot because he'd seen him kill a man in San Antone. In doing so, he'd saved Colter's life. Colter had invited Boley to join him on the trip to the Wyoming Territory, and the young man had agreed that perhaps Texas wasn't going to be such a good place to be when the dead bounty hunter's brothers found out what he'd done.

When Kinyan herded several cows past the end of the ramp, Hercules took one whiff and crashed down the incline in a hurry, head up and bellowing. Hoss cut the bull off, heading him in the direction the cows had taken, which Hercules was perfectly willing to follow.

"He's magnificent!" Kinyan breathed, coming up behind Colter on Gringalet.

"That he is," Colter agreed proudly.

The rangy bull, his horns spreading a majestic seven feet from tip to tip, was the last of Colter's stock to be unloaded, and as Hercules shoved his way to the front of the stretched-out herd, the cowboys began to move the beeves away from Cheyenne toward the Triple Fork.

"Petey will make sure you get home, Kinyan. We ought to be able to cover the fifteen miles to the Triple Fork in two days, so you should expect us on Sunday."

"I don't want to go home."

"We've been through all this before. I'm not going to argue with you. It's just too dangerous."

If she hadn't already made up her mind to follow Colter surreptitiously, Colter's last statement would have goaded her into it. Saying no to Kinyan was like waving a red flag in front of a bull. You could expect the response to be both spontaneous and dangerous.

"All right," Kinyan said with a cheerful smile. "This time I give up. I'll find Petey."

Colter was too busy admiring Hercules to catch the flash of defiance in Kinyan's eyes. If he'd known his wife better, he would not have trusted her easy yielding.

"You ready to go now, Miz Holloway . . . uh, Miz Colter?" Petey asked, blushing fiery red at his mistake. Although the young cowboy had been honored to be asked to escort the boss's wife home, he looked longingly at the herd trailed out before him. Petey had never been on a trail drive before and it seemed a shame he was going to miss most of this one. It was not much comfort to know that as soon as his charge was safely home he could come back to help. By then, Petey thought, half the grand adventure would be over.

"Let's go, Petey. I'm ready," Kinyan said. She resented Colter setting a guard over her to make sure she went home, but she'd been outwitting minds a lot sharper than Petey Watkins' for a lot of years. The pink-cheeked cowboy didn't stand a chance.

They had only been riding an hour past the herd when Kinyan stopped to wipe her brow with her bandanna. "Petey, this is ridiculous. I can get myself home fine."

"But the boss said—"

"Yes, I know my husband wants to protect me, Petey, but it just isn't necessary, and I know he needs your help."

Petey's chest puffed out a notch. "Well . . . "

"Then it's settled," Kinyan replied with a brilliant smile that had Petey blushing again. "I'll go home alone, and you can join the trail drive."

"Yes, ma'am," Petey agreed. As he rode away, Petey made a mental note to keep out of Colter's sight for a while, just so no questions arose about how he'd got all the way to the ranch house and back so fast.

Kinyan's brows rose in contemplation. She let her hat slide down her back to hang by its string tie and quickly rolled her single-braided plait of hair up so it would fit neatly under the hat. Then she put the hat back up on her head and tugged it down hard. She stepped down off Gringalet and pulled the chaps and leather vest from their hiding place in her saddlebag. She even had a darker shirt to put on over the one she was wearing. Now attired like an ordinary cowhand, she pulled her bandanna up and tied it around her nose. Since it would keep the dust out of her nose and mouth as well as hide her face, the disguise was both efficient and practical. Colter and Frank were riding point for the long procession of men and cattle, so she decided she would be safest from detection riding drag, at the opposite end of the herd.

The lowliest cowboys were assigned the task of riding drag, where the dust was thickest and where stragglers had to be constantly harried to keep up. It was a dirty, thankless job, but she wasn't about to complain, counting herself lucky to be able to be a part of the trail drive at all.

Josh and Jeremy had fared far better than Kinyan. She would have much preferred their job as wranglers for the remuda, but it pleased her that not only had Colter allowed the boys to come along, but he had also conceived a way to keep them out of danger. Herding the cowboys' extra horses would keep them out of the way of the cattle. Not that the herd was particularly dangerous, but there was always the chance of stampede. She should also be perfectly safe riding drag. After all, if the herd stampeded, it would be running away from her, wouldn't it?

In the billowing dust, Kinyan had lost sight of Petey, who

was also riding drag, and could only barely make out the shape of two of the four hands a little farther ahead riding flank, let alone Boley Snow and the other three hands riding swing near the front of the herd. There was just too much dust in the air. All too soon, Kinyan began to regret her impetuous behavior. Teeth gritty from dust, choking on dust, blinking dust from her eyelashes over red-rimmed, teary eyes, dust settled on her clothes, in her boots, in her hair, in every pore of her body, Kinyan's world had diminished so she was oblivious to the twelve cowboys who surrounded the cattle to keep them moving. Her world consisted only of herself, the horse beneath her, the stubborn, bawling, unhappy cattle, and dust, dust, dust.

Kinyan had heard Colter warn the hands that the first morning would be the hardest, since the cattle weren't used to traveling together and would all try to go their own way. Petey's horse did most of the work for him, setting its nose to a steer's face and anticipating the steer's movements until the dumb animal gave up and rambled back in line. Kinyan was not fortunate enough to have a trained cutting horse. Gringalet was untiring in his willingness to go after a steer, but it was Kinyan who needed to guess which way the steer was moving and rein her horse to cut the animal off. After several hours of that kind of effort in the heat and dust, both horse and rider were exhausted.

Kinyan blessed Colter's call for a noon stop. At the same time, she wondered how she was going to manage to get another horse without being detected. She hadn't realized how the work would exhaust Gringalet. Then it occurred to her that her goal could be easily accomplished by including one of her sons in her masquerade.

Kinyan rode confidently to the string of horses waiting near the chuck wagon and dismounted.

"I'd like another horse," she said.

Jeremy gave the unidentified cowboy a querulous look. "Sure. Soon's you tell me which one of these mangy critters is yours."

Kinyan pulled the dusty bandanna down to reveal her nose and mouth, then quickly pulled it back up again.

"Is that you, Ma?"

"Shh! Yes, Jeremy, it's me. Can you saddle a horse for me? Gringalet's worn out."

"Colter's gonna skin you alive, Ma, if he finds out you're here!"

"Well, he won't find out if you'll hurry up with that horse," Kinyan snapped.

"You had anything to eat, Ma?"

"I brought some food along with me," Kinyan said. "Don't worry. I'll be fine."

"Where you gonna sleep tonight, Ma?"

"I'll be nearby."

"You sure, Ma?"

"I'm sure! Please, Jeremy. Don't ask any more questions. Just do as I ask."

Kinyan set a boot in the stirrup, grabbed the horn, and pulled herself up onto the large buckskin Jeremy had saddled for her. "Don't breathe a word about this to Colter."

"Don't worry, Ma," Jeremy said with a quick grin. "I ain't gonna let myself in for that kinda trouble."

Kinyan put her palm to Jeremy's cheek, then pulled down her bandanna and leaned over to kiss him before quickly replacing the mask.

"Aw, Ma!"

Jeremy blushed and glanced around to see if anybody had been watching to see that he'd been kissed by what, to all appearances, was another cowboy.

"I'll see you again when Colter calls the night stop," she said. "Take care of yourself until then."

"Hey, cowboy," Colter called out.

Kinyan ignored the voice, pretending she hadn't heard it.

"You, on the buckskin," Colter called again.

That could not be ignored. Kinyan lowered her voice and said as gruffly as possible, "Yeah? What?"

"What's your name?"

Kinyan lowered her voice another octave and coughed. "Ken," she said.

"Ken, I need some help with a cow that's stuck in a mudhole. You can always count on the female of the species to get herself into trouble," he said with a companionable chuckle.

Kinyan choked out a "Yes, sir," before Colter added, "Well, let's go rescue our damsel in distress."

Kinyan grimaced her disgust to Jeremy behind Colter's back before she spurred the buckskin to follow him.

178

The cow was stuck in the mud all the way to its shoulders, and bawling to beat the band. The harder the animal struggled, the deeper it sank.

"You can dig out around her," Colter ordered, "and then pull her out by the horns."

Kinyan stared at Colter from above her bandanna with incredulous eyes. Wasn't he going to help?

"Here's a spade I picked up from Cookie's wagon." Colter handed Kinyan the spade and rode away.

Apparently not.

Kinyan's eyes narrowed in speculation. Colter must have discovered her disguise, she thought. It was just too coincidental that she'd been chosen for this horrible, disgustingly dirty job. She checked her costume. No, she thought. The outfit was perfect. It must just be her own bad luck to be in the wrong place at the wrong time.

Kinyan ground-tied the buckskin and walked to the edge of the mudhole. The cow turned to her with big cow eyes, opened her big cow mouth, and stuck out her big cow tongue, mooing for all she was worth.

"All right, all right," Kinyan grumbled. "I'm coming."

She slogged carefully into the mudhole until she stood at the front end of the cow, the mud sucking at her legs all the way to her hip. Then she began to dig. The muscles in her wounded arm shrieked at her for a while but then settled into a low throbbing. It was backbreaking work. The mud was heavy and there was a lot of it. Even with gloves on, in fifteen minutes the blisters on Kinyan's hands had both formed and burst. Yet she kept on digging. She wouldn't let Colter discern her disguise by failing this job he had given her.

When she had cleared the mud down to the cow's belly, Kinyan decided to give the rope a try. As she slogged her way out of the bog hole, she lost her footing and fell backward into the mud. A string of unladylike expletives rumbled out in succession. She was breathing so hard through the bandanna that it sucked into her mouth and huffed back out again like a sail in a shifting wind.

Muddy though she was, Kinyan climbed back into the saddle, made a comfortable loop in her lariat, and swung it in a neat circle over her head, releasing at just the right moment so it settled over the cow's horns. Colter should be here, she thought smugly, to see one of the few cowboy skills she had. Before the loop could slip farther down, she dallied it around the horn of her saddle and backed the buckskin up until it was tight.

Inch by mucky inch, the cow began to come free. When at last the animal stood on dry ground, Kinyan learned a quick lesson on cow thankfulness. The ungrateful animal, which had pleaded so woefully to be free, now put down her head and charged Kinyan.

"Hellfire!" she yelled, unconsciously using Colter's favorite expression. She spurred the buckskin away at the same time she flicked the noose free from the cow's horns. Then she used the tail end of the lariat to whip the cow into line and head it back to the herd.

Kinyan was filthy. What wasn't dusty was muddy. What wasn't gritty was soggy. And she was having, she decided, the absolute most fun she'd ever had! With a superior grin to celebrate her success in freeing the cow, she trotted the buckskin back to take her place riding drag. The mud and dust could be washed off later, for she knew Colter planned the evening stop close enough to the Triple Fork that she could slip home for a bath.

It was at dusk, when the cowboys were most weary and the cattle leery of the mythical dragons created by their own shadows, that the trouble began.

At first Kinyan was only aware that the cattle seemed to be milling and shifting more than normal, bellowing anxiously. She headed off at right angles from the herd to chase a lone steer so she was away from the main body of the herd when, without warning, without apparent rhyme or reason, they took off at a run.

"Heeeerrrrddd's brooooooke!" came the mournful wail, carried on the wind. "Heeeerrrrddd's brooooooke!"

Because of the stampeding cattle, Kinyan never heard the rattlesnake that struck her horse. Suddenly the animal was lunging upward out of control, and just as suddenly she was flat on her back on the grassy ground.

Kinyan was never so relieved as when she realized that although she was on foot, the cattle were stampeding in the opposite direction. She was safe!

Then Kinyan heard the familiar frightening rattle begin.

* * *

Colter rode hard to catch up to his brindle bull at the head of the mindless mass of animals that had taken off like scared rabbits with a very hungry fox in pursuit. The best way to stop a stampeding herd was for some cowboy to get in front of it and turn it back on itself. It was a dangerous job, especially at dusk, because for a few moments the cowboy would put himself in the path of the thundering herd. If his horse should stumble in the dark, both of them would disappear beneath the churning mass.

Colter saw Frank riding hard on the far side of the herd. Neither cowboy allowed himself to think of the danger. There was simply a job to be done, and they were the best ones to do it. As Colter reached the front of the herd, he realized Hercules was nowhere to be seen. Where had his prize bull disappeared to? There was no time to worry about a single animal now. Colter and Frank turned first one steer and then another until the herd began to circle back on itself. Then, to Colter's consternation and dismay, a shocking torrent of gunfire started the milling cattle running hard in the opposite direction.

"I'll horsewhip the bastard who fired those shots!" Colter's threat was lost beneath the thundering hooves of the herd. He hoped the cowboys riding swing and flank would have the sense to turn the herd again at the other end.

Colter saw Jeremy riding hell-bent toward him and swore again. He'd told the boys to stay out of the way if the herd broke!

"Colter!" Jeremy yelled. "Help!"

Colter kicked Hoss into a flat-out gallop toward Jeremy, pulling him to a sitting stop in front of the boy.

"What's wrong?"

"It's Ma," Jeremy shouted hysterically. "She's ridin' drag! *The herd's stampedin' toward her now!*"

CHAPTER 15

"WE FOUND HER HORSE, boss."

"And?"

"There wasn't much left of 'im," Frank admitted hoarsely.

"Did you find any . . . " Colter couldn't continue.

"Were there any remains of the woman?" Boley asked in a clipped voice.

"Didn't see none, but—"

"Then she may be alive," Colter said. "Get back out there and look some more."

"With them clouds, it's too dark to see yer nose in front of yer face now," Frank argued.

"You heard what I said! No one stops looking until we find her!"

The anguish in Colter's voice penetrated the night and sent a shiver down Boley's spine. The man had it bad, Boley thought. He really loved the woman. And she was more than likely dead.

Frank reined his horse away from Colter, shaking his head as he disappeared into the cloudy darkness.

Josh and Jeremy flanked Colter on horseback, their faces grim.

"You ain't gonna be my pa," Josh repeated like a litany under his breath. "I'd rather be an orphan. You ain't gonna be my pa."

"Boley, would you take the boys back to camp? I'm going to look some more."

"If only I hadn't given her that buckskin," Jeremy wailed. "If only Ma had stayed on Gringalet."

"She wasn't on Gringalet?" Colter questioned, startled by Jeremy's revelation.

"I saddled Petey's buckskin for her at noon."

"Buckskin? Buckskin! I sent the cowboy on that buckskin to dig a cow out of a mudhole."

"That was Ma," Jeremy confirmed.

"Hellfire! What was your ma thinking? Her hands'll have blisters so big—"

Colter stopped abruptly. He was worrying about blisters when it was very likely they wouldn't even find enough of Kinyan to bury.

"Take the boys back to camp, Boley. I'm going to keep looking." Colter had no idea he had repeated himself.

Hoss trembled with fatigue, yet when Colter asked, the cowhorse responded with a shambling trot. He could keep that rocking trot up all night if he had to. And he did.

It took them two days to round up the stampeded cattle. Colter continued the search alone for another week. But he never found the brindle bull. And he never found Kinyan.

Once back at the ranch house, Colter closed himself in the parlor and didn't come out for two days. He sat in John Holloway's chair, which fit him like a glove, and reached over to rest his hand on the leather chair where Kinyan should be sitting. He could see the wear on the leather where her nails had scraped each time she grasped the arm to rise.

He had loved her. Improbable, impossible, unlikely that love could have touched him so quickly, but it had. He had loved her without ever possessing her, and now she was dead. *How stupid can one man be?* Colter raged. He'd promised himself he would not love another woman. How blind he had been not to foresee this tragedy!

Colter spent most of his first day alone blaming himself for Kinyan's death. He should have known she would try to come along. He should have let her come along in the first place and kept an eye on her himself. He should have noticed her disguise when he sent her to the mudhole. But all the should-haves in the world wouldn't bring her back now.

The agony of blame receded on the second day as Colter began to recount in his head the events preceding Kinyan's disappearance. He had already turned the herd on itself, effectively ending the stampede, when the shots were fired that started the animals running again. He had questioned all the hands and each swore he hadn't fired any shots. However, neither had any of them seen anyone else fire any shots. It was a mystery.

Not so deep a mystery, Colter reasoned, when he considered the loss of the hundred head of cattle they hadn't recovered and the disappearance of the brindle bull. Those facts strongly suggested the existence of rustlers. Colter swore under his breath. He would have given them the whole damn herd to have Kinyan back!

Then another outrageous idea emerged. Could the rustlers possibly have kidnapped Kinyan? That thought was both comforting and terrifying. Colter didn't know whether it was worse to imagine Kinyan suffering the violation of some other man or the horrifying alternative that she'd been hurt and had crawled away somewhere to die alone, eaten alive by scavengers.

Was it possible Kinyan was still alive out there somewhere? Could her horse have thrown her before the stampede? Could she be safe somewhere, trying to make her way home on foot? He had searched everywhere, but then the stampede had wiped out most of the signs. How far could a woman get on foot without food or water? If she had been anywhere nearby, surely he would have found her.

Colter went round and round, knowing he was looking for any excuse to believe Kinyan wasn't dead, until at last he brought himself to thoughts of the living. There were three lives that had been left in his charge by Kinyan's disappearance (or, he reluctantly admitted, death). Colter heaved a giant sigh as he considered Kinyan's children.

Josh had eluded Boley and disappeared the night of the stampede. Colter would have searched for the boy, but Jeremy had assured him that Josh was safe and that his brother needed this time alone. Colter had been willing to accept that explanation because it allowed him to indulge his own grief. He'd not given another thought to Josh or to Jeremy, who had gone on with Frank, Boley, and the rest of the hands to the Association roundup.

Colter leaned his head back against the smooth leather and closed his eyes. What was he going to do about the children?

He and Josh would no doubt slug it out over the years, but with Jeremy as a buffer, Colter hoped that someday they might come to an understanding. It was Lizbeth who concerned him. Colter tried to imagine what it would have been like if Hope had lived when Sarah had died. Would he have been able to raise his daughter by himself? Of course he could leave Lizbeth to Dorothea, but when Colter thought of how alone Hope would have been without Sarah, his heart opened to the motherless waif left in his charge. Accepting responsibility for Lizbeth was the least he could do in memory of the woman he had loved.

Colter roused himself from the comfortable chair. He'd already missed the first week of the Association roundup. It was dark, but Colter had no idea whether it was early evening or early morning. He stumbled to the door of his refuge and flung it open. He paused, blinded momentarily by the lantern light in the hall. He could hear voices upstairs and followed the sounds until he arrived at Lizbeth's room. Dorothea was reading a story to the child. She stopped abruptly when Colter appeared at the door.

He's done grieving, Dorothea realized as she took in Colter's ravaged appearance. His eyes were red-rimmed and sunk deep in their sockets. Heavy black beard stubbled his gaunt face, and his hair—well, his hair had been through a tornado at least.

"What are you reading?" Colter asked.

" 'Sleeping Beauty,' " Dorothea responded.

"I'll finish if you like."

As naturally as if Colter read to Lizbeth every night, Dorothea rose from the padded rocking chair beside Lizbeth's brass-railed bed and handed the book of fairy tales to him.

"I'll just go finish up the supper dishes," she said. Then Dorothea left the room.

"We were at the part where the princess pricks her finger on a spindle and goes to sleep for a hundred years," Lizbeth said to an awkward Colter.

Colter looked down at the book in his hands and found the place. He moved to the willow rocker and sat down like a very old man.

"I already know the rest of the story, so if you don't want

185

to read, you don't have to," Lizbeth reassured him. "But I would like it if you did," she added in a small voice.

"I said I would."

Colter's voice boomed in the small room, startling both of them. Tears of fright came into Lizbeth's eyes, and Colter swore under his breath. This wasn't going to work!

Colter reached over to wipe a tear from Lizbeth's cheek with his thumb. "I'm not very good at this, Lizbeth," he admitted with a ragged sigh. "I guess you're going to have to teach me what to do."

Lizbeth's eyes rounded. "I will. Oh, I will."

The little girl seemed so sure of herself, so self-confident that Colter's lips quirked up in the semblance of a smile. Encouraged by this small break in the man's forbidding visage, Lizbeth offered, "Maybe you should just kiss me good night."

Colter tucked the sheet carefully around the little girl, then brushed a strand of silky black hair away from her brow. She looked so much like Kinyan! Colter leaned over to press his bristly cheek to Lizbeth's face, and her fingertips came up to catch his other stubbled cheek and hold him there.

"You feel like . . . my pa," she said timidly. She felt Colter stiffen, and his breathing stopped entirely. Then he angled his head to kiss Lizbeth's baby-smooth cheek.

"Good night, Lizbeth."

"Good night . . . Colter." Lizbeth sensed it was too soon to say more. She could be patient. Someday she would call him Pa—and he would like it.

Colter blew out the lantern. He stopped at the door to look back at the child.

"Sleep well," he said. "I won't see you for a while. I'll stay with the roundup crew."

"Come home soon," she responded sleepily. "I'll miss you, Colter."

Colter kept those words in mind while he worked with the Association members on the cooperative roundup. Although Ritter had attempted to cast suspicion on Kinyan's sudden disappearance, his tale gained little credence with Sheriff Potts. There were too many Triple Fork cowboys loyal to John Holloway's widow who could testify to Colter's innocence, not the least of whom was Petey Watkins, who knew that Kinyan was supposed to be safe at home at the time of the stampede.

Colter simply ignored the talk, finding it easier to cope with his grief by immersing himself in the repetitious, grueling demands of the roundup.

They worked in teams of five, a cutter on horseback and four cowboys on foot at the branding fire. Colter worked as cutter, heeling a calf with his lasso, then pulling the calf's hind legs out from under him. With the rope dallied around the saddle horn, he dragged the bawling calf to the branding fire and turned it over to Boley and Petey, who were working as flankers.

His back and shoulder muscles rippling with the effort, Boley reached across the calf's back with both arms, grabbed the animal under the throat and under its hind leg, and lifted it completely off the ground, dropping it on its right flank. Then he dropped his right knee onto the calf's neck, while he sought the left forefoot and bent it back as high and as far into the air as he could. At the same time, Petey grabbed hold of the left rear leg, pulled it high, and stood with both feet on the calf's right rear leg waiting, nose averted, for the third member of the branding team, the iron man.

Frank stood ready with a cherry-red Triple Fork brand, which he pressed to the calf's left hip. Jeremy was the fourth member of the team, and with a razor-sharp knife he notched the ear brand and castrated the male calves. The entire branding process took less than half a minute.

Hoss was such a good cutting horse and Colter such an excellent roper that he could do his job endlessly without paying much attention to it. It was because he wasn't paying attention that Colter accidentally snagged the mossyhorn.

The ancient steer was branded with a Circle C, the same as the cattle Colter had just brought with him from Texas, and for a split second he wondered how one of his new herd had gotten mixed with the Triple Fork steers they'd rounded up. But his second look at the animal he'd thrown his loop around sent a chill of foreboding down his spine.

Colter had shipped breeding cows and some two- and three-year-old steers from Denver. This animal was twelve or thirteen years old, a steer so old the cowboys joked that moss was growing on its horns. Such an animal was long past its four-year-old prime for being sent to market. This steer was old enough to have been stolen from Colter's Circle C ranch in Texas eight years ago! How had this mossyhorn gotten mixed up with Triple Fork stock? Then Colter remembered Kinyan's remark about a Texan who had come to the Triple Fork right after the war, and he found himself forced to accept the fact that while he had been searching vainly in Texas, one of the murderers of his wife and daughter could have been here.

"I'm taking a break," Colter shouted at the branding team. "I'll see you later."

Since it was a full hour until noon break, the four cowboys on the ground watched Colter ride away in some consternation.

"What the hell got into him, I wonder?" Frank said.

"Don't suppose it takes much of a magician to guess," Boley replied. "I'm surprised he's managed to last this long without this whole business getting to him."

Boley's hooded eyes slid to the quiet youth with the bloody knife in his hand. Jeremy had worked alongside the three men seemingly unmoved by his mother's death. The kid didn't even appear distressed. Boley hadn't seen him shed a single tear. It wasn't natural, Boley thought.

Jeremy was aware of the three sets of eyes focused on him, and he shifted uncomfortably, cocking his hip in a gesture that was unconsciously reminiscent of his father.

"We can't work without a cutter. I'll go see if I can find somebody to take Colter's place," Jeremy said.

A frown crossed Boley's face as he watched the youth head for his horse. The kid was like ice, and in this September heat that was some trick.

"However it might look to you, he loved his ma," Frank said to Boley, correctly interpreting Boley's disgusted expression. "He always did look on the practical side of things, though. He must have figured out some way to make sense of all this."

As he mounted and rode away, Jeremy suffered the effects of Boley's scathing scrutiny, Frank's confused concern, and Petey's guilty remorse. They just didn't understand. How could he grieve when he had hope his ma was still alive? Until he saw her dead body, Jeremy planned to keep on hoping. It was the only way he could keep from breaking down and bawling like a baby.

Colter took his questions about the mossyhorn to the man who had been friendliest to him at the Association meeting. To Colter's surprise, Warren MacDougall's branding team included Ritter Gordon. Warren squatted on his heels in front of a fire, where the branding iron had been exchanged for a coffeepot, pouring himself a cup of the black concoction from the soot-blackened tin pot. His son, Andy, sat cross-legged next to him. Ritter leaned against a nearby cottonwood, letting the shade keep him cool and unruffled. The other members of Warren's team were nowhere to be seen.

"Howdy, Warren, Andy. Who's watching that telegraph key while you're out here, Andy?" Colter teased the boy.

Andy shot a quick look at Ritter, who subtly shook his head. Andy forced a weak smile.

"Uh, I'm not here working the roundup. I just came to . . . uh . . . to see my pa."

Warren was taken aback at the lie. Why hadn't Andy just said he'd brought Ritter a telegram? Warren looked at Ritter and saw the look that cautioned not to interfere.

Warren didn't approve of Andy's fabrication, but he wasn't about to put his own son on the spot. Neither, on the other hand, was he about to let the boy be manipulated further by Ritter.

"Well, now that you've seen me, I guess they'll be expecting you back at the telegraph office." His dismissal of Andy was clear, and the boy tipped his hat at Colter and Ritter, mounted his horse, and rode away. Before he got far, however, Andy looked back over his shoulder, trying to catch a last glimpse of Colter. Ritter had gotten his answer from Texas, but the telegram he'd rushed out here to deliver to Ritter hadn't told Andy anything. There were just those two names. Two names. What did they mean?

"Hello there, Colter," Warren said in greeting. "What brings you to our humble campfire?"

"I found a Circle C steer in with the Triple Fork calves we're branding."

"Circle C? Don't know that brand. Ritter, you heard of any of the smaller outfits uses the Circle C?" Warren asked.

"Can't say as I have."

"It isn't a Wyoming brand. It's a Texas brand."

"Well, if you knew it was a Texas brand, what're you askin' me for?" Warren said irritably. He'd had to do double work half the morning, since Ritter was late arriving, and having Andy ride out here was a reminder that although his son relented so far as to attend Association meetings, Andy didn't want anything to do with ranching. Warren wasn't in much of a mood for riddles.

"I thought maybe you knew of somebody who might've sold a herd of Circle C cattle around here seven, maybe eight years ago," Colter said casually.

"Now let me see," Warren said, wiping the sweat from his throat with his bandanna. "We've really only been having these joint roundups for a couple of years now, so that long ago somebody coulda been running Circle C cattle and I'd never've known it."

"How about you, Ritter?"

"I've seen a few Circle C cattle here and there over the years," he admitted cautiously. "Don't know where they came from, though."

"How long a period are you talking about?" Colter asked, a tingling beginning between his shoulder blades.

"Guess I started seeing them three or four years ago," Ritter lied.

Ritter's comment confused Colter. Supposedly, Kinyan's mysterious Texan had come through right after the war. If Circle C cattle had only showed up around here three or four years ago, that would mean this mossyhorn had probably been bought by someone unconnected with its original theft. If so, why hadn't the Circle C on its hide been branded over by some trail brand or some new owner's brand?

Colter pulled his hat off to rake his hands through his hair, then pulled the hat back down, the brim hiding his eyes. He had to stop thinking about finding that third man. It was a waste of time and a waste of his life. He had other responsibilities now, and it was time he got back to them.

Ritter waited for Colter to press the issue, and when he didn't, Ritter wasn't sure whether he was irritated or relieved. Strange Colter should ask about that Circle C steer now. He hadn't thought after all these years there'd be any left. He'd been very careful to sell them all through an agent so they couldn't be traced back to him. Still, it was eerie how that Circle C mossyhorn had shown up in Colter's herd. Ritter didn't like it at all. The fates had a way of dealing low and dirty sometimes.

Ritter examined the face that had seemed so familiar the first time he'd seen it. As soon as he'd read the two names on the telegraph, he'd remembered where he'd seen Colter before. Too bad he hadn't placed the cowboy sooner, but it had been a long time ago and there had been a lot of faceless victims. Ritter was in no hurry to deal with Colter. Now he knew he would have his revenge for the slights the drifter had dealt him. He would make sure that before Bart Jefferson killed Colter, the bounty hunter made it very clear exactly who Ritter Gordon was and what he had done to Benjamin Colter's wife and child.

"Where's the rest of your branding team?" Colter asked Warren.

"Seems Jason Sawyer got gored by some outlaw bull back on the Bar 7. The rest of the boys were good friends of Jase's, so they went back to see how he was doing and to see if they could locate that outlaw bull. A bull that goes crazy like that can leave a horse and rider in ribbons. Better to kill it now, before it comes after some other unsuspecting cowboy."

"You had problems with this outlaw bull before?"

"Naw, this is a first. Don't worry, though. Those boys are good trackers. We'll be having beefsteak tonight."

"Well, I'll leave you to enjoy it. I better get back to work," Colter said. He gave Ritter one last look, which Ritter returned with a sanguine smile. Colter turned Hoss and rode back to his own branding fire.

Colter spent the rest of the afternoon with the image of Ritter's evil smile stuck in his mind. It stayed with him even when he had dropped, exhausted, into his bedroll in the dark. He couldn't shake the suspicion that Ritter had something to do with Kinyan's disappearance. He had half convinced himself that Ritter had her hidden away somewhere when he realized he was merely desperate for some scapegoat to take the blame for the tragedy that had occurred. His own guilty conscience wanted an answer to the mystery. What had happened to his wife?

Colter slammed the door on his thoughts. His imagination

was too vivid, and the picture in his mind of his first wife in death was so horrible that he simply refused to think of Kinyan at all. So Colter feared he had gone mad when he suddenly heard her name whispered in the dark.

"Kinyan."

Without moving a muscle, Colter allowed all his senses to come alert. Tonight, as he had every night during the roundup, Colter had sought out a place away from the rest of the cowhands. He had purposely picked a spot in the open so no intruder could approach without being detected. Yet he felt rather than heard or saw the presence of another man. The touch on his shoulder was all the more surprising because he hadn't believed the man to be so very close.

The name was repeated.

"Kinyan."

The intruder allowed his face to be perceived in the moonlight, and Colter suddenly understood the reason nothing more had been said. He rose without question and followed the caller into the night.

CHAPTER 16

AT FIRST, KINYAN had no idea where she was. It was dark, and some external force seemed to restrain her. Within moments, the familiar feel of the soft buffalo robe beneath her fingertips and the thick smoke that burned her eyes and assailed her nostrils confirmed that she was confined in a tepee. She listened, and heard the rustle of cottonwoods as the wind moaned through them. Then she heard the sound of children playing, calling to each other in Sioux. She must be in her parents' tepee. But no, where was Wheat Woman's white buffalo robe? Kinyan's heart skipped to her throat when her eyes locked on Rides-the-Wind's eagle-feather headdress and then on his blue-and-white-beaded ceremonial shirt. How had she ended up in his tepee?

As her eyes adjusted to the shadows, Kinyan made out the banked fire in the center of the round space, and a small, buckskin-clad figure huddled there.

"Josh?"

"Ma?"

Josh crawled quickly over and hunkered down on his knees before his mother. When she reached out to stroke his forearm, he dropped his head on her chest and began to sob uncontrollably.

"It's all right," Kinyan crooned. "Everything's fine. Don't cry, dear one. Everything will be fine."

Kinyan smoothed the narrow shoulders that heaved under her hand. She let her son cry until the sobs had become gasps and then gulps, and he finally lay silent, his arms grasping her tightly around the waist.

"Josh," Kinyan said quietly. "How did we get here?"

Quite embarrassed now at the way he'd expressed his relief that his mother had regained consciousness, Josh jerked himself up and backed away from her a foot or so to sit cross-legged, his arms folded solemnly across his chest. He had to clear his throat before he could speak.

"You've been real sick. I thought you were gonna die."

"I've been sick?"

When Kinyan tried to sit up, she realized she couldn't move. There was no strength at all in her upper body.

"Josh, am I tied down?" Kinyan asked incredulously. She couldn't see her left arm beneath the animal skins that covered her, but it would not respond to her commands.

"Rides-the-Wind said you were struck by a rattlesnake," Josh explained. "Your arm was swollen somethin' terrible from the poison, and I s'pose it's still pretty bad. You've been crazy out of your head, Ma."

All at once Kinyan's memory of the events leading to the rattler's attack came flooding back.

"The stampede! Is everyone all right?"

"Nobody got hurt that I know of 'cept you," Josh said. "And everybody thinks you're dead, 'cause they found that buckskin you were ridin' and he was trampled down to nothin'. I told Jeremy I was going to stay with Grandfather. When I got here, I discovered that Rides-the-Wind had found you and brought you here."

"Rides-the-Wind found me? What was he doing on Triple Fork land?"

Now Josh rushed headlong to break the news he'd been holding until he was fit to burst.

"Ma, it's Ritter who's responsible for all the trouble! Rides-the-Wind heard some of the young bucks sayin' how they'd been promised rifles by Ritter if they'd use 'em to start a stampede and kill Colter's brindle bull. Rides-the-Wind wanted to make sure it wasn't some kinda trap, so he came along. That's when he found you. He brought you here and insisted on takin' care of you himself."

The news that Ritter had incited the Sioux to attack the trail drive was distressing, but it was Josh's other announcement that sent shivers up and down Kinyan's spine. The fact she was in Rides-the-Wind's tepee, being cared for by him, could only mean he'd claimed her as his own. He could only

194

do that if he'd given her father a bride price that Soaring Eagle had accepted or if she was his captive. Either way, she was in deep trouble.

"Have you sent word to let Colter and Jeremy know I'm all right?" Kinyan questioned.

"Well, not exactly."

"Josh, does Colter know I'm here?"

Josh flushed. "Well, prob'ly by now he does."

"What does that mean?"

"Well, I didn't say nothin' 'bout Colter at first, so nobody knew to say nothin' to him. But, Ma, how could I know Rides-the-Wind was gonna keep you for his wife?"

"Oh, Josh!"

"If I'd've known, I'd've told straightaway 'bout you already bein' married to Colter. Honest I woulda, Ma. Then I was scared to tell Grandfather, 'cause he seemed kinda pleased by the way things turned out. But you kept callin' Colter's name and Rides-the-Wind was askin' questions, so finally I told 'em both, and Rides-the-Wind, he was powerful angry, Ma. I've never seen him so mad. Grandfather left yesterday to find Colter."

Kinyan's head was pounding, and her left arm and shoulder throbbed. She wanted to go back to sleep and wake up safe in her bed at home. How was she going to unravel this mess?

"If only I'd seen that rattler!" she muttered to herself.

"What happened, Ma? How'd you get bit by that rattler?"

"Yes, I'd like to hear the answer to that myself," Colter said as he rose to his full menacing height after coming through the flapped doorway of the tepee.

For the smallest second Kinyan saw relief and concern on Colter's face. Then it was masked by the controlled fury that filled the tepee along with his presence.

Rides-the-Wind stepped into the buffalo-hide shelter behind Colter, his onyx eyes purposely expressionless even though his body was strung tight as a bowstring. Though the Indian couldn't understand Colter's words, the cowboy's tone of voice was unmistakable. This fierce attack wasn't what he'd expected from the man Kinyan had cried for ceaselessly during her illness.

Colter bristled further when Josh inched closer to his mother to protect her.

195

"Get out of my way, boy!" Colter snarled ferally.

"Shall I kill him?" Rides-the-Wind asked Kinyan in Sioux, his hand on the knife hilt at his waist.

Rides-the-Wind had his answer from the look of horror that rose on Kinyan's face even before she answered, "He is my husband. His anger is not without cause. I disobeyed him."

At that admission, Rides-the-Wind admonished softly, "You were ever too willful, Kinyan." He hadn't believed it when Josh had said Kinyan was married, and to another white-eyes. Did she not care for him at all? If she loved him, why had she gone so eagerly to the white man's bed? He would not have thought he could hurt so much. "Why did you not wait for me, Kinyan?"

Kinyan's stricken blue eyes met the dark eyes of the Sioux who loved her. She shut her eyes to the agony she found there, but saw it still in her mind's eye.

"I . . . I . . ." Her pleading eyes went to Josh and then back to Rides-the-Wind.

"We will speak alone later. Little Hawk," he said, addressing Josh by his Indian name, "this matter is between a husband and a wife. We do not belong here."

"I don't want to leave. I want to hear what happened!" Josh argued in English.

Colter hesitated a moment, his fists clenching and unclenching. Soaring Eagle hadn't been able to tell him anything during the long ride to the agency camp, but he certainly hadn't expected to be confronted by this powerful young Indian buck when he'd arrived. Soaring Eagle had deferred to the Sioux brave and it was only by the young man's grudging leave, after a heated exchange with Soaring Eagle, that Colter had been allowed to enter the tepee where Kinyan was held. From the look on Kinyan's face, the young brave obviously meant something to her. But what? And what was she doing alone in his tepee?

Perceiving Colter's agitation and the rippling undercurrents of pain that held Rides-the-Wind's questions temporarily in abeyance, Kinyan attempted to soothe the frayed tempers as best she could.

"I'll tell you all about it later, Josh," she said. "Go now." There was also an unspoken promise to speak with Rides-the-Wind.

Josh looked at the three tense faces that surrounded him. This was not the time to argue. He gave his mother an encouraging look and shot Colter his special evil eye before he rose proudly and exited the tepee with Rides-the-Wind close on his heels.

"Now, my disobedient wife," Colter said in a voice more dangerous because of its softness. "Tell me how you ended up where I had expressly forbidden you to be."

Colter paced the four or five steps before the low slant of the tepee forced him to turn back in the other direction again.

Kinyan was distracted by Colter's nervous movements. Her eyes followed him as he strode back and forth, back and forth, while she tried to concentrate and remember exactly what had happened when the stampede started.

"You mustn't blame Petey," she began. "I told him I was going home, but instead I changed clothes and came back to ride drag. I was off away from the herd chasing a steer when I realized the cattle had stampeded."

"So you got out of the way where you'd be safe, right?" he rasped angrily.

"I would have," Kinyan spat back, unwilling to be unjustly accused when Colter didn't have all the facts, "except a snake struck at the buckskin, and he reared. I lost my balance and fell off." She paused, "Then I remember hearing the rattles close by my face."

Kinyan shivered as she recalled her feeling of helplessness before the coiled snake.

Colter felt a chill run up his spine, prickling his neck hairs, and he stopped pacing to watch the emotions flit across his wife's face.

"I stayed very still, and for a few moments I thought it wouldn't strike me. Then the steer moved behind me. I whirled at the sound and the snake bit into my forearm. I don't remember any pain, because by then I could see the cattle coming toward me and I knew I was going to die. I guess the snake striking me didn't seem so important when I was going to be trampled to death by a stampeding herd of cattle in a few moments anyway.

"I jumped up and ran until I thought my heart would burst from the effort. I stumbled down a ravine and fell under an overhang of grass. I remember I could see the roots of the

197

grass coming through the dirt above me. I tried, but I just couldn't get up. I could hear my heart pounding, and then it became the pounding of thousands of hooves and I could feel the vibrations of the earth and the falling stones and dirt as the herd passed by.

"When they were gone, I was still alive. I remember being so relieved because I was safe. Then my arm began to hurt and I was sure I was going to die from the snake bite. It really was a very funny moment. I even laughed out loud."

Colter held his breath at the bemused smile on Kinyan's face as she recalled the moment.

Then she finished, "That was when Rides-the-Wind called to me."

"You're lucky as hell to be alive!"

Colter began pacing once again. Finally, stopping with his back to her, he said, "What am I going to do with you?"

It was more a query to himself than to her. Colter had allowed hope to flow within him when Soaring Eagle had summoned him and then had suffered the agonies of the damned because the Sioux had been unable to communicate whether he was taking Colter to Kinyan or to her remains. Colter's relief at finding his beloved alive was so intense that he'd wrestled mightily with the desire to pull her into his arms and forgive her everything. But he knew that it would lead to only one thing, and if Colter hadn't learned his lesson about caring the first time, then he'd surely learned it the second. In the future, there would be nothing between him and this woman except their common name.

On the other hand, Kinyan, who had twice within a matter of minutes seen her life snatched from her and twice had it handed back, had learned that life was too fragile a thing to put off living it. She was not going to make the mistake of denying her feelings for Colter any longer. She had chosen this man as her husband, and she intended to be a wife to him from now on in every way.

"Better you should ask what we're going to do about Ritter," Kinyan said with asperity.

Colter whirled around to face her.

"Ritter!"

"It was Ritter who supplied the guns to start the stampede. He offered new Winchesters to some of the young braves here at the camp if they'd stampede your herd and kill the brindle bull."

Kinyan watched the blood drain from Colter's face and hurried to finish. "Rides-the-Wind came along with the braves to keep an eye on things and that's how he happened to be there to find me. But I don't know how we can prove anything against Ritter. No one will believe the word of an Indian against that of a white, and we have no other evidence that Ritter is responsible. Besides, I have no wish to cause enmity between the whites and the Sioux by making this incident known."

Colter hoped the Indians had seen what a fine animal Hercules was and stolen him rather than following through on Ritter's orders to kill the beast. He'd envisioned such wonderful progeny from the brindle bull! He tried not to let Kinyan see his disappointment.

Colter was not surprised, however, to learn that Ritter was at the bottom of this incident. With the precedent of planting three outlaws on Triple Fork land, bribing Indians to start a stampede was not out of character at all. Colter made careful note of the fact Ritter rarely did his own dirty work. In the past two instances, it had been Ritter's hired help of which Colter needed to be wary. Of course that made it more difficult to determine where the danger lay, but Colter had spent years evading those bent on having his hide and he'd learned a few tricks himself along the way.

"I'll handle Ritter," he informed Kinyan. "You just let me worry about him. How soon before you'll be able to ride?"

Colter asked the question so curtly, and with so little consideration for Kinyan, that she gasped aloud.

"I don't know," she said, trying to keep her hurt feelings from her voice. "I can't seem to move at all." And then there was the matter of whether Rides-the-Wind was going to let her go anywhere . . .

As though she were no more than a dog with a thorn in its paw, Colter crossed to Kinyan and tore the soft animal skin covering away from her body. Kinyan lay naked to his gaze.

Her hands rested on her smooth belly, hiding her navel from view. Her sharp hipbones protruded beyond the flat plane of her stomach, and a triangle of dark curls adorned the juncture of her tapered legs. Her breasts looked smaller, curving mounds with only the large brown nipples, puckered from sudden exposure to the cooler air, rising above her chest. Only the slightly swollen arm and the bruises and scratches scattered here and there testified to her grim ordeal.

Kinyan was proud of her body. She knew it had pleased Colter when he'd bathed her. But she saw in Colter's eyes none of the pleasure he'd enjoyed that time. The sapphire orbs were dark, but not with passion. They had become bottomless wells, stony and cold.

Colter fought a battle with hell. His jaw tightened. His heart lurched. His muscles tensed. His loins ached. His good intentions faltered. He righted them again. He reached for Kinyan. He stopped himself. He turned her hands over, barely brushing the soft skin of her belly with his knuckles. Then he found the remnants of the blisters on her palms. And lost the battle.

"Hellfire and damnation!" he whispered.

He reached out and pulled Kinyan into his arms, crushing her against his chest and pressing kisses to her face and throat.

"I thought I'd lost you," he breathed. "I thought you were gone and I didn't know how I could live without you."

Colter held her in his lap and rocked her like a baby, crooning endearments, unwilling to think now of the future. He would set her aside again when he was sure she was well. He had lived without her before. He would live without her again. Only he knew this time it would be harder. Much harder.

Kinyan was very tired, and Colter's soothing voice, the gentle rocking, lulled her. He cared. Despite his vow not to, he cared. But so did Rides-the-Wind, and she'd hurt him terribly. She must explain to the Sioux warrior. She must tell him that she loved Colter.

When Kinyan fell asleep, Colter laid her back down on the buffalo robe, gently covered her with the silky furs, and left the tepee. He found Josh and Rides-the-Wind sitting cross-legged in the shadow of the tepee waiting for him.

"As soon as she's well enough, I'm taking your mother home," he told Josh. "I want you to come too."

"I'm staying here," the boy replied stubbornly. "And I don't think Rides-the-Wind is gonna let Ma go either."

"What do you mean?"

"He says he's gonna marry Ma."

"Your ma's already married to me."

"He knows that," Josh replied.

Colter squared his shoulders. His hand dropped to where his Colt should have been, and he remembered he'd removed it at Soaring Eagle's request. He still had the knife in his boot, but he had a feeling this wasn't a battle that would be fought with a weapon. Colter came down on his haunches before the handsome Sioux. He could feel the man taking his measure. He took the time to do the same.

What he found was a fearless man, as strong of heart as of body. He would have liked to match strength sometime with the Indian, for the fun of it. But where Kinyan was concerned, Colter wasn't willing to play games. The sooner the Sioux recognized Colter's right to the woman, the better. Colter picked up a handful of dust and let it sift slowly through his fingers before he spoke.

"I want you to translate for me, Josh," Colter said. "Tell Rides-the-Wind that Kinyan belongs to me. And that when I leave here, I will take her with me."

Colter watched the Sioux's face remain passive as Josh gave him the message. Then the Indian spoke.

"I can't tell him that!" Josh blurted.

"Tell me what?" Colter asked.

Rides-the-Wind commanded Josh to answer.

"He says perhaps you won't leave here," Josh said, his face flushed. Josh wished he could reassure Colter that Rides-the-Wind didn't mean what he'd said, but if there was one thing he'd learned from his grandfather and the Sioux warrior at his side, it was that their word was sacred. If Rides-the-Wind had threatened Colter, then there was a good chance Colter would have to fight his way out of here.

Colter smiled ferally. "What else does he have to say?"

Rides-the-Wind spoke again, his eyes steadily meeting Colter's while Josh translated.

"Kinyan has been mine from the time of our childhood," the Sioux brave said. "Her father gave her to the white man John Holloway against her wishes. Otherwise she would have been my wife long ago. Now John Holloway is dead and Kinyan is mine. We will be together now as we should have been then."

"If what you say is true," Colter questioned calmly, "why did she choose to marry me?"

When Josh translated, the Sioux seemed momentarily perplexed. Indeed, Rides-the-Wind didn't understand why Kinyan had married Colter unless she didn't believe he was serious about the plans that were being made to rid the land of the white man. Yes, that must be it. He would explain to her about the great congregation of Sioux that would meet in the spring in the land to the north, near the valley of the Little Big Horn. Not just the Oglala, but all the tribes of the Sioux would band together to make war against the white man and send him from the land. Then Kinyan's children and their children, too, would live and grow as a proud and strong people in the land of their forefathers.

"I must speak with Kinyan and hear from her mouth the truth of her reasons. Then we will see whom she will have as husband," Rides-the-Wind said. With that, he rose and went inside the tepee.

When Colter started to follow, Josh put a hand on his arm.

"You can't go in there unless Rides-the-Wind invites you, and he hasn't done that."

"I'm not leaving Kinyan in there alone with him!"

It was apparent the two men would come to blows unless Josh did something fast, and for reasons he didn't care to examine too closely, he didn't want to see a confrontation between Colter and the Sioux.

"Rides-the-Wind wouldn't refuse to invite Grandmother in, and if she's there, nothing's goin' to happen to Ma that you wouldn't approve."

Colter hesitated a moment. "Where's your grandmother now?"

"Follow me."

When Kinyan awoke, she found Rides-the-Wind sitting cross-legged next to her and her mother settled comfortably in a far corner of the tepee beading a new buckskin shirt for her father. She knew without being told the reason for her mother's presence. Colter must have insisted upon it. And since Rides-the-Wind had allowed her a chaperone, he must be reconsidering his claim upon her.

"Welcome back among us," Rides-the-Wind said.

"Where's Colter?" Kinyan asked anxiously.

202

"You seem exceedingly concerned for the white-eyes. Why?"

"He's my husband."

"Again I ask, Why? I thought you would wait for the time that we might be together always as husband and wife. Yet you have taken a white husband. I thought you cared for me as I care for you. Did I mistake your feelings, Kinyan?"

Kinyan glanced guiltily at her mother, but Wheat Woman didn't raise her eyes from the intricate work before her.

"I should have told you sooner that I . . . that I don't love you as a wife should love a husband," Kinyan managed to say.

"For how long have you known this?"

"A long time."

"How long!" the warrior snapped.

"From the birth of my sons."

Rides-the-Wind said nothing. He thought back to all the years he had nursed his love for this woman, all the years he had foregone the pleasure of a wife to comfort his nights, to greet him when he came from battle, and to have his children, only to discover that this same woman had not returned that love! Had she ever told him how she felt? Had he missed a sign she might have laid in his path? She had told him once he should marry, but he'd thought that was only because she couldn't bear to think of his loneliness.

"Do you love the white-eyes named Colter?"

It seemed cruel to answer the question truthfully, yet Kinyan dared not lie.

"Yes."

So, Rides-the-Wind thought, it was not just the poverty and hunger of the tribe that had made her choose to live among the white man. His love, his life, had found a soulmate among the white-eyes. Rides-the-Wind now had one more very good reason for hating the white man, and it strengthened his resolve to join the Sioux gathering beyond the Powder River. He would have his revenge upon all white men in the great war that was to begin in the spring. As for Colter, even though Josh had protested he didn't like the man, he'd said no ill of him. And Kinyan loved him. He should have hated the white-eyes. He only envied him.

"You never planned to return to live among us, did you, Kinyan?" Rides-the-Wind asked finally.

"No." The single word came out as a croak.

It would be better, he thought, to cut all ties between them. He could not bear to be near her and know she would not be his. So he let her feel his disdain, untempered by his love.

"Yet never were you strong enough to speak the truth to my face. I am grateful I was spared the burden of such a cowardly and dishonest wife."

Kinyan winced at the bitterness that spilled from the lips of the Sioux, cringed at the loathing in the voice that said, "You may have your white-eyes, Kinyan, but you are welcome within this tepee only until you are well enough to leave it. I will stay elsewhere. As soon as may be, take your white-eyes and leave here. I do not wish to look upon you again."

With those words, Rides-the-Wind rose and, without looking back at Kinyan, left.

Kinyan hadn't thought she could feel such pain, like unto the death of a brother, and for almost a minute she didn't even breathe. Then she drew breath in a sob that brought Wheat Woman to her side.

Kinyan moaned, feeling Rides-the-Wind's pain as her own. "I did love him once. I should have told him the truth long ago. I just couldn't. If Father hadn't sent me from the village, I would have married him. I would! I will never forgive Soaring Eagle! Never!"

Kinyan pressed a fist to her mouth and bit down hard on her knuckles to prevent the sobs that threatened to break free.

"Why not aim your anger at the one who deserves it," Wheat Woman said. "It was I who forced your father to send you among the white man."

"What?"

Wheat Woman sighed and set aside the buckskin shirt, which was still in her hand. The war between the white man and the Sioux she had always feared was nearly upon them. When the great battles had been fought, the Sioux would be no more. This, Wheat Woman believed. And, knowing that Kinyan would very likely never see her father again after they left for the gathering in the north, Wheat Woman had determined that Soaring Eagle should once again know his daughter's love.

It had been a selfish thing she had done, to bind Soaring Eagle to the promise, when she was pregnant with Kinyan, that the child should be sent among the white man for a time when it was older. Then John Holloway had come along, searching for a woman who had been stolen by the Sioux, and Soaring Eagle had offered his daughter to the white man instead. He had fulfilled his promise. But it had broken his heart and turned his child against him.

After Soaring Eagle had fulfilled his promise, Wheat Woman had been selfish again. She hadn't told Kinyan the truth because then her daughter's anger would have fallen upon her. No one understood Kinyan's motives in keeping the truth from Rides-the-Wind better than her own mother. And, like Kinyan, Wheat Woman knew she must now pay the painful price for her selfish lie.

"Your father was only keeping his vow to me when he sent you among the white man. If the choice had been his, he would never have let you go. So, you see, I am to blame for everything that has happened."

Kinyan closed her eyes and tasted the blood on her knuckles. Her heart pounded within her chest. She could feel the scream rising in her chest at the betrayal she felt, but what finally came out was hysterical laughter. All those wasted years! All those years she had shut her father out of her life! All those years Rides-the-Wind had been alone!

Kinyan's laughter became deep, wrenching sobs of sorrow. Kinyan groped for her mother, and when Wheat Woman's welcoming arms surrounded her, Kinyan laid her face upon her mother's breast and let the ravaging regret run its course.

"Are you feeling any better now?" Wheat Woman asked much later.

"Yes. I want to see Father. I want to explain to him—"

"That you still love him."

"Yes."

"I'll find him and send him to you."

"Mother . . ."

"Yes, Kinyan."

"I understand why you didn't tell me the truth. And I don't blame you for it."

"I thought you might understand, Kinyan. I hoped you would. I wished for you only what I thought best."

When Josh saw Wheat Woman leave the tepee shortly after Rides-the-Wind, his curiosity sent him inside.

When he entered the tepee, Josh sat down cross-legged next to his mother. Once his eyes were accustomed to the dim interior, the sight of her tear-ravaged face sent his next words spilling from his mouth.

"Rides-the-Wind didn't look none too happy when he came outta here, Ma. He ain't gonna go lookin' for Colter, is he?"

"No, I don't think so. Would you be concerned for Colter if he did?" Kinyan asked.

"I don't know," Josh replied. "It'd be like two bobcats tangling if they ever did get together. The fur'd fly for sure! I wouldn't mind havin' either one of 'em on my side in a knockdown fight, but I don't think I'd wanta bet against Colter. He's always surprisin' me."

"Does that mean you don't hate him anymore?"

Josh darted a look at his mother, suddenly cautious.

"I didn't say that."

"Because I love him," she continued. "As much as I loved your father."

Josh let out a deep breath of air. "I kinda thought you felt like that. I guess he must care for you too. He told Rides-the-Wind he wasn't gonna leave here without you."

"He did?"

"Yeah." Josh thought about the threat that had been implicit in the Sioux brave's response but decided not to burden his mother with it. Colter had seemed more than ready to meet the challenge if it came. "I don't know how I feel about Colter anymore, Ma."

"Could you give him a chance, Josh?"

The youth hesitated to agree because he feared it would be the last step in a long line of inroads the tall man had made on his initial impression of him. Josh wouldn't go so far as to say he liked Colter, but he respected him. During the week they'd spent together, he'd found himself wanting to please the Texan, seeking ways to earn his approval, because he felt good inside when Colter praised him. *Just like with Pa.* But Josh wasn't ready yet to give up John Holloway.

"I can't just forget about Pa."

"I'm not asking you to do that," Kinyan replied.

206

"I don't know, Ma. It's like sometimes Colter will say something and I hear Pa. It's eerie. Sometimes he . . ."

Josh stopped speaking when Soaring Eagle entered the tepee. The Sioux paused for a second to let his eyes adjust to the darkness, then crossed to sit beside his grandson.

"Wheat Woman said you wished to see me, Kinyan. But continue, Little Hawk. I did not wish to interrupt your words."

"I was just talkin' 'bout Colter," Josh admitted. "Sometimes he reminds me of Pa."

"That is a good thing, is it not?"

"Yeah," Josh mumbled. "I guess so."

"It is a hard thing to be a father," Soaring Eagle said. "One cannot always know the right decision to make. Nor does a child always know the reasons behind a decision that must be made," Soaring Eagle continued. "So the child must simply trust that his father is doing what is best for him."

Kinyan's eyes began to blur.

"But why should I trust Colter?" Josh asked.

"Because he cares for you and wants to do what's best for you," Kinyan said. "Even if it doesn't seem like it at the time."

Josh chewed his lower lip thoughtfully. "Well, I guess I better get outta here and let you two talk."

When Josh had gone, Soaring Eagle and Kinyan looked at each other for a moment without speaking.

"Welcome back, my daughter."

"It's good to be home, my father."

Then Soaring Eagle held out his arms, and Kinyan lurched into them, burying her face in the strong shoulder that had always been there waiting for her.

CHAPTER 17

"ALL RIGHT, LET'S GET those cattle moved! Remember, let your horse do the work."

Colter shouted the order to Kinyan from his position atop a hillock in the Laramie Mountains. She was down in an arroyo with a small herd of steers who were starving to death but too dumb to find their way out of the area that had become denuded of grass. Josh and Jeremy worked with Kinyan, all three of them equally liable to become the object of Colter's criticism as he fulfilled his promise to teach them what he knew. Jeremy slapped an ornery critter with the tail of his lariat, then broke from the edge of the herd and came straight up the incline to interrupt Colter's discerning vigil.

"Hey, Colter!"

"What, Jeremy?"

"Ma's worn out. She's been at it all afternoon. Don't you think it's time to take a break? She's only been home a week and—"

"I've already told your ma once she could stay home and rest, but she wanted to come. She's welcome to quit anytime."

"But she don't wanta quit. You oughta know by now how stubborn she is. She'd fall over in a faint before she'd admit she couldn't take it, 'specially since the stampede. You gotta let her rest!"

Two days after his ma had arrived home, she'd started coming on these daily sojourns, but it was clear she wasn't really feeling well enough yet to manage a whole day without a break. Colter had seemed to be aware of that, and Jeremy had watched him come up with excuses to stop so she could rest—until today. Today, for some reason, he'd worked Ma extra hard, and he'd shown no signs of letting up.

Come to think of it, both Ma and the cowboy had been acting mighty peculiar since her return. First off, they weren't sleeping in the same bedroom anymore. Colter had moved himself to the guest bedroom that first night home, saying that Ma needed the privacy to recuperate. Since then, Ma had been walking around Colter like he was patched in by eggshells, and Colter had been treating Ma pretty much like a hen with a rotten egg—knowing something was wrong, but not sure exactly what to do about it.

Jeremy watched for a break in the guarded expression on Colter's face, and when it came, it was so short-lived that if Jeremy had blinked he'd never have seen it. But it was there all right, plain as the freckles on his face—concern. Why was Colter hiding what he felt? Why couldn't the cowboy just admit he cared for Ma?

Colter's lips pressed into a thin line and the wrinkle appeared at the bridge of his nose that Jeremy had learned to expect when Colter was thinking. Finally, Colter called out, "Kinyan, come here a minute."

"What do you want?" Kinyan asked as she rode up. She pulled her hat off with her right hand and wiped the sweat from her brow with her sleeve. The days were still sweltering even though the late September nights were cool. A break in the weather could come anytime, but so far, autumn hadn't made itself felt and Kinyan suffered from the heat.

"If you're tired, take a break."

"Who says I'm tired?" Kinyan asked belligerently. She was sticky with sweat, gritty with dust, and her irritability increased as she recognized the trembling in her limbs that signaled just how close she was to collapse. She took a quick look at Jeremy, who hung his head, then kicked his horse, and mumbled, "See you later," before he rode away.

"You don't have to prove anything to me," Colter said quietly.

"Who says I'm trying to prove anything?"

But she was, and Kinyan knew it. If she didn't take a break soon, she was going to end up prostrate. She might as well sit down and eat a little humble pie while she still could, before her face fell in it from sheer exhaustion.

"All right," she admitted reluctantly with a whooshing sigh of weariness. "I'm tired. How about a short break? I'll be fine if I can just rest a minute."

Colter couldn't fathom how his wife had kept going as long as she had. By all rights she should have keeled over hours ago. She looked tuckered out, and there were dark circles under her eyes that proved she wasn't as well as she professed to be. The dark circles were not enough to hide her loveliness and Colter damned the persistence of his need for her. Ever since he'd seen Kinyan in the tepee, his mind's eye had created images of the two of them, her uptilted breasts pressed to his hairy chest, her soft, smooth thighs pressed to his hard ones. The past week had been hell. It was too damn hard having her around and not being able to touch her. But he wasn't about to make that first move, because he wasn't sure he could have her body without giving her his soul.

The physical desire he'd been fighting all week on the range had been exacerbated by Kinyan's actions at home. When he'd moved into the guest bedroom to sleep, Kinyan had actually seemed disappointed. That didn't seem possible, since there had been three weeks left until their bedtime bargain ended. He'd ignored her signals and stuck to his guns. Yet each morning when he came back to Kinyan's bedroom to dress, he had cause to regret his decision. She was always asleep when he entered, but just the sight of her dusky rose skin, her black hair spread across the white pillowcase, her breasts rising and falling with each breath had tantalized him, spurring his desire.

Because they were no longer sleeping in the same room, Kinyan had made a habit of staying at the dinner table with him while Dorothea put the children to bed. She'd asked him inconsequential questions until he'd found himself sharing his dreams about the cattle and the ranch and especially his brindle bull, Hercules. He'd come to enjoy the time they spent conversing before they each turned to their own bedroom. And then she'd started touching him.

At first Colter had thought the touches were accidental. A brush of her fingertips against his when handing him his coffee. The press of her breast against his back when she leaned over to take his plate from the table. Her thigh laid against his when he continued the reading and writing lessons. But last night she'd come up behind him and rested her hands on his shoulders and then leaned down to his ear to speak. Colter shivered at the memory of her moist breath in his ear.

No, Kinyan was bent on seduction all right. Subtle, but effective. What he wanted to know was why she'd decided to give herself to him now. What had changed her mind? More importantly, how was he going to resist the physical need that made itself felt more urgently each time she touched him?

All day he'd been nursing the notion of working his wife so hard that she'd give up and go home. Then he couldn't be tempted to give in to the urge to pull her off Gringalet and hold her in his arms. He should have known better than to try to get her to quit. Hadn't he tried that once before and failed? Still, what other choice did he have? Colter eyed his true love, and his lips quirked at Kinyan's mulish expression.

"Can't you just give it up?" Colter pleaded softly, admiring her tenacity at the same time as he questioned her sanity.

"I can't!" Kinyan said fiercely. "Nothing's changed. If anything, it's even more important than before that I know everything I can about the ranch."

Now, Kinyan knew, there was no turning back. Before, if she had failed with the ranch, there had always been the thought in the back of her head that she could return to the agency camp. Only now there wasn't going to be any camp. There was going to be a war between the white man and the Sioux.

Besides, Kinyan wanted to stay close to Colter as much as she could. Once she'd made up her mind to consummate the marriage, Kinyan had tried different ways to back down on her demand for a six-week period of adjustment without admitting she was doing it. She had thought she could simply drop hints and let nature take its course. She had done her best to let Colter know he was welcome in her bedroom, but he had been unbelievably honorable about their agreement. Finally she'd realized that if she wanted to couple with

Colter before the six weeks was up, she was going to have to seduce her husband.

Kinyan had teased Colter mercilessly, always making sure she was seductively posed when he came in to dress in the morning, thinking that would be sufficient to provoke him to make the first move. Yet Colter had resisted the temptation she laid in his path. Then she had resorted to tentative touches and finally, last night, to something even more explicit. When he'd lurched out of the chair and stomped off, she knew she was making progress.

Well, Kinyan thought, she might as well take advantage of the break Colter had offered to get some rest. Perhaps tonight she could try something even more direct to convince Colter she wanted to be his wife in every way.

Before Kinyan could step down from her horse, Jeremy came tearing back up the hill.

"Ma! Colter! You gotta come quick. It's Josh. He's found the brindle bull!"

Colter felt a surge of joy at the news his brindle bull was both alive and on Triple Fork land. So high was his euphoria that it came as a more horrifying shock when he arrived at the carnage that lay at the far end of the arroyo where the brindle bull had passed.

"My God," Colter breathed. "The beast must be mad!"

"Josh! Where are you?" Kinyan shouted. "Answer me! Where are you?"

"I'm up here, Ma."

Fifteen feet up on a rocky ledge, Josh hugged the rough stone. At the base of the ledge, Josh's horse lay with its entrails spilling upon the ground. The animal was not yet dead, and it flailed and screamed until Colter pulled his .44 and released it from its misery.

"What the hell happened?" Colter demanded.

"I didn't do nothin'. He attacked my horse, Colter," Josh sobbed. "He charged at me, and I couldn't get outta the way."

"Let him come down first, Colter," Kinyan said sharply. "Come down, Josh."

"Where's the bull, Josh?" Colter asked. Only if the crazed brindle had gone would it be safe to allow Josh to come down.

"I . . . I don't know," the boy mumbled. "He gored my horse, and when I climbed up here, he raked my horse once or twice more with his horns. Then he took off. But, Colter . . ."

"What?"

"He's hurt, Colter. Somebody sliced him up pretty bad. His whole body was a mess of cuts. He bellowed some with pain, but mostly he was just plain mad."

"Hellfire!"

Colter had heard of outlaw bulls in Texas that attacked the smell of humans, and he recalled that Warren had mentioned an attack on one of his cowhands during the roundup by an outlaw bull. He wondered briefly whether Hercules was responsible for the attack on the Bar 7 cowboy. He hoped not. The cowboy had died.

There was always speculation as to what turned the bulls mean, but the mutilation Josh had described made the explanation pretty apparent in the case of his brindle bull. However, such an animal was a menace, and there was only one course of action that could be taken. The thought of destroying Hercules brought a pinched look to Colter's face.

"Come down now, Josh," Kinyan coaxed. "Relax and come down easy."

Josh obeyed his mother's soothing tone and soon stood once more upon solid ground.

"Mount up behind Jeremy," Colter ordered. "Until I know where that bull is, I don't want anybody on foot. Is that understood?"

Colter waited for the nods from his wife and her sons.

"Now, you three get those cattle moved out of the arroyo. Then go home. I'm going to find that bull." Colter didn't add, *and destroy it*. Perhaps Josh had been wrong. Perhaps there had been some good reason for the bull's attack. Now that there was a chance he had his bull back, he wasn't going to give up his dream so easily.

That evening, after the boys and Lizbeth were in bed, Kinyan slipped into the small wooden tub she'd set up in the bedroom she shared with Colter. She had braided her hair into a single plait, which she flipped outside the edge of the tub when she leaned her neck against the metal-tipped rim. She pulled her knees up higher and scooched down more comfortably to think. It really was too bad about Hercules. She had never seen Colter as animated as when he talked about the calves he'd get out of his great brindle bull.

Kinyan lathered herself with a special cake of lavender essence, a belated wedding gift from Dorothea. She paused when she heard Colter's greeting to Dorothea, listening for his tread upon the stairs. She checked to see what parts of her showed above the soapy water—only her head and shoulders and her knees—before Colter opened the door and entered the room.

Colter stopped in the doorway and nearly turned around and left when he found Kinyan in the tub. Tonight he was feeling the need of comfort and he was afraid that if she offered it, he would be likely to accept. But when he thought of leaving this haven, the outside world seemed too cold. So he placed his battered hat upon the bedside table, crossed to the wardrobe, and with his back to Kinyan, began to undress.

"Did you find him?" Kinyan asked.

It was an invitation to unburden himself, but Colter chose to mistake it as a question that required a simple answer.

"No."

Kinyan pursed her mouth in a rueful grimace. How could she help if he shut her out? She turned in the tub to watch Colter as he unbuckled his spurs, then removed his chaps and finally his gunbelt, which he hung on the bedpost at the head of the bed. He pulled off his black leather vest and unbuttoned his black shirt, and stood, unmoving, as though in a trance. Worry sat heavy upon his brow, slipped down to sag his shoulders, bound his feet to the floor. Kinyan felt a surge of sympathy that left her anxious to share his burden and lighten his load.

"Did you find tracks? A trail? Have you any idea where Hercules is?"

Colter winced under her prodding, then turned and barked a painful response.

"I found Petey. He'd been gored. Said it was the brindle bull. He died before I could help him."

"Oh no," Kinyan breathed. "Oh no."

She rose in the tub, lifted by the agony in Colter's blue eyes. The water streamed from her body like rivulets of tears for the youthful cowboy who'd died unmourned on the

214

prairie. Not thinking to reach for a towel, Kinyan crossed to Colter and stood before him, a sleek offering worthy of the gods but presented to mortal man.

Colter let his eyes touch her. He caressed the wispy tendrils that framed her face, the fine arch of her throat, the gentle undercurve of her breasts, the indentation of her waist, and the fullness of her hips. Then his eyes made the same leisurely journey from the juncture of her slim legs upward, noting the goose bumps that had risen on her forearms from the chill in the room. He ached with the need to cover her as the stallion covers the mare, warming her body, searing her soul with the fullness of him. Colter closed his eyes and waited, unmoving. He needed her. She had caught him in her web of desire and he was helpless to do other than as she bade him.

Kinyan felt the naked power she wielded over the man standing spread-legged before her. For a moment she considered yielding him his freedom, but the thought was fleeting and quelled when she lifted her hand and caressed a sharp cheekbone. Colter exhaled fully, a deep, sighing sound of surrender, and turned his head slightly to kiss her palm. Kinyan brought her other hand up to frame his face and then stepped closer to him.

Always in the past Colter had dressed in the darkness, hiding the scars that crisscrossed his chest. Now, as a last defense against her seduction, he shrugged from the black shirt and stood in the rosy glow of the single lantern, his ravaged body bared to Kinyan's gaze. Slowly, slowly, she lowered her eyes from his cherished face only so far as the scar at his throat. Her lips followed to heal the hurt. Colter shuddered under her touch. Kinyan raked her fingertips through Colter's silky hair until they rested at his nape. She could feel the rising tension as Colter waited for her reaction to his scarred body, which had so repulsed the other women he had known.

Emboldened by his taut control, Kinyan's fingertips slid to Colter's sinewy shoulders, lean and hard, then down to the chest, which had been slashed so many years ago. Colter flinched as Kinyan traced first one scar, and then another and another. Her lips followed her hands until Colter trembled with a mixture of gratefulness at her loving acceptance of his tortured body and tightly reined desire.

"Oh, my love," she whispered. "How you must have suffered."

Her words burst the dam of control Colter had erected, and he swept Kinyan's slick, wet body against his fiery flesh. He lifted her in his arms, bringing her mouth up to connect with his own in a flood of passion. He splayed his large hand across the base of her spine, urging the wet curls protecting her femininity against their masculine counterpart, still bound by his restraining Levi's.

Colter pulled his mouth from Kinyan's long enough to gasp, "I need you," then brought her lips back to his own, searching for the solace she could bring.

Colter's embrace was so tight it forced the breath from Kinyan, and she dug her fingernails into his shoulders to free herself. Dimly aware of Kinyan's struggle, Colter abruptly released her. While she sucked huge gasps of air to fill her tortured lungs, Colter's hands went to his belt buckle, then to the buttons as he released his Levi's. He leaned against the bedpost and yanked off his boots and socks, then lowered the jeans to reveal even more scars on his upper thighs.

The state of his need was plainly, intimidatingly visible, and Kinyan was startled to discover how terribly ignorant she was of men. It was all too apparent from the virile evidence before her eyes that all were not the same. In this way, as in others, they differed from one to another. It did not seem possible that she could accommodate Colter, and so it was with trepidation that she awaited his stalking move toward her.

"Colter, I . . ."

Kinyan stopped when she acknowledged that she desired the consummation of this marriage as much as she now feared it.

Colter did nothing to lessen her anxiety. Rather, the glazed brightness of his hooded eyes left no mistake as to his single-minded purpose as he approached Kinyan.

"My beautiful wife . . ." Colter murmured. He reached around to pull the single plait of black hair forward over her shoulder. He released the tie and unwound the braid, spreading the silky mass so that the tips of Kinyan's breasts jutted from the raven tresses that shielded her from view.

Colter caressed Kinyan as though he were admiring the fine work on a porcelain figurine. His fingertips traced each

216

smooth line of her face, disbelieving of the sculptor's skill in creating such a work of art. His hands rested on the curve of her throat, his thumbs at the pulse points there, feeling the rising excitement his touch evoked in his wife. He brushed aside the obscuring tresses and reached to cup Kinyan's breasts in his hands, letting his thumbs graze the nipples, his own body jerking as he witnessed the instant reaction.

He lowered his head slowly, his eyelids closing as his lips surrounded an erect nipple. Sweet! Oh God, she tasted so sweet!

Kinyan arched her entire body into Colter's, her head falling back and her breasts rising into his hands and mouth. Abruptly, Colter pulled away from her and stepped back. Kinyan stared at him, dazed by the swiftness of his retreat, not entirely recovered from his assault on her senses.

"Oh no," he growled low. "You'll not tempt me, or we'll be done before we've started. I've waited a long time for this evening, and I'll not be cheated of the satisfaction of knowing that our desire is equally matched before we mate."

"I do desire you," Kinyan admitted candidly with a shy smile.

"Not as much as I want you," Colter countered with a rueful grin.

"How can you possibly tell that?" Kinyan asked, genuinely curious. She had already anticipated joining with Colter with far more yearning than she'd ever imagined possible. His mere touch had brought her to readiness, and when she'd felt the liquid warmth spreading within her, she had, quite naturally, thought he would bring their closeness to its expected culmination.

"You're still able to talk, aren't you?"

"You mean I'm to be speechless with desire?" Kinyan asked in disbelief. "I had no idea you so much enjoyed having the last word."

"Oh, but I do."

A bubble of laughter, husky and low, escaped Kinyan when Colter swept her into his arms. He crossed to the bed and laid her crosswise upon it. When she tried to scoot around to put her head on a pillow, Colter's weight came down upon her to hold her in place.

"Huh-uh. Don't move. This is just perfect."

Kinyan's laugh sounded again at the novelty of his demand. It was a little thing but, all the same, something John had never done.

"All right, cowboy," Kinyan taunted. "Take my breath away."

It was both the right thing and the wrong thing to say. Colter's almost instantaneous physical response to her words left Kinyan without doubt as to his ability to rise to the occasion. When she would have commended him for his ardor, he dropped his mouth to her breast and suckled so strongly that he did, indeed, take her breath away. The blood swooshed through her veins, heading for her center, tingling all the way, then raced back up to her breasts, engorging them for Colter's pleasure.

Colter was caught up in an oblivion of sensation. He wanted. He needed. He yearned. He sought. He found. His callused fingertips searched over Kinyan's rib cage, identifying each rib, then slipped down to span her waist. His lips followed his hands, and he kissed his way across her chest. His thumbs locked on her hipbones while his mouth followed her concave belly down to the juncture of her legs, to the heat and heart of her.

Kinyan had allowed Colter's dizzying touch to bring her to a plane of exhilaration beyond rational thought. When his tongue dipped inside her to sip at the fount of life, her back arched off the bed and her hands flew to his hair to stop him. John had never done this! She couldn't form the words to stay his fingers and mouth. Instead, his touch sent her into a frenzy of action. With her hips and legs, she thrust toward freedom; with her hands, she held him captive to her need. A feverish groan wrenched its way from deep in her throat as the building tension roiled and convulsed within her, erupting finally in a shaking, shuddering release that left her lost in a whirling vortex of passion.

Colter rested his head on her thigh, a satisfied smile breaking across his contented features.

"Kinyan."

His only answer was the heavy panting of an animal that has run its full course and now, totally without energy to flee, is at the mercy of the hunter.

Colter raised himself to the length of his arms and moved his knees between Kinyan's thighs, spreading them even

218

further apart. Then he shifted to brace his palms on either side of her head. Her eyes were closed, her mouth open to draw in ragged breaths, her nostrils flaring with the extra effort to simply stay alive.

Colter kissed her temple, each closed eyelid, then one regal cheekbone and the other. His mouth went to her ear, and he took the lobe in his teeth and nipped it before he breathed, "You're not talking."

A smile broke on Kinyan's face, and a gusty laugh came from deep within her.

"That was . . ." she panted, the smile becoming a grin, "truly wonderful. But as you can . . . plainly hear . . . I am not yet . . . speechless."

"I guess we'll have to remedy that now."

Kinyan's eyes widened as Colter let his weight down onto his forearms, joining their hips. His mouth claimed hers in a sighing kiss so gentle it teased her mouth up to search for his. He ran his tongue along the sensitive inner skin of her upper lip, then tasted her more fully, dipping, plunging, ravaging. Kinyan's tongue came out to meet Colter's and she found herself with the urgent need to nip, to bite, to give back in full measure all she had received. Kinyan satisfied her craving, letting her mouth find Colter's face, his neck, his shoulders. She bit him once hard enough to rouse a growl, followed by an equally evocative tasting of her shoulder that sent shivers scattering.

Colter pulled away from Kinyan, searching her face, for he knew not what. Yet what he had unconsciously sought was there in full measure. Kinyan glowed with his loving, glowed with love for him.

Colter's eyes darkened with passion, and he came up on his arms once again and set himself between her legs, his aroused shaft probing at the entrance to her. She was so small! He pressed further and she opened to him, at last sheathing him fully. Then Colter began to thrust, the muscles in his buttocks contracting with each driving movement within her. Kinyan's legs wrapped tightly around him as though to keep him forever inside yet released him each time as he backed to thrust again. His strokes were so powerful Kinyan was pushed across the bed, until her head had fallen off the edge. She grasped at Colter's arms to keep herself from falling, and still he thrust. Higher and higher she pulled

219

herself along his body. Passionately she clung to him, wildly, fiercely fought to counter the savage thrusts that sent her soul beyond herself.

Then she was falling, spinning away, caught in a storm where the furies howled, where the angels raved, and she had only one source of hope. She reached out for it and held on tight while the furies were overpowered, the angels overcome, and she became one with Colter.

There were no words to describe what had happened. So Kinyan did not speak.

CHAPTER 18

COLTER PULLED KINYAN to his breast and lay back upon the pillows, holding her in his arms as much to comfort himself as to comfort her. What he had just experienced was beyond his comprehension. In the moment of extremity he had cried out with joy. Even now, the memory of the fulfillment he had found overwhelmed him. He couldn't help his quirking lips when he realized that except for her gasps of ecstasy, Kinyan hadn't spoken. He'd kept his promise better than even he had thought to do. Colter opened his mouth to speak and was appalled at the words on the tip of his tongue. He had been prepared to say, "I love you." Colter controlled the impulse, emptying his mind of all feeling. He would just rest a moment and then he would go.

Colter was so tired and satisfied, however, that sleep claimed him before he could rise and leave. Several times during the night he turned to the woman next to him to bid her good-bye, but each time he ended up making love to her instead. In the early dawn he awoke with a vague feeling of unease. As he lay in bed watching the sky change from purple shadows to pink delights, he knew what troubled him. He was asking to be ripped asunder if he let himself love Kinyan.

With the thought of saving himself, Colter gently set his wife away from him and rose from the bed. He wouldn't love again. He couldn't love again. He grabbed for his Levi's on the floor and yanked them up, then sat to pull on socks and boots. He crossed to the wardrobe and picked a clean shirt, tucking it into his jeans before buttoning them up and then buckling his belt. As he retrieved his gunbelt, he glanced at the ripe, wanton pose of the well-loved woman in his bed. Hellfire and damnation! It was too late. He already loved her. What was he going to do about it?

Still half asleep, Kinyan's sultry eyes drifted open when she heard Colter beside her. Seeing him completely dressed, Kinyan fought to remember if Colter had mentioned why he needed to leave her side.

"Where are you going?" she asked lazily.

The seductive tone of Kinyan's husky voice cinched Colter's determination to get away before he took her once more into his arms. He wanted some time alone to think. There was a valid reason for his absence that would not raise questions, so he felt no compunction about using it.

"I'm going after Hercules. You stay here and get some rest. You're exhausted. Besides, I don't want you or the boys on the range again until the brindle is caught. Do you understand?"

"No, I don't," Kinyan said, her shoulders coming up from the bed. "I should be out there helping you. I should be by your side."

"If you want to help," Colter replied, "make sure Josh and Jeremy stay home. I don't want to have to worry about scraping up the pieces of them that the bull would leave."

Colter whirled and fled the room.

Ignorant of Colter's emotional struggle, Kinyan smiled and hugged her arms about her, dozing fitfully. Colter had not said he loved her, but he'd given too much of himself not to have cared a little. And if he cared even a little, then that was a good start.

Kinyan's flushed appearance at the breakfast table brought raised brows from Dorothea, a concerned frown from Josh, and a suppressed smile from Jeremy, who, having noticed that Colter's bed hadn't been slept in, had made assumptions far beyond his years.

"Colter said we had to stay around the ranch house today while he hunts down his brindle bull," Josh complained. "How does he expect us to learn anything if he treats us like babies?"

"If it's any comfort to you, he's treating me the same way," Kinyan admitted. "As long as you have to be around anyway, you can do me a favor," she continued. "How about giving me some more writing lessons today?"

"I thought Colter was gonna do that," Jeremy said.

"I haven't been a very apt pupil," Kinyan conceded with a wry grin.

"What makes you think we're gonna have any more luck than he did?" Josh asked.

"I wasn't trying very hard before. I can see now it would be a good idea to know how to write, so if you boys are willing, I'd appreciate your help."

"Sure, Ma," they agreed. The idea of teaching their mother was different enough to catch their fancy. Lizbeth joined them, and the two boys eagerly spent most of the morning coaching their mother and sister on the alphabet. Amazingly, by noon Kinyan had mastered it.

"Now all you gotta do is learn how to put the letters together to make words," Jeremy said, commending his mother for the speed with which she had acquired the basics.

"First I think you should all take a break to eat," Dorothea said, interrupting them. "Anybody hungry?"

"As a bear," Josh said, grinning.

"As a seven-foot grizzly bear," Jeremy rivaled.

"As a seven-foot grizzly bear with three cubs," Kinyan finished with a laugh as she mussed Josh's and Jeremy's hair in turn. When the boys squirmed away, she pulled Lizbeth's pigtails and the little girl shrieked once in mock pain before leaping into her mother's arms.

It was a meal of leftovers, and Kinyan's mind was elsewhere while she ate. The previous night's energetic activities combined with her full stomach to make her sleepy. She was glad of the opportunity to take Colter's advice and rest.

"I'm ready for a nap," Kinyan confessed when she'd finished eating. "Lizbeth, would you like to join me?"

Although Lizbeth really was in no mood to sleep, it was tempting to lie down close to her mother.

"Will you look at a book with me?"

"Will you sleep when we're done?"

With an affirmative answer received for each question, mother and daughter headed upstairs.

"You boys stay around the ranch house," Kinyan reminded from the top of the stairs.

"What are you two going to do this afternoon?" Dorothea queried.

"Guess we'll hang around the bunkhouse," Josh said.

"We'll have supper at sundown. Don't stay too late. And don't make trouble!" Dorothea warned.

Josh grinned broadly and spread his arms wide.

"Who? Me?"

At Dorothea's clucking response, Josh and Jeremy headed for the bunkhouse. However, when they arrived, they found it abandoned.

"There's nobody here," Jeremy announced unnecessarily, plopping down on the trunk at the foot of Frank's bed.

" 'Course not. They're all out huntin' for that bull. Just like we would be if Colter weren't runnin' things." Josh hiked his foot up and rested his boot against the edge of the trunk where Jeremy sat, then leaned over to rest his forearm on his bent knee.

"He sure was countin' a lot on that bull," Jeremy said. "Think how awful it must be to know he's gonna have to destroy it."

"Yeah," Josh admitted. "I guess it must be pretty awful for him, all right. Why can't he just catch it? Maybe when it heals up it won't be so mean anymore."

"How's he gonna catch it? That bull won't let nobody get close without attackin'!"

"Let's go, Jeremy. I've got an idea."

Josh grabbed Jeremy by the arm and led him toward the barn, outlining his plan as he went.

"What if we could think of a way to catch Colter's brindle without gettin' attacked?"

"Boy, Colter'd sure be thankful if somebody could do that, all right," Jeremy agreed. "But we're supposed to stay off the range."

Josh threw a blanket over his horse's back and then added the saddle.

"Come on, Jeremy. Get saddled up," Josh urged. "Colter's gonna be so grateful we saved his bull, he's not gonna remember we disobeyed him."

224

Despite his better judgment, Jeremy followed his brother's lead.

Once on their way, the two boys began to plan carefully. They knew the bull had to be pretty crafty to catch Petey off guard, and Josh had firsthand experience as to the quickness of the animal. Neither boy was unaware that what they did was dangerous, but that only added to the fun of it.

They decided to set their trap at the watering place on Little Horse Creek where Hercules had last been spotted. In both previous attacks, Hercules had gone for the horse as well as the rider, so they left their mounts tied to a tree some distance away. Then they clambered over each other getting up the unevenly spaced branches of an ancient cottonwood that overhung the water and waited with their lariats looped and ready for the bull to come to drink. Their plan was simple. When the brindle was beneath them, they would snag him with their lassos, which were tied off in the tree. In their treetop hideaway, they would be perfectly safe from the massive bull's horns and hooves.

After several hours of sitting on a narrow branch in the shade of the tree watching the sun move lower in the sky, the merits of their plan began to pall.

"I'm thirsty," Jeremy admitted at long last.

"Me too."

"Ma's gonna be lookin' for us."

Both boys realized at the same time that if they lowered themselves from the tree, they were sitting ducks for the brindle if he showed up. In fact the longer they had waited, the more imminent the bull's arrival seemed and the more dangerous it appeared to be to get down and retrieve their mounts. They hadn't really thought so far as to plan how to get out of the tree if they didn't capture the bull.

"I'm goin' down," Josh said.

"Josh, don't!"

"You're bein' silly, Jeremy. That bull ain't gonna show."

Jeremy pursed his lips and put his thumb in the way of an ant trail along the cottonwood. As the tiny insects marched up and over his thumb, he said, "That bull can squash us as easy as I can squash these ants." To prove his point, he pinched his thumb and forefinger together, ending the lives of several of the tiny marchers.

Josh snorted in disbelief. "What're you talkin' about? That bull ain't within miles of here."

"A second ago those ants were safe," Jeremy countered. "If you're scared, I'll go get the horses and bring 'em back."

"Don't go, Josh," Jeremy pleaded. "I'm scared."

Josh laughed. "You baby! I can't believe what I'm hearin'."

Josh scrambled down the tree. He dropped as nimbly as a monkey from branch to branch. When he was on the ground, he grinned up at Jeremy through the leaves.

"I'll be back in a few minutes. Stay put till then."

"Be careful, Josh," Jeremy warned. "You just be careful."

Josh had been gone from sight for several minutes when Jeremy heard the first neighing scream. It was followed by a trumpeting whinny and more shrieks of fear and pain. The sounds were bone-chilling, and the hair stood on end all over Jeremy's body. He waited for his brother's shrill cry to pierce the dusk, but it never came. The screams of the horses continued, accompanied now by the grunting of the angry bull. The bull had followed their scent to the horses!

Josh was out there on foot!

The bile rose in Jeremy's throat. He swallowed it, but the burning sensation remained. His palms were cold and clammy and he rubbed them on his jeans in an attempt to wipe away his fear. He felt sorry for the horses and for Josh, but he felt more sorry for himself—because he knew his brother needed his help and he was too scared to go to him.

"Joooooosh! Answer me! Joooooosh!" he cried over and over. "Where are you? Are you all right? Where are you?"

As he watched the great orange ball of sun disappear between the pine-covered peaks of the Laramie Mountains to the west, Jeremy still had no answer to his mournful plea.

Kinyan rose from her nap well rested and spent the balance of the afternoon practicing her letters. She copied words from the primers Josh and Jeremy had used and found, to her delight, that writing was not so difficult once you got the hang of it. She couldn't wait to surprise Colter with how much she'd learned.

It never occurred to Kinyan to seek out her sons, for they had often idled away their free afternoons listening to stories in the bunkhouse or learning some new skill, from whittling to lassoing, from one of the cowhands. However, when supper time arrived and the boys still didn't show up, Kinyan set off for the bunkhouse to find them.

"I ain't seen 'em, Miz Colter," Frank told her. "I'll ask around, but there wasn't nobody here when we came in this afternoon."

Kinyan headed for the barn, afraid of what she would find. The two missing horses confirmed her worst suspicions. What could they have been thinking? So great was Kinyan's fear that when Colter dismounted before the barn just as the sun was leaving the sky, she threw herself into his arms, clinging tightly to his neck.

"I'm so glad you're home!"

Colter was no closer to an answer about how to deal with loving his wife than he had been when he left. So it was with some uncertainty that he accepted Kinyan's embrace. It was not until it dawned on him how desperately she held him that he realized something must be wrong. He pulled his wife's hands from around his neck and held her at arm's length as he asked, "What's the matter?"

"It's Josh and Jeremy," Kinyan said, her eyes round. "I've looked everywhere for them. They're not here, and their horses are missing. I'm afraid they may have gone after the bull."

"Hellfire! I thought I told you to keep them out of trouble."

When Kinyan paled from his censure, Colter drew her back into his arms.

"Don't blame yourself," he consoled her. "Nobody could make those two imps toe the line if they made up their minds to cross it. But we can't search for them tonight. God knows I'd go if I thought we had any chance at all of finding them, but it's pitch black out there and we haven't even got an idea where to start looking for them. I'm not giving that bull any more easy targets. We'll have to wait until tomorrow."

It was a solemn gathering at the supper table, and not much of the beans, steak, and biscuits were consumed from their plates.

"Where are Josh and Jeremy?" Lizbeth inquired.

"They're staying out tonight," Colter answered when Kinyan remained mute. "They'll be home tomorrow," he reassured Lizbeth.

At this response, Kinyan looked at Colter with such hope and trust that his lips thinned and he thrust his hand through his hair. She had no right to believe he could save the boys. If the bull found them first, they would very likely be killed. The two youthful faces came to his mind's eye, along with the picture of what had been left of Petey after the bull had stomped and gored him. The thought of losing those two innocents racked him with tremors. It was then Colter glanced from Dorothea to Kinyan to Lizbeth and realized that he had come to love not only his wife, but her family as well. It was a shocking admission and one that left him feeling trapped.

As he had every evening since he'd made his peace with her, Colter tucked Lizbeth in for the night. When he had accepted her kiss and kissed her in return, he met her bright-eyed gaze with a troubled stare of his own.

"Don't worry," Lizbeth whispered conspiratorially as she patted Colter's hand comfortingly. "You'll find Josh and Jeremy."

A rueful grin found its way to Colter's lips. "Not much gets by you, Lizbeth, does it?"

"I snuck out to the barn when I was supposed to be napping and I heard Josh and Jeremy talking. They were gonna try to catch your bull 'cause they know how much he means to you."

Colter felt a warmth rising inside him at this evidence that his feelings for the boys were reciprocated, but he forced it down to give his attention to the more important information Lizbeth had just unwittingly provided.

"Did they say where they were going?"

"No. Are you gonna be able to find them, Colter?"

"I'll find them, Lizbeth. Now you get some sleep."

"I love you, Colter."

"Good night, Lizbeth."

Colter stopped at the door to the guest bedroom, then turned down the hall to Kinyan's room. He told himself he just wanted to see her. He told himself he wasn't going to

228

stay. He entered the room noiselessly. Kinyan lay with her eyes closed, and he admired her for a moment before he realized she wasn't asleep.

"Colter?"

"Yes, Kinyan."

"Will you hold me?"

Colter sat down next to her, then reached over to bring Kinyan within his embrace. Her head fit the niche in his shoulder, and he could feel her moist breath on his throat.

"They're so young."

Kinyan had spoken so quietly Colter barely heard her.

"Try to get some sleep. We can't help them tonight. We'll get an early start in the morning, and we'll take Frank and Boley along with us."

Colter felt Kinyan's frantic grip tightening, just like the invisible ties binding him to this woman and her children. For a moment he felt suffocated by the demands they made on him, but then he forced himself to relax and the feeling eased. He lay down beside her and held her until he felt her relax into sleep. The knowledge that he must make a decision weighed upon him like a millstone around a drowning man's neck. He knew he should leave, but he couldn't go. For better or for worse, he was committed. Whatever the new day brought, it would bring it to them as a family.

By the break of dawn, Kinyan, Colter, and the two cowboys were well on their way to the spot on Little Horse Creek where the brindle bull had last been seen and where the twins were most likely to have started searching for him. Colter's efforts to persuade Kinyan to stay home had been futile, as he'd known they would be, but he made sure she brought along her Winchester rifle and that she was ready to use it.

They heard the sounds of the bull long before they reached the creek. Its hooves pawed the ground, and every so often they could hear it bellow in rage. As they passed under a stand of cottonwood, Kinyan thought she heard Jeremy's voice. When the faint call came again, she stopped Gringalet to listen.

"Ma."

The croaking call was more distinct, and Kinyan turned her horse back toward it.

"Colter! Back here. It's Jeremy."

"Boley, you and Frank keep an eye out for the bull," Colter cautioned. "Maybe we're going to be lucky after all."

Kinyan sat her horse at the base of the cottonwood where Jeremy was perched high above her. Her gaze was focused on the fresh gouges in the trunk, where the bull had evidently vented his ire.

"Son, are you all right? Is Josh up there too?"

Colter was unconscious of his use of the term *son* but to Jeremy, Colter's voice and his use of the familiar address were most welcome.

"Josh went to get the horses. He never came back," Jeremy rasped. "You gotta find him."

Jeremy had yelled so long and so loud that he'd made himself hoarse, but not before he'd attracted the bull's attention. The brindle had come and spent part of the night at the base of the tree, raking it with his horns, pounding it with his shoulder as though to shake his quarry from the limbs. The night of exposure to the cold had left Jeremy shivering, but it was the certain knowledge of what must have been Josh's fate that made it impossible for him to control his muscles sufficiently to climb down from the tree.

"Can you get down, Jeremy?"

"I can't move, Ma. I'm too stiff."

"I'll get him."

Before Kinyan could warn him to be careful, Colter had slipped off Hoss and started up the tree. When he reached Jeremy, he could see the boy was suffering from exposure.

"Can you hold on to my neck?"

"I'll try."

Colter turned his back to Jeremy, and the boy grasped Colter's shoulders and throat and hung on as they descended the cottonwood. When Colter reached the ground, he crouched, so when Jeremy let go, he fell back prone in the grass. The youth was too exhausted to raise himself and he simply lay there. Colter turned and lifted Jeremy into his arms, cradling him like a baby. Colter raised his eyes to Kinyan and there was the unspoken admission that this might be the only son they had left. It was a thought too painful to be accepted, and Kinyan abruptly wheeled Gringalet.

"We have to find Josh," she said curtly.

"Frank, take Jeremy up with you." Colter gently raised the boy into Frank's arms, and the cowboy's embarrassed flush told how moved he was to be made the trustee of the child. "Stay here and wait for us," Colter ordered as he mounted Hoss.

Colter, Kinyan, and Boley had no difficulty following the noise to the bull's location. It was a grim sight that met their eyes. The mutilated bull swayed back and forth in an open space surrounded by a copse of cottonwood. It stood guard over the carcasses of the two dead horses. Also visible was a child's foot, extending on the ground beneath one of the horses.

A red wall of fury rose behind Kinyan's eyes when she saw the booted foot. Without thought, she pulled her .44 Winchester from its buckskin scabbard and, shooting crazily, charged the brindle bull.

Colter saw a bullet hit the bull's shoulder, but it only seemed to further enrage the animal, which put its head down and charged just as crazily toward Kinyan. As the distance closed between them, Colter pulled the Winchester from the leather sheath on his saddle and aimed between the rolling white eyes of the onrushing beast. In the milliseconds before he pulled the trigger, the hopes and dreams he'd lived with along the difficult trek from Texas flashed before him. When he heard the whine of the bullet and saw the magnificent animal crash to the ground in front of Kinyan, Colter felt the death of his dream as surely as he felt the lifeblood oozing from the dying beast. The brindle had killed and therefore deserved to die, but the beast had been mad with pain, and it was man who had made it that way. With the death of his dream came a roiling rage at the man who had caused its loss. Ritter Gordon would pay.

Kinyan was already on the ground next to the dead horses, trying to retrieve Josh's body. Boley had come down off his horse and was trying to keep her out of the bloody mess. It could only worsen her grief to see what was left of Josh.

"Josh!"

It was a cry of agony wrenched from Kinyan's depths. Tears he was unaware of slid down Colter's face as, together with his wife, they grieved the loss of their son.

"Ma! Colter! Get me out of here!"

The muffled voice coming in the still aftermath of Kinyan's cry left all of them aghast. Within moments, Kinyan was yanking and tearing at the horse, while Colter and Boley rushed to help her. As they pulled the boy from inside one of the downed horses, it was impossible to tell whether they should be encouraged, for he was covered in blood.

"Oh my God," Boley breathed.

When they finally freed him from the horse's belly far enough to see his features, a shaky grin split Josh's face.

Kinyan burst into tears of joy. Colter plucked the boy from the morass and held him tight against his chest, while Kinyan put her arms around them both.

Josh was bursting with the need to explain what had happened.

"I'm all right, Ma," he choked out over his own tears, which had started when he saw the wet faces that surrounded him. "I was gettin' the horses when the bull showed up. He gored my horse right away, and then he went to work on Jeremy's. I was half under my horse when it fell down anyway, and the bull had gutted it, so I just slipped inside. It was warm, and it was safe. I could hear Jeremy yellin', but I didn't wanta excite the bull by makin' any noise. Hercules went away, but I was afraid he'd come back, so I just stayed where I was."

Kinyan thought of the night her son had spent in the dark, bloody cavern while the bull, smelling the boy within but unable to reach him, had hacked steadily at the horse with its horns. She shuddered at how close she had come to losing her sons, and would have collapsed except for her hold on Colter.

Having heard the shots, Frank rode up to join them. When Jeremy first saw the bloody bundle in Colter's arms, his face paled. When his brother turned to smile at him, Jeremy shook his head in disbelief.

"I called you," he rasped to Josh angrily. "Why didn't you answer me? I thought you were dead!"

"It's a wonder you aren't both dead!"

Colter's furious voice crackled in the quiet of the glade,

and Josh stiffened in the man's arms. "There'll be time enough for explanations later, and I'll have one from each of you before I'm done."

On that ominous note, Colter handed Josh up to Boley.

"I ain't a baby," Josh mumbled, embarrassed to be held thus by the cowboy.

"When you two boys start acting a little more grown up, I'll treat you a little less like infants."

Colter helped Kinyan mount Gringalet and threw his own leg over Hoss's back. His stern visage left no doubt that there would be repercussions when they got home that would cause the twins to think twice before they started on their next escapade.

Kinyan glanced at Colter, and a sense of peace flowed within her. Here was a father for her sons. Concern was etched on his features. He had promised discipline, but she knew it would be tempered with love. If only, she thought, he could learn to love her as much.

Josh and Jeremy traded guilty glances. Then the two boys grinned at each other. It had been a great adventure, however frightening at moments, and they were alive and safe and on their way home. Colter had yelled at them, but Jeremy remembered that Colter had called him son, and Josh remembered that Colter had cried when he thought him dead. The sun was shining, and it was going to be a wonderful day.

"I'm not going back to the ranch with you," Colter announced.

Kinyan waited for an explanation.

"I'm going into Cheyenne."

"I'll go with you," she offered.

"No. I'm going to settle a debt. I won't need your help, Kinyan. This is personal. You boys get yourselves cleaned up, and stay around the house until I get back," he instructed. "Frank, I'm leaving you in charge. Boley, I want to talk to you before I go."

Colter took Boley aside and spoke privately with him. Boley glanced up once or twice at Kinyan with a look that aroused her curiosity. Boley nodded once, then held his horse up when Colter kicked Hoss and waved a cursory good-bye.

When they arrived back at the ranch house, Kinyan

gratefully accepted Boley's offer to take care of the horses while she took the twins in to get cleaned up. Once she got into the house, however, Kinyan realized she'd left her .44 Winchester in her scabbard on the saddle. She'd been taught well about the care and cleaning of the rifle by Colter, so once she had Josh in the tub, she trudged back out to the barn to retrieve it. Kinyan paused just inside the open barn door when she heard voices.

"Colter plans to have it out with Ritter in town 'bout that brindle. Hell, we drove that ornery critter all the way from Texas. Sure was a shame to put him down like that," Boley said.

"Colter and Ritter—that's one meetin' I'd surely like to be there to see, all right," Frank said with a low whistle of appreciation. "You ever seen Colter draw, Boley? It's sure a pretty sight."

"Once. He's fast, all right."

"Well he beat Ritter before," Frank said. "Don't s'pose he'll be much bothered to do it again, 'cept that Ritter, he don't always fight fair. Wouldn't take much for Sheriff Wiley Potts to look the other way if Ritter don't cheat obvious like. Hell, wish he'da let one of us come along with 'im. Surely wouldn't like to see the missus become a widow again so soon, nor them children lose their pa, neither."

"I'm just glad he didn't let his wife know where he was goin'," Frank continued, shaking his head. "Way she followed us on that trail drive, no tellin' what she'd do if she heard 'bout this."

"Yeah," Boley agreed. "She's some woman, all right. Colter wasn't taking any chances. I'm stuck here in the barn watching her horse to make sure she don't go nowhere."

"Well, it's gonna be a cold one. Hope you got yerself a warm blanket."

When Frank left the barn, Boley lovingly set his saddle on a sawhorse and went to work with the saddle soap. He was right proud of that hand-tooled saddle. His pa had given it to him ten years ago, and except for some natural wear around the horn, he'd kept it looking near new.

So engrossed was Boley with the memories of home and family that working with the saddle always raised, he failed to see the slight figure that slipped from the shadows and slid out through the barn door.

Kinyan made it to the settee in the parlor before the trembling in her legs made her knees buckle and she landed with a jounce on the horsehair stuffing.

According to Boley, Colter had gone into Cheyenne for the express purpose of engaging Ritter in a gunfight! How could he take such a chance with his life when she needed him, when she loved him and hadn't even told him so yet?

After the trail drive, Kinyan had been obliged to promise Colter she would obey him strictly from now on in order for him to take up his lessons where he'd left off. And she'd meant with her whole heart to keep that promise. So she hadn't argued once Colter had said he didn't want her to accompany him to Cheyenne. She'd dutifully obeyed him and come straight home. And she had to admit he hadn't actually lied about where he was going. He was going to Cheyenne to settle a debt.

However, with the information supplied by Frank and Boley, Kinyan reconsidered the situation. If what Frank said was true, Ritter might catch Colter in an ambush. Maybe those two cowboys were willing to trust Colter to his own devices, but she had too much at stake!

Kinyan could name at least one superb reason why she should follow Colter—his own safety. But there was a good chance that if Colter caught her disobeying him again, she would have no hope of convincing him to continue teaching her about the ranch. But that was a minor consideration compared to the prospect of Colter being wounded or, perish the thought, killed.

She would follow Colter, but she wouldn't interfere unless Ritter tried something underhanded. She'd keep her presence a secret from Colter unless and until she was needed. But hellfire! That meant dressing up like a cowboy again. Without a disguise, she wouldn't be able to get close enough to Colter to help. Then she saw a second advantage. If her help wasn't needed, she could spur Gringalet back home, and Colter would never be the wiser.

She'd have to act quickly. She didn't have much time if she wanted to be sure to get to Cheyenne before Colter confronted Ritter. Kinyan stood up and realized her legs had stopped shaking. She wiped her sweaty palms on her Levi's, then pulled her .44 from its holster and checked the rounds. There was something vaguely comforting about the feel of the heavy weapon, and Kinyan held it a moment longer before she returned it to its holster. If Ritter Gordon tried anything, he'd soon find out he was no longer dealing with a helpless, defenseless widow.

Now, Kinyan thought, how am I going to get Boley out of the barn?

CHAPTER 19

IT WAS NEARLY DARK when Kinyan rode into Cheyenne. The weather had taken care of Boley before she'd needed to use the elaborate plan she'd concocted. Incredibly, fall not yet having arrived, it was snowing. Boley had concluded nobody would be stupid enough to ride to Cheyenne when a winter storm was on its way and had left his lonely post in the barn for the warmth of the bunkhouse. That's when she had ridden out on Gringalet.

Kinyan hunched down into the fleece-lined coat under her yellow slicker, trying to keep the cold out. For once there was absolutely no wind, and the powdery flakes came down so slowly and softly it created a world of mystical enchantment. There was a fine clean layer of white on the ground, and Kinyan almost hated to walk Gringalet down the street knowing he was destroying that perfection.

It was Tuesday night, and the saloons, gambling palaces, and variety houses were suspiciously quiet. Perhaps others were wiser than she and unwilling to challenge the weather. Kinyan only hoped she and Colter got back home before a real blizzard broke. The Wyoming weather had a tendency to be downright scary at times.

Kinyan searched the few animals tethered to the hitching posts and finally spotted Hoss in front of the Variety Palace. Second thoughts rambled around in her head. What would Colter say if he found out she'd followed him? If she loved her husband as she professed to, shouldn't she have shown a little more trust in him? She did trust Colter, Kinyan argued to herself. It was Ritter she didn't trust.

237

The first thing she had to do was stable Gringalet. If Colter saw the stallion, he would know she was in town. Kinyan headed for the stable a few streets over, and after she'd boarded her horse, she looked to her appearance. She tucked her braided hair up under her hat, then pulled the hat down low. She hunched down once again in the yellow slicker, which entirely engulfed her figure. If she kept her head down, she ought to be able to pass for a very short cowboy.

It took a great deal of courage for Kinyan to push through the heavy door that had been closed over the threshold of the Variety Palace. She had never before entered a saloon. Once inside, the heat, the smell, the joyous life of the place assaulted her senses. Her eyes nearly bugged out at the garishly bright costumes worn by Rosie's girls as they entertained the few cowhands at the tables in the saloon. Kinyan's eyes narrowed in their search for Colter, and her heart sank when she didn't find him in the room. Of their own volition, her azure eyes followed the curving banister to the upstairs. Surely he hadn't gone up there!

When Kinyan might have turned and fled, she heard Colter's laugh from the back of the room. His laugh? Perusing the layout of the Palace, she realized that if she stood at the bar on the left, she would be able to watch Colter from the mirror above it. So, without allowing herself to think and perhaps chicken out, Kinyan stepped up to the far end of the mahogany bar, stuck her boot on the brass rail, and ordered a drink.

"Whiskey or beer?"

"Uh . . . beer," Kinyan decided.

The bartender set the drink in front of her but didn't move away.

"Pay as you go. Five cents," he clipped out.

"Oh." Kinyan was rattled. She hadn't brought any money with her. "I . . . uh . . ."

At that moment, Rosie appeared at Kinyan's elbow with her arm around Colter's waist.

Kinyan hunkered down even farther into the slicker and pulled her hat down to cover her eyes.

"Some problem, Jake?" Rosie asked.

"Just asked him to pay for the beer, Rosie."

"Guess I left my wad in the bunkhouse," Kinyan mumbled an octave lower than her own voice.

"I'll take care of it, cowboy," Colter said. "I've been there myself."

To Kinyan his voice sounded husky, sexy, and a fire kindled deep inside her and insidiously wound its way up to her face, and she blushed a deep, dark red. This fire was unlike any Kinyan had ever experienced and had nothing to do with desire. This fire was born of a dragon—the mythical green-eyed monster—and Kinyan felt its raging heat burning within her. Colter actually had his arm draped around that painted woman's bare shoulder! And that woman had her hand tucked into the belt of Colter's jeans!

"Thanks," Kinyan grated. It was a strangled sound lost in Rosie's next words.

"Come on upstairs, Colter," Rosie cooed. "Ritter won't be back from Chicago till next week. You might as well stay and enjoy what I have to offer. You seemed to like it well enough last time."

Last time?

Kinyan closed her eyes to fight the dizziness that swept over her. Colter's voice had faded, and Kinyan realized he and Rosie had moved toward the stairs.

Colter hadn't planned to be with the whore. That much was plain from what the woman had said. Her invitation hadn't suggested any prior arrangements. But it was also clear he had been with her before. Had she sent her husband into this woman's arms when she'd refused him her bed? The thought sickened Kinyan.

"You all right, cowboy?"

The deep bass voice rumbled next to her, and Kinyan jerked herself upright to greet this next challenge.

"I'm fine."

Kinyan spoke before she thought, which was a good thing, because if she'd thought first she probably would have choked on her words. Kinyan shivered involuntarily. The man standing next to her was the most viciously ugly creature she'd ever seen. Large, vacant black eyes dominated the square face. He had no lips, just a thin line where they ought to be, and when he spoke a black cavern appeared, lined with crooked, fanglike teeth.

Although he was obviously a young man, his hairline had already begun to recede and his bald scalp, decorated with a wisp or two of long black hair just at the center of his forehead, glistened in the light from the chandelier above the bar. His dark, bushy eyebrows seemed intent on compensating for the lack of hair on his head, straying here and there above his browline. A thick black, gray, brown, and yellow beard adorned the weak chin and pouchy cheeks, doing its part along with the eyebrows to alleviate the nakedness of the man's head. He had let the little hair he still had grow long and stringy, clubbing it back in a tail that hung down over his collar.

The gruesome head didn't fit with the body of the man, which shouted strength, virility, and toughness. He wore a flashy red sateen shirt, a concha belt, and Mexican chaps over his jeans, and he smoked a long, thin black cigar. Kinyan realized with a start that he must be up from the south. She gaped at the huge hand he had extended toward her.

"Name's Bart," the brute said.

What was she supposed to do? Did Bart the Brute want something? When she didn't reach to shake the hand, vacant eyes crinkled at the corners and the nonexistent lips opened to reveal snaggled teeth.

"Man of my own heart." The brute chuckled, clapping Kinyan on the back. "Don't trust a soul till you know him," he whispered in Kinyan's ear.

Kinyan was too frightened to do more than nod quickly. She choked on the fetid breath that came from the gaping maw. On top of everything else, Bart the Brute was undeniably drunk.

"That fellow, now," the brute continued, gesturing toward Colter. "Who'd think he's a murderer, nice-looking cowboy like that?"

Kinyan's amazed expression wrought another chuckle from Bart the Brute.

"It's true. I oughta know. Came all the way from Texas to claim the reward. There's two thousand dollars on his head, dead or alive. I sure ain't thinkin' to take 'im back alive," Bart said with a pleased guffaw. "Jus' gotta make my plans, that's all. Gotta make plans."

The brute turned his head back to the whiskey in front of

him and mulled over the color of the liquid, the shape of the glass, the smoothness of the counter, then idly squashed a cockroach that scurried across the shiny surface.

Kinyan turned pleading eyes toward Colter. Whatever he'd done in Texas and for whatever reasons, he was her husband and she didn't want him killed by riffraff. She wished she'd never come. She wanted to be home. She wanted Colter home safe with her to explain what Bart the Brute had said. And to explain about the whore.

Kinyan surreptitiously observed the pair at the stairs. Their heads were close in intimate conversation. Rosie pressed her lips to the scar at Colter's throat and Kinyan's stomach revolted. Colter pushed Rosie back away from him gently and Kinyan could see him laugh and shake his head. Then Rosie seemed to be pleading again, and at long last, Colter bent and spoke earnestly to her. Rosie nodded her head twice, spoke again, and a smile came to her lips. Then they kissed each other tenderly on the mouth. Kinyan's fingers curled into claws. She could have raked Colter's eyes out at that moment had she been within touching distance. Perhaps it was just as well that she wasn't.

"I gotta go, cowboy," the brute announced to Kinyan. "I promised someone I'd deliver a message to that man from Texas before I kill him." The brute was watching Colter, and his eyes registered so much pleasure at the prospect of cold-blooded murder, it rocked Kinyan back on her heels.

"What're ya gonna do?" Kinyan asked with a nonchalance she certainly didn't feel.

The brute's eyes narrowed calculatingly. "Don't you go gettin' no ideas to help yourself to this reward," he warned. "I ain't gonna share it with nobody. Least of all some baby-faced cowboy."

Kinyan reddened. "I never thought—"

The brute grasped Kinyan at the throat of her slicker with a hairy fist and raised her off the ground, bringing her face close up to his. Kinyan kept her chin lowered, fearing the brute would recognize features that were too feminine to belong to even a youthful boy. "Just mind your own business. Understand?"

"Y—yes, sir . . . Bart," Kinyan stammered.

The brute laughed deep from his belly and dropped Kinyan. She staggered unsteadily before she regained her footing. She hesitated to run for the door, not wanting to meet Colter, but a quick check showed he was gone. Kinyan raced for the threshold with the coarse, bass guffaw following her into the night. Right away, Kinyan noticed Colter's horse was gone. At least he hadn't gone upstairs with Rosie! She raced for the stable where she'd left Gringalet.

Kinyan planned to follow Colter for a short way to make sure Bart didn't come after him tonight, but then she'd push Gringalet so she could be home in bed when Colter arrived. She didn't trust herself to talk with him tonight. She wanted some time to think over everything that had happened.

The fact Colter was wanted by the law could be explained and excused. Hadn't he told her he'd taken revenge on some men who'd hurt his family? Yet that knowledge hadn't changed her feelings about him.

But this matter of infidelity was different. In the first place, fidelity was a part of their marital bargain. He'd agreed not to have other women! But that was before he'd known she would turn him away from her bed. Kinyan groaned. She should have known Colter would need a woman. But Kinyan couldn't forgive or excuse him so easily. She needed time for the hurt to reach manageable proportions. The thought of Colter's lips on those of the painted woman stabbed at her like a knife.

Kinyan's jealous rage grew, and by the time she reached the stable, she was ready to spit nails. Her yank on the stable door would have pulled it off the hinges, except the door was locked and nearly tore her arm out of its socket instead. She was locked out, and Colter was on his way home! He would find out she was gone and she'd have to explain everything. The consequences of that eventuality sent Kinyan stomping off to find the hostler.

It took Kinyan nearly half an hour to hunt down the elderly man. By then her fury had mushroomed so much that when the poor fellow tried to tell her a blizzard was on its way and she had no business traveling, Kinyan pulled her Colt. She wasn't taking no for an answer! Believing in the power of the Peacemaker, the hostler quickly acceded to Kinyan's wishes, and she found herself mounted on Gringalet and on her way out of town.

But by now Kinyan was far behind Colter, and the storm

was worsening. The wind had returned with a vengeance and the few gentle snowflakes had become whirling flurries of icy chips. It was going to be a long, frigid trip home, but Kinyan was grimly determined to make it.

Kinyan was not the only one determined to travel in the inclement weather. Bart "the Brute" Jefferson had decided the snow would provide the perfect conditions to ambush Colter. The Texan couldn't be far ahead of him, and he'd already discussed with Ritter the various places for waylaying Colter between Cheyenne and the Triple Fork ranch. Ritter had left the details of the ambush up to Bart and had taken off for Chicago, where no suspicion could fall on him for Colter's death, but Ritter had been adamant that Bart deliver a message before he killed the cowboy.

"I don't want him killed before he knows I'm responsible for the death of his wife and his child. And I want him to know that I'll have Kinyan when he's gone," Ritter had said.

"Be safer just to kill 'im," Bart had replied. "I don't like takin' chances."

Ritter hadn't exactly been sympathetic to Bart's concerns. He countered with, "You owe me."

"Owe you? Shit, I don't *owe* you nothin!" Bart argued. "I'm doin' you one damn big favor just showin' up in this ball-freezin' territory."

"When you needed me, I came through for you."

"I ain't never gonna be rid of that debt, is that it? I ain't never gonna be square with you for gettin' Ma off my back twenty years ago. How many men have I killed for you, Ritter, to settle that debt? Eight? Nine?"

"Eleven. Colter makes twelve."

"Shit, Ritter. I know I wouldn't even be alive now if you hadn't beat the crap outta Ma that time she came after me with a whip, but you lit out and left me to face that no-good bastard fourth—"

"Fifth," Ritter inserted.

"—fifth husband. He hadn't figured out yet what a black widow spider our Ma was, and he thought what you done wasn't much in keepin' with the honorin' of your ma that the Good Book calls for. He damn near killed me outta Christian kindness after you left."

"But Ma never bothered you again, did she?"

"Shit, no. You killed her."

"I repeat. You owe me."

Bart had sighed and admitted, "All right. Shit. I owe you."

Bart didn't think he was ever going to get over that feeling of obligation to his older half-brother. Ritter was born of their mother's first husband. He'd been born six years later, of the third. Both of her children had been serious mistakes and total pains in the ass as far as Madeline Sampson Gordon Bellows Jefferson Thomas Flynn was concerned, and consequently they'd both survived more beatings than Bart could count. They'd also survived an endless series of husbands with a voracious desire for the voluptuous Madeline. But in each case, when their money had run out, the black widow woman had found a way to rid herself of her mate.

Ritter and Bart had never been sorry to lose a one of those fathers—except that "in between husbands" was the worst time for them because it left Madeline with a bad temper and no one to take it out on except her two sons. It got so they couldn't wait to get their next pa. However cruel the men were, they couldn't hold a candle to an unmarried Madeline. It was during one of those unmarried moments, however, that Madeline had come after Ritter, only to discover that he'd finally gotten big enough to fight back. After that, she'd ignored Ritter and turned all her motherly attentions to Bart.

Ritter had left Bart to fend for himself against their ma, and Bart had taken a lot of lickings before that final one. That's why he'd been so surprised that night when Ritter had told their ma to leave off hitting him with the whip. Ritter hadn't had much trouble taking the whip from Madeline, and it seemed like she was willing to just forget the whole thing when Ritter spit on her. She went crazy then and scratched his face, and Ritter responded like a wild man himself, pummeling their ma long past her ability to resist his attack, beating her to death.

Once Madeline was dead, her fifth husband had inherited everything. Then he died a month later in an accident, and Ritter got it all. Bart had often wondered later if Ritter hadn't planned to get rid of them both. It wouldn't have bothered Bart one bit. Ritter convinced Bart the local orphanage was the best place for him, and looking back, Bart had to agree that the beatings hadn't been near as bad as at home. Ritter had told Bart to look him up when he got out of the orphanage, that he'd be waiting for him then, and Bart had looked forward to it and done his time at the orphanage patiently.

Sure enough, when he got out, Ritter suggested a job for him. There was a man with a price on his head giving Ritter trouble. If Bart killed the man, he could have the reward money. It had seemed like a simple enough thing to do, and once he'd killed the man, Bart knew he'd found his niche in life. Bounty hunting was legal, it was pleasurable, and it paid good money. Normally, Bart didn't like to leave the warm, dry San Antonio weather, but he'd come to Cheyenne at Ritter's behest because the reward was good, and after all, he would always owe his brother for ridding them both of the black widow woman.

Bart focused his thoughts on his quarry and knew he'd chosen the most opportune occasion for his attack. Tonight, Colter would be tucked down into his slicker to stay warm and wasn't likely to be watching where he was going. Tonight, the first-quarter moon danced with the clouds that bore the gusting flurries. At intervals, the clouds dipped to reveal the moonbeams that gave Bart the light he needed to be able to wound, but not kill, on the first shot. He'd make sure the cowboy was incapacitated but alive when he got to him. Yes, tonight was going to be absolutely perfect.

As though he'd read Bart's thoughts, Colter pulled up the sheepskin jacket he wore under his slicker to cover his ears and hunkered over to let Hoss's body cut the wind. It was bitter cold, but soon he'd be with his wife and family and he would never leave them again. He hadn't found Ritter in Cheyenne, but the information he'd gotten from Rosie had helped him decide on the best way to settle his debt. He would hit Ritter where it would hurt the pompous man most. He was going to take Ritter's place as head of the Association. It might not happen right away, but he was going to prove the value of his open range ideas and convince the Association members that he'd be a better guide for their future endeavors. He'd made a stop at the telegraph office before he'd left town and sent for his library of books. He wanted to teach Kinyan all about the new ideas he planned to suggest to the Association.

Colter replayed his conversation with Rosie in his head. He hadn't been physically tempted by the woman. He'd only wanted to be home with his wife. So when Rosie had cajoled him to stay, he'd finally admitted to her what he had never admitted to Kinyan. He loved his wife. He wanted to be with her. At the thought of Kinyan, he felt his body rouse even in this frigid cold. Colter grinned. Kinyan wasn't going to get any argument out of him tonight!

Colter had ridden half the distance to the ranch before he suspected he was being followed. He turned his head casually, as though inspecting his saddlebags, and saw it again— a flash of movement. Colter tried to think who might want to follow him, but he drew a total blank. Unless Ritter had sent someone. He looked again. A yellow slicker! The young cowboy at the bar? The youth hadn't seemed particularly dangerous, but then most killers didn't look like what they were.

While Colter's attention was focused behind him, a hundred feet to his left, Bart the Brute settled himself in the thin layer of snow. He lay prone, the Winchester held propped in his arms, while he squinted to take aim at Colter. He'd hit the cowboy with his first shot, then take care of the horse with his second shot to make sure it didn't carry his prey away. Bart took a deep breath, held it, and squeezed the trigger.

The impact of the bullet in his upper thigh threw Colter out of the saddle, so although Bart couldn't stop his second shot, he at least raised the rifle enough for the bullet to miss the roan. He hadn't really wanted to destroy the animal, but he would have done so if it had been necessary. Bart scrambled down the slight incline to where Colter lay unconscious. The awkward fall from the saddle had worsened Colter's injury by breaking his leg. Bart yanked Colter's gun from his holster and, checking for other weapons, found the knife in Colter's boot.

"Wake up!" he snapped, kicking Colter brutally in his wounded leg.

The excruciating pain brought Colter to groggy consciousness.

"I got a message to give you from Ritter Gordon before I kill you. Ritter said to tell you he remembers your wife and kid. He said to tell you your wife was real good in bed and he

246

was real sorry to have to kill her. And you should have shut the kid up. He just couldn't take all that whinin' and cryin'. He's real sorry he didn't put you out of your misery with the two of them eight years ago, but he sent me here to do it for him. It's my pleasure."

Colter couldn't have saved himself if he'd wanted to, such was the shock of hearing that Ritter Gordon had murdered his wife and child. He'd held Ritter within his gunsights and hadn't killed him! Oh, how he regretted letting Ritter live! And now there would be no one to avenge him. Ritter Gordon was going to get off scot-free! With a savage cry of frustration, Colter tried to rise, and the broken bone poked through the skin of his leg. Unfeeling of the pain, he struggled harder. But the leg simply would not support him, and he fell back to the ground.

Bart the Brute laughed. It was a diabolical, maniacal sound. He was so much enjoying Colter's agony that he let the tip of his rifle slide downward and waited, smirking, for the wounded man to further harm himself fighting the cruel, inescapable trap.

The wind kept Kinyan from hearing what Bart was saying to her husband, but it was clear that if she didn't interfere, he was going to kill Colter. She could have shot Bart the Brute in cold blood. A bushwacker like him probably deserved it. But that would make her no better than he was. She knew all about the cowboy code: "Never shoot an *unarmed* man; never shoot an *unwarned* man." Even weasels like Bart were entitled to their chance. So Kinyan did the honorable thing and hoped she wouldn't regret it.

"Drop your gun!"

Bart didn't stop to consider that the voice that had ordered him belonged to a woman. He simply pulled up the rifle and fired at Colter before he whirled and fired again at Kinyan. Because he'd shot first at Colter, Bart hadn't had time to aim at Kinyan, and the bullet merely cut a hole in her slicker and disappeared into the snowy darkness behind her.

Kinyan took a second to think, just a second, but it was enough time to remember all Colter had taught her. This time she didn't fire wildly as she had at the brindle bull. This time she didn't jerk the trigger or commit any of the hundreds of errors Colter had corrected when he'd taught her to fire the gun. She took careful aim at the center of Bart's chest and gently squeezed the trigger. The kick of the gun rocked her upper body back in the saddle, but she righted herself in time to see the dark red stain spread before Bart the Brute fell backward into the snow.

Kinyan dismounted and crossed to the ruthless villain's body. Bart the Brute was dead. She had vanquished her enemy. Never again would she be a helpless, defenseless widow. And she owed her newfound confidence to Colter. Kinyan focused on the blood staining the pure snow as it streamed from the wound to Colter's head. She was a widow again. And she was furious with Colter because she didn't want to feel so much regret for the death of a man who had betrayed her with another woman.

"A fine mess you've gotten us into now," she chided aloud. "How am I supposed to get you home in this weather?"

"What the hell are you doing here?" Colter muttered.

Kinyan gasped and fell to her knees beside Colter's body. "You're not dead!"

"Not yet," Colter admitted dryly. "Where's the man who shot me?"

"He's dead. I killed him."

"How long have I been out?" he asked.

"Just a few moments."

"A few moments?" Colter tried to tell from the sting of the wind if the storm had worsened. "What happened to the moon?"

"What?"

"It's so dark out, I can't see a damn thing," he said irritably.

Kinyan could see Colter clearly in the moonlight despite the snow flurries. Colter's eyes were wide open, yet he said he saw nothing. There was only one conclusion Kinyan could draw, and she hadn't the courage to voice it.

The same thought had come to Colter, but he refused to accept it, because now he knew who the third man was and he must be whole to take his revenge. Why hadn't he recognized Ritter sooner? Because the man who had abused his hospitality had weighed fifty pounds more. Because the man who had defiled his wife had possessed a full beard and mustache. Because the man who had battered his child had spoken with a heavy Southern accent. Because the man who

248

had sliced him to ribbons had kept his hat down over his eyes—the snake eyes that would have led Colter to his quarry. It wasn't possible that he was now blind. God couldn't be so cruel as to show him his enemy and then take away the means to smite him!

Colter reached out a hand and touched Kinyan's knee. She was so close, yet he couldn't see her! He reached back to touch his own eyes and became furious when he found them open.

"My eyes are open. Why can't I see?"

"The second bullet grazed your head. I can only guess that it blinded you." Kinyan spoke with a calm that belied the turmoil inside her. "Colter, your leg is broken pretty badly. It needs to be set. I'm not sure I can do it by myself. The storm is worsening and we need to get to shelter, otherwise we'll freeze to death. I can use a blanket and some rope to make a sling between our two horses and carry you that way. We're halfway between home and Cheyenne. I'd rather go home, unless you have some objection to that."

"No. I have no objection to that."

Colter lay quietly while Kinyan rigged the sling. She laid the blanket out flat on the ground and helped Colter struggle onto it. He gasped when she first moved him, but at least he didn't faint until she had him centered on the sling. She tied the corners of each end with a length of rope. She attached both ropes to one saddle horn. Then she tied the opposite corners of the blanket with ropes and tied those off on the other saddle horn. By separating the two horses, she was able to tighten the tension on the ropes and lift Colter from the ground. Kinyan walked in front of the horses with her arms held wide to keep the animals apart.

The gentle swaying of the sling was not enough to further aggravate Colter's injuries, but when he regained consciousness, he began a plaintive moaning, almost a lamentation, Kinyan thought, as sad, as mournful, as the wailing wind. She talked to Colter constantly, attempting to keep his mind off the pain. But he never answered her. She never asked him the things she wanted to know. Why was he wanted by the law? Was he a murderer? Did he love her? If so, why had he sought out the woman in the saloon?

The walk seemed interminable, and it was long past bedtime when Kinyan arrived at the Triple Fork. She had long since stopped talking to Colter. He'd fainted again, or was frozen from the cold for all she knew. She kept walking, for once they were home, all could be made right again. Kinyan brought the horses close enough together to lower Colter to the ground and untied the ropes that had held the sling to the saddles. She left the horses standing in the yard, their heads bowed low against the wind. She grasped the big brass doorknob and entered the house.

Kinyan walked up the stairs and down the hall to Dorothea's room, and when she reached the closed door, she knocked twice. When there was no answer, she knocked harder and then began to pound. When the door was yanked open suddenly, Kinyan's fists continued to pound futilely against Dorothea's breast as she gave way to the fear and frustration and fatigue she had so carefully controlled over the long trek home. Dorothea's questions were drowned out by Kinyan's sobs. Then three words finally found their way to Kinyan's lips.

"Colter's been shot."

Then Kinyan swooned at Dorothea's feet.

CHAPTER 20

DOROTHEA SPENT A WEEK traversing from one end of the upstairs hall to the other, tending the two very sick loved ones in her care. Kinyan had suffered from exposure, and while she didn't lose any fingers or toes to frostbite, a sickness had developed in her chest. Colter's leg had needed a better doctor, but Dorothea had done her best and could only hope that he would walk again. Josh, Jeremy, and Lizbeth had spent equal time at the bedsides of their mother and new father, worry etched on their very young faces. Dorothea was exhausted, as much from trying to hide her own concern from her grandchildren as from her efforts to heal the pain of their parents.

That pain, Dorothea had realized as she listened to their delirious mumblings, was more than skin deep. She was convinced Colter and Kinyan loved each other despite the fact that Colter had apparently betrayed Kinyan with another woman. She'd been surprised to discover that Kinyan had killed the brute who'd come after Colter. But it made more sense when she found out from Colter's ramblings that the brute had come to deliver the message that Ritter Gordon had murdered Colter's first wife and child.

It was knowledge Dorothea would rather not have had, because it left her anxious to do something, and uncertain exactly what to do. She wanted to hear a coherent version of the whole story from the two young people. Until then she could only wait and watch and hope. For a woman of action, that was a heavy cross to bear.

Kinyan regained her senses first. She opened her eyes to discover herself in the guest bedroom with Lizbeth sprawled at the foot of the bed playing with her rag doll.

"Good morning, Lizbeth. Is Grandma Thea upstairs?"

"She's sittin' with Colter. He doesn't feel very good."

At least he's still alive, Kinyan thought, breathing a sigh of relief. "Would you go ask Grandma Thea to come see me, please?"

Lizbeth crawled the length of the bed on all fours and laid her head on the pillow next to Kinyan.

"You've been sleeping a lot. Are you all well now, Mama?"

Kinyan mentally assessed how she felt. Her body ached and her muscles were sore, but otherwise she could find nothing wrong. She tried to sit up, but the weakness in her limbs and her dizziness convinced her to stay prone.

"I will be soon, Lizbeth. I suppose I just need to rest a little bit more and then I'll be up and around."

"Will Colter be well soon, Mama?"

"What does Grandma Thea say?" Kinyan asked cautiously.

"She just says we have to hope and pray. I have been praying, Mama. God wouldn't take away another pa, would he?"

Kinyan drew the girl into her arms and smoothed the hair away from her forehead as she said comfortingly, "No, Lizbeth. I don't think he would."

But Lizbeth's words had alarmed Kinyan, and she asked again to see Dorothea. Lizbeth willingly scampered from the bedroom, and within moments Dorothea appeared.

"I'm glad to see you're feeling better," Dorothea said with a smile.

"How's Colter?"

"As well as can be expected."

Kinyan shot Dorothea an exasperated grimace. She regretted her impatience because she could see from the dark circles under Dorothea's eyes, her sagging jowls, and the disheveled state of her dress and hair that taking care of two invalids had run the older woman ragged. Yet Kinyan's need to know about Colter overshadowed everything.

"He's still unconscious," Dorothea continued, unperturbed by Kinyan's irritability. "He's had a fever, but it seems to be less and less every day. With the blizzard, there was no way to get Doc Stewart here from Cheyenne, so I set his leg as best I could with Boley's help. It hasn't gotten infected, and it seems to be healing. I guess the head wound must be keeping him unconscious."

"Then you haven't been able to tell whether he can see or not?"

"What?"

"Right after he was wounded, Colter was conscious for a little while." Kinyan paused and swallowed before she added, "He was blind."

"God help him," Dorothea whispered. A picture flashed through her mind of a helpless Colter facing a vindictive Ritter. Yes, Colter was going to need all the divine help he could get. But the cowboy wasn't without friends, Dorothea realized. Frank and Boley would come to his aid, and Kinyan had already proved her mettle. No, Benjamin Colter would not need to face Ritter alone if his blindness turned out to be permanent.

As soon as Kinyan felt well enough to walk, she went down the hall to see her husband. It was a beautiful, crisp fall day. Kinyan paused at Colter's side for a moment, and when she saw he was asleep, she crossed past him to the window to observe the glorious profusion of orange and yellow leaves on the cottonwood trees along the creek.

"It's beautiful."

Kinyan was unaware she had spoken aloud until Colter responded, "What's beautiful?"

"I thought you were asleep. The cottonwoods," she said, crossing back to sit next to Colter on the bed. "They're wearing their fall splendor. You should see them."

Of course he couldn't see them! Colter's blindness had been confirmed upon his regaining consciousness.

"I'm sorry!"

"Don't apologize." Colter reached out for Kinyan's hand, and when she gave it to him, he brought it to his lips to kiss her palm.

"Dorothea told me what happened. I haven't thanked you for saving my life, even though I should tan your hide for being in Cheyenne in the first place," Colter said, his voice low and husky with feeling.

"I wanted to help. I was worried you'd be hurt."

253

The words warmed Colter. She cared. Or at least she had cared before he'd been blinded.

Kinyan enjoyed the caress until the ugly thought arose that these were the same lips that had kissed the painted woman. Had his tongue teased Rosie just so? Kinyan slowly withdrew her hand from Colter's.

Sensitive to Kinyan's every nuance, Colter asked, "What's wrong?"

Kinyan knew Colter had given her the perfect opportunity to ask about Rosie, but it seemed ridiculous under the circumstances to bring up the subject. Her jealousy seemed a petty concern after her husband had been accused of being a murderer and had almost been murdered himself. Besides, now that he was blind, Colter was hardly likely to go riding into Cheyenne to be with Rosie. So Kinyan didn't confront Colter. But neither did she forgive him.

"Nothing's wrong, I . . ." To excuse the action, she settled on the other issue. "The man I killed said you're a murderer. He said you're wanted by the law in Texas."

Colter exhaled. So that was it. She thought he was an outlaw. "I'd already told you I killed those two men. Believe me, they deserved it."

"What would happen if the law found out you're here?"

"I suppose they'd take me back to Texas for trial. But there's not much chance of that. And most Texas bounty hunters don't get this far north. I could have cleared myself with the law if I'd stayed around to do it. I just didn't want to have to talk in court about my reasons for killing those two men. If I ever had to, though, I would."

"Unless some bounty hunter kills you first."

"No one's ever succeeded in the past."

"You weren't blind then!"

Colter's face turned ashen. He'd spent the time since he'd regained consciousness trying to come to grips with being blind. He'd convinced himself in the dark solitude of his room that he could still function almost like a normal man. But Kinyan had voiced the fears that plagued him as well. She had vividly exposed his vulnerability.

"I'll manage," he replied evenly.

"How?" Kinyan snapped. She wasn't angry with Colter, merely feeling sympathetic frustration when she added, "You won't be able to ride. You won't be able to shoot. You

254

won't even be able to see the danger when it's right in front of your face!"

Colter was all too aware Kinyan had only married him because she needed someone to teach her how to manage the ranch. While she'd apparently come to care for him, what if she'd now decided she had no use for a cripple? It was a bitter thought, but one Colter forced himself to acknowledge. After all, what use was a blind man to her now? She'd learned a great deal in the little time he'd worked with her, and maybe she'd decided she would be better off handling the Triple Fork on her own than if she were saddled with him. There was only one way to find out.

"Have you made any plans about how you're going to manage the ranch until I'm back on my feet?"

Colter's question was a total surprise to Kinyan. She hadn't thought about the ranch at all. Every waking moment had been spent thinking and worrying about Colter. But from the way Colter had worded his question, Kinyan felt certain he expected her to shoulder the responsibility of the ranch until he could take his rightful place again. Even if Colter couldn't ride or shoot, with his knowledge of ranching and with help from Frank and Boley, the plans and dreams for the Triple Fork they'd discussed could still become a reality. It only took Kinyan a moment to make her decision, but she knew it was the right one.

"Now that we've had the first snow, I can implement your plan to distribute hay to the stock. I'll start by setting a schedule with Frank and Boley of when and where to drop the feed. Then I guess I'll work with Frank to decide who'll do the winter line riding," Kinyan said.

Colter's lips tightened, and he turned his sightless eyes away from Kinyan. Nowhere in her plans had she included a crippled husband. She hadn't even bothered with the pretense of asking for his advice.

What had she said wrong? Kinyan wondered, watching Colter battle for control.

"Of course, if you want to do anything differently, I'll be glad to listen," she hurried to add.

"No, it sounds like you have everything well in hand."

Colter's voice reflected the cynicism he felt. Kinyan was going to do quite well without him, it appeared. That last grudging offer, a blatant attempt to salve his pride, was too little too late. He didn't need, couldn't bear her pity when what he wanted was her love. And now he would never know how she really felt. He didn't think he could stand to be merely tolerated.

Colter raged against his fate. He'd been so close, so very close to finding a new love. Why had God chosen to blind him? *Why me? And why now?* Then Colter accepted that God had nothing to do with it. The woman he loved was lost to him. Ritter Gordon had robbed him again.

His bitterness was compounded by his knowledge that Ritter had murdered Sarah and Hope, and that he was helpless to wreak his vengeance. Colter kept his own counsel. No one could help him now. It might have been some comfort if he'd believed in God's mercy, but Colter had asked God once for a miracle and been refused. He wasn't about to go begging again.

"I'm glad to see you'll be able to manage the Triple Fork by yourself, because I'll be leaving as soon as my leg is mended," Colter said finally.

If Colter had been able to see, the shocked look on Kinyan's face would have told him he'd drawn the wrong conclusions. Kinyan didn't have the ghost of an idea what had gone wrong between them. She only knew she couldn't let Colter leave.

"Your plans will have to wait," she shot back.

"What?"

"First rule, Colter: the ranch comes first," Kinyan responded in a steely voice. "I'm going to need your help to get through the winter. When spring comes, you're welcome to leave—with my blessing." It would be a long winter. By spring Kinyan hoped she could convince Colter he was where he belonged.

"You can't keep me here," Colter replied, his voice raw with pain and anger.

"You can't very well leave on your own. You're blind. And nobody here is going to help you."

"Get out of here. Leave me alone."

The tone of his voice was frightening, but Kinyan couldn't afford to be afraid.

"Gladly. I find your company leaves something to be desired right now. When you're ready to act a little older than Josh and Jeremy, let me know."

A knock at the door rescued Kinyan from having to say anything more.

"There's someone here to see you, Kinyan," Dorothea said.

"Who is it?"

"I think you better come find that out for yourself."

From the look Dorothea shot at Colter, Kinyan surmised the older woman didn't want the injured man to know who was there.

"I'm coming."

Without another word, Kinyan left Colter alone to mull over her ultimatum in the darkness. It was always going to be dark for him from now on, she thought. As she descended the stairs, Kinyan thought of all the different ways she was going to bring golden sunshine and soft white moonlight back into Colter's life.

When she reached the parlor, Kinyan knew why Dorothea hadn't spoken the name of their visitor. Kinyan probably would have shrieked at Colter, and the list she'd compiled on her way downstairs would have been altered considerably. For Rosie McLaughlin had settled her body, buxom bosom and all, on the frail settee. The low-cut, bright pink satin dress she wore clashed with the muted burgundy velvet. And Rosie looked no more comfortable or happy than Kinyan felt.

It was not hard to see what Colter found to like in the woman. Those caramel-colored eyes were soft as a doe's. Her figure was lush and every movement graceful, certain to entice a man to want to hold her in his arms, to have her in his bed. The henna-colored hair was Rosie's crowning glory, and Kinyan's mouth flattened into a straight line when she imagined Colter's fingers entwined in those curls. Kinyan forced down her jealousy and asked with calm if somewhat breathless dignity, "How can I help you?"

Rosie was aware how much of an imposition it was for good folk to allow a whore into their home even if she had come to do them a favor. Hadn't she been spurned by ladies like this often enough on the streets of Cheyenne? But Dorothea Holloway had asked her into the parlor just like she was a real lady come to call, and if she hadn't already felt she owed Colter, she would have spoken now out of gratitude for Dorothea's kindness.

"I got somethin' I gotta tell you." Rosie licked her lips nervously and moved a stray curl that had fallen across her forehead. "Maybe you two ladies oughta sit down."

Dorothea and Kinyan exchanged a glance of trepidation but proceeded to the two chairs across from the settee.

Rosie took a deep breath and said, "Ritter Gordon is a regular customer of mine." Rosie wouldn't have believed she could blush, but she could feel her cheeks pinkening. Before her embarrassment tied her tongue, she continued, "Sometimes he brags to me about the things he's done. He's told me some pretty awful things." Rosie paused and gathered her courage. She focused on Kinyan and said, "Your husband didn't die in an accident. Ritter Gordon killed him. He had some men knock John out and then tie him to his horse and drag him till he was near dead."

The blood drained from Kinyan's face. Her fingers tightened on the arms of the leather chair, her nails scraping the soft leather.

Dorothea put a hand on her chest as though to still the heavy beating of her heart, then slowly leaned her head back. She closed her eyes and breathed deeply.

"Vengeance is mine, saith the Lord."

Dorothea had spoken her thought aloud. It didn't help. She imagined her gnarled arthritic fingers around Ritter Gordon's throat.

"Thank you for coming," Kinyan managed to whisper.

"I'm not done yet," Rosie said.

Kinyan and Dorothea gave their attention to her again.

Rosie found she couldn't look the two women in the eye when she spoke, so she dropped her head and pretended an interest in the little finger of her black net glove.

"The Triple Fork boys have been talkin' in Cheyenne. Is it true Colter is blind?"

When Kinyan nodded, Rosie said, "Colter was . . ." Rosie cleared her throat and tried again. "Colter treated me . . ." Rosie paused again.

Kinyan could see the difficulty Rosie was having and sought to ease her way.

"I know my husband cares for you. I saw him kiss you at the Variety Palace." Kinyan's voice was ragged before she finished the two sentences.

Rosie had heard the story of how Kinyan had disguised herself and followed her husband into Cheyenne, how she'd killed Bart, then made a sling to carry Colter and walked the whole way home to the Triple Fork on foot. As far as the Triple Fork hands were concerned, Kinyan Colter walked on water. In Rosie's opinion, she was just the sort of woman Colter deserved. And she'd hate to think that Colter's actions in the Variety Palace that night might have caused a rift between the two.

"Oh no, Miz Colter," Rosie said, realizing that Kinyan must have misconstrued the situation. "He doesn't care none for me. I wouldn't have you mistake that kiss. He was just bein' kind to me, lettin' me down easy. He was tellin' me that he loved his wife. He was kissin' me good-bye."

"I heard you say you . . . had been with him," Kinyan persisted, blushing furiously.

A grin cracked Rosie's face. "Well yes, ma'am, that's true, and I'd be lyin' if I said it wasn't a pleasure. But," she reassured, "that was before he married you." Rosie still hadn't said what she'd come to say, and she wanted to leave her message and get back before Ritter noticed she was gone. She only had another week before she planned to make her escape to San Francisco, and it wouldn't do at all to get caught visiting the Triple Fork.

"Your husband treated me like a lady, and I'm grateful to him for that."

Kinyan felt herself flushing again. How she'd misjudged her husband! She was so caught up in chastising herself for her unwarranted jealousy that Rosie's next words slipped past at first without sinking in.

"Colter didn't deserve to be blinded by a man like Ritter."

Then the import of Rosie's statement registered.

"Ritter's responsible?"

Rosie hurried on to end the confusion she'd created. "Bart Jefferson was Ritter's brother. Well, his half-brother, anyway. Bart stayed in Texas when Ritter came north. Ritter didn't like Colter hornin' in at the Association, and he was fit to be tied when Colter snatched you away from him along with the Triple Fork. So he asked Bart to check and see if Colter was wanted by the law. He was. When Bart told

259

Ritter the names of the men Colter had killed in Texas, Ritter remembered where he'd seen Colter before."

Dorothea had a horrified feeling she knew what was coming. "He remembered Colter?" she asked.

"Miz Colter, the awfulness of what I'm about to tell you is what brought me here. Eight years ago in Texas, Colter was married to a woman named Sarah. He had a daughter named Hope, 'bout the age of your Lizbeth. Ritter and two other Confederate soldiers stopped at Colter's ranch and accepted his hospitality. After they ate dinner, they all three helped themselves to Colter's wife. They forced Colter to watch while they raped her, and then they killed her before his eyes. When his little girl cried for her mama, they stabbed her too. They left Colter for dead. The two men he killed in Texas—they were Ritter's friends. Before he killed Colter for the reward, Bart was supposed to tell Colter what Ritter done to his family."

A low, keening moan broke from Kinyan's lips. Her hands came up to cover her face and her head dropped to her lap, while the muscles of her heart squeezed and squeezed until she thought it would break. All the times she'd glared at Colter when he'd slighted Lizbeth came back to haunt her. If only he'd told her he'd lost a daughter, she would have understood. Why hadn't he just explained the tragedy? Unless it was still too painful. Then an equally disturbing thought occurred to Kinyan. Was he still in love with the wife who had died so long ago? Was that why he had never proclaimed his feelings toward her?

That last fear was not long-lived. Kinyan knew from her own experience that you might treasure a memory, but you loved flesh and blood. And she was here, now, and planned to see that their lives together were everything that Colter had been denied by the loss of his first wife and child.

Dorothea's eyes had closed and her lips were moving in what seemed a silent prayer. But it was not a prayer. She was merely ceding before God her claim to vengeance upon Ritter to another who had been hurt far worse than she by that fiend's villainy.

Rosie found the two white faces across from her comforting. They cared for Colter. That was good. And they'd see that he was safe from Ritter Gordon. She would make sure of that.

"I don't know if Bart got a chance to deliver his message to Colter or not. I just thought you oughta know, Colter bein' blind and all, so you can protect him when Ritter comes after him." Rosie paused before she added, "And he will come after him. Make no mistake about that."

"Thank you," Dorothea said, "for warning us."

Rosie met Dorothea's wise gray eyes and knew her message had come across loud and clear.

"Yes, thank you," Kinyan said, still dazed by Rosie's revelation.

"I guess I'll be leavin' now." Rosie stood up and began to make her way toward the door. Before she could get far, Kinyan came to her and embraced her.

"Thank you for caring for him," Kinyan whispered in Rosie's ear.

A lump came to Rosie's throat that kept her from speaking, but she grunted a choked "Uh-huh," that expressed how much she wished a Benjamin Colter had showed up at her door a long time ago.

Kinyan stood at the front window and watched until Rosie's carriage was out of sight. It was not until she tried to move that she realized Dorothea's arm had been around her waist the whole time. It was a simple thing to turn into Dorothea's arms, to put her head on the older woman's breast and be comforted like a child and give comfort.

"We'll go to Sheriff Potts," Dorothea said. "We'll tell him what Ritter did. We'll have him arrested."

Kinyan raised her head so her eyes met those of the older woman, but kept her arm around Dorothea.

"We don't have any proof. Besides, Colter's wanted by the law. He says nobody from Texas is liable to come after him, but if we go to the sheriff, there's no telling what Ritter will do or say."

"What's to keep Ritter from going to the sheriff anyway?" Dorothea asked.

"Why hasn't he already done it? I don't think he will. It's not his way of doing things. We'll have to keep an eye on Ritter ourselves." The two women remained arm in arm, gazing out on the snow-covered plains, their thoughts running over worn but divergent paths.

That was the way Josh and Jeremy found them when they came to the front door.

261

"Who was that just left?" Josh asked.

Kinyan and Dorothea stepped back from one another.

"A friend," Kinyan said simply. "Josh, I want you and Jeremy to go talk to Colter."

"He's been awful crotchety the last few days, Ma. What if he don't wanta see us?"

"As long as he's stuck in bed with that leg, he can't make you go away."

"And if he wants to get rid of us badly enough he'll get well, huh, Ma?" A quirking smile lit Jeremy's face, and Kinyan met it with a tremulous smile of her own.

"That's right. You boys know what you have to do. Now get to it."

"Just leave it to us, Ma," Josh said as he whipped past her up the stairs. "Colter'll be on his feet in no time!"

"Do you really think you should have done that?" Dorothea asked. "They'll drive Colter crazy long before the bone has mended enough for him to be up on his leg."

"It'll be good for him. In fact I think I'll have Lizbeth listen to her story in his bedroom every night, and you'll need to sit with him while he eats, and of course, I'll be needing lots of advice about how to run the ranch. Colter may have lost one family to Ritter Gordon, but we're not going to let that sonofabitch Ritter tear *us* apart!"

CHAPTER 21

IT WAS NEARLY THANKSGIVING, and Colter's blindness and broken leg had kept him captive in the four-poster for six long weeks. Kinyan had been as patient with Colter as a cat waiting for a mouse to break from its hole, but so far her patience had gone unrewarded. Colter showed no signs that he ever intended to leave his pillowed prison.

Colter hated being fed, so Kinyan had agreed to let him feed himself. He did the job so awkwardly that he often gave up eating long before his stomach was full. Kinyan had watched his lean, powerful physique waste away to skin and bone. Nowhere was his gauntness more pronounced than his face, where his sightless blue eyes shone with feverish brightness in recessed sockets and sharp cheekbones stabbed at his skin from the inside, threatening to tear their way out.

To make matters worse, Colter rarely slept. When he did finally succumb to exhaustion, his nightmarish ravings for Sarah and Hope were evidence enough as to why he fought that vulnerable state. Kinyan despaired of Colter ever recovering even though Dorothea had declared Colter's leg was healed well enough for him to be walking on it.

And then Ritter came to visit.

Dorothea had answered the door and was as cordial to Ritter as the spider to the fly. Kinyan couldn't believe her ears when Dorothea came upstairs to tell her Ritter was waiting in the parlor and wanted to speak with Colter.

"Send him up," she heard herself say.

Ritter was dressed the same as always, except his blue shirt was made of wool. Kinyan noticed he wore a Colt under his heavy sheepskin overcoat, which Dorothea hadn't invited him to remove downstairs. Kinyan vacillated for a moment before deciding it wasn't necessary to ask Ritter to remove the weapon. Even Ritter wouldn't be so stupid as to use his .44 where there would be so many witnesses. Besides, bushwhacking was more his style.

Ritter ignored Kinyan and came to stand beside Colter. A grim smile rose on his face when he saw Colter's poor condition. The man was half dead already.

"Colter, there's someone here to see you," Kinyan said as calmly as she could.

"Hello, Colter," Ritter said.

Colter's eyes blinked once, but his body remained perfectly at ease. Colter had also been waiting—as a cat for a mouse, as a spider for a fly—for his victim to come to him, and at long last his wait had been rewarded.

"Leave us alone, Kinyan," Colter said.

"But, Colter. . ."

Colter angled his head so his feverish blue orbs stared at Kinyan.

"I'll be fine. Leave us."

It was not a request. It was a command. And it was the first sign Kinyan had seen that Colter did not intend to roll over and die. Without looking at either man again, she whirled and left the room.

"I've been wondering when you'd show up," Colter drawled. "Vultures usually start picking at the carcass long before the lifeblood has ebbed away."

"I take it Bart gave you my message before he was killed. I wondered."

"You're a walking dead man, you know. I'm going to kill you, but not right away. I want you to wonder when it's going to happen and worry how it's going to happen. I'll make sure you suffer a long time. Did you hear how your friends died? It was slow, Ritter, and it was painful. And they weren't men anymore when it was all over."

"Big talk for a blind invalid."

Colter tensed at Ritter's taunt.

Ritter's barking laugh curled his upper lip into a snarl. "I want you to know I intend to have Kinyan. I'll use her the way I used your Sarah, but I won't give her the release of death. I plan to keep her around a long, long time. Of course, I have no use for the children or the old woman. They'll meet with a tragic accident. I *will* have the Triple Fork. You can be sure of that. And I'll have your wife. Again. There's no way you can stop me." Ritter's barking laugh sounded again and was cut off when he raised his eyes to the .44 Colt pointed straight at his belly.

"You're making a big mistake," Ritter said. "I've had a gun on you from the moment we were alone together. You might hit me, but it's more likely you'll miss. I'll claim self-defense. You'll be a dead man, but I'll be alive and I'll have your wife."

As much as Colter was tempted to shoot, for he believed he would have heard Ritter pull the gun from his leather holster, he couldn't take the chance that Ritter was lying. He'd have to wait.

"Get out."

Colter heard Ritter's short-strided steps as he moved to the door. He listened for the click of the catch as the door opened and then closed behind his enemy. Colter expelled a deep breath of air and realized he was trembling. He would have been happy to die and take Ritter with him, but that opportunity was past. What was horribly clear was that for the second time in his life, Ritter was threatening his family!

There was no question now of leaving Kinyan. Even if she no longer cared for him, he wasn't going to abandon her to the clutches of that fiend. Nor was he going to allow Ritter to harm anyone else in this family. He was going to have to find a way to remove the threat Ritter represented. But how? Hellfire! He felt weak as a baby and helpless as a child. How was a blind man going to corner a snake like Ritter? There were too many rocks he could slither under and wait for a chance to strike. Colter felt a deep, gnawing fear. For the first time in his life, he faced a foe he wasn't sure he could vanquish.

Ritter's visit was also a turning point for Kinyan. She no longer planned to wait patiently for the mouse to come out of its hole. It was time to reach into the darkness after it. So that evening, after the boys had bid Colter their customary good night, after Lizbeth had given and received her kiss, after Dorothea had checked to make sure Colter was comfortable and didn't need anything from the kitchen, Kinyan went into the master bedroom, where Colter had slept for six weeks alone, and closed and locked the door.

Kinyan had no way of knowing Ritter's visit had considerably altered Colter's outlook on life. She had no way of knowing he was now as determined to get well as she was to have him that way. She and the children and Dorothea had spent six weeks giving Colter all the loving attention they could muster and it hadn't done one bit of good. Now she was going to try something different. If Colter couldn't be cajoled into wanting to get well, then perhaps he could be angered into it. She planned to make love to Colter and then tell him she no longer needed him for any other purpose. It was a desperate measure, but she was desperate.

Kinyan had done a great deal of planning for her seduction, knowing she would need to appeal to other senses besides sight. Josh and Jeremy had lugged bucket after bucket of heated water up to fill her wooden bathtub. When Colter had objected to her use of "his" room, Kinyan had pointed out that the master bedroom was the only upstairs one with a fireplace, and she couldn't very well be expected to take a bath in the winter cold without staying very near a fire. That had shut him up.

When Colter heard the bolt close on the bedroom door, a shiver of anticipation had raced up his spine. He listened as Kinyan's dress dropped to the floor. He felt the bed dip as she sat down to remove her boots and socks, then move when she stood up again. He heard her grunt as she pulled her chemise up over her head, and he listened for the rustle of cloth against skin as her pantalets came down. When Kinyan padded barefoot to the tub, he waited for the splash of water as she stepped in.

Colter's lips quirked when he recognized the satisfied sigh as Kinyan settled into the steamy water. Then the scent of lavender assailed his nose. It was the same essence she had used the first time they had made love. He would never forget that smell.

Kinyan stayed in the tub until the water was tepid. She lathered herself all over and even washed her hair with the lavender-scented soap. She smiled to herself when she realized Colter had begun to shift restlessly in the big bed. She stood up and wrapped her body in one towel and her hair in another, then stepped from the water onto the braided rug. She stayed close to the fireplace while she dried her hair with the smaller towel. The glowing heat from the fire warmed the towel that was wrapped around her. For a long time after she had finished, she just sat on the rug in front of the fireplace and stared into the orange and blue flames.

"I hope you're planning to be done soon."

Colter's agitation was plain in his voice. Kinyan smiled broadly.

"Oh? why?"

"Because I need to get some sleep."

Kinyan gathered her courage and walked to the foot of the four-poster. She climbed up onto the end of the bed and, holding the towel around her body with one hand and keeping her balance with the other, made her way up the bed until she found herself on her knees next to Colter. She sat back on her heels and waited.

"What are you doing?"

There was a breathless excitement in Colter's question that caused Kinyan's face to flush.

"I'm tired of sleeping alone," Kinyan replied. "I thought since you're almost well now, it would be all right for me to join you again in this big bed."

"I don't . . ."

Kinyan's fingers covered Colter's lips. He brought his right hand up to cover hers.

"I've missed you," she whispered.

Kinyan let the bath towel fall free. She took Colter's right hand in both of hers and brought it to her naked breast. She quivered as Colter's fingertips rested lightly on her flesh.

"Touch me," she pleaded. "Love me."

Colter sighed raggedly. She wanted him. She needed him. And he feared he would fail her when she needed him the most. Would he be able to protect this tender flesh from Ritter's poisonous grasp?

Tentatively, Colter closed his hand and felt the turgid nipple press against the center of his palm. A vivid image of Kinyan's warm honey-brown nipple, puckered to his touch, rose before him and he felt himself swell with the memory. He cupped a breast in each hand. His head came up from the pillow and his mouth unerringly found one engorged nipple. This had not changed. Oh God, she tasted the same. So sweet!

Kinyan had no intention of letting Colter take control of their lovemaking, despite her plea to be loved. She wanted to make a point. He had many senses besides sight upon which he could rely, if he would only make the effort. Kinyan intended to make sure he utilized every one of them. So she leaned away from Colter, gasping aloud when his teeth latched on to her nipple at the last second before it fell away from his mouth.

"No biting," she purred. "Or I'll bite back."

Colter promptly bit Kinyan on the neck.

When the shivers had finished their course down the length of her throat, Kinyan shoved Colter back down flat on the bed.

"You'll pay for that," she taunted.

Kinyan's hair fell forward onto Colter's belly, caressing him. Then she leaned across him, her breasts pressing into his chest, and suckled a flat nipple that peeked through the wiry black curls surrounding it. Colter grabbed her hair as though to pull her away, then changed his mind and held her there as the nipple rose and tightened. Kinyan switched her attention to the other nipple, and Colter groaned in response to her titillation.

"You're not well," Kinyan said. "Let me see what I can do to help you feel a little better."

Colter felt weak, all right, but he doubted that right now it had much to do with the state of his health.

Kinyan pulled the sheets down to reveal Colter's naked form. His hipbones protruded above a flat stomach and his ribs stood out along his chest. Colter's thinness firmed Kinyan's determination to follow through with her plan. She would have her husband whole again no matter what she had to do!

"I've wanted to go riding with you for a long time."

Colter gasped aloud when Kinyan mounted him as though he were her stallion, sheathing him within her. He had never taken the time to do more than cover his casual lovers with his body to assuage his physical need. He had experienced no desire to play with the women he paid, and he'd apparently been intimidating enough that none had dared play with him. So Kinyan's desire to "ride with him" had come as a total surprise. But not an unwelcome one. Colter grasped Kinyan's hips and seated himself more deeply within her.

Kinyan allowed him that liberty, but then took his hands away.

"Soon," she promised. "First I want to play a game."

"You want to play?" Colter said dryly. "You tempt me beyond reason and you want to play a game?"

"Where am I?" Kinyan asked.

A guffaw burst from Colter's chest.

"You know damn well where you are!"

"How do you know? You can't see me, can you?"

"Witch! Teasing witch!" Colter rose to a sitting position and wrapped his arms around Kinyan. "I can feel you all around me."

Kinyan was grateful Colter couldn't see the full blush that statement provoked.

"If I took a deep breath, I'd suffocate in the lavender essence of you."

Well, maybe she had overdone it a little.

Colter pulled Kinyan's lips down to his and dipped his tongue teasingly into her mouth. He tempted her tongue into his mouth, and then sent his tongue back to sip the sweetness of her. Then he tasted the tangy salt of sweat along her temple, where she had warmed at the fire, and gathered a breast in his hand and flicked his thumb across the nipple once before he sucked it into his mouth.

"Mother's milk," he muttered.

"Wh—what?"

"You taste as sweet as mother's milk."

Kinyan's breathing had quickened, as had Colter's, so everything they said now came out between rapid pants.

"Do you . . . hear what you're saying?" Kinyan rasped as she kissed Colter's temple and nipped the lobe of his ear.

"I'm saying . . . I love the taste of you."

"No, not that," Kinyan contradicted.

"Then what?"

"I forget what . . . I wanted . . . to say."

"Don't worry. I'll help you remember. Later."

Kinyan clung to Colter as though she were drowning and he were the lifeline while he grasped her hips and moved her in rhythm to his need. Their bodies merged from lip to breast to thigh, the man within the woman, the woman surrounding the man, until there was no Colter and Kinyan, only one fleshbound soul seeking a heaven and finally, finally, finding it on this small piece of earth.

Colter had fallen back on the bed with Kinyan lying across his chest, still gasping. There was something she was trying to prove to Colter. Oh yes, now she remembered. She was going to prove that he had more senses than just sight to rely on—touch and smell and hearing and taste. Her tongue flicked out to taste Colter's salty chest. Ah yes, taste!

"Whoa!" He chuckled. "I'm not in good enough shape to take you on again right away."

Kinyan had been more successful in accomplishing her goal than she knew. All of Colter's senses had become highly developed over the years he'd been prey for an endless stream of bounty hunters. He'd suddenly realized, as Kinyan undressed in the room, that he knew exactly what she was doing every minute of the time. He could have placed her within an inch of where she was. And what he could find, he could kill. It only remained for him to hone that skill with a gun.

What was even more wonderful was the fact that Kinyan had come to him. Maybe there was a chance for them after all. Colter found himself clinging to that hope even though no words of love had been spoken. Right now it was enough just to be close to her. Besides, he hadn't recovered from the throes of their lovemaking enough to speak without sounding as winded as he was.

Colter's remark about the shape he was in gave Kinyan the perfect opening for the attack she'd planned. She dreaded what she had to do now and steeled herself for the anger that was sure to follow.

"It's a good thing I've learned to get along without you," she said lightly. Kinyan felt Colter's muscles tense beneath the hand that played with his nipple. "I'd be in pretty bad shape myself if I'd been counting on you to help me out, wouldn't I?"

Colter couldn't help taking offense at her words, but if he were honest, what she said was true. Still, he wanted to see how deep her dissatisfaction ran. He took Kinyan by the shoulders and shoved her into a sitting position.

"What exactly does that mean?" he asked.

"Only that I've found out I can manage fine without your help. Except in bed," she added, sticking the knife in deep. "I still need you in bed."

A strangled sound came from deep within Colter before he drawled, "Well, if you're done with me for the evening, ma'am, I'd like to get some sleep. I have a lot to do tomorrow. But do come see me anytime. It'll be my pleasure to service you."

Colter's voice cut deep and Kinyan was hurting at least as badly from the wounds he'd just inflicted as he must be from hers.

"Well in that case, I'll let you go. I have quite a few things to do myself tomorrow."

When Kinyan heard from Josh and Jeremy the next day that Colter had actually gotten out of bed and walked a few steps, her heart leaped with joy before it stumbled on the mess she'd made of things getting him on his feet. Her only consolation was the promise she'd made to herself that when Colter was really and truly well, she would tell him of her deception. Until then, she would have to continue the charade.

The rest of the winter passed in a blur for Kinyan.

There had been good news at Thanksgiving. She and Colter had rejoiced together when they heard Ritter had taken off for San Francisco. No one knew exactly why he'd left, but the rumor was that he'd gone after Rosie McLaughlin. Kinyan couldn't imagine why Ritter would care one way or the other about Rosie leaving Cheyenne, but she hoped the woman was safe. And she hoped Ritter Gordon never came back.

Kinyan discovered something very important about herself during the bitter cold, frost-fettered months of deep winter. She liked managing the ranch. What was more, she was good at it. All it took was the determination not to give up or give in. She had not, of course, been able to handle everything by herself, and it had seemed the natural thing to come to Colter for advice.

Colter had suggested she learn to read so she could make use of his books about ranching. Kinyan had honed her skills by reading aloud to Colter, and they discussed what she read. It became habitual for Kinyan to consult Colter on almost everything. And even though she always made a point of arguing with him over what course they ought to take, she was frequently grateful to have the benefit of his experience.

In March, there was news of Sioux raids in the north. Kinyan heard that more soldiers had been called in to solve the "Indian problem." General George Armstrong Custer, it was said, could not afford politically to have sympathy for the Indian plight. Then her mother and father had come secretly at night to bid her farewell before they fled north from the Red Cloud Agency camp to join the other Sioux at their ancestral hunting grounds.

Her father had seemed happy to be going north. Her mother's expression had been bleak. Kinyan asked about Rides-the-Wind and was told he had married Fawn. Rides-the-Wind had paid many ponies to her father for the youthful bride, and he had smiled at her when he took her as wife. Kinyan sent a message to the couple through her parents, wishing them well and expressing her hope that they would enjoy a long and happy life. She had hugged her parents to her, and then she had watched them ride away. Kinyan cried that night after they left. Colter comforted her.

Kinyan continued coming to Colter's bed, and he made love to her each time with a passion that seemed boundless. She treasured those brief moments when they laid aside all enmity, but she was always careful to set the barb again before she left him, although it hurt her more each time to do so. The days dragged, but Kinyan was patient, because she could see the changes for the better in Colter.

His leg improved, but slowly, because the bone hadn't set exactly right. It appeared, as the months passed, that he would have a permanent limp. And he had so much to learn about how to live without his sight! He was impatient with himself, angry when he tripped on the furniture, disgusted when he spilled his food, furious when he felt he was being patronized. Yet Kinyan noticed he was consistently even-tempered with Josh and Jeremy, almost indulgent with Lizbeth, and considerate of Dorothea. She alone appeared to be a fair target for his temper, which he unleashed only occasionally, but with disastrous results for her.

Spring could not come soon enough for Kinyan. When the crocus burst from the ground, it was as though she had burst the confining shell that had contained her over the frigid months. She had the satisfaction of knowing that Colter's plan for feeding the cattle had worked. They'd lost fewer cattle to starvation than the other ranchers, and the cattle had stayed bunched rather than drifting with the weather because they'd looked forward to the free meal the line riders provided.

Her plan had worked too. Colter seemed a new man. Kinyan waited for the day when she could tell him she loved him and that she needed him in all ways, always.

Colter had also been waiting for spring, because even though he'd never prayed for it, God had gifted him with a miracle. At first he hadn't believed the fuzzy gray outlines, thinking he must be hallucinating. But the fuzzy gray outlines had become clear black and white outlines, and then colored figures, and finally he was seeing perfectly again. It was when his sight first returned that he made the most important discovery of his life.

The first night Kinyan came to him after he was able to see clearly, he was especially bitter because now he had back what he thought was most precious to him—his eyesight—and realized he would have traded it for Kinyan's love. He greeted her that evening, as he always did, with sharp words so she wouldn't suspect anything was different.

"You're early tonight. Do you think the ranch can manage without you?"

Then, though she replied sharply, "It's doing fine without you," he could see the tears build in her eyes.

"Well, I may give you a run for your money this spring," Colter taunted.

"You do that," Kinyan replied sarcastically. "But don't expect me to make it easy for you. Rule number two, Colter: you have to be willing to fight for what's yours."

But her face didn't fit her words or her tone of voice! On her face was a look of such tenderness, such love, that Colter hardly believed what he saw. He tested her further.

"Give me a kiss."

Colter kept his eyes open and watched Kinyan closely as she bent to him. Her eyes searched his features tenderly, and the tears spilled over before her mouth reached his.

"Tears?" he questioned, shifting his mouth so he intercepted the streams of salty liquid.

"I had a hard day," she excused. "I lost three calves to wolves."

Yet the whole time she kissed him, her eyes ate him, overflowing with love and caring. Why on earth had she maintained that uncaring facade? The truth was not long in coming to him. He thought back to the day she'd first suggested this crazy arrangement—the day of Ritter's visit. Truth to tell, before then he'd lain in bed without the will to get out. He could hardly blame her for seeking a way to goad him out of bed with the specter of Ritter's fiendishness hanging over them all.

Colter's heart soared on eagle's wings. He almost blurted out to Kinyan that he could see, but he stopped himself. It was important he continue his masquerade until Ritter returned from San Francisco. Then he'd confront Ritter before the villain had a chance to attack him. The fact he could see would be too difficult a secret to keep once it was out. Kinyan, Dorothea, and the children must all continue to react to him as though he were blind in order that Ritter not be forewarned.

That night, Colter didn't send Kinyan away after they made love. He held her in his arms. He noticed that she questioned his actions with her eyes, yet she didn't speak, nor did she attempt to leave him. Then she gave him the gift he hadn't known he wanted. He watched his wife mouth the words *I love you* before she tucked her head beneath his chin and went to sleep.

Colter hugged his wife fiercely to him. Someday soon he would be free to tell her the words he was aching to say.

Beautiful woman, my wife, my life: I love you too.

CHAPTER 22

"HEY, COLTER! ARE YOU gonna ride with us today?" Josh shouted to the upstairs window.

Colter pushed aside the curtains and enjoyed the picture of the grinning youth on horseback with the budding cottonwoods along the creek behind him.

"No. I think I'll stick around close to the house today."

"You gonna practice with your Colt?" Jeremy asked. He sat his horse next to Josh. "I wanta be here when you do. It's somethin' how you can hit those peach tins just by listenin' to where they smack the ground."

"Not today, Jeremy."

Colter smiled because despite the fact he could see as well as Josh and Jeremy, he really did use his hearing to locate the targets. Josh had suggested that Colter join their game when he came upon them down at the creek one day shooting at tin cans. They'd been watching him so closely, he'd had to be careful not to use his eyesight. To his surprise and delight, he'd discovered he could be amazingly accurate if he just listened for the sound of the can hitting the spring grass.

"Are you sick or somethin', Colter?" Jeremy asked. "It isn't like you to stay at home."

Colter grinned ruefully. Sometimes his family tended to be a little too protective. Right now, though, he couldn't afford to have them suspicious. He'd had Boley stay in town to watch for Ritter's return and had gotten word last night that

Ritter was back. He'd hesitated this morning about letting Kinyan go out on the range, then kept silent, working it out so Boley would stay with her and the boys. After today, Ritter wasn't going to be a problem.

"I'm fine, Jeremy. I thought I'd hang around the house for a while."

"All right. If you change your mind, we'll be back at noon and you can go with us then."

Colter felt a thread of excitement when he saw the twins ride away. According to Boley, Ritter had brought Rosie back with him. If Ritter held to his usual schedule when he spent the night with Rosie, he wouldn't leave her room until just before noon and then he'd ride straight to his ranch. Colter had left a cowboy in Cheyenne to warn him in case Ritter varied his routine. He planned to meet Ritter between Cheyenne and Ritter's ranch sometime in the early afternoon, so Colter had a few free hours on his hands.

Since it was also the first time for weeks that both Kinyan and the boys had left him alone in the house for any period of time, he wanted to take advantage of the chance it gave him to check the books and see how they'd come through the winter. Kinyan had told him his feeding program was a great success, but since he was supposed to be blind, he couldn't very well ride the range alone to check her story. And as much as he now knew she loved him, he wouldn't have put it past her to have exaggerated to keep him from knowing his idea had failed.

Colter waited until Dorothea headed out to do her morning chores in the barn and slipped into the parlor. He seated himself at John Holloway's oak rolltop desk and searched until he found what he was looking for. So immersed was he in the columns of figures that he didn't hear the bare feet that crossed the floor behind him. The small voice in the large room took him completely by surprise.

"What're you readin'?"

"Lizbeth!" Colter whirled as he spoke and, thinking quickly, answered, "I wasn't reading." How could he have been so careless as to forget about Lizbeth! But he hadn't actually forgotten her. Usually, she slept much later.

"You're up early."

"It was too quiet," she explained, then accused, "You were too readin'."

276

The little girl's disbelief had registered on Colter even as he'd told his lie, and he realized now that although he could fabricate a story, she was more likely to give him away if he did so than if he simply took her into his confidence and swore her to secrecy.

"Well, maybe I was reading."

"Then you can see?"

"Yes, Lizbeth. I can see."

"That's wonderful! Does Mama know you can see?"

"Come here, Lizbeth."

When Lizbeth was close enough, Colter lifted the little girl into his lap.

"My sight came back a little bit at a time. At first I didn't believe it was really happening, so I didn't tell anybody. I'm planning to surprise your ma, but I've been waiting for just the right time to do it. It's been my secret, and now I need you to help me keep it."

"Nobody else will know except us?"

"Nobody. It's very important, Lizbeth, that you keep my secret. Do you think you can?"

"Of course I can!" the child replied indignantly.

Dorothea appeared at the door and stuck her head in to say good morning before she took the milk to the kitchen.

"Grandma Thea, guess what?" Lizbeth shouted.

"What?" Dorothea responded absently, barely pausing on her way past the door.

Lizbeth cocked her head and grinned up at Colter, whose hands had tightened around the little girl's waist as though he wished they covered her mouth.

Lizbeth winked saucily at Colter and, daring him to stop her, announced, "Colter's gonna take me for a ride this mornin'."

Colter grinned back and hugged Lizbeth in relief.

"Little rascal talked me into it," he confirmed.

"That sounds like fun, Lizbeth. Now, don't you tire Colter out."

"I won't," the sprite assured her grandmother. "You want me to keep watch?" she whispered to Colter.

"No. I've had enough close calls for one day. How about if we go for that ride?"

"You mean you're really gonna take me?"

"Sure, why not? Secret pals have to stick together."

Colter took Lizbeth's hand and walked her out to the barn, making it appear as if she were walking him. Then he saddled Hoss, set the small child on the roan, and mounted up behind her.

"Now, where shall we go?" he asked.

"Let's go find Mama."

"I don't know, Lizbeth . . ."

"Please?"

"All right."

When Colter got to the general area where Kinyan and the boys had said they'd be working with the other hands, he found no one there. They'd been rounding up cattle all week along the boundary line the Triple Fork shared with the Lazy 6. From the signs, he could tell that there had only been three riders here, Kinyan and the boys. Where the hell was Boley? He'd wring Kinyan's neck if she'd sent Boley off on some wild-goose chase! Then he'd give Boley a dressing down he wouldn't soon forget!

Colter was worried. The three riders had left here in a hurry. He searched for spent shells that would have indicated real trouble, but found none. Now he was in a quandary. Should he take the time to go home and drop Lizbeth off, or should he bring her along and hope he wasn't taking her into a dangerous situation?

When Colter heard a gunshot, the decision was taken out of his hands.

"Hang on, Lizbeth."

Colter spurred the roan in the direction of the shot, not slowing from a gallop until, from his position at the top of a sharply dropping slope, he recognized Kinyan and the twins being held at gunpoint in the grassy valley below by three masked riders. Before he could be seen, Colter backed Hoss down into the narrow gully on the opposite side of the slope from the riders. He dismounted and pulled Lizbeth down out of the saddle. Colter crouched next to the little girl and looked into her eyes as he spoke.

"Lizbeth, your mama and your brothers are in trouble, and I have to help them. I want you to *stay right here*. Don't move and don't make any noise. Do you understand?"

"Yes. Nobody's gonna get hurt, are they, Colter?"

"I hope not, Lizbeth. I hope not."

"Please be careful. I love you, Colter." Lizbeth squeezed Colter tightly around the neck and hung on.

"I love you too, Lizbeth," he replied. "Do what I say, hear?"

He mounted the roan and headed toward the masked riders without waiting for her answer.

Kinyan knew who held the gun on her despite the mask. Did Ritter think she wouldn't recognize the costume he always wore? But, she realized, Ritter didn't really care if she recognized him. His mask only guarded against a stray cowboy happening upon them. It appeared his precaution had been necessary, for there was a rider approaching in the distance.

"Kinyan, are you out there?" the cowboy shouted.

It was Colter! Somehow Colter had made his way out here alone. She had to warn him. Kinyan opened her mouth to scream, and a huge hand clamped down over it and she was yanked from her saddle onto Ritter's lap. Kinyan's thoughts raced to the day Colter had pulled her from her horse just as roughly. She had feared kidnapping by a villain then and discovered instead a knight in shining armor. This time her danger was real, and her knight had come to meet his foe without armor or shield.

"You say one word other than what I tell you to say and I'll have your brats shot," Ritter grunted in her ear. Then he dropped his hand from her mouth, confident that given the choice, Kinyan would choose to save her sons over her husband.

Kinyan remained mute, but in agony over the decision that still must be made.

"If you brats make a sound, I'll shoot your ma," Ritter warned.

Colter stopped about fifteen feet away. He had a difficult time not giving himself away when he realized who was holding Kinyan. So, he thought, the bastard got tired of waiting and came after what he wanted. How had Ritter gotten out of Cheyenne without being seen? Colter knew he'd made a mistake. He'd fallen into the trap he'd hoped to set for Ritter. He'd underestimated his enemy.

"Tell him hello. Ask him how he found you," Ritter rasped.

"It's good to see you, Colter. How'd you find me?"

"I just counted on Hoss. He's almost as good as a hound dog sometimes."

Colter felt an inner satisfaction when he saw the scowl on Ritter's face, but he forced his own features to remain impassive. "Then I heard the shot," he continued. "So I followed the sound. What happened?"

"One of the boys shot at a jackrabbit," Kinyan said, repeating the words Ritter hissed at her.

"Which one of you boys did that?" Colter asked.

Neither Josh nor Jeremy dared answer without Ritter's approval, so each sat his horse in miserable silence.

"Josh? Jeremy?"

"They don't have to answer to you. You're not their pa," Ritter muttered in Kinyan's ear.

Kinyan turned and glared at Ritter. She knew the interpretation Colter would put on that statement. When she clamped her lips tightly together and shook her head, Ritter grabbed a hank of her hair and forced her face around to him.

"Tell him," he spat. "Or I'll kill those precious twins of yours right before your eyes."

Colter had gone hot and then cold when he saw Ritter handle Kinyan so roughly. It took every ounce of willpower he had to retain his bland expression.

"They don't have to answer to you. You're not their pa," Kinyan blurted. Then she waited for the pain to show on Colter's face.

Josh looked guiltily at Jeremy. At one time he would have said something very nearly like that. But not anymore. Would Colter take Ma seriously? He sure hoped not . . .

"No, I'm not their pa," Colter replied calmly. "But I love them both very much. I hope they know that."

Colter wanted that said in case he didn't live beyond the next few minutes.

Ritter sneered. He nodded to Cletus and Dobie, who sat on their horses to the left and behind Josh and Jeremy. The outlaws pulled their Colts, then waited for further orders from Ritter.

Josh and Jeremy exchanged anxious glances. The end was very near now.

Ritter freed his .44 and aimed it at Colter's belly. It took a

280

gut-shot man a long time to die. He planned to tell Colter the fate he had planned for Kinyan and the boys before he left him to the buzzards. He found his pleasure infinitely greater knowing that Colter loved them all.

Kinyan struggled with the choice Ritter had forced upon her. Did she dare warn Colter at the risk of her sons' lives? How much longer would Ritter let any of them live once Colter was dead? Why, oh why had she sent Boley off to find a mother for that stray calf? She should never have let down her guard. She should have known something like this might happen!

When she felt Ritter's body tense in preparation to fire his gun, Kinyan braved a quick glance at Josh and Jeremy and jerked her head slightly. Then, the instant before Ritter pulled the trigger, she thrust her whole weight down on his gun arm and shouted, "Colter, look out!"

Everything happened at once.

Before Cletus and Dobie could react, Josh and Jeremy slid to the sides of their ponies and, whooping and shrieking, sprinted their horses toward Colter. Bullets whined past the spots where they had been.

Colter drew his .44 and killed the two outlaws, then turned his gun on Ritter.

"Drop it!" he ordered.

Ritter abruptly stopped struggling with Kinyan, and his head snapped around in amazement. Kinyan took advantage of Ritter's shock to knock the gun from his hand.

Something was very wrong.

"How'd you do that?" Ritter choked out to the supposedly blind man.

"My pa can hit a target just by *hearing* where it is!" Josh bragged proudly.

Colter's throat closed with emotion. Josh the warrior, Josh the rebel, Josh the indignant digger of post holes, had called him pa.

Ritter's mouth gaped in disbelief.

"Then I expect your *pa* can *hear* the gun I have aimed at your ma," he finished furiously.

Although he'd lost his gun in the scuffle with Kinyan, Ritter had managed to snake his arm around her throat at such an angle that he need only apply the proper pressure to snap her neck. A quick gesture of his head to both Josh and

281

Jeremy warned they were not to contradict or interfere lest he abruptly end their mother's life.

Colter could see for himself Ritter had no gun. He could also see Kinyan's precarious predicament.

"Hand me your gun, butt end first, Colter," Ritter commanded. "It's all over."

Colter said nothing, but his mind searched frantically for a way to save Kinyan.

Ritter hadn't reckoned on Kinyan fighting back, and that was a grievous error. For now that there was no way Ritter could threaten her family, the way was clear for her to try to free herself. And she had an idea.

Kinyan had occasionally come across an unflappable cowhorse, one that was not as scared as the rabbit when the two met accidentally. In most cases, however, a cowhorse was a flighty sort, likely to bolt at its shadow at the most inopportune moment. Kinyan was counting on Ritter's palouse to be just such an animal. She bent her knee and jabbed her spur as hard as she could into the horse's chest.

The Appaloosa backed so quickly from the unexpected pain that it almost sat on its haunches. Ritter yanked on the reins to keep himself from falling, and that brought the horse up off its front legs. It was so overbalanced by the flailing humans on its back that it went completely over backward.

Trying to save himself, Ritter let go of Kinyan, who, being prepared, rolled free and scampered toward Colter.

While the horse was down, Ritter's full attention was focused on locating his gun. He turned to fire at Colter as soon as he had it in his hand. His too-quick shot just nicked Colter's side.

Colter shot reflexively, instinctively, and unerringly and Ritter's gun flew several feet in the air past his horse's head before it skidded into a clump of buffalo grass. Before Colter could fire again, his shot was blocked by the palouse, which struggled to rise.

As Ritter's gun flew past its ear, the skittish horse panicked and bolted. Ritter realized with horror that his boot had not come free of the stirrup and that he was about to become a victim of the most feared of cowboy fates. One scream was all Ritter had time for before his Appaloosa took off at a full gallop across the plains.

Kinyan watched in astonishment as the spotted horse

raced away. Even though Ritter was responsible for John's being dragged to death, she couldn't wish that fate on any man.

"We have to stop his horse!" she cried.

Colter sat on Hoss undecided for only a moment before he urged, "Get up here!"

"You can't see. I'll go!"

"I can see just fine! Get up here!"

There was no time for Kinyan to question Colter's revelation as he pulled her up behind him on Hoss.

"You boys stay here!" Colter ordered.

Then Colter and Kinyan were gone, chasing after the frantic animal with its wildly bouncing unnatural appendage. They heard a scream of agony and then saw that the palouse, although still galloping wildly, had lost its grisly burden. Colter pressed Hoss to run faster.

When they reached Ritter, he was conscious and whimpering piteously. His body had been caught between two rocks, yanking him free of the stirrup, but his right boot, along with the foot inside it, had been torn off. Colter stopped Hoss a short distance from Ritter, and he and Kinyan dismounted.

"You don't want to see this," Colter warned Kinyan.

"I have to."

After a short pause, he replied, "All right."

Ritter's beautiful face was no more. One eye was still open in the bloodied mess, and when Ritter comprehended who had come to help him, he snarled, "Get away from me!"

Colter could see Ritter's back was broken, and the unnatural angle of his legs showed they were broken in several places as well. Ritter was losing blood from the torn ankle stump at an alarming rate. Colter knew it was only a matter of time before Ritter was a dead man.

Ritter knew it too, and he couldn't bear the thought of these two witnessing his demise.

"Get out of here!"

Ritter's words came out in a ghoulish gurgle, since he was bleeding internally, and he spat blood as he spoke. When neither Colter nor Kinyan moved, Ritter hissed, "I enjoyed your wife, Colter. She was a good . . ."

A spasm of pain distorted Ritter's features and cut him off before Colter could do so. The malevolent glitter in Ritter's open eye left no doubt that even at death's door he remained a ruthlessly cruel creature. It took several moments for Colter and Kinyan to realize that Ritter had died, his once-beautiful face frozen in a horrible, mutilated mask that revealed the vicious inner man.

Colter felt numb. Ritter Gordon was dead. A sense of peace settled on him all at once. And wonder. For what he felt was not relief that Sarah and Hope had finally been avenged. It was relief that Kinyan and her children were safe forever from the malicious intent of this demon.

"Colter? Are you all right?"

Kinyan stood at Colter's side. The glazed, faraway expression in his eyes frightened her. She could see the hole in his leather vest and the growing stain on his shirt below it.

Colter turned to Kinyan, and his eyes narrowed on his wife's face. He seemed to be searching for something.

Kinyan met his gaze openly, honestly, all the love she felt there for him to see. His perusal reminded her that Colter was not only looking at her, he was actually *seeing* her.

"You *can* see!"

"Yes I can," he answered soberly, without further explanation. "There's nothing we can do here. Let's get back to the boys."

Colter turned back to Hoss, leaving Kinyan confused, her questions about the miracle of his sight unanswered. Yet in the aftermath of Ritter's death, she willingly kept silent on the ride back to where Josh and Jeremy waited for them.

"Ritter's dead," Colter announced when they arrived.

"Hey, Pa, can you really see?" Jeremy questioned tentatively.

"I don't understand how. . ." Kinyan ventured.

"I don't understand either, but it's a fact. I can see," Colter interrupted, a small smile teasing at the corners of his mouth.

"How long have you been able to see, Pa?" Josh asked suspiciously. "No wonder you could hit those cans every time."

"I hit those tins by listening to where they landed," Colter countered.

"But you *coulda* seen them," Josh argued.

"I could have, but that would have been cheating," Colter replied, his smile growing.

284

Ritter had been momentarily forgotten while the Colter family immersed itself in the joy of arguing like a family. That reminded Colter there was someone missing from the group.

"We'll have Boley come pick up these bodies. The horses are ground-tied. They shouldn't stray."

When Kinyan would have left Colter's lap, he stopped her.

"Kinyan, you can ride with me."

The initial surprise and wonder of Colter's returned sight had worn off quickly. Now Kinyan had to clamp her jaw shut to keep from screaming. Colter had made a fool of her! All the time she'd been pitying him, walking on tiptoes around his blind temper, he'd been able to see! Why hadn't he told her so and relieved her concern?

Colter felt the rigidity of his wife's body but didn't let it dissuade him from holding her even closer in his arms.

"I have something special I left a short way from here that I need to pick up," he said mysteriously.

Their curiosity aroused, Josh and Jeremy quizzed Colter the entire distance back to the gully where he'd left Lizbeth.

When she saw them coming, Lizbeth ran out to meet them. Kinyan slipped off Hoss and ran to scoop her daughter into her arms.

"Aw, Pa. That's just Lizbeth," Josh spouted in disgust as Colter stepped down to greet Lizbeth.

Lizbeth readily came into Colter's arms.

"Lizbeth is your sister. As her older brother, it's your responsibility to protect her and keep her safe," Colter said as he set the little girl in the saddle in front of Josh. "She's my only daughter and therefore very special to me. I'm entrusting her to you. Think you're up to the job?"

Lizbeth beamed and looked adoringly up at Josh.

Josh's cheeks darkened and he opened his mouth to answer, but no words came out.

"Sure he is," Jeremy said, rescuing his older brother. "And if he runs into any trouble, he can always count on me."

"Thanks, Jeremy," Colter said with a smile.

Kinyan's rigidity persisted the long ride home, and she spoke at dinner only so much as was necessary to get through the meal. Dorothea had taken the return of Colter's

285

sight in stride, and noting the children's frequent use of *pa* to address Colter and his proud willingness to be so called, she trusted Colter to sway Kinyan, who seemed to be the last holdout against their being a family once more.

It was Colter who took charge of getting the boys and Lizbeth headed upstairs to bed.

"You boys keep the noise down in here tonight," Colter admonished before he blew out the lantern on the table by the door.

"Yes sir, Pa."

"Sure, Pa."

When Colter arrived in Lizbeth's room, she had her nightgown on but was having trouble with the tie at the neck. Colter finished the bow, then tucked Lizbeth under the covers.

"Will you read me a story?"

"Not tonight, Lizbeth."

Colter leaned down to kiss Lizbeth on the cheek, and she put her hands behind his neck and held his bristly cheek close to her baby-smooth one.

"Good night, Pa," she whispered in Colter's ear.

"Good night, Princess."

Lizbeth's wide smile fattened her cheeks against Colter's.

Colter gave Lizbeth a quick hug. "Sleep well," he said, and he blew out the lantern and left the room.

Colter went to his bedroom, thinking Kinyan had retired there, but when he didn't find her, he headed back downstairs. He found Dorothea, but no wife.

"Have you seen Kinyan?"

"I heard the front door close a few minutes ago. Maybe she went outside to get some fresh air."

Colter's frown caused Dorothea to add, "She loves you very much, Colter, no matter what she may have said or done these past months."

Colter turned the shiny brass doorknob to open the front door but stopped long enough to say, "Thanks Dorothea," before he set out in search of his wife. Colter started looking in the spot where he went when he wanted to be alone. He lit a lantern at the door to the barn and made his way to Gringalet's stall. The stallion was alone.

Consternation wrinkled Colter's brow. He stopped to pat

Hoss on the withers and, as was his habit, spoke aloud to the understanding animal.

"Guess I really did it this time, huh, partner? I knew she was going to be upset, but I thought if I had a chance to explain everything, she'd understand why I kept my secrets. Where do you suppose she's disappeared to anyway? It's too cold for her to be running around outside."

Several pieces of straw floated down from above Colter. He scratched Hoss between the ears and continued.

"I couldn't tell Kinyan about Sarah and Hope. I wanted to, but it was much too painful to talk about them. You see when I lost them, I thought I'd die, it hurt so much. But I didn't. I woke up every day knowing their killers were out there somewhere. That thought began to eat away at me until I couldn't do anything except go after them."

Colter had stopped scratching and Hoss whickered and butted his head against the large hand that rested on his forehead. Colter moved to a second favorite spot, under Hoss's chin, and began to scratch again as he picked up his story.

"I found two of the murdering bastards in Laredo and I killed them. I'm not proud of how I did it. I was half insane with grief and the need to spill blood. But no matter how long I searched, I never found that third man.

"One day I finally came to my senses, Hoss. That's when I drove my herd north to start over, far away from those memories. How could I have known that the third man was Ritter Gordon and that he'd been here all that time? It's a strange thing, though, Hoss. When I killed Ritter, I wasn't thinking of Sarah and Hope."

Hoss shook his head as though in disbelief.

"Don't believe me, huh? Well, it's true. I was thinking of my family—Dorothea, my daughter Lizbeth, my sons Josh and Jeremy, and my wife Kinyan. I wanted them to be safe. That's why I had to keep my sight a secret, Hoss. I needed that extra edge I got from Ritter not knowing I could see."

Colter brought his hand around to pat Hoss's smooth jowl.

"You know, Hoss, it's amazing the things you can see clearly for the first time when you're blind." Colter chuckled. "I never wanted to love Kinyan, you know. I desired her so much I ached all the time, but I had no intention of loving her. It wasn't until I thought I'd lost her in the stampede that I realized how much she meant to me. Just when I planned to tell her how much I'd come to love her, I got shot. Then it appeared she could get along without me just fine, and I got caught between feeling proud of all she'd learned and feeling sorry for myself 'cause she didn't need me anymore.

"My sight began to return a little bit at a time, and I could see that while Kinyan spoke those bitter words to me, saying how she really didn't need me, there were tears on her face. And then, Hoss, I saw her looking at me and she said, not so's I could hear, you understand, she just mouthed the words, *I love you*. And I could have cried 'cause of course I loved her, too."

A single sliver of straw wafted down, landing on Hoss's shoulder. Colter brushed it off and spoke again.

"I've told Kinyan how much I love her a thousand times—in my head. I planned to tell her to her face and keep on telling her for the rest of her life. But I guess she isn't going to forgive me for keeping secrets from her. We'd have made a great team, Hoss, that girl and me, working this ranch."

The barn, pungent with horsy smells and musty hay, remained quiet. Colter picked up the lantern and patted Hoss one last time.

"I'm going down to the creek, partner. All this talk about Kinyan has had the same effect it always does, and if the lady's angry with me, I better cool off before I go back to the house. She's probably wondering where I am right now while I've been out here yakking with you."

Colter blew out the lantern and put it in its place by the barn door. It was several moments before the hay in the loft crackled with the movement of an animal much larger than the cats and mice that challenged each other for control of the barn. A booted foot came down the vertical ladder and then another, until Kinyan stood on the straw-covered floor.

Had Colter known she was there? It seemed impossible he would have bared his soul so completely had he not. It seemed she had another choice to make. She could either return to the house alone or she could meet Colter at the creek and walk back with him.

Kinyan stepped outside the barn. It was cold now. The

creek would be colder. She thought of Colter, naked in the moonlight, his long, lean body bared to her gaze, and she shivered—but not from the cold. She thought of everything she wanted to say to him. While she thought, her feet moved her beyond the house and down the hill toward the creek.

He was there, an Adonis of flesh and bone, standing hip deep in the creek. Kinyan left a trail of clothing, like Gretel's breadcrumbs, leading to the rushing water. She stood at the edge of the creek, a marble sculpture of Venus come to life, letting the moonlight splay over her opalescent skin. She reached out her hand, and Colter came out of the water toward her one step at a time. He extended his hand to her and their fingertips entwined, ivy and oak, as they touched. Kinyan led Colter between the branches of the weeping willow that trailed its limbs over the water. Inside that protected bower, the lovers turned to one another.

It was dark, yet as the willow shifted in the wind the moonlight flickered on their skin like tiny mirrors, reflecting their love.

"I think I first began to love you when you rescued me from my own sons," Kinyan said with a chuckle as she let her fingers roam across Colter's scarred chest. "You earned Dorothea's trust and the twins' respect. You gave Lizbeth back her pa. You were my teacher and then my lover. I was afraid of you because I couldn't control what I felt, and you made it clear you wanted no commitment."

"Kinyan, I . . ."

She placed two fingers on his lips to silence him.

"I've known about what Ritter did to your wife and child for a long time."

Colter's expression remained blank, but Kinyan could feel his entire body tense beneath the hands she had returned to his chest.

"Rosie came to visit some time before Ritter did and told Dorothea and me everything," she explained. "He killed John too—for the ranch."

"I'm sorry," Colter breathed.

"I'm sorry too, for the things I said—about not needing you except for loving. I didn't know what else to do. I had to make you want to live. Third rule, Colter: if you have to fight, make use of all the ammunition at your disposal. So I pretended not to need you. But I do."

Kinyan raised her eyes to meet Colter's.

"I was in the barn, Colter."

"I know."

"I thought you knew," she said with a smile. "I spilled enough hay on you trying to get you to notice me."

"I meant everything I said, Kinyan. You'd do to ride the river with."

Kinyan flushed with pleasure. Colter had just paid her one of the highest cowboy compliments.

"Did you really say *I love you* a thousand times in your head?" she asked with a flirtatious grin.

"Well, maybe only several hundred," he conceded. "I wasn't actually keeping count. I love you, Kinyan."

Colter had his arms around Kinyan and as he pulled her close, the icy droplets of water on his belly and thighs drew a gasp from her. Then he was nipping the lobe of her ear while he cupped a breast in his hand, and she was suddenly very warm all over.

"Kinyan."

"What?" Kinyan replied distractedly.

"I had a lot of time to think over the winter. And . . . I'd like another child. A child from us."

Kinyan jerked out of Colter's arms.

"I . . . uh . . . well . . ."

"Well, what?" he asked in exasperation. Colter had been expecting a quick response, and his body protested Kinyan's hesitation.

"There's something I need to tell you."

Kinyan's words left Colter wary. He tried to mask his disappointment. Maybe she couldn't have any more children. Or maybe she just didn't want any more children. Then Colter frowned. Hellfire! He didn't have to like it if she felt that way, did he?

Kinyan's lips quirked and a tinkling laugh spilled out to fill their lover's haven.

"Don't frown like that or I'll never be able to confess."

Before she could say another word, Colter had Kinyan flat on her back on the grass and had come down on top of her, pinning her hands on either side of her above her head.

"Tell me!" he barked. "And be done with it!"

"There's already a baby on the way."

Colter came up off Kinyan like he'd been stung by a bee in clover and stood over her aghast, balled fists hanging at his sides. Kinyan's mischievous blue eyes gleamed back at him in the semi-darkness.

"Why didn't you tell me sooner?"

He paced like a wolf inside the shifting tent of willow limbs. He had absolutely no experience with pregnant women. He'd been gone the entire time Sarah had been with child. Finally, Colter came down on his knees beside Kinyan and placed his hands gently on her belly as though to touch the child inside her.

"Did I hurt you? I mean, did I hurt the baby lying on you like I did?"

The gentle laughter sounded again, and Colter felt it touch him everywhere. The ache in his groin was excruciating. Did this mean they could no longer make love with one another? Colter paled.

"No, you didn't harm either of us. In fact we very much need to be held exactly like that. Come, dear one," Kinyan coaxed. "I'm chilled. Cover me."

Like a man receiving manna from heaven, Colter obeyed, reverently extending his naked form over hers. Gently, he kissed. Gently, he touched. Yet Kinyan would not let him be gentle. She teased. She taunted. She tantalized until Colter gave her what she demanded, the wild fullness of him deep within her, loving, giving, becoming one.

"Colter," Kinyan sighed much later.

"Ummm," he replied, nuzzling Kinyan's throat.

"I have another confession to make."

Sated as he was and as pleasant as her first confession had turned out to be, Colter merely kissed his way down to a softly rounded crest before he murmured, "Ummm?"

"I ordered some barbed wire."

Colter's head shot up off his soft pillow.

"You what?!"

"I ordered some barbed wire."

"I heard what you said! What did you do that for?"

"Well, when you explained at the Association meeting how much time it saved on the roundups in Texas, I thought it would make that much more time we could spend together doing more pleasant things."

Kinyan suited her actions to her words, and her lips closed over one of Colter's nipples and her tongue came out to gently lave it.

"Oh."

It was a sigh of pleasure.

"When you put it that way, the idea begins to sound a lot more appealing," he said.

Kinyan switched to the other nipple and Colter moaned.

"But I'm warning you, Kinyan. Ahhh. Next time. Ohhh. Let's talk it over first."

"Yes, Colter," Kinyan replied meekly.

Colter's head had dropped to her shoulder, and his teeth nipped while his tongue bathed.

"We'll talk everything over from now on. Ahhh. What do you think of the names Cody and Cassidy?"

Kinyan caressed the hard length of Colter's shaft.

"Names?" he choked as a groan started deep in his throat. His hands went to Kinyan's buttocks, his tongue to the curve of her shoulder.

"Didn't I tell you? Ohhh. We could have twins."

"I thought we were going to talk everything over first."

"What do you think?"

"I think it's great. Kinyan?"

"Ummmm?"

"I love you."

"I love you, Colter. I . . . what are you doing?"

Colter pressed Kinyan down flat on the cool grass and covered her body with his.

"Shouldn't we talk this over first?" Kinyan said with a grin as she felt Colter seat himself deep within her.

"Some things don't need to be discussed," Colter replied with a sigh of satisfaction.

She agreed wholeheartedly with her husband. So Kinyan did not speak.

JUDE DEVERAUX

A Unique New Voice In Romantic Fiction

Jude Deveraux is the finest new writer of historical romances to come along since Kathleen Woodiwiss.

The Montgomery Annals

_____ **The Velvet Promise** 54756/$3.95
_____ **Highland Velvet** 60073/$3.95
_____ **Velvet Song** 60076/$3.95
_____ **Velvet Angel** 60075/$3.95

POCKET
BOOKS

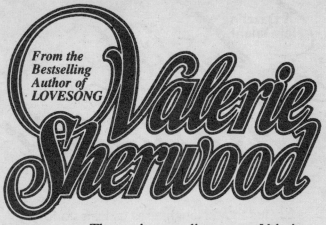